Only one
woman can
tame this devil...

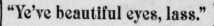

"Ye've beautiful eyes, lass."

"So do you," Evelinde whispered.

A smile tugged at the corners of his lips right before his mouth covered hers.

She stiffened at the unexpected caress. His lips were soft yet firm and wholly inappropriate. She was about to say so when something prodded at her lips. She tried to pull back, but his hand was at the back of her head, preventing her retreat. Suddenly, she found her mouth invaded by his tongue.

No one had ever kissed her before. No one would have dared.

When he broke the kiss, he didn't release her as she expected; instead his mouth simply trailed its way across her cheek.

"Sir," she murmured, thinking it time she introduce herself and tell him he had to stop. She had no fear he wouldn't. The moment she mentioned being betrothed to the Devil of Donnachaidh, he'd probably thrust her away himself.

Everyone feared the Devil, she thought, as he began to nuzzle the side of her neck.

By Lynsay Sands

DEVIL OF THE HIGHLANDS
THE ROGUE HUNTER

The Argeneau Family

VAMPIRE, INTERRUPTED
VAMPIRES ARE FOREVER
THE ACCIDENTAL VAMPIRE
BITE ME IF YOU CAN
A BITE TO REMEMBER
A QUICK BITE

Coming Soon

THE IMMORTAL HUNTER

LYNSAY SANDS

DEVIL OF THE HIGHLANDS

AVON

An Imprint of HarperCollinsPublishers

AVON BOOKS
An Imprint of HarperCollins*Publishers*
10 East 53rd Street
New York, New York 10022-5299

Copyright © 2009 by Lynsay Sands
Excerpts from *Tempt the Devil* copyright © 2009 by Anna Campbell; *Devil of the Highlands* copyright © 2009 by Lynsay Sands; *Bride of a Wicked Scotsman* copyright © 2009 by Sandra Kleinschmit; *Confessions of a Little Black Gown* copyright © 2009 by Elizabeth Boyle
ISBN 978-0-06-134477-0
www.avonromance.com

First Avon Books paperback printing: February 2009

Avon Trademark Reg. U.S. Pat. Off. and in Other Countries, Marca Registrada, Hecho en U.S.A.
HarperCollins® is a registered trademark of HarperCollins Publishers.

Printed in the U.S.A.

10 9 8 7 6 5 4 3 2 1

chapter

One

Northern England
1273

y lady!"

That anxious cry made Evelinde pause in what she was saying to Cook and glance around. Her maid was rushing across the kitchens toward her, expression both angry and worried. It was a combination usually only engendered by Edda's actions. Wondering what her stepmother had got up to now, Evelinde quickly promised Cook they would finish their discussion of menus later, and went to meet her maid.

Mildrede caught her hands the moment they

reached one another. Her mouth turned down grimly as she announced, "Your stepmother is calling for you."

Evelinde grimaced. Edda only sent for her when she was in one of her foul moods and wished to cheer herself by abusing her unfortunate stepdaughter. For one moment, Evelinde considered ignoring the summons and finding a task away from the keep for the rest of the day. However, that would only make the woman's mood—and the subsequent abuses—worse.

"I had best go see what she wants then," Evelinde said and squeezed Mildrede's hands reassuringly before moving past her.

"She's smiling," Mildrede warned, following on her heels.

Evelinde paused with her hand on the door to the great hall, trepidation running through her. A smiling Edda was not a good thing. It usually meant Evelinde was about to suffer. Not that the woman ever dared hit her, but there were worse things, tasks so unpleasant one would almost prefer a beating. Biting her lip with worry, she asked, "Do you know what has set her off this time?"

"Nay," Mildrede said apologetically. "She was railing at Mac for not pampering her mare properly when a messenger arrived from the king. She read the message, smiled, and called for you."

"Oh," Evelinde breathed faintly, but then forced her shoulders straight, raised her head, and pushed through the door. It was the only thing she could do . . . That and pray that someday, she would be free of her stepmother's control and abuses.

"Ah, Evelinde!" Edda was indeed smiling—a very wide, beaming smile that really didn't bode well.

"I was told you wished to speak with me?" Evelinde said quietly, aware of Mildrede hovering at her back. The woman always offered her support during Edda's little attacks.

"Aye." Edda continued to flash a wide, toothy smile, although toothless would have been as good a description. The woman was missing half her teeth. and those remaining were brown and crooked. Edda rarely smiled, and certainly never widely enough to show off the state of her mouth. Her doing so now made Evelinde's anxiety increase tenfold.

"Since your father's death, seeing to your welfare has fallen to me, and I have been most concerned about your future and well-being, my dear," Edda began.

Evelinde managed not to sneer at the claim of concern. Her father, James d'Aumesbery, had been a good man and a faithful baron to their king. When Henry III had requested he marry the troublesome Edda and remove her from court, where she was making a nuisance of herself, her father had bowed to the task gracefully. Edda had not. She'd resented being tied to a man who held only a barony and had seemed to take an instant dislike to Evelinde on reaching d'Aumesbery.

It hadn't been so bad at first. With the presence of Evelinde's father and her brother, Alexander, Edda had at least behaved cordially to her. However, Alexander had ridden off to join the Crusades with Prince Edward three years earlier. While the prince had since returned and been crowned king on his father's death, Alexander was still in Tunis. Worse yet, no sooner had he left than their father died of a chest complaint.

James d'Aumesbery hadn't even been placed in the family crypt before Edda dropped any pretense at civility and let her true feelings show. These last three years had been a hell Evelinde feared she would never escape. Her only hope was to await her brother's homecoming so that he might see her married and settled far away from the woman. Unfortunately, Alexander seemed in no rush to return.

"I have decided 'tis well past time you married," Edda announced, "and the king agrees with me."

"She means the king decided you should marry, and she was forced to agree," Mildrede muttered behind her, low enough that Edda couldn't hear. "You don't think she'd willingly give up tormenting you. It's her favorite pastime."

Evelinde barely heard her maid, she was too busy trying to absorb what Edda was saying. Part of her feared it was simply a cruel attempt on Edda's part to get her hopes up, then dash them.

"And so I chose a husband for you, and the king negotiated a marriage contract," Edda announced grandly. "I have just received a message that 'tis all done. You will be married."

Evelinde simply waited, knowing there was more. Edda would either explain it was all a jest, or name some perfectly horrid, smelly old lord that Evelinde would surely be miserable with.

"Your betrothed is on his way here from his home even as we speak. He is the laird of Donnachaidh," she announced triumphantly, pronouncing it Don-o-kay.

Evelinde gasped. This was worse than a smelly old lord, this was—"the Devil of Donnachaidh?"

Edda's expression was full of evil glee. "Aye, and I wish you all the unhappiness in the world."

"Bitch," Mildrede hissed furiously from behind Evelinde.

Ignoring her maid, Evelinde managed to force away the horror and dismay and keep her features expressionless. She would not add to Edda's pleasure by revealing how deep this blow had struck. The Devil of Donnachaidh? The woman didn't just hate her, she despised her if she was willing to hand her over to that infamous Scottish laird.

"Now be gone," Edda said, apparently having had her fun. "I do not wish to look on you anymore."

Evelinde nodded stiffly and turned, catching Mildrede by the arm to lead her out of the great hall and the keep itself.

"Cow!" Mildrede snapped, as soon as the keep doors closed behind them.

Evelinde merely urged her quickly across the bailey toward the stables.

"Vile, ugly, cruel creature," Mildrede continued. "She has a heart of stone and a face to match. The Devil must have been laughing the day the king forced your father to marry that she-devil."

Evelinde flashed Mac, the stable master, a grateful smile when she urged Mildrede into the stables and saw her mount saddled and ready next to the reddish brown roan he favored.

"I saw the smile on Edda's face when she received her message," the stable master explained. "I figured ye might need a ride when she was done with ye."

"Aye. Thank you, Mac." Evelinde urged Mildrede up to the mare.

"Your father must be rolling in his grave," the maid snarled, as Evelinde boosted her up onto the mount.

With a little help from Mac, Evelinde swung herself up onto the horse behind the older woman as she continued her rant. "And your dear sainted mother must be frothing at the mouth, wishing she was still alive so she could tear the wench's hair out one mud brown strand at a time."

Evelinde put her heels to her mare to urge her into a canter, aware Mac had mounted and was following close behind.

"I should poison the nasty harpy's mead," Mildrede threatened as they rode across the bailey at a sedate canter, heading for the gate and drawbridge. "Every single inhabitant of the keep would be grateful for it. She's the most unpleasant, grasping, cold-hearted, mealy-wormed—Ack!"

Evelinde smiled faintly at her squawk. They'd reached the halfway point on the drawbridge, and she'd given Lady her head. The mare immediately tossed her mane with a whinny of joy and bolted into a dead run. Evelinde didn't bother to look behind to check on Mac; she knew he would be keeping up. Besides, her hands were full with keeping her seat and holding on to the reins as Mildrede began clawing at her as if she thought she might slide out of the saddle.

Only when Mildrede's grip began to weaken did Evelinde draw gently on her mare's reins. Lady responded at once, used to this routine. Every time Edda did something cruel or mean, Mildrede lost her temper, and Evelinde took her for a ride to prevent her from saying or doing something that might see her punished.

Once Lady slowed to a sedate canter again, Mac urged his own horse up beside them and raised an eyebrow, but Evelinde just shook her head. She had no desire to explain Edda's "happy news." It would just upset Mildrede all over again, and she was distressed enough herself. Rather than waste her time soothing her maid, she wished time to herself to think over the situation.

"You can turn around now," Mildrede said. "I'm calm. I'll not say or do anything to the vile creature. 'Tis a waste anyway. I'm sure the Devil has something special in store for her when she finally dies. Though 'twould be nicer for all of us did she do so soon."

Evelinde managed a faint smile but didn't have the energy to respond. Instead, she drew her horse to a stop and glanced toward the stable master. "Will you see her home, Mac?"

"Ye'll no return then?" he asked with concern.

"Not right now. I should like a moment to myself first."

Mac hesitated, but then nodded and easily lifted Mildrede from Lady's back to place her on his own horse. The man was not very tall and had a wiry build, but he was surprisingly strong.

"Don't go much farther else ye might run into trouble," he warned. "And don't stay out here too long, or I'll come looking."

Evelinde nodded, then watched them head back toward the castle at a much more sedate pace than they'd taken riding out. The way he kept bending his head to Mildrede told her the woman was probably explaining what had taken place and what was still to occur.

Marriage. To the Devil of Donnachaidh.

Evelinde swallowed back the fear that immediately clawed its way up her throat. She turned her horse away, heading for a nearby clearing she favored. The spot was small and alongside an area of the river with a small waterfall. The fall was no taller than she but delightful just the same.

Evelinde urged Lady to the water's edge so the mare could drink, then slid off her back, running an absent hand along her mount's neck as she peered into the water.

She had always found this spot soothing. It was where she brought all her troubles and cares. Usually, the tinkle of the water and the mist in the air from the falls washed away her worries, and Evelinde left feeling better. She wasn't sure it would succeed very well this time, though. She suspected it would take a lot of water to wash this worry away.

Grimacing, Evelinde moved to sit on a large boulder at the water's edge and removed her slippers. She then bent and reached between her feet to catch the hem at the back of her gown, brought it forward between her legs, and tucked it into the front of the loose belt she wore over her gown. That accomplished, she moved back to the river's edge and daintily dipped one toe into the water, smiling at the cool rush of liquid over her flesh. Evelinde stayed like that for one moment before she stepped right in, a pleased sigh slipping from her lips as the water closed around her feet and halfway up to her knees.

Closing her eyes, she simply stood there, trying not to think about marrying the Devil of Donnachaidh. Evelinde wanted a few moments of peace and calm; then she would consider her future.

Her few moments didn't last, for the hem of her skirt unraveled and dropped around her feet in the water.

Crying out, Evelinde tried to hop back out of the river but got her feet tangled in the wet hem of the skirt and stumbled sideways. She threw herself forward at the last moment, arms outstretched, hoping to break her fall. However, her hand skimmed the side of a boulder before continuing on to the river bottom, then the boulder rammed into her ribs and hip with a painful blow even as her head continued down, slamming the side of her jaw into another stone.

Evelinde gasped in pain and sucked in a mouthful of water as she was briefly submerged. She came back up at once, spitting water and coughing up what little bit had gone down her throat as she ignored the pain in her side and pushed herself to a sitting position in the water. Placing one hand to her ribs, Evelinde felt the tender spot, relieved to find that, while it ached, she didn't think she'd broken anything. Her hand then dropped to her sore hip as well, and she muttered a pained curse as exasperation overcame her.

Was not this perfect? Evelinde had never been the most graceful of women, but rarely did something as clumsy as this. It seemed luck had abandoned her this day.

Shaking her head, she dragged herself to her feet and staggered out of the river. Her mare, she noticed, had backed away and was now eyeing her balefully. Evelinde supposed she must have splashed the animal as she fell. She didn't bother apologizing but simply moved back to sit on the boulder, shivering.

The water had been nice on her toes, but her gown was now completely soaked and cold where it touched her skin, which was everywhere.

Grimacing, Evelinde tried to hold the skirt away from her legs but soon gave that up. She could hardly sit there holding the skirt away from her skin until it dried.

Muttering under her breath, she set to work on her laces, and struggled to get out of the gown. It was an almost impossible task. While the dress had slipped on easily enough when dry, it was a nightmare to remove when wet. Evelinde was flushed, breathless, and sweating by the time she got it off.

Dropping it on the ground with relief, she plopped herself back on the boulder again, but the heat she'd generated with her efforts soon faded, and Evelinde found herself once again shivering in her damp chemise. However, she wasn't going to remove that and sit there naked. While people rarely intruded on her favorite spot, they did on occasion, and she wasn't going to risk being caught in such a state.

Evelinde wasn't foolish enough to sit there shivering either. She needed to find a way to dry herself, her chemise and her gown—and quickly—else she might catch a chill.

Her gaze slid to her horse. Lady had given up glaring at her and was once again at the riverside, partaking of the crystal-clear water. Evelinde hesitated a moment, considering the practicalities of the idea that was tickling the edges of her mind, then stood, picked up her gown, and moved to the mare.

Cullen was the first to see her. The sight made him rein in so sharply, his horse reared in response. He tightened his thighs around his mount to help keep his seat, moving automatically to calm the animal, but he didn't take his eyes off the woman in the glen.

"God's teeth. What is she doing?" Fergus asked as he halted beside him.

Cullen didn't even glance to the tall, burly redhead who was his first. He merely shook his head silently, transfixed by the sight. The woman was riding back and forth across the clearing, sending her horse charging first one way, then the other and back. That in itself was odd, but what had put the hush in Fergus's voice and completely captured Cullen's tongue was the fact she was doing so in nothing but a transparent chemise while holding the reins of her mount in her teeth. Her hands were otherwise occupied. They were upraised and holding what appeared to be a cape in the air so it billowed out behind her above her streams of golden hair as she rode back and forth . . . back and forth . . . back and forth.

"Who do you think she is?" Rory's question was the only way Cullen knew the other men had caught up as well.

"I doona ken, but I could watch the lass all day," Tavis said, his voice sounding hungry. "Though there are other things I'd rather be doing to her all day."

Cullen found himself irritated by that remark. Tavis was his cousin, and the charmer among his men; fair-haired, handsome, and with a winning smile, it took little effort for him to woo women to his bed of a night. And the man took full advantage of the ability, charming his way under women's skirts at every opportunity. Were titles awarded by such an ability, Tavis would have been the king of Scotland.

"I'd first be wanting to ken why she's doing what she is," Fergus said slowly. "I've no desire to bed a wench who isna right in the head."

"It isna her head I'd be taking to me bed." Tavis laughed.

"Aye." Gillie said, his voice sounding almost dreamy.

Cullen turned a hard glare on his men. "Ride on. I'll catch up to ye."

There was a moment of silence as eyebrows rose and glances were exchanged, then all five men took up their reins.

"Ride around the meadow," Cullen instructed, when they started to move forward.

There was another exchange of glances, but the men followed the tree line around the meadow.

Cullen waited until they had disappeared from sight, then turned back to the woman. His eyes followed her back and forth several times before he urged his mount forward.

It hadn't appeared so from the edge of the meadow, but the woman was actually moving at high speed on her beast, slowing only to make the turn before spurring her horse into a dead run toward the other side. The mare didn't seem to mind. If anything, the animal seemed to think it was some sort of game and threw herself into each run with an impressive burst of speed.

Cullen rode up beside the mare, but the woman didn't immediately notice him. Her attention was shifting between the path ahead and the cloth in her upraised hands. When she finally did glimpse him out of the corner of her eye, he wasn't at all prepared for her reaction.

The lass's eyes widened, and her head jerked back with a start, unintentionally yanking on the reins she clenched in her teeth. The mare suddenly jerked to a halt and reared. The lass immediately dropped her hands to grab for the reins and the cloth she'd been holding swung around and slapped—heavy and wet—across Cullen's face. It both stung and briefly blinded him, making him jerk on his own reins in surprise, and suddenly his own mount was turning away and rearing as well.

Cullen found himself tumbling to the ground, tangled in a length of wet cloth that did nothing to cushion his landing. Pain slammed through his back, knocking the wind out of him, but it positively exploded through his head, a jagged blade of agony that actually made him briefly lose consciousness.

A tugging sensation woke him. Blinking his eyes open, he thought for one moment the blow to his head had blinded him, but then felt another tug and realized there was something over his face. The damp cloth, he recalled with relief. He wasn't blind. At least, he didn't think he was. He wouldn't know for sure until he got the cloth off.

Another tug came, but this was accompanied by a grunt and a good deal more strength. Enough that his head was actually jerked off the ground, bending his neck at an uncomfortable angle. Afraid that, at this rate, he'd end up with a broken neck *after* the fall, Cullen decided he'd best help with the effort to untangle himself from the cloth and lifted his hands toward his head, intending to grab for the clinging material. However, it seemed his tormentor was leaning over him, because he found himself grabbing at something else entirely. Two somethings . . . that were covered with a soft, damp cloth, were roundish in shape, soft yet firm at the same time, and had little pebble-like bumps in the center, he discovered, his fingers shifting about blindly. Absorbed as he was in sorting out all these details, he didn't at first hear the horrified gasps that were coming from beyond the cloth over his head.

"Sorry," Cullen muttered as he realized he was groping a woman's breasts. Forcing his hands away, he shifted them to the cloth on his head and immediately began tugging recklessly at the stuff, eager to get it off.

"Hold! Wait, sir, you will rip—" The warning ended on a groan as a rending sound cut through the air.

Cullen paused briefly, but then continued to tug at the material, this time without apologizing. He'd never been one to enjoy enclosed spaces and felt like he would surely smother to death if he did not get it off at once.

"Let me—I can—If you would just—"

The words barely registered with Cullen. They sounded like nothing more than witless chirping. He ignored them and continued battling the cloth, until—with another tearing sound—it fell away, and he could breathe again. Cullen closed his eyes and sucked in a deep breath with relief.

"Oh dear."

That soft, barely breathed moan made his eyes open and slip to the woman kneeling beside him. She was shifting the cloth through her hands, examining the damaged material with wide, dismayed eyes.

Cullen debated offering yet another apology, but he'd already given one, and it was more than he normally offered in a year. Before he'd made up his mind, the blonde from the horse stopped examining the cloth and turned alarmed eyes his way.

"You are bleeding!"

"What?" he asked with surprise.

"There is blood on my gown. You must have cut your head when you fell," she explained, leaning over him to examine his scalp. The position put her upper body inches above his face, and Cullen started getting that closed-in feeling again until he was distracted by the breasts jiggling before his eyes.

The chemise she wore was very thin and presently wet, he noted, which was no doubt what made it transparent. Cullen found himself staring at the beautiful, round orbs with fascination, shifting his eyes left and right and continuing to do so when she turned his head from side to side to search out the source of the blood.

Apparently finding no injury that could have bloodied her gown, she muttered, "It must be the back of your head," and suddenly lifted his head, pulling it up off the ground, presumably so she could examine the back of his skull. At least that was what he thought she must be doing when he found his face buried in those breasts he'd been watching with such interest.

"Aye, 'tis here. You must have hit your head on a rock or something when you fell," she announced with a combination of success and worry.

Cullen merely sighed and nuzzled into the breasts presently cuddling him. Really, damp though they were, they were quite lovely, and if a man had to be smothered to death, this was not a bad way to go. He felt something hard nudging his right cheek beside his mouth and realized her nipples had grown hard. She also suddenly stilled like prey sensing danger. Not wishing to send her running with fear, he opened his mouth and tried to turn his head to speak a word or two of reassurance to calm her.

"Calm yerself," was what he said. Cullen didn't believe in wasting words. However, it was doubtful if she understood what he said since his words came out muffled by the nipple suddenly filling his open mouth. Despite his intentions not to scare her, when he realized it was a nipple in his mouth, he couldn't resist closing his lips around it and flicking his tongue over the linen-covered bud.

In the next moment, he found pain shooting through his head once more as he was dropped back to the ground.

chapter

Two

"Oh!" Evelinde gasped when she realized she'd dropped the man on his injured head again. She hadn't meant to, but she'd suddenly realized where she'd pressed his head while searching for the wound. At first she'd simply frozen, mortified at what she'd done, and when he'd tried to speak, his mouth against her breast had caused the oddest tingling sensation to shoot from where his mouth moved. It had been stunning in the pleasure it caused. So, of course, she'd released him. Anything that felt that good must be bad.

The man rolled onto his side, his tartan shifting so that she had a lovely view of his legs almost all the

way up to his personal bits. Evelinde forced herself
to look away from the intriguing sight and instead
leaned forward to peer at the wound on the back
of his head. He was a Scot, but that didn't worry
her. Her father had several friends who were Scots,
mostly highlanders he'd met at court or on his trav-
els. They'd had many visitors over the years from
Scotland, and Evelinde supposed this was another,
and expected he'd treat her with the same respect
and kindness the others had. She'd found that Scots
weren't nearly the primitive heathens they were re-
puted to be.

A curse of pain from the man brought Evelinde's
attention back to his head wound. There had been
a good deal of blood on the gown, and there was
still more caught in his hair. However, she found it
impossible to tell how bad the wound was with the
blood and dirt obscuring the injury.

"Are you all right?" she asked worriedly, shifting her gaze to what she could see of the side of his
face. He was grimacing in pain, his one visible eye
squeezed tight shut. Evelinde shifted on her knees
and glanced around the meadow as she tried to
think what to do. Then she asked, "Do you think
you can stand?"

A grunt was his answer. Unsure if that was a yes
or no, she stood up herself, then bent to catch his
arm and try to help him to his feet. "Come. We have
to tend your head."

"Me head is fine," he growled, but would have
been far more convincing if he weren't still grimacing in pain.

His words, spoken with a heavy burr, reminded her that he was Scottish, and Evelinde found herself leaning anxiously over him again as she asked, "Do you know the Devil of Donnachaidh?"

The way he suddenly stiffened suggested he at least recognized the name though most people did. It was the name parents all over England and Scotland used to terrify children into good behavior. *'If ye don't behave, the Devil of Donnachaidh will get ye,'* was an oft-repeated warning by nursemaids and mothers.

When the man started to sit up, Evelinde quickly sat back to give him room. Much to her dissatisfaction, however, he didn't answer her question but simply stared at her, his expression closed.

"Do you know him?" she asked fretfully.

"Aye. I'm the Duncan," he said finally, and Evelinde frowned, not sure what that meant. Was Duncan his name or title? She suspected it was his title, but wondered if the Duncans were a neighbor of clan Donnachaidh? She opened her mouth to ask, but then decided it didn't matter. What was important was that the man knew the devil she was supposed to marry.

"Is he as cruel as they say? He is not, is he?" she asked hopefully. "'Tis just a rumor, is it not? Tales told by the fireside that grow all out of proportion? I am sure he will be a fine husband. Really, he could not be more cruel than Edda. Could he?"

The man wasn't answering any of her questions, which Evelinde thought was terribly rude. Then she saw the streak of red running down his neck and recalled his injury. It really was not well-done of her to sit here pestering him with questions when he was wounded.

"You are bleeding badly," she said with concern. He reached to feel the back of his head, and Evelinde saw pain flash through his eyes at just that tentative touch.

Snatching up her ruined gown, she stood and glanced around. Much to her relief, he'd taken his tumble at the end of the meadow nearest the river. She hadn't paid attention to where they were when their mounts had reared—her attention had been taken up with keeping her seat—then she'd been more worried about him than anything else as she'd rushed to dismount and reach him. Fortunately, they merely had to walk a short path through a narrow band of trees to reach the water.

Turning back to the man on the ground, she held out a hand. "Come. We should tend to your injury."

The man noted her offered hand but got to his feet without accepting her help.

Men can be so proud, Evelinde thought with an exasperated shake of the head.

"Wait here, and I shall retrieve our horses," she instructed. Both animals had moved a good twenty feet away. Her mare was standing still, studiously ignoring the other horse, who was nosing at her side.

Evelinde had only taken a step in that direction when a piercing whistle made her pause. Eyes wide, she glanced back to the Duncan, then gasped in surprise when he caught her arm as his horse suddenly

charged over and presented himself with a proud
flick of the head.

Evelinde waited long enough to see the Duncan
murmur a soft word of praise to the animal and run
a hand over his mount's neck. She then turned and
headed off to collect her mare.

"There is a river just through the trees here," she
announced, returning with Lady. "We can wash
your wound, and I can get a better look and see how
bad it is."

"I be fine," the Duncan muttered, but followed
when she moved past him with her mare and started
through the trees.

"Head wounds can be tricky, sir," Evelinde said
firmly as she led him into the clearing on the edge
of the river. "It needs to be cleaned and tended. And
you need to be careful about sleeping and such for a
bit. You lost consciousness after the fall."

"I be fine," he repeated, his voice a growl.

"I shall be the judge of that," she announced,
releasing Lady's reins and moving to the water's
edge. Once there, she knelt, found a clean bit of
skirt on the gown she carried, and dipped it in the
water. She'd been hoping the wind would dry her
dress, which was why she'd been riding back and
forth, holding it over her head. It probably would
have worked better had she simply taken Lady
for another, heart-pounding race, but she hadn't
wished to be seen charging through d'Aumesbery's
woods in naught but a chemise. The meadow was
surrounded by trees, and she'd hoped to dry the
dress without being seen. Her plan hadn't worked

too well, obviously. She'd been seen, startled off her horse, and her gown still wasn't dry.

Grimacing, Evelinde stood up with the now-sopping skirt in her hands. She turned to find the Duncan, only to pause and stare when she saw he'd removed his boots and was standing knee deep in the river, bent forward, with his head under the waterfall.

"Well, bother!" Evelinde muttered, wishing she'd thought of that rather than soaking her skirt again. Sighing, she laid the gown out to dry on the boulder she'd sat on earlier and crossed the clearing to stand on the bank near where he was letting the water wash away the blood.

"Come, let me see," she ordered, when he straightened, pushed the hair out of his face, and started back out of the water.

The man raised an eyebrow at her demanding manner, but paused before her and turned away. Evelinde stared at the wide wall of his back and rolled her eyes. He was nearly a foot taller than she. She couldn't see a thing.

"Here, you need to sit down." Catching his hand, she tugged him to a fallen tree trunk lying at the edge of the clearing. She urged him to sit, then stepped between his legs and clasped his head to bend it forward so she could see the back of it. With Mildrede's help, Evelinde had taken over tending to the injured and ill when her mother died. It wasn't a task Edda had bothered claiming when she'd become the new lady of d'Aumesbery, so Evelinde had carried on with it and was used to bossing grown soldiers about like they were children. Quite honestly, in her experience, that was exactly how the men tended to act when injured or ill. They were worse than any child when ailing.

"Hmm," she murmured, examining the abrasion. It was still bleeding, but head wounds tended to bleed a lot, and it was really more of a small scrape than a deep gash. "It does not look so bad."

"I told ye I was fine," he rumbled, lifting his head.

"You lost consciousness, sir," she fretted. "Let me see your eyes."

He lifted his face, and Evelinde clasped him by both cheeks, her gaze moving slowly over his eyes. They looked perfectly fine to her, however. More than fine. They were really quite beautiful; large and a deep brown so dark they appeared almost black. They were also fringed by long black lashes. The rest of his face was rugged, however, with sharp planes, an arrow-straight nose, and his lips—

Evelinde's eyes paused there, noting that his upper lip was thin, but the lower one was full and looked as if it would be soft to the touch. Before she could think better of it, curiosity made her shift one thumb to rub it over the pillowed surface, and she found it was indeed soft. Then Evelinde realized what she'd done. She could feel a sudden blush rise to cover her face and released him abruptly.

"There was a bit of dirt there," she lied, trying to step away at the same time, but his legs immediately closed on either side of her. Finding herself trapped between his knees, Evelinde felt her first moment of disquiet with the man. Not fear, exactly. For some reason she felt sure she had nothing to fear from this man, but the action did make her nervous.

She opened her mouth to ask him to release her, then sucked her breath in on a hiss of pain when his hands rose up to catch her by the hips. His hold eased at once, but he didn't let her go. Instead, he held her in place and lowered his gaze to the spot he'd touched, a frown claiming his lips.

"Ye took some punishment in the fall as well," he growled, sounding displeased. "Ye've a bruise on yer hip."

Evelinde bit her lip and tried to pretend she was anywhere else but there as his gaze rose along her side, one hand following the path, then pausing again on the side of her chest just below her left breast. The action stirred an odd tingling along her skin.

"And here."

She glanced down with confusion. The bruising would be from her fall in the water, but there was no way he could see through her chemise to the bruises he was—

Evelinde's thoughts died as she saw that her still-damp chemise was transparent. She could clearly make out several dark patches through the clinging cloth. One was the large mottling bruise on her hip, the other another even bigger bruise on her ribs, but the others were not bruises at all. Her darker nipples were clearly displayed in the damp shift, and the dark gold at the apex of her thighs stood out against her pale skin.

A gasp of horror caught in her throat, but before

Evelinde could pull away and cover herself, he'd taken hold of her arm.

"And here."

She peered distractedly down at the arm he'd turned slightly. She had seen all these bruises earlier, the result of her tumble in the river, not from falling from her horse as he supposed. She was more concerned with other issues at the moment, like her near nudity. When he leaned a little closer to see her upper arm better, Evelinde sucked in a startled gulp of air. His breath was blowing hot and sweet on her chilled nipple through the damp chemise. The effect was almost shocking.

Evelinde stood completely still, holding her breath as he examined her injury. He took an exceptionally long time doing so, much longer than he had with the other bruises. And the whole time he did, he was inhaling and exhaling, sending out warm puffs of air over the trembling nipple. Each time he did, an odd little tingle went through Evelinde. Then he suddenly raised a hand to run a finger lightly around the discoloration on her arm, and his wrist brushed against her nipple through the damp cloth.

Evelinde was sure it was accidental, and he did not even notice, but the effect it had on her was rather startling. She closed her eyes as an odd pleasure rolled through her body, finding herself suddenly torn between putting some space between them and staying put to enjoy more of the astonishing effect he had on her. When he finally released her arm and unclasped her legs, she opened her eyes to find him standing up. Before Evelinde could regain enough of her senses to go find her gown and draw it on to cover herself, he'd clasped her head in one hand and tilted her face up to his as he brushed his finger lightly in a circle along her left jaw.

"Ye've another here," he growled.

"Oh," Evelinde breathed, as his finger apparently followed the edge of the bruise past the corner of her lips. That, too, was from her fall in the river, but she couldn't seem to untangle her tongue enough to say so as his finger trailed over her skin.

"Ye've beautiful eyes, lass," he murmured, peering into those eyes now rather than at the injury he was tracing.

"So do you," Evelinde whispered before she could think better of it.

A smile tugged at the corner of his lips right before his mouth covered hers.

Evelinde stiffened at the unexpected caress. His lips *were* soft yet firm, but kissing her was wholly inappropriate. She was about to say so when something prodded at her lips. Evelinde tried to pull back, but his hand was at the back of her head, preventing her retreat. Suddenly she found her mouth invaded by his tongue.

Her first instinct was to push him away, but then his tongue rasped along hers, and Evelinde stilled again. The caress was surprisingly pleasant. She found herself holding on to his arms rather than pushing him away, and her eyes closed as a little sigh slipped from her mouth to his.

No one had ever kissed Evelinde. No one would have dared. She had never left d'Aumesbery and, as the daughter of the lord, was forbidden to dally with the knights and servants of the castle. This was a first for her, and she really wasn't sure if she liked this kissing business. It was interesting, and was causing little stirs of excitement in her, but they were faint and well overshadowed by her confusion. Evelinde wasn't terribly disappointed when he broke the kiss. But he didn't release her as she expected, instead his mouth simply trailed its way across her uninjured cheek.

"Sir," Evelinde murmured, thinking it time she introduce herself and tell him he had to stop. She had no fear he wouldn't. The moment she mentioned being betrothed to the Devil of Donnachaidh, he'd probably thrust her away himself. Everyone feared the Devil, she thought, then stilled again as he began to nuzzle the side of her neck.

Her breath caught in her throat at the havoc sent rioting through her. Evelinde found her eyes drooping closed again, and a murmur of surprised pleasure slipped from her lips as she tilted her head to allow him better access. She even shifted a little closer to the man, her hands now clutching at his arms and urging him nearer rather than pushing him away. All sorts of tingly sensations were rushing through her as his mouth moved over her skin to her ear. He concentrated there until Evelinde found herself standing on her tiptoes in the circle of his arms, gasping and moaning.

His mouth finally returned to hers, and this time, she was not quiescent. Evelinde kissed him back, her tongue now wrestling with his. His hands began to move then, releasing the hold he'd kept on her head and sliding down her back until they slid over her bottom. Clasping the curve of each cheek, he lifted her off her feet and pressed her against him.

Evelinde groaned into his mouth as a hardness ground against the apex of her thighs through their clothes. It sent a sharp new excitement shooting through her, and she found herself shifting her hips and tightening her arms around his neck as she tried to get closer still.

When he suddenly broke their kiss, she moaned in disappointment, but when he then reclaimed his seat on the fallen log and tugged her forward to tumble into his lap, some of her common sense resurfaced.

"Oh, nay, sir! We should not be doing this. I am betrothed to the Devil of Donnachaidh."

Evelinde had expected that to bring an abrupt halt to the proceedings, but the man merely muttered, "I am the Duncan and would have a kiss."

His mouth descended on hers again, and Evelinde gave up her feeble struggles. One kiss did not seem so bad, she thought, as his tongue invaded her again, resurrecting her excitement. At least she would have these memories to warm her in her cold marriage bed, she thought, then—conscience soothed—Evelinde stopped thinking and allowed herself to enjoy his kiss.

It was much nicer sitting in his lap. She was surrounded by him, cocooned by the hard lap beneath her and the warm chest and arms around her. Relaxing against the arm at her back, she slid her own arms around his neck again, careful to avoid the sore spot on the back of his head as she kissed him enthusiastically. Evelinde shuddered and pressed against him as his hands slid over her back, and then gasped and arched as his hand moved around to find and clasp one breast through her damp chemise. Clutching at the cloth of his plaid, Evelinde groaned into his mouth and held on for dear life as he kneaded the round orb, and she was inundated by a whole new swell of sensations.

When his thumb brushed over the excited nipple through the cloth, it sent shocks of pleasure through her, and she couldn't keep from wiggling in his lap. Her hips moved of their own volition as they ground her bottom down against the hardness under her.

This seemed to have an electrifying effect on the Duncan, his kiss immediately became more demanding. The hand at her back shifted to her head to tilt her one way, then the other as the fingers at her breast tightened and began to pluck at her nipple through the quickly drying cloth.

This time Evelinde turned her head to give him better access when his mouth moved to her ear once more. His attention there soon had her gasping and moaning. Other than to dig her fingers more firmly into his shoulders, she hardly noticed when he leaned her back against his arm so his mouth could travel down her neck. His hand was still doing delightful things to first one breast, then the other, and that, combined with his lips nibbling over the flesh of her throat, had her giving one long, seemingly unending moan. By the time he reached the shockingly sensitive area of her collarbone, she was a mass of excitement, wiggling in his lap in response to the liquid heat now pooling in her lower belly.

So distracted was she, Evelinde didn't realize he had tugged aside the top of her chemise, revealing one breast, until his lips suddenly left her collarbone and dipped to close over the naked nipple.

She cried out then with both shock and excitement and tugged frantically at his plaid as he suckled and drew on the nipple, his tongue flicking over it repeatedly.

Evelinde knew she shouldn't be allowing this. She was betrothed to someone else. Even if she hadn't been, however, as an unmarried lady, she shouldn't be allowing it . . . but it felt so *good*. And really, if she was going to be married off to the Devil of Donnachaidh and left to wither away in misery, or possibly beaten to death by the man, it did seem less of a sin to allow herself the momentary pleasure of a kiss or two.

Besides, it was the most amazing thing she had yet experienced in her life. Evelinde had never felt so . . . alive. She was afire with passions she'd never even imagined existed, her body reacting of its own volition as it pressed and rubbed against him, seeking something she didn't understand.

The excitement he was causing in her was a living thing that built and built until Evelinde couldn't bear it anymore. Only then did the Duncan let her nipple slip from his mouth with one last rasp of the tongue and lift his head to cover her mouth again. If his earlier kiss had been passionate and demanding, it was nothing compared to this one. He wielded his tongue like a weapon, thrusting it into her mouth as if thrusting a sword into an opponent. Evelinde welcomed it and parried with her own.

His hand was again at her breast, fingers cupping and squeezing as his thumb rubbed back and forth over the sensitive nub. Evelinde groaned and found herself squeezing her thighs together as heat pooled there.

When his hand drifted away from her breast, she felt a keen sense of regret. However, that quickly turned to alarm as she felt it begin to drift up her leg, pushing the hem of her chemise before it. Evelinde squawked into his mouth and immediately began to struggle. This was definitely further than she was willing even to contemplate going.

She must have caught him by surprise, for Evelinde was sure he could have held on to her had he wished to, but he didn't. He removed both hands at once, and she quickly pushed herself from his lap, managing to send herself tumbling to the ground at his feet.

The Duncan immediately reached for her, but Evelinde scrabbled backward out of his reach, then scrambled to her feet and rushed over to snatch up her wet dress. Aware he was following and afraid he would try to drag her back, she kept moving, circling the clearing as she struggled to drag the gown on over her head, babbling anxiously as she tried to stay out of his reach.

"Pray, sir, you must stop. I should not have allowed even the one kiss. I am betrothed to the Devil of Donnachaidh. He's said to have a vile temper and—"

Her words died on a gasp as he caught her from behind and whirled her around to face him. He couldn't kiss her, however—her gown was wet and recalcitrant and caught on her head. Evelinde expected him to rip it back off and continue his barrage of kisses. Instead, however, he tugged at it, helping her to don it. It seemed mention of her betrothed had stopped him after all.

Relieved he wouldn't tempt her to further sin, Evelinde beamed a smile at him as soon as the cloth was tugged down from her face, and said, "Thank you."

The Duncan finished tugging the dress into place, then straightened and peered into her face.

Evelinde stared back, trying to memorize his features to take out and examine in the long miserable years to come, sure this face was the one bright spot she would have in her life once she was married off to the Devil of Donnachaidh. She was sure it was his eyes she'd remember best. They spoke of what he was feeling. At the moment, they were afire with a hunger she suspected was mirrored in her own. It was madness, she didn't know this man, but in truth, all she really wanted to do at that moment was forget everything, strip off her gown and chemise, and make him kiss her again. She wanted his hands moving over her body, making the fire jump and run under her skin as he had moments ago. It was something Evelinde had never experienced before today and something she suspected she'd never experience again as the wife of the Devil of Donnachaidh.

Apparently it was something the Duncan wanted to do, too, because his head started to lower, his mouth aiming for hers, but Evelinde stepped quickly away. "Nay. I pray you, Sir Duncan. No more."

He hesitated, a frown claiming his lips as if he was confused by her refusal. "Ye liked me kisses. Doona deny it. I ken ye did."

"Aye," she admitted sadly. "And I would give a lot to have more of them, but not your life. If he lives up to his reputation, the Devil of Donnachaidh would probably kill you if he found out about the kiss we already shared. I would not see him kill you for something that will be a lovely memory and will no doubt sustain me through many a dreadful night in my marriage bed."

He blinked at her words, then shook his head. "Lass, I am *the Duncan*."

"Duncan," she repeated softly. "I shall never forget your name."

He rolled his eyes with disgust, then explained, "Duncan is me clan name, I am Cullen . . . the Duncan," he said meaningfully.

"Cullen," she breathed, thinking it much nicer than Duncan.

Frowning now he said, "Duncan in Gaelic is Donnachaidh."

Evelinde's eyes widened with a dawning horror. This was just awful, the worst thing she could imagine. If he was a member of her future husband's clan, then she would no doubt see a lot of him. He would be there day in and day out, a temptation she would have to resist for both their sakes. Their very lives would depend on it.

"Oh this is awful," she breathed, imagining years of torture ahead. "You are kin to my betrothed.

"Nay," he said with exasperation. "I *am* yer betrothed."

chapter

Three

You cannot be."

Cullen's eyebrows rose at that dismayed whisper from Evelinde d'Aumesbery, his bride-to-be. Moments ago, she'd been warm and willing in his arms, and now she appeared utterly horrified. Mouth turning down grimly, he assured her, "I am."

"Nay, you cannot be the Devil of Donnachaidh," she assured him. "He is . . . well a *Devil*. Everyone knows that. And you . . ." She peered at him help-lessly. "You are handsome and sweet and have kind eyes. And you made me feel . . ." She paused and shook her head firmly. "You cannot be the Devil."

Cullen's expression softened at her words. She found him handsome? He could do without the sweet and kind eyes nonsense, but he liked that she thought him handsome.

"What did I make ye feel?" he growled, moving closer to slide one hand up her arm, suppressing a satisfied smile when she shivered and gasped at the light touch.

"My lady!"

Cullen froze and nearly cursed aloud at the interruption as he became aware of the sound of hoof-beats closing on them. Scowling, he turned a glare on the hapless man who charged into the clearing on a light reddish brown roan.

"Mac." There was no missing the relief in her voice as Evelinde pulled away and turned to greet the man.

"There ye are. I was starting to worry. I—"

Cullen's eyebrows rose as the man's words died and his expression darkened with rage. He followed the fellow's gaze to Evelinde and immediately understood. The woman was a complete and utter mess. Her dress was still damp and torn in at least three places; the worst of which was a long rent from shoulder to waistline. It left one side of her gown gaping open like a flap, giving them both a perfect view of the bruise on her side, visible through the still-damp cloth of her chemise. If that wasn't enough to convince the man his mistress had been attacked, there was also the darkening bruise on her chin, her lips, swollen from his kisses, the knotted mass her hair was, and the still-stunned look on her face.

The fury on the man's expression made Cullen positive he was going to get some welcome exercise to work off the unsatisfied desire still rolling through him, but then he noted the man didn't have a sword. A servant then, he realized with disappointment.

"Ye'd be the Donnachaidh, then?" the man asked, his voice shaking with fury.

"Aye." Cullen answered, supposing his men must have reached the castle before this man had ridden out. If they had mentioned coming across a woman in the woods and their laird staying behind with her, it might even be the reason he'd headed out in search of his mistress. It suggested he was protective of her, and not a coward if he was willing to face the infamous Devil of Donnachaidh for his lady.

As he caught Evelinde by the arm and urged her to her mare, Cullen considered easing the man's mind by explaining he was not the cause of any of her injuries, but then decided against it. He rarely bothered to explain anything. Cullen preferred to let people make up their own minds about things, which was part of the reason he had such a fearsome reputation. Left to their own devices, people almost always chose the most damning explanation for events. That usually worked to his advantage, however. It was quite handy being considered the cruel, heartless Devil of Donnachaidh. His reputation assured most battles were won before they even began. He'd found there was no better weapon in the world than the fear inspired by the ridiculous tales of the Devil of Donnachaidh.

"Thank you," Evelinde murmured, when he lifted her onto her mare.

He glanced at her then to find she was eyeing him with an expression that was both worried and perplexed. For some reason that made him want to kiss her again . . . so he did. Ignoring the watching servant, Cullen caught her by the back of the neck and drew her head down for a brief hard kiss that made her gasp in surprise. Then he released her, and she sat back up in the saddle. Apparently, the action hadn't been reassuring to her. If anything, she looked more worried as well as more perplexed.

Women are like that though, Cullen thought as he caught the reins of her horse in hand and led it to his own mount. *Always thinking, always fretting, and never logical, but that was why God had made men, to protect the silly creatures from themselves.*

He hauled himself up into the saddle and turned to eye the servant expectantly. The man glanced from him to his mistress, then ground his teeth together and urged his horse out of the clearing. Cullen followed, drawing Evelinde's horse behind.

With any other woman he would have paid her no more heed than that, but Cullen found himself glancing repeatedly over his shoulder as they rode. He couldn't seem to help himself. Every time he looked back, it was to find her returning the stare, and her expression was different each time. Perplexed, worried, thoughtful . . . When Cullen glanced back to find a soft smile on her face, it was too much for him. He stopped his horse, drew her mare to a halt as it cantered alongside his mount, and reached out to draw her onto his horse before him.

"Who is he?" Cullen asked as he urged his mount to start moving again.

"Mac," she answered. "He is our stable master . . . and a friend."

Cullen considered the back of the grizzled man's head, but quickly decided he was no threat. The stable master was not an amorous interest to the girl he was sure. The man's influence was probably more fatherly in nature. From her complete lack of finesse when he'd first kissed her, it seemed obvious his betrothed had never been kissed before. She'd learned quickly though, he thought with satisfaction and allowed the hand he had around her waist to slide up to rest just below one breast. She would please him in bed.

"He thinks I raped ye," he announced, and she jerked in his arms.

"What? No! Why would he think that?" she asked, twisting around to look at him.

Cullen merely raised one eyebrow, his gaze sweeping over her. Evelinde followed his gaze and groaned as she took note of the state she was in, then caught the gaping flap of her gown and tried to draw it up to cover herself, but his arm and hand were in the way.

Sighing, she gave up the effort, and asked, "Why did you not explain?"

Cullen shrugged, the action bringing his hand up higher so it brushed against the bottom of her breast. "I am the Devil of Donnachaidh."

Evelinde peered up at him silently, and Cullen felt himself suddenly uncomfortable under that gaze. He suspected he'd revealed more than he'd intended with those words.

Scowling, he snapped his mouth shut and turned his gaze forward. This was exactly why he didn't like talking.

Cullen remained silent for the rest of the ride, but Evelinde didn't mind. She was caught up in her own thoughts, but found it somewhat difficult to concentrate with his hand brushing repeatedly against her breast. Each time it did, an arrow of anticipation shot through her as her body recalled the pleasure he'd given her in the clearing.

And that was a problem. Evelinde was terribly confused. The Devil of Donnachaidh, or the Duncan as he kept calling himself, wasn't at all what she'd expected. She hadn't felt any fear at all of the man. Even when he'd first appeared in the meadow, she hadn't been frightened so much as startled to find someone next to her.

Evelinde hadn't had much time to think about her upcoming marriage to the Devil of Donnachaidh, but she was sure she wouldn't have imagined he could inspire the passion in her he had. The Devil was supposed to be a cold, heartless, and cruel bastard. He was supposed to have murdered his father and uncle to gain his title as laird of his clan. He was also supposed to have killed his first wife because she produced no bairns for him. Perhaps Evelinde was naive, but it seemed to her a man like

that should look cruel and heartless. He should inspire fear in a body the moment one laid eyes on
him, and he shouldn't be able to stir the concern and
passion in her that Evelinde had experienced back
in the clearing.

That was only one of her worries, however. The
other was that she feared—after her wanton behavior
in the clearing—the man might think her free with
her affections. And she hadn't even known he was
her betrothed. Did he think she was not just wanton
but also the sort of woman who would be unfaithful? Because she *had* been unfaithful. Perhaps not
technically since it turned out he was the man she
was to marry, but Evelinde hadn't known that when
she was letting him kiss her so passionately and do
those other things, and now she was ashamed of
herself and afraid of what he thought of her.

Cullen's thumb suddenly brushed across the
bottom of her breast, distracting Evelinde again.
Glancing up, she noted they had arrived back at
d'Aumesbery and were crossing the drawbridge.
Her gaze lifted to the men on the wall, and she
frowned as she noted how silent they were and how
grim their expressions. Obviously, they had noted
her condition and were thinking the worst.

Feeling herself blush with embarrassment,
Evelinde bit her lip on the instinct to shout out that
she hadn't been raped and merely turned her face
forward as they passed into the bailey.

Edda was waiting for them at the doors of the
keep as they crossed the bailey. Five rugged-looking
men in plaids stood around her.

"Your men?" Evelinde asked, her gaze sliding over them. Each and every one towered over Edda, and Edda was not short. Her stepmother stood at least four inches taller than she, so it seemed obvious they were all good-sized men. They stood with arms crossed over their chests and grim expressions on their faces. They didn't look particularly pleased to be there.

Edda, on the other hand, looked like the cat who found the cream. Her smile widened with every step Cullen's mount took as she was better able to see the state her stepdaughter was in.

Evelinde had no doubt the woman was coming to the same conclusions that Mac had, only her stepmother was apparently enjoying these conclusions. She wasn't really surprised. Edda had never liked her and had made no bones about letting her know it. No doubt she'd convinced the king to choose the Devil of Donnachaidh as Evelinde's betrothed in the hopes of ensuring her a miserable future. In fact, she suspected Edda would probably be most upset to know what had really happened. If the odious woman thought for one moment that Evelinde had gained her bruises—not from this man—but in a fall in the river, or that the Duncan had but kissed her and—worse yet—that she'd enjoyed his kisses and caresses, Edda might very well find some way to end this betrothal.

That thought gave Evelinde pause. When she'd ridden out of the bailey the idea of finding a way to end her betrothal to the Devil of Donnachaidh would have been a welcome one. Was it still?

She twisted to look at the man behind her. Cullen's chin was high, his eyes on the people on the stairs, his expression as grim as those of the men they were approaching . . . but she recalled the soft words of praise he'd given his horse and the affectionate pat he'd offered the animal. His kisses had been passionate and yet not roughly so, while his caresses and touch had been gentle. And when she'd begun to struggle, he'd released her at once, even though, as her betrothed, he really needn't have. He had also handled her gently when he'd lifted her onto her mount, and again when he'd lifted her from her mount to join him on his own horse on the return journey.

All of this made Evelinde wonder now how many of the terrible tales about him were simply that: tales. People assuming they knew what happened and he allowing them to do so.

It was little enough to go on, but more than she'd known before their meeting in the meadow.

Evelinde wasn't yet sure of much about this man, but she was sure about one thing. She was not afraid of him. Her instincts were telling her she was safe in his hands.

It made her positive she did not wish Edda finding out the truth of things. She would not risk the woman bringing an end to this betrothal, only to marry her off to someone she *was* afraid of, or whom she would find sharing a bed with to be thoroughly repulsive, because Evelinde was quite sure she would not have that problem with this man. He had already stirred passions in her she hadn't known existed.

No, Evelinde decided, she would allow Edda and everyone else to think the worst . . . and marry this man.

When Cullen reined in his mount and slid off the back of the horse, Evelinde immediately started to slide off unaided, but he was there to catch her by the waist before her feet hit the dirt. Their eyes met briefly as he set her gently on the ground, and she almost smiled her thanks, but then she remembered Edda and glowered instead. She saw surprise flash through his eyes and nearly blurted an apology, but caught it back and instead murmured, "Forgive me, my lord, for what is about to take place. I shall explain later. Just, pray, be the Devil of Donnachaidh as you were with Mac."

Much to her relief, he didn't demand an explanation. One eyebrow merely arched slightly on his forehead, but that was the only reaction he showed.

She turned to walk forward, her steps slow and a bit rigid as her bruising began to pain her. Stiffness was setting in, she realized with a grimace. No doubt it would only worsen in the coming hours.

Her gaze slid to Edda to see the woman was almost in the throes of ecstasy as she watched her approach. Hiding the disgust she felt, Evelinde forced her face to remain solemn and emotionless and paused before her. She wasn't surprised when Edda ignored her altogether and instead turned a wide, approving smile on Cullen.

"Laird Donnachaidh," Edda greeted. "I see you have met our Evelinde. I do hope you are pleased with the betrothal."

"Aye," Cullen grunted, and Evelinde noted the way his eyes shifted to his men in question. Each met his gaze in turn and some silent message seemed to pass between them. Evelinde couldn't read what the message was but suspected it had something to do with Edda.

"Good, good." Her stepmother smiled widely, then quickly tempered the smile to hide her teeth and slid her arm through his to turn him toward the door to the keep. "I should tell you I am the one who chose you to marry our Evelinde, and I admire a man who begins as he means to go on. You need not spare the girl. Beat her as often as you wish. She is healthy and strong and can withstand much. In fact, she is so strong I often wonder if there is not peasant stock somewhere in her ancestry." She ended the little insult with a laugh that faded uncertainly as she tried to lead Cullen to the door of the keep only to find he didn't move.

"Yer priest," Cullen growled when she turned a confused expression up to his face.

Her eyebrows rose. "Father Saunders?"

"Fetch him. We wed and we leave."

"So soon? I—You—" Edda paused, then, apparently deciding she liked the idea of ridding herself of Evelinde so quickly, her wide smile returned. "I shall send for him at once."

Cullen gave a curt nod, caught Evelinde by the arm, and urged her past Edda to enter the keep.

Evelinde bit her lip on the protest that she couldn't possibly be ready to go so quickly. Instead, she tried to think how she could manage to get all her things

packed and ready to go in such a short time. The idea
of leaving d'Aumesbery was both a painful prospect
and a pleasure to contemplate. There were many
here she would miss. She had grown up with these
people and was now leaving them behind. The idea
of being free of Edda, however, was a pleasant one,
Evelinde thought, as Cullen left her at the bottom of
the stairs and she started up them.

It wasn't until she started up those steps that she
realized how much of a problem her injuries were
going to be. While walking raised aches and com-
plaints, lifting her legs to mount the stairs made her
suck in her breath as pain shot from hip to knee. Oh
yes, traveling was going to be most unpleasant, she
thought with a sigh.

Gritting her teeth, Evelinde forced herself to ignore
the pain and continue upward, telling herself it
would pass. A day or two and she would be fine. It
was just bruising and stiffness setting in now. She
could handle the pain until her body mended. But she
knew it would only grow worse over the next hour or
so. The thought of having to rush about packing was
not a pleasant one, but the thought of riding after the
ceremony was enough to bring tears to her eyes.

Her room was empty when she entered. Evelinde
put off changing for now and began to pack, working as quickly as she could. She hadn't grown much
since she was sixteen years old and had always taken
care with her gowns, so while Edda had refused
to allow her even one new dress since her father's
death, Evelinde still had many clothes from while
he'd still lived. They were all somewhat old and

faded, perhaps, and a little frayed here and there, but still wearable. She was slowly folding away one such gown in her chest when her chamber door burst open and Mildrede rushed in.

"Oh, my lady! Mac told me—Dear God in heaven," the maid breathed, coming to an abrupt halt when Evelinde straightened and turned to face her.

It was only then Evelinde recalled her bedraggled and bruised state. Wishing she'd taken a moment to change as Cullen had ordered, she quickly assured her, "Cullen did not do this."

"Nay, that Devil you're supposed to marry did," Mildrede said grimly.

"No, I—"

"Mac told me everything. Never fear, we have a plan," she assured her, hurrying forward. "We shall run away. 'Tis not far to the Abbey. We can—"

"Cullen is the Devil," Evelinde interrupted, stepping back as the woman reached for her, then realized that hadn't come out right. "I mean, he is not really the Devil. But—Cullen is Lord Donnachaidh," she said finally, exasperated with herself. "And he did not do this. I fell in the river."

"Oh, aye." Mildrede paused before her, open disbelief on her face. "And falling in the river ripped your bodice wide open, did it?"

"Nay," she admitted. "Cullen did that."

Mildrede nodded and grabbed her by the arm. "We are fleeing. Mac is preparing three horses as we speak."

"Nay," Evelinde cried, tugging at her arm, but her maid was determined to save her and held fast. "He did not mean to rip the gown, he was just trying to get it off . . . of him," she added quickly, when Mildrede clucked with disgust.

That brought her to a halt. Turning back with wide horrified eyes, she asked, "He is one of those? He was wanting to wear your dress?"

"Nay," Evelinde gasped, shocked at the very idea. Really, she couldn't imagine Cullen or any other man wanting to don a dress. "It was on his head."

That explanation did not soothe Mildrede. If anything, it seemed to be exactly what she'd expected.

"The randy Devil!" she said with disgust, beginning to tug her forward once more. "Forcing his way under yer skirt on first meeting you! And the two of you not even wed yet!"

"Mildrede!" Evelinde cried with exasperation. "'Tis not what you think! Pray, stop and let me explain. This is all just a muddle. He really did not hurt me."

"You can explain on the way to the stables. 'Tis —" Her voice died as she opened the door only to find herself confronted with several servants bearing a tub and pails of water.

"The Dev—Lord Donnachaidh ordered a hot bath for you, my lady," one of the men at the front of the tub announced. "He said we were to make it as hot as you could stand. 'Twould soothe your aches and pains from your fall."

"See." Evelinde tugged her arm from Mildrede's grasp and moved a couple of steps away just to be sure she didn't grab it again. "I told you I fell."

Mildrede hesitated, then instructed the men to set

the tub by the fire, before moving closer to Evelinde. "So he did not strike you? Not one of those bruises you are sporting are from his fists?"

"Nay. 'Twas the fall in the river that bruised me, though I think he thinks I fell from my horse as he did," Evelinde assured her in a whisper, her gaze moving nervously to the men now emptying pail after pail of steaming water into the tub. She didn't wish them to hear and possibly report to Edda. Drawing Mildrede to the far corner of the room, she quickly whispered the string of events that had led to her returning in the state she was in.

"So his head was not under your skirt?" Mildrede said slowly, once Evelinde had finished. "He did not touch you in that way at all?"

"Well . . ." Evelinde blushed and avoided her gaze. Then seeing the suspicion on the woman's face, she sighed and admitted, "He kissed me."

Mildrede stared at her silently and quirked an eyebrow. "And?"

Evelinde hesitated, but knew if she didn't convince her maid all would be well, Mildrede and Mac would risk themselves to try to make her escape, and she really had no desire to escape the marriage at this point. In fact, she was beginning to feel the first bit of hope for her future she'd had in a long time. She would be the mistress of her own home, without Edda there to make life miserable, and truly, she was beginning to have hope she might deal acceptably well with Cullen.

"He has really been quite kind," Evelinde assured

her in a low and solemn voice. "And I feel no fear
with him. He has kind eyes and"—she took a deep
breath, and admitted—"I enjoyed his kisses . . . Very
much," she added when Mildrede hesitated, still
looking uncertain. "Besides, look how thoughtful he
was in ordering a bath for me to ease my aches," she
pointed out, and shook her head. "He is not what
his reputation claims him to be, Mildrede, any more
than Edda is the sweet, biddable, and adoring stepmother everyone at court thinks she is."

A slow sigh slid from the maid's lips, then she
glanced to the men as they finished their work. She
watched them leave the room before turning back
to Evelinde to suggest, "Get you into the tub. I shall
nip down to the stables to reassure Mac all is well . . .
for now. Howbeit, do you change your mind, we can
still—"

"I will not change my mind," Evelinde assured
her, and was quite positive she wouldn't. She then
cautioned, "Make sure no one is near when you tell
Mac the truth of what happened. I would not have
Edda learn any of this before the wedding takes
place."

"Nay. The old cow would probably find some way
to break the betrothal and force you to marry another," the maid muttered, confirming Evelinde's
own thoughts on the matter. "Shall I help you with
your gown?"

Evelinde opened her mouth to refuse the offer,
but then hesitated. It wasn't just her leg stiffening
up as time passed. She had noticed her arm was be-

ginning to ache as she'd packed, and suspected between that and her bruised ribs, undressing would not be the easy task it normally was.

"Aye. Thank you," she murmured.

Mildrede nodded and set to work, removing the gown quickly. She pronounced it beyond repair and tossed it in a corner, then helped remove Evelinde's chemise, tsking with concern as the bruises she bore were revealed.

"You cannot ride like this, my lady," Mildrede said with a frown as she urged her into the tub. "You will be in horrible pain."

"I hope the bath will help," Evelinde said quietly, wincing as the hot water seemed to scorch her skin. She was panting from the heat by the time she lowered herself fully into the tub, but it soon became more bearable, and it did start to ease her aches and pains almost right away.

"Can you not ask him to remain a day or two to allow you to heal? If he is as kind as you claim, surely he would allow it?"

Evelinde bit her lip, but then shook her head. "He has already seen them and yet desires to leave at once. He must have his reasons. Besides, what is a little pain beside the pleasure of escaping Edda?" she asked dryly.

Mildrede smiled reluctantly at the words and sighed. "I shall put a little tonic in your mead for you to drink. 'Twill make it more bearable."

"Thank you. I would appreciate that," Evelinde admitted.

Mildrede nodded and turned away. "I shall bring

the mead and tonic back when I return from speaking to Mac. You just relax and soak."

Evelinde nodded silently, her eyes closing as she allowed the water to work its magic.

She must have fallen asleep in the hot water, for the next thing Evelinde knew, Mildrede was back, three maids on her heels and the water she reclined in was now tepid.

"Father Saunders is here, and your betrothed wants you below for the wedding at once," her maid squawked in a panic. She tossed her bag of medicinals on the chest by the bed, then hurried to the tub, where Evelinde was forcing herself to sit up. "Come. We have to wash your hair and get you dressed."

"How long have I been soaking?" Evelinde asked blearily as she noted her fingers and toes were wrinkled from the water.

Mildrede took a moment to bark at the other three maids to get packing, then answered, "Quite a while. It took me longer than I intended to convince Mac all was well, then Edda demanded I do first one thing and another for her."

The maid shook her head with disgust as she picked up a pail and splashed it over Evelinde's head to dampen her hair. "I will not be sorry to see the back of that woman."

Evelinde murmured an agreement and closed her eyes as Mildrede began to wash her hair with scented soap. She heard the door open again and blinked her eyes open, risking getting the soap in her eyes, to see a maid hurry in, a mug in hand.

"I brought the mead, Mildrede," the woman said, hurrying toward them.

"Put a little of my tonic in it, Alice," Mildrede ordered. She nodded toward the chest by the bed. "'Tis in my medicinal bag on the chest. A smaller leather pouch with an x scratched into it."

The maid did as instructed, and Evelinde closed her eyes again as Mildrede grabbed up a pail to rinse her hair.

"I am sure I will be fine without the tonic, Mildrede," she said once the maid finished pouring out the first pail of water.

"The tonic will help. 'Tis better to be safe than sorry," she assured her, pouring another pail over her head.

Evelinde didn't bother to protest further. She supposed it couldn't hurt.

"There. Up you come. We have to dry your hair and dress you." Mildrede wrapped a linen around her when Evelinde stood, then held her hand to brace her as she stepped out of the tub. She urged her to a chair by the fire.

"Alice, where is the—Oh good," Mildrede muttered as the maid rushed over with the doctored mead. Handing it to Evelinde, she said, "Sit there and drink your tonic while I figure out what you should wear."

Evelinde accepted the mug with a smile of thanks for Alice, then lifted it to her nose and sniffed. That was enough to tell her this was going to be one of those tonics that caused more pain going down than it eased. She considered refusing to drink it, but rather than argue with Mildrede, she plugged her nose and tipped the mug to her lips. No amount of nose holding could cover the foul taste of this brew, however, and Evelinde nearly gagged on the pungent liquid the moment it hit her tongue.

"Gawd, Mildrede, 'tis horrible stuff," she complained with a shudder as she lowered the mug.

Mildrede turned from the gowns she was sorting through to shake her head. "'Tis not. You should barely be able to taste it."

It was what the woman always said to get her to drink her medicine, and Evelinde gave her usual disbelieving snort, then plugged her nose and downed the rest of it.

"Do I have to eat the dregs?" she asked reluctantly when she recovered from downing the last of it and found the bottom of the mug full of small bits of crushed leaves and twigs.

"What?" Mildrede was suddenly at her side, snatching the mug from her. She peered at the contents, and then cursed and whirled to Alice. "What did you put in here, girl!"

Evelinde felt trepidation rise up along her spine at the panic in the woman's voice.

"I—the one you said to. With the x," the hapless Alice gasped, following Mildrede when she rushed to snatch up her medicinal bag and dump its contents on the bed.

"Which one did you use?" she asked.

"That one." The girl picked up a small pouch.

"Nay!" Mildrede gasped in horror.

"Is it wrong? You said the one with the x on it," Alice cried with distress.

"That is not an x, 'tis a cross," Mildrede snapped. She glanced down into the mug with a frown, and asked, "How much did you put in?"

"I—You said just a little," Alice answered evasively.

"Aye, I did, but this pouch was full and is now half-empty."

"Well, it tipped a bit as I was pouring it in," the girl said apologetically.

"Dear God," Mildrede breathed.

"What is it, Mildrede?" Evelinde asked, alarmed when her voice came out terribly slurred. She tried to gather the linen around herself to stand and cross the room, but found her hands incapable of holding the cloth. The material simply slipped through her fingers like sand. "What—?"

" 'Tis all right," the maid said reassuringly as she headed back toward her, though the worry in her voice detracted somewhat from the words. " 'Twill not kill you. 'Twill just—" Mildrede broke off and rushed forward to catch her as Evelinde began to slide out of the seat.

chapter

Four

Did ye na tell that maid to hurry? What is taking so long?"

Cullen managed not to grimace at Tavis's complaint. His cousin had never been a patient man, but at that moment he was in full agreement with him. He'd sent the maid up to fetch his bride more than an hour past and Evelinde still had not appeared.

"Ye doona think she doesna wish to marry ye and fled, do ye?" Tavis said fretfully. "Yer reputation as the Devil of Donnachaidh may have scared her off. Maybe we should check the stables and be sure her mare is still here."

Cullen frowned at the suggestion. From what Evelinde had said in the clearing, he already knew his reputation as the Devil of Donnachaidh had preceded him. Still, he didn't think she was afraid of him. In fact, after their tryst in the clearing, he would expect she'd be less afraid of him and even looking forward to the marriage bed. He certainly was.

"Nay," he said finally. "There's no reason for her to run."

"Women don't need a reason," Fergus said dryly from his other side. " 'Sides, I wouldna be so sure. She could be mad. She certainly didna seem all that right in the head, riding about the meadow waving a flag as she was."

" 'Twas her gown," Cullen snapped.

"What the devil was she doing waving it around as she was?" Fergus muttered.

"It looked wet to me," Tavis said, when Cullen didn't trouble himself to explain. "She was probably trying to dry it."

A round of relieved murmurs sounded from the other men. Cullen knew they'd feared their new lady would be mad since discovering she was the lass from the meadow.

"How did she get herself all bruised?" Gillie asked suddenly.

"No doubt she took a spill from her mount," Fergus surmised when Cullen remained silent. "That's what happens when ye act foolish and doona ride proper. Hopefully, the lass has learned her lesson."

Cullen didn't comment. His gaze had moved to

the top of the stairs in hopes of seeing his betrothed appear, but the stair head was still empty.

"I am glad we are na staying here tonight," Gillie commented, drawing his attention again. "Her stepmother is a horrible woman."

"Aye," Tavis muttered, and Cullen noted his gaze shifting along the table to where Edda d'Aumesbery was talking with Father Saunders. His cousin shook his head with incomprehension, and added, "I doona understand the woman at all. From what she said while we awaited yer return, she obviously believes all those tales about the Devil of Donnachaidh."

"Aye," Gillie muttered. "And yet she doesna seem the least afeared of ye."

"Nay, she's too pleased at the prospect of her stepdaughter marrying our laird and being miserable," Fergus commented with disgust. "She sees our laird as an ally because of it and hasna the sense to be afraid."

Tavis blew out a silent whistle at the suggestion, then nudged Cullen. "If that's the case, I suspect the woman has made the lass's life miserable as can be until now."

"Aye," Cullen grunted, his gaze shifting to the Englishwoman. She was a vile creature. It hadn't taken him more than a glimpse of Edda's obvious pleasure at Evelinde's state when they returned to the keep to realize getting the lass away from here as quickly as possible was the best thing he could do for her. His opinion hadn't changed in the time he'd waited below. Edda had spent the interval spewing out insult after insult about her absent stepdaughter and telling him what a trial the girl had been to her.

The woman kept insisting Cullen would have to beat her into shape. She seemed to think he should take a stick to Evelinde morning, noon, and night to ensure good behavior . . . but the more she talked, the more he felt like taking a stick to Edda. Cullen didn't think the woman had dared to raise a hand to Evelinde herself, but he had no doubt that Tavis was right, and the bitch had made Evelinde's life here as miserable as she could since Lord d'Aumesbery's death. It had been a relief when Father Saunders arrived, and they'd been able to break away from the nasty cow and move farther along the table to confer. It had saved him from strangling his betrothed's stepmother . . . probably not the best memory for Evelinde to have of their wedding day.

Cullen's gaze slid back to the top of the stairs again, and he wondered where his bride was. He was eager to get her out of this cursed castle.

"Well," Edda d'Aumesbery suddenly stood. "Evelinde is obviously taking her time. I shall have to go chivvy her along, else we shall, no doubt, be left here awaiting her pleasure all afternoon." She turned a gaze full of happy anticipation to Cullen. "I do hope you can take the girl in hand and teach her to be more prompt and obedient. I fear her father spoiled her horribly, and she needs a strong hand."

Cullen ground his teeth but simply stood, and announced, "I shall go up."

The catlike smile that immediately claimed the woman's face rubbed his nerves raw. He had no doubt she was anticipating his taking his fists to the lass for her dallying. Cullen had never raised a hand to a woman in his life. He'd have liked to at the moment, however. He wanted to slap that smug smile off Edda's face. Mouth tightening, he strode to the stairs and bounded up. He could not get out of this castle quick enough.

Cullen reached the top of the stairs just as a maid slid out of one of the doors and hurried up the hall toward him. Her steps slowed, and her eyes grew wide with alarm when she spotted him.

"Where is Evelinde's room?" he growled, impatient with her fear. Truly, a little caution around strangers was healthy, but the servant's open terror was insulting. Still, he supposed he brought it on himself by letting everyone think the worst.

When the girl turned and gestured silently back to the room she'd just left, Cullen nodded and moved swiftly to it. He didn't knock. He pushed open the door, stepped in, and opened his mouth to demand to know what was taking so long, only to have his jaw sag. There were two women in the room with his bride—her lady's maid and another younger maid. Neither had noted his arrival. They were too busy dragging a naked Evelinde across the floor with her arms pulled over their shoulders. She hung limp between them, head sagging forward and legs—apparently unable to hold her weight—dragging behind.

Cullen slammed the door closed to get their attention, and the women paused at once and peered his way. All except his bride, who simply continued to sag between them.

"What the hell is wrong with her?" he snapped, crossing the room to the trio. The maids immediately began to back away, dragging Evelinde with them.

The younger woman simply shook her head frantically in response to his question. It was the older one, the one he believed was Evelinde's maid, who explained, "I told Alice to put some tonic in Evelinde's mead. It was to help soothe her sore muscles."

"Oh, aye, her muscles are soothed," Cullen snapped, lifting Evelinde's head to see she was conscious, but dazed and seemed incapable of holding up her own head. He gently eased her head back to rest against her chest again and glowered at the maid. "If I'm ever ill, doona even think to treat me."

"Alice gave her the wrong medicinal," Mildrede snapped. "And too much."

Cullen just pursed his lips doubtfully, his gaze sliding back to his bride. "How long will it take to pass?"

Mildrede hesitated, considering the matter, then shook her head, and admitted, "I am not sure. A while."

"But it'll na harm her?" he asked.

Mildrede shook her head.

"Can she speak?"

"Aye." The word was little more than a slur from his bride's bent head.

Cullen nodded, then scooped Evelinde away into his arms. "Then we can be wed."

"Just a minute!" Mildrede squawked, as he turned to head to the door. "You cannot take her like that. She is naked!"

Cullen paused to look down at the woman in his arms. He'd been so upset and worried by her state he'd quite managed to forget she was naked. He had to wonder how that was possible as he peered at her now, his gaze traveling over her breasts, down her stomach to the golden thatch of hair nestled at the apex of her thighs, and finally over her shapely legs.

"Come, set her on the bed, and we will dress her," Mildrede said.

Cullen scowled at the peremptory order, but laid Evelinde on the bed. He looked down at his bride as Mildrede sent the younger maid to fetch a chemise and gown.

"She took a bad tumble. Those are some nasty bruises she's carrying," the maid said with a sad shake of the head.

"Aye," Cullen agreed, his eyes traveling over lovely, milky white skin, interrupted by several black bruises. "She looks like a cow."

Mildrede turned a horrified gaze on him at the comment, but he was more concerned by the choked sound that came from his bride. He really hadn't meant it as an insult, but it seemed the women were taking it so.

"I just meant the coloring," Cullen muttered, wondering why he was bothering to explain himself.

Mildrede shook her head and turned to take the

shift from the younger maid when she rushed back with it. She immediately began to try to put it on the lass, but Evelinde was unable to help at all, and it was obvious it was not an easy job. The two women had to hold her in a sitting position, raise her arms, and maneuver the chemise onto her at the same time. Even with the younger maid trying to help, Mildrede was struggling with the task.

An irritated sound slipping from his lips, Cullen moved around the bed to help. He was holding her upright with her hands in the air for Mildrede to work the chemise onto her when a knock sounded. The younger maid was just hovering nervously by the side of the bed, so she was the one who went to answer it.

"This will teach me to trust anyone else to mess with my medicinals," the maid muttered as she finished getting the chemise over one hand and turned her attention to the other.

Cullen's only response was a grunt as he shifted his hand about, first down the arm, then back up as Mildrede worked that hand through the sleeve.

"God's teeth! With all that bruising on her lily-white skin she looks like a cow," Tavis said, appearing at his side.

"That's what I said," Cullen agreed, feeling vindicated. He wasn't at all surprised his cousin had managed to talk his way around the maid. However, when Evelinde made a groaning sound, her head flopping against her chest with distress, it suddenly occurred to him that his cousin was staring at his betrothed's lily-white skin, mottled or not. It mattered little that in the normal course of events, Tavis, as well as all the rest of the men, would have got an eyeful during the bedding ceremony. This was not the bedding ceremony, and there probably wouldn't be one. There was absolutely nothing normal about this wedding so far.

"Turn around," he snapped. "What are ye doing here anyway?"

A grin tugging at his lips, Tavis did as ordered, and explained, "Ye've taken so long, Edda was threatening to come up and check on ye, so I said I'd come." He glanced back toward the bed, and asked, "What's the matter with her?"

"They drugged her," Cullen said dryly.

"It was an accident," Mildrede protested. "Alice got my tonics mixed up."

Tavis raised his eyebrows, but simply asked, "Can the wedding go ahead?"

"Aye," Cullen said firmly. "We just need to get her dressed."

Tavis nodded. "Diya need me help?"

Cullen hesitated, then shook his head. "Nay. Jest guard the door and keep that bitch stepmother of hers out of here."

"Aye."

The moment he moved away, Cullen turned his full attention to getting Evelinde dressed. Mildrede now had the shift on her arms and over her head and was tugging it down over her upper torso.

"Can you lift her up?" the maid asked.

Cullen lifted Evelinde by her hands so her bottom was off the bed, and the maid quickly tugged the chemise down to cover her.

They were working to get the gown on her when the next knock came. Cullen glanced back to see Tavis positioned beside the door, inside the room. He was leaning against the wall, arms crossed, watching the whole process, but straightened and turned to answer the knock.

Cullen spotted Fergus on the other side when it opened and shook his head with disgust as he turned back to what he was doing. Edda was obviously eager to find out what was happening. At this rate, every one of his men would be in the room ere they got Evelinde dressed.

"Nay. You will consummate the marriage now. I will not have you take Evelinde from here, change your mind, and return her to have the marriage annulled later. This marriage will not be undone," Edda insisted firmly.

If Evelinde's head were not already hanging down, it would be now at the insinuation that Cullen would soon find her lacking. Her wedding day was turning out to be one of the most humiliating of her life to date. She was battered, bruised, apparently resembled a cow, and completely incapable of supporting herself.

Once they'd dressed her, Cullen had been forced to carry her below, then hold her upright by pressing her to his side with one arm around her waist and his other hand holding her head up so she could see the priest. When she'd had to say her vows, they'd come out as little more than a grunt because her mouth wouldn't move properly. The priest had been upset and reluctant to accept it as a vow, and Cullen had begun to lose patience with the man. Fortunately, Mildrede had saved the holy man by pointing out that Evelinde could nod. When the priest had looked at her, Evelinde had done so, though it was more like a flop than a nod. She had very little control over her muscles.

And so she had nodded rather than spoken her vows. She'd been terribly relieved to have it over and done with until Cullen had announced it was time to leave, and Edda had spoken up with her insistence they consummate before they leave. The woman was mad, of course; there was no way they could consummate it as she was.

Apparently, Cullen felt the same way, and snarled, "How are we to consummate it? The woman cannot even move."

Edda didn't seem to see this as a problem. Unconcerned about pricking Cullen's temper—probably because his hands were hampered holding Evelinde upright—she said with amusement, "While I have been widowed two years, I do recall enough to know she need not move for it to be consummated. You need not even do more than lift her skirt to accomplish it if you do not wish."

"Lady d'Aumesbery!"

Evelinde recognized Father Saunders's shocked voice, but was more concerned by the way her husband had suddenly gone stiff against her. She suspected he was very angry, and his expression must have said so, because Edda sounded defensive as she added, "'Tis not as if she will feel it, and I am merely pointing out that if he is in such a rush, he can accomplish the deed quickly."

Evelinde heard the low growl that rumbled in the chest next to her ear and felt the anger in the increased pressure on her side where his fingers held her. She suspected that in his fury the man was bruising her without meaning to, but only felt a very slight increase of pressure, not pain thanks to the tonic, and supposed one more bruise would not matter.

"What will it be, my lord?" Edda asked determinedly. "Do you consummate now or wait for her to recover enough and leave a day or so later?"

Cullen's answer was to shift Evelinde away from his chest to sweep her up into his arms and head for the stairs.

Evelinde supposed she should be horrified at the idea of what was to come, but she really wasn't all that sure what was coming. Everything had happened so quickly, Mildrede hadn't had the chance to tell her what to expect from her wedding night, and there had been no need ere this. Even if she had known what was coming, she didn't think she'd be afraid. The man had been nothing but gentle in his dealings with her until now, and she wasn't afraid of him. Evelinde was just rather resigned. She should have been prepared for Edda to make this as humiliating and uncomfortable as possible.

She would just have to lift her head and bear it one more time, Evelinde supposed. Not literally, of course; she simply wasn't physically capable of raising her head at the moment.

Cullen carried her above stairs and along the hall to her bedchamber, muttering under his breath the whole way. Clearly she was not the only one who found Edda trying.

He paused at her door, reached out with the hand under her legs to open it, then whirled back as Edda huffed her way up behind them.

"The bedding ceremony—"

"I hope, Madame, that ye doona intend to insist on witnessing the consummation," he growled in a warning tone.

Evelinde had no doubt Edda wanted to do exactly that. It would mean more humiliation for her to enjoy.

"I—" the woman began, but Cullen continued speaking.

"Because my temper is frayed, and I'd hate to hit a woman on me wedding day," he growled.

Evelinde really wished she could see her stepmother's face at that point. She was positive she heard her swallow thickly, and her voice certainly sounded shaken as she said, "Nay, of course not, my lord."

Cullen waited, and Evelinde could see the skirt of the woman's dress backing away. When it was out of sight, he turned to the men who had apparently followed Edda, and said, "Prepare the horses, we will be below in a trice."

A trice? Evelinde thought with dismay. He wasn't really going to just lift her skirt and . . . ?

Cullen turned away and entered her chamber, then apparently kicked the door shut with his foot, because she heard it slam behind them. He then carried her to the bed. He stood there for a moment and Evelinde wished she could see his expression so she would have some idea of what he was thinking. Then, he turned away and carried her across the room to lay her on the fur in front of the fireplace. Cullen was very gentle about it, even bunching up the end of the fur to act as a cushion beneath her head. His gaze met hers briefly and he nodded, before straightening and walking away.

Evelinde was left wondering what the nod had meant. Was it supposed to have been reassuring? she wondered, following him with her eyes.

Cullen walked back to the bed, grabbed the linens and furs, and tugged them aside. Then he did something that just confused her: He slipped his sgian dubh from his waist, sliced himself on the arm, then rubbed his blood on the bed. He straightened then and moved back to her. Evelinde watched him approach, unsure what he was doing. She didn't worry, however, until he murmured an apology and reached for the hem of her skirt.

Evelinde's eyes widened as he eased her legs apart. She felt a very faint and brief pressure on her leg, and then he was tugging her skirt back into place and shifting to lift her into his arms again.

Cullen carried her back to the bed, set her on it right where the blood was, then paced briefly around the room. Evelinde followed him with her eyes as much as she could, but he suddenly moved to the corner where her open chests were and out of her sight. She heard him rustle about down there, but could see nothing, and eventually the strain of trying to turn her eyes so far began to make them ache, and she had to close them for a moment to ease the strain.

When she felt hands slipping under her body, she opened her eyes again as Cullen scooped her up. He then walked to the door, using the hand under her legs to open it, and shouted for Edda before turning away and moving back to stand by the bed with her in his arms.

" 'Tis done," he lied, as Evelinde heard several pairs of footsteps entering the room.

A moment of silence passed during which she presumed Edda was examining the bloodstain on the bed, then her stepmother said, "I want her examined."

"I have wasted enough time on this foolishness," Cullen snapped. "I'm no waiting for some pasty-faced—"

"I *will* have her examined," Edda insisted, and turned to the door. "Bet."

Evelinde would have bitten her lip at that point had she been able to. Bet had been her mother's maid and healer alongside her mother, much as Mildrede was for her. She hoped she might preserve Cullen's lie, but couldn't be sure. It would bring horrible punishments down on the old woman were she found out.

Cullen growled under his breath, bringing her eyes back to him as he turned back to lay her on the bed. He did not leave her alone. He stood grim and silent beside the bed. She heard Bet's slow, limping tread enter the room and then Edda and Bet came into her line of vision and approached the bed. Evelinde closed her eyes at that point. She just did not want to be there, though she was aware of it when her legs were pulled open.

A moment passed, then Bet said, " 'Tis done."

"You are sure?" Edda asked. " 'Twas very quick."

"You can see the blood on her thighs for yourself, my lady," Bet said with exasperation and Evelinde opened her eyes and met the wrinkled, old woman's gaze as she tugged her skirt back into place. She hoped the woman could read the gratitude in her eyes and thought she might have when Bet gave her a quick wink before turning away.

Evelinde now knew what Cullen had been doing under her skirt by the fur. He'd been clever enough to know Edda would subject her to all the humiliation she could and insist on her being examined. He must have rubbed some of the blood from his wound on her thighs to help convince Edda.

"Are you quite satisfied?" Cullen snapped.

"Aye. 'Tis well and truly done. You cannot return her." Edda beamed her satisfaction, then glanced down at Evelinde. "Farewell, stepdaughter. May your life be all that I hope for you."

Evelinde knew exactly what the woman hoped for her future and would have snorted at the words were she able. It was Cullen who did so as he picked her up. He then carried her out of the room.

They were down the stairs and out the front doors in a trice. One of his men was beside them the moment the door closed behind them, so Evelinde supposed he'd been waiting. Her husband spoke quickly to him in Gaelic as he carried her to his horse, then she found herself passed over to the man as her husband mounted. She was then passed back up to him once he was in the saddle. Cullen took a moment to arrange her in his lap, and they were off.

It all happened so fast Evelinde was left gasping. Where was Mildrede? And what of her things? Her gowns, the bits of her mother's jewelry her father had told her to hide so Edda would not steal them, the portrait of her mother, which had been hidden in her room ever since Edda's arrival at d'Aumesbery because she'd ordered it removed and destroyed. The portrait of her father that had been hidden there for the same reason after his death . . .

There were so many things she would not have left behind. However, Mildrede was the most important. And she'd hoped to be able to speak to her husband about possibly bringing Mac with them. He was a Scot and should have fit in at Donnachaidh, and she worried about leaving him behind with Edda. The woman would have to turn her frustration and anger on someone else now that Evelinde was no longer there to abuse, and Mac would be her most likely target.

But she had nothing. Evelinde did not even have a small bag with a change of clothes as far as she knew. She was going forth into her new life with nothing but the clothes on her back, she realized, and felt fear and anxiety claim her.

It was what every girl had to face when she reached marriageable age, and really Evelinde had been fortunate in not having to do so when much younger—as most girls had to. She would have, had fate not intervened. First, her betrothed drowned when he was twelve. Before her father had found a replacement for him, her mother had fallen ill, and his time had been taken up with worry over her. When Margaret d'Aumesbery had passed away, her father had put off finding Evelinde a husband, wishing to keep her close after losing the woman he hadn't known when he'd married but whom he'd soon grown to love. He'd finally begun searching for a husband for Evelinde just before the chest complaint had taken him.

Still, despite being older than most girls were when they started a new life with their husbands far away from everything and everyone they had ever known, Evelinde didn't think it was any easier. Her husband was a complete stranger, and her new home was a distant place she knew nothing about. It was all terribly scary.

Something else for her to lift her head and bear, she supposed. There seemed to be a lot of that in a female's life. Realizing she was making herself weepy and miserable, Evelinde closed her eyes and decided to try to sleep. There was little else she could do at this point.

chapter

Five

W e're home."

Evelinde opened her eyes and glanced up at her husband. She then sat up a little straighter in his lap and followed his gaze to the dark castle towering ahead in the darkness. Trepidation immediately slithered through her.

Truly, Donnachaidh was a grim and gloomy fortress cloaked in night as it was, she decided, as Cullen urged his mount up the hill toward the gates. Evelinde settled back against his chest and rubbed her hands over her face, trying to wake up properly. She'd nodded on and off through most of the three-day journey. Not because of Mildrede's tonic, but just because it was long and monotonous and seemingly without end. The first time she'd woken was the morning after they left d'Aumesbery. She'd been stirred from sleep to find most of the effects of the tonic gone. It had been a relief since it had been a burning need to relieve herself that had dragged her awake. Wouldn't that have been embarrassing had she still not had control of her muscles?

Cullen had only stopped long enough for her to take care of business, then had hurried her back to his horse. He'd set her in the saddle, mounted behind her, and they were off again. A few moments later, he'd retrieved an apple, some cheese, and bread from a bag hanging from his horse and offered it to her. It was then Evelinde had realized they would not be stopping except to take care of personal needs.

They'd ridden through the day, traveling at a speed that didn't allow for conversation unless she wished to risk biting off her own tongue. The only other stops they'd made had been to change horses once a day.

Evelinde would have liked to ask why they were in such a rush. She would have liked to ask where the rest of his men were, too. She hadn't realized it when they'd first left d'Aumesbery, but once she'd been able to lift her head and look around, it was to see that their party was made up of herself, Cullen, and a man named Fergus. The other four men were not with them. But Evelinde had feared did she open her mouth, the first question to pop out would be to ask how he could carry her away from d'Aumesbery without her maid, her mare, and her belongings. Not wishing to start the marriage on a note of strife, she'd kept her mouth shut, remaining as silent as her husband was.

Evelinde glanced curiously around as they entered the bailey of her new home. Due to the hour there was little activity and even less to be seen in the darkness covering everything. All she could make out were shapes and shadows.

Giving up on trying to examine her new home in this light, Evelinde settled against her husband with a little sigh and waited impatiently to be able to get off the horse. Truly, Evelinde had never wanted anything in her life as badly as she wished to get off his mount at that moment. She'd never left d'Aumesbery ere this and hadn't realized how uncomfortable, wearying, and just plain boring travel could be. She sincerely hoped she'd not have to travel again for the rest of her life.

Cullen drew his horse to a halt at the foot of the stairs leading up to the keep. He slipped off the back of his mount and reached up to lift her down before she could stir herself to follow. Evelinde clasped his hands anxiously once he set her on her feet, waiting for her legs to find their footing once more. As they had the few times they'd stopped on the journey, her legs were weak and sore and threatening to buckle under her. But as they had also done each time, they soon regained their strength and agreed to hold her weight.

Cullen usually gave her the time to recover so she might walk under her own steam, but this time he

simply scooped her up and carried her up the stairs
to the keep.

Glancing over his shoulder, Evelinde saw Fergus
leading Cullen's mount away to the stables and supposed the stable master at Donnachaidh had already
retired for the night.

The great hall was dark and silent when they entered, but certainly not empty. By the light of the
fire in the hearth, Evelinde could see that every bit
of space on the floor appeared to be taken up with
sleeping bodies. Male and female, old and young,
they filled the floor sleeping side by side, leaving
just a path from the doors to the stairs and another
from the doors to another smaller door she presumed was the kitchens.

When Cullen carried her to the stairs, Evelinde
found herself clutching nervously at his shoulders
as they ascended into darkness, leaving the weak
light from the dying fire behind. Her husband apparently had no need of light, however. His steps
were confident as he carried her along a landing
that left her blinking owlishly at the darkness surrounding them.

"Open it."

Evelinde reached out blindly and felt a wooden
panel she assumed to be a door. She found the lever,
pushed the door gently open, and Cullen carried her
inside. He set her down on a soft surface she presumed was a bed, then moved away. She wasn't sure
where he'd gone until she heard the soft click of the
door closing.

Evelinde followed the sound of his returning and

moving around the room to the opposite side of the bed. There was a soft thump of something hitting the floor, the jangle of his removing his sword and belt, then a soft whoosh followed by a rustle she suspected was his plaid landing on the rushes. Then she felt the bed depress as he climbed in the opposite side.

"Sleep."

The soft order was followed by silence, but Evelinde simply sat where he'd placed her. She'd spent a good deal of time worrying about her arrival at her new home during the journey here. She'd worried about what her new people would think of her, about whether they'd accept her. She'd fretted that she'd arrive looking less than her best after three days and nights in the saddle. She felt that first impressions were important, and she'd also been concerned about what her husband would expect, fearing he might wish to consummate their marriage the night they arrived.

Apparently, all her worry had been for naught. Her new people had slept through her arrival, and her husband definitely had no interest in bedding his new bride. The man was already snoring next to her.

Evelinde shook her head with a little sigh and lay back fully clothed on the bed he'd set her on. Really, she should have realized he'd be interested in nothing but sleeping on arrival. While she had slept quite a bit the last three days despite the jolting ride, he and Fergus had not slept at all. The two men had traveled a bit more slowly through the night, but both had remained awake the two nights and three days of the journey. In truth, she was amazed her husband had maintained the energy to carry her up here to what must be his room.

She supposed now she just had a whole day more of fretting over the bedding to come. Meeting her people, however, would happen the moment she awoke, Evelinde thought, and closed her eyes and drifted off to sleep to the sound of her husband's soft snores.

"What are ye doing, Mogg! Ye blethering—Ye'll drop the damned tub do ye no watch where yer going. Stop staring at the lass and pay attention!"

Evelinde opened her eyes at that exclamation, then sat up abruptly on the bed to stare with confusion at the crowd of women moving about in the space between the foot of the bed and the fireplace in the far wall. At first, she was completely befuddled as to where she was. *This wasn't her room at d'Aumesbery* was the only thing rattling through her poor, sleep-muddled brain, but then she shifted on the bed and gasped as pain radiated through her hips, and she recalled the events of the last few days.

She was at Donnachaidh, Evelinde recalled, and presumably in her husband's chamber. Hers now, too, Evelinde supposed, glancing curiously around. The room was twice the size of her chamber at d'Aumesbery. The bed she lay in was also twice as big as her own had been. Two plain wooden tables stood, one on each side of the bed. The one on the far side held an unlit candle, the one beside her held a mug of what looked to be mead.

Evelinde peered at it curiously, then turned her attention to the rest of the room. A large open space sat between the foot of the bed and the far wall. It was a nice spot for a couple of chairs and perhaps a small table, a place where the lord and lady, she and Cullen, might relax on a night. However, there was nothing there at the moment but a tub and several female servants rushing about pouring in pails of steaming water.

"She's awake," one of the women announced, flashing her a wide smile.

Evelinde found herself unable to resist smiling back, then glanced to the plump little woman, who glanced around and suddenly broke from the group to rush to her side.

"Oh, yer awake, lass," the woman greeted her with a smile as she grabbed up the mug of what Evelinde had thought might be mead and turned to offer it to her. "I've brought ye some honey mead, and we're preparing a bath fer ye. Cullen said ye'd be wanting one."

Evelinde stared at the woman blankly for a moment, slow to decipher her thick Scottish burr and understand what she said. While her husband had a definite accent as well, his words were so few she had no problem understanding him. However this woman had rattled on so quickly, it took her mind a moment to comprehend the meaning behind what she said. Finally, thinking she'd grasped their meaning, Evelinde reached for the offered drink, murmuring, "Thank you . . . ?"

"Elizabeth Duncan, but you can call me Biddy,

lass. Everyone does," the woman answered the silent
question. Clasping her hands before her skirt, she
beamed at her expectantly. "Mairghread makes the
finest honey mead in Scotland. I'm sure ye'll agree."

Evelinde raised the mug to her lips and sipped
as she deciphered the words. Once she thought she
knew what the woman had said, she let her gaze
skate to the servants milling about at the foot of the
bed. It appeared the task of filling the tub was finished, and now the women were staring at her with
unabashed curiosity, while edging closer to the bed
like a litter of shy puppies.

Evelinde smiled at them all a trifle shyly herself
as she lowered the mug, then pronounced, "I believe you may be right, Biddy. 'Tis indeed fine honey
mead."

Biddy beamed at her, then glanced to the people at
the foot of the bed as one of them bumped against
an empty pail, sending it toppling on the rushes.

"Well? What are ye waiting fer? If yer done, be off
with ye. Ye've all things to do," Biddy said, though
her tone of voice was not as angry as her words
would have suggested. She sounded more exasperated than annoyed with the group. She watched
them out the door before turning back to Evelinde,
to say, "They're all loves, lass, but ye need to be firm
else they'll get nothing done."

Evelinde merely nodded, still feeling disoriented.

"I shall leave ye to yer bath then, I—Oh!" Biddy
had moved toward the door as she spoke, but paused
when she glanced back, a small frown curving her
lips. "I've sent them all off, and ye need help un-

dressing." She hesitated, glancing toward the door and back, then clucked her tongue and returned to her side. "I guess I shall have to help ye."

"Oh, no, that's all right—" Evelinde began, but then paused as she shifted her legs off the bed and the small movement made pain shoot through her from hip to knee. Sighing, she managed a smile and nodded. "Aye, I would appreciate help if you do not mind."

"Not at all," the woman assured her, concern now in her eyes. " 'Tis a long ride, and Cullen said he rode straight through. No doubt yer feeling it now. Do ye need help standing up?"

"No, I think I can . . ." Evelinde let the words trail away as she got to her feet. She sucked in a breath at the pain that caused, but her legs held her up without trembling for the first time in what seemed like days. Assuring herself that was a good sign and hopeful she would mend quickly now she was no longer sitting in one position on a horse's back for hours on end, Evelinde let out a slow breath and offered a grateful smile as Biddy set to work at helping her undress.

"Dear God in heaven, lass," Biddy breathed once the gown and chemise were off. Walking around her slowly, she examined the bruises. They were an unattractive mixture of purple, blue, and black. Evelinde hoped that meant they were starting to fade, but they still looked ugly.

"What did ye do to gain these?" the maid asked, shaking her head.

"Cullen did not do it," Evelinde said at once, used

to everyone assuming he had. "I fell in the river."

"O' course he didna do it," Biddy said with a laugh that suggested the very idea was ridiculous, then she sobered, and said solemnly, "Pay no mind to those tales about the lad. He's no Devil, but a good man like his da before him. He's got a good heart. He'd no hit a woman."

Evelinde relaxed with a little sigh. Despite her lack of fear of the man who was now her husband, and her own instincts prior to this telling her he was a good man, it was nice to have someone else verify it.

"I've a special salve. I'll fetch it after yer bath and rub it into yer sore spots and ye'll be right as rain in no time," Biddy assured her as she urged her into the tub.

This, too, was bigger than the tub at d'Aumesbery, Evelinde noted as she relaxed in the water.

"Where is my husband?" Evelinde asked, as Biddy moved back to collect her gown and chemise from the floor.

"Out with the men, checking on things," Biddy answered. "He's a hard worker, is our Cullen. A good man and a good leader. The clan is lucky to have him." Her mouth firmed, and she added, " 'Tis just a shame they've no the sense to ken it."

Evelinde raised her eyebrows curiously at the words. "Are his people not happy with him?"

"Oh." She waved one hand with exasperation, then continued her folding as she said, " 'Tis just that half of them believe those nonsense rumors about his father, uncle, and wife, and think he should step down. They forget that we've enjoyed peace and prosperity since he became the laird."

Evelinde was silent for a moment, then admitted, "I have heard the rumors."

"Aye. All of Scotland and most of England have," Biddy said dryly, and shook her head once more as she crossed the room to the tub. " 'Tis all nonsense. Cullen was not even here when his father, the old laird, died. He'd ridden out to visit our neighbors the Comyns when it happened. He rode out that morning, his father died that afternoon at the foot of the cliffs, and someone started the rumor the lad was seen there. By the time he arrived home, the rumor was firmly entrenched, and it mattered little that he could produce witnesses that he was not here. The rumor was started, and nothing could stop it. Tip yer head back, lass, and I'll wet yer hair to wash it."

Evelinde tipped her head back and closed her eyes, but asked, "So his father's death was an accident?"

Biddy snorted as she poured water over her head. "Of course it was, though ye couldna convince half the people here of it. I think even Cullen thinks it was not."

Evelinde fell silent, considering the matter as Biddy began to work a lovely scented soap into her hair, then asked, "Who was this witness that claimed Cullen was there?"

"I told ye, Cullen wasna there," Biddy said with a scowl.

"Aye, obviously this witness was mistaken, but who was it?"

Biddy paused and frowned briefly before picking

up a pail of water and raising it to rinse her hair as she admitted, "In truth, I doona ken. It was just told to me that 'someone' saw him there."

Evelinde kept her eyes closed as a second pail of water was poured over her head, then asked, "And the uncle?"

Biddy shook her head. "An accident. He was out hunting with the men and took an arrow in the chest."

"That does not sound like an accident," Evelinde said dryly.

" 'Tis no the first time it's happened and willna be the last," she assured her.

Evelinde nodded, then asked quietly, "And his wife?"

Biddy was silent for a long time before sighing, and saying, "I fear she may not have been an accident . . . and I also fear she may have brought her death down on herself."

Evelinde's eyes blinked open with surprise at the words. "How?"

Biddy was silent for another few moments as she continued to rinse her hair, then said, "It troubled Maggie that Cullen's name was tainted by his father's death. She loved him."

Evelinde felt herself tense and wanted to ask if he'd loved her back, but instead simply queried, "Did he talk more to her? He seems to keep his thoughts to himself with me, and I worry he does not—"

"Cullen isn't much for talking," Biddy interrupted reassuringly. "He tends to keep his own counsel. He used to be more talkative when his father was alive, and when he and Tralin were boys, you couldn't shut either of them up, but since the trouble . . ." She shrugged.

Evelinde sighed at this news and found herself wishing she could resolve the mystery around all these past deaths. Perhaps then Cullen would open up and talk a bit more.

"Maggie found his silence a bit hard going as well and feared he didn't care for her," Biddy said sympathetically.

"Did he?" Evelinde asked, unable to stop herself this time. "Did Cullen love Maggie?"

"I think he grew to have affection for her," Biddy said carefully, then sighed. "There are different kinds of love, lass. For the most part, our Cullen treated Maggie with the easy affection of an older brother. In truth, I think she set out to find his father's killer in the hopes of gaining his love. And I fear that may be what got her killed."

"I am not sure I understand," Evelinde said slowly.

"The silly lass got herself broken on the cliffs. No one kens how. She may have just fallen, or . . ." She paused and then admitted, "I've often wondered if she did not come close to solving the matter, if she did not fall so much as was pushed. Ye ken?"

Evelinde nodded, then just as quickly shook her head, confusion rearing up in her. "But if Cullen's father and uncle were not murdered, why would anyone kill Maggie for looking into their deaths?"

Biddy appeared startled by that logic. "Aye. That's true enough."

Evelinde took in her troubled expression and decided Biddy obviously wasn't as certain they weren't murdered as she'd like others to believe. Closing her eyes as the woman began to pour another bucket of water over her head, Evelinde asked, "How did the rumor start that Cullen killed her?"

Biddy released a sound of disgust. "How does any rumor start? Someone spoke it and, nonsense though it was, it spread like wildfire. They say he killed her because she had produced no bairn. Howbeit, the lass was with child when she pitched off those cliffs."

"She was?" Evelinde gasped, and peered at her with horror. "Are you sure?"

"Aye. She'd missed her woman's time three moons in a row, though she wasna showing yet."

"Did Cullen know?"

"It would be hard for him to miss, with them sleeping in the same bed," she said dryly.

"Aye," Evelinde murmured, a blush rising to her cheeks. She hadn't considered what it would mean to be married. She would now be sharing a room and a bed with the man. He would know everything about her; every flaw on her body, and even when her woman's time was. She bit her lip at the realization, then shook the matter away with a sigh. There was little to be done about it. It was the natural way. It was just embarrassing to realize Cullen would soon know her even better than her own lady's maid.

"There, lass. Yer hair is all done. Now I shall go take yer gown and chemise below to be cleaned and fetch that salve for ye. It'll take me a minute to mix it up, so ye go on and soak a bit if ye like, then dry off, but doona dress. Lay yersel' on the bed on the linen, and I'll be back to spread it on ye."

"Thank you, Biddy," she murmured, as the woman bustled from the room. Evelinde remained in the tub a few more minutes while she contemplated all she'd learned, but her thoughts died abruptly as she realized she had no fresh clothes to don.

A displeased mutter slipping from her lips, Evelinde carefully got out of the tub and began to dry herself. She then wrapped the linen around her body and plopped onto the side of the bed to consider her situation. Much to her dismay, all she had in the world was the wrinkled and filthy dress she'd worn on the journey. It amazed her that a man who had shown such care and consideration in other ways could be so dense about things such as this. Shaking her head, she dropped back on the bed and closed her eyes, but then winced as her hip began to ache.

Standing, Evelinde removed the linen and laid it out on the bed to protect it from any salve dripping on it, then lay down again, this time on her stomach. She then crossed her hands as a pillow and laid her cheek on them, her eyes closing as she tried to sort out how she was to deal with the issue of having only one gown. Perhaps Biddy would have an idea, she thought hopefully. She would have to ask her when she returned with the salve.

So far, the woman really seemed very sweet, and she was glad to have her there, but it didn't stop her missing Mildrede. Sighing, she closed her eyes and soon found herself drifting off to sleep as she waited.

Evelinde woke to the feel of a warm salve being spread over her back. She smiled sleepily as strong hands massaged the salve into the bruise over her ribs on her side and back. The touch was as soothing as the salve, the way the abused flesh was kneaded, easing away the last of the knots in her muscles.

"That's lovely, Biddy, thank you."

The grunt that came in answer made her eyes pop open and her head swivel in alarm.

"Cullen!" she gasped.

"Wife," he said calmly.

"I thought you were Biddy." It was the only thing she could think to say as her mind screamed that the man was kneeling on the side of the bed, her naked back and bottom displayed before him.

Cullen didn't bother to say she'd been wrong, but simply pushed her back to lie flat with one hand on her shoulder blade and continued his ministrations.

Biting her lip, Evelinde lay stiff beneath his efforts, even squeezing the cheeks of her bottom tight together.

Cullen worked in silence for another moment, then growled, "Relax."

Evelinde tried. However, it was simply impossible while his hands were moving over her skin and his eyes were drinking in her naked state.

Cullen continued to work on her side for another moment while she struggled to relax, failing miserably. He then stopped, caught her by the waist, and flipped her onto her back.

Evelinde gasped in alarm, her eyes going wide, and then his mouth covered hers. She stilled at once, not rejecting him, but not exactly welcoming either. She was too stunned by the speed of everything, but then his tongue slid into her mouth, and she relaxed beneath him with a little sigh, her arms creeping up around his neck as his mouth and tongue worked their magic.

He really was a very good kisser, Evelinde thought dreamily, then blinked her eyes open in disappointment as he suddenly broke the kiss. In the next moment, he'd flipped her onto her stomach again as if she was a child and began to work the salve into her back once more. It was only then she realized he'd only kissed her to make her relax.

It had worked, too, Evelinde realized. She'd become loose and limp in his arms after just one kiss. Mind you, now that he wasn't kissing her anymore and her mind was functioning again, she was remembering she was lying naked before him, her bare behind in his face. It was having a rather deleterious effect on her relaxed state, slowly bringing the tension back to her body as she wondered if her bottom was as pink as she was sure her face was at that moment.

Cullen removed his hands, and she glanced around to see him scoop up a handful of some goop from a bowl on the table beside the bed. He worked the salve between his hands for a moment, warming it, then turned back to smooth it over her back.

Much to her surprise, he wasn't just using it on her bruise, Instead he was spreading it over her whole back, running it up her spine and kneading it into her shoulders, before sliding down her back again. She was just beginning to relax under the gentle kneading when his hands reached her backside.

Evelinde winced when his hands slid to the sides of her hips, smoothing the salve into the tender areas there. She even began to squirm a little, instinctively trying to withdraw from the touch. Cullen didn't comment, merely worked the salve into the skin gently until she began to relax as the pain eased and faded. He then shifted his attention to her lower back and finally her buttocks.

Evelinde had to bite her lip and squeeze her thighs tight together to keep from reacting to the touch. She was most relieved when his hands continued down to her legs, smoothing the salve across the backs of her thighs and down to the backs of her knees. However, when his fingers began to trail up again, moving along the inside of her thighs, every muscle in her body jerked tight.

"Roll over."

Evelinde glanced over to see him concentrating on scooping out more salve from the bowl. She briefly considered refusing the order, but he was her husband, and he'd certainly already seen everything, she told herself. He'd had to help dress her on their wedding day.

Cow indeed, she thought with disgruntlement as she recalled the comment, then heaved out a breath and reluctantly turned over. Still, Evelinde couldn't prevent her hands from instinctively moving to cover herself.

When Cullen turned back with the salve, he didn't comment on her modest efforts but simply began by rubbing the salve into her throat and shoulders. Evelinde watched his face as he worked, but as usual it was expressionless. His eyes, however, were not, and she found herself fascinated by the slow burn building in them as he met her gaze.

She didn't resist when he took the arm she'd laid across her breasts and began to massage the salve into it. Cullen started at her fingers, then moved on to her hand, wrist, and elbow, feeding her arm through his hands so it was between them. He'd reached her upper arms when Evelinde realized her salve-slick hand had brushed against the bit of plaid that crossed his chest over his tunic as he worked.

"There is some on your plaid," she said apologetically.

Cullen glanced down and frowned. He released her to try to brush at the spot, only to make it larger. Scowling, he reached for the broach that pinned the plaid in place, then paused to stare at his salve-covered hands. Raising his head, he said, "You do it."

Evelinde hesitated, then reached out with her still-clean hand and quickly unclasped the pin. The plaid fell away at once to pool around his waist, but she knew it was just lying there loose and could slip away at any moment.

"The shirt, too."

Evelinde glanced uncertainly at his face. His expression was closed, waiting. Biting her lip, she sat up on the bed, wiping her greased hand on the linen as she did. She then reached for the hem of the loose shirt and lifted it up his chest, her eyes widening as inch after inch of flesh was revealed.

Unlike her, his chest looked perfect, without a bruise to be seen, but then he'd landed on his back, she thought, as he lifted his arms and leaned forward for her to remove the shirt. Evelinde did and then sat back to look at the suddenly half-naked man before her.

Lord in his heaven above! He was beautiful. Muscles rippled through his shoulders and chest as he was freed from the shirt and lowered his arms. She had the most curious urge to run her hands over his chest, and briefly considered scooping up some salve as an excuse to do so.

"Lie down."

Evelinde dropped back on the bed as ordered, but couldn't seem to make her eyes stop their exploration of the wall of male chest before her. The man had to be twice as wide as she.

Cullen distracted her from his chest by bending to his work again. His hands were still slick with the salve as he turned his attention to massaging her side where the biggest bruise was. Evelinde winced at the first touch, but the salve soon eased the tenderness there. She hardly noticed when his hands began to move in wider circles over the spot . . . until his fingers brushed lightly over the side of one breast.

Evelinde caught her lip in her teeth, her eyes fastened on his face as he worked. Truly, at first she thought it was merely an accident. There was nothing about his expression to suggest otherwise, but then his fingers brushed lightly over the side of her breast again, a little higher this time.

On the third pass, Cullen's eyes suddenly shifted to her face, and he caught her gaze and held it as his fingers glided up again, this time, sliding so high they came perilously close to brushing her nipple. Evelinde's breath caught in her throat, then he removed his hands and turned to scoop up more salve and, again, he warmed the substance between his hands. Evelinde watched the process with interest, her gaze sliding between his hands and his face. She was watching his face when he apparently decided the salve was warm enough and suddenly brushed her arm out of the way and covered both her breasts with his hands.

Evelinde gasped, her body jerking as he began to knead the flesh there. Her eyes closed as his fingers worked magic, drawing responses that left her breathless and even panting. It was exciting and frightening, all at the same time. He'd touched her before, but then she hadn't felt quite so vulnerable and . . . well . . . naked. It did not help that he was watching her the whole time, his eyes hooded and hungry.

She wanted to ask him to stop. She wanted to beg him not to stop, and she wanted him to kiss her, but he touched her with nothing but his hands, squeezing, kneading, plucking then rubbing by turn, until Evelinde thought she couldn't bear it another moment. Just when she opened her mouth to protest, to ask him to at least kiss her as he touched her, his hands slid away, and he turned to scoop up more salve.

Evelinde bit her lip to keep from speaking and clenched her fingers to keep from reaching for him as he warmed the salve. When he turned back, he ignored her upper body altogether and instead turned his attention to her lower legs. He massaged and caressed her feet, her ankles, her calves, her knees . . .

Evelinde watched him turn away to collect more salve, aware her breathing had become uneven and labored. It was a combination of what he was doing and anticipation of what was yet to come, then he turned back, and his hands glided over her legs just above the knees. Evelinde was stiff as a board, her entire body waiting. When his hands moved higher and crested over her upper thighs toward the juncture between her legs, she gasped and caught her hands in the linens she lay on.

She did not know if it was the salve, or his massage that was doing it, but her aches and pains were completely gone; the only sensation she was experiencing was pleasurable anticipation.

"Relax," he growled again, and Evelinde sighed as his hands moved back down her legs: rubbing, massaging, and kneading the kinks out of her muscles. This time, when his hands began to move higher along her thighs, she didn't stiffen up but squirmed slightly, her legs easing open under his touch.

What he was doing was making her eyes droop closed so she was peering at him through bare slits. She watched his face, noting the concentration and care on his expression and once again wished he'd kiss her. Evelinde liked it when he kissed her. She liked to taste him when his tongue thrust into her mouth, she liked the way it rasped across her own. These thoughts frittered away like cobwebs, and she gasped and found herself clutching at the linens again as his hands moved over her upper thighs, his fingers brushing lightly across the flesh at the apex.

Evelinde was suddenly aware that as he'd massaged her he'd spread her legs wider, leaving her open to him. A flash of embarrassment claimed her, but not enough, she thought, to make her close them and hamper his touch. And then his fingers brushed over her core again, and her legs snapped closed, stopping the caress and trapping his hand at the same.

It was an instinctual reaction. Evelinde couldn't have stopped it had she tried. Biting her lip, she opened her eyes and found him looking back at her. They stared at each other for a moment, neither of them moving, then, still meeting her gaze, he used both hands to ease her legs open again and shifted to kneel between them so they couldn't close. As he did, his plaid slipped until she was perilously close to seeing the hardness that was presently raising the cloth.

Evelinde watched him silently, aware her chest was rising and falling in rapid shallow breaths, as his fingers brushed over her skin again. Her legs tried to snap closed but were prevented by his presence, so instead she closed her eyes and clenched her fists and moaned, her hips instinctively trying to shift and arch as his fingers danced over her flesh.

If she'd thought he'd built a fire in her by the riverside at d'Aumesbery, it was nothing compared to what he was doing now. Evelinde actually began to ache with a need she didn't understand and had barely tasted at the river. Her hips began to move of their own volition, the urge so strong his hold could not completely stop it. And then he suddenly withdrew those magic fingers.

Evelinde's felt the absence keenly, and her eyes shot open at once. She met his gaze and saw the smile curve his lips before he suddenly leaned forward to dip his head between her legs, replacing his hand with his mouth. She cried out with shock and started to sit up to grab for his head and try to draw him away, but then his tongue rasped over her heated, sensitive flesh, and she froze, even her breathing stopping. A second rasp sent the breath she'd been holding out on a whoosh, and Evelinde dropped back on the bed, her body taking over from her shocked mind.

Her knees rose, her heels dug into the bed, and her hips began to undulate as a high, ululating moan began to stream from her mouth. It soon turned into a somewhat louder, uh uh uh . . . and then an Oh God, oh God, oh God.

Evelinde had begun to twist her head desperately back and forth on the bed when she felt something enter her, his finger, she thought, and the excitement that had built in her suddenly exploded, rushing over her in a wave that left her incapable of making any sensible sound at all. Lost in the sensation claiming her, she never noticed him rising up, tearing his plaid away to drop it on the floor, and shifting his position between her legs.

Evelinde was vaguely aware of a gentle prodding, then he suddenly plunged into her, filling her until she thought she'd break apart around him. He froze. She opened confused eyes to see his were now closed, an expression that appeared almost to be pain on his face. After a moment his eyes opened, and he watched her face silently as he eased halfway out.

Evelinde felt her body clench around him, protesting his leave-taking, then he eased back in again, and she closed her eyes once more, giving herself over to the sensations bursting back to life inside her.

She felt him catch her by the bottom and lift her hips, and groaned as he pushed back into her again, his body rubbing against her sensitive core. Her moan seemed to act like a release for Cullen. The speed picked up then, his hips moving faster, his body pounding into her over and over again, enflaming their passions until they both cried out with release.

chapter

Six

Evelinde opened her eyes, smiled at the spot where her husband had slept, and stretched happily. She decided that she quite liked marriage. It was the most exciting and invigorating adventure she'd ever known. At least it was with Cullen. She was so pleased with herself, her husband, and her marriage, that Evelinde thought were Edda there right then, she might be tempted to throw her arms around the woman and give her a great big kiss on the cheek in thanks.

Well, perhaps that was going a bit far, but a letter to express her gratitude might be in order. A glowingly happy letter that would probably make the woman pull her hair out and throw a temper tantrum.

The last thought made Evelinde frown, and she decided no, she had better not. If Edda realized how happy she was, the woman really would be in a fury, and she'd take it out on the people at d'Aumesbery. Evelinde wrinkled her nose at the thought. She wouldn't see anyone pay for her happiness. She'd just have to forgo sharing her joy with her stepmother.

Ah, well . . . Shrugging philosophically, Evelinde rolled happily out of bed, then paused and moved her leg about as she realized it was hardly paining her now. She didn't know if it was the salve, or her husband's massage, or even just not being in the saddle, but it felt much better.

It was a wonderful day, Evelinde decided, and turned to move toward her chest, only to pause as she recalled she didn't have one. She had arrived with just the dress on her back. And she didn't even have that, Evelinde realized with dismay, because Biddy had taken it and her chemise below for cleaning.

Her smile slowly slipping away, Evelinde dropped onto the side of the bed. She didn't have a thing to wear she realized and sat there for several moments, at a loss as to what to do. It was not as if she had many options. She could hardly walk around Donnachaidh naked. She wasn't even terribly comfortable just sitting there on the side of the bed naked, Evelinde acknowledged, and reached for the top linen, drawing it around herself.

Then she just sat there feeling rather numb and unhappy . . . and trapped.

Grimacing, Evelinde stood and began to pace fit-
fully around the room, her gaze sliding with disin-
terest over the few items scattered about the large
chamber. Other than the bed and the two small
tables, there wasn't really very much to distract her,
just three chests.

Her gaze landed on the largest one, and Evelinde
contemplated it silently. It really wouldn't be well
done of her to go snooping in her husband's chests,
she knew, but there might be something in there she
might wear; one of her husband's shirts, say. 'Twould
be better than standing around wrapped in a linen.

Moving to the largest chest, she knelt to open it,
eyes widening as she peered over the contents. It was
filled with dresses. If this was her husband's chest,
he had some odd customs, indeed, Evelinde thought,
and smiled faintly as she recalled trying to explain
that Cullen had ripped her gown while trying to get
it off himself and Mildrede asking if he'd been wearing it. Her maid would be amused at the sight of all
these gowns, she thought, and felt a pang for the
woman who had been her lady's maid most of her
life. She was going to miss Mildrede terribly.

Sighing, Evelinde reached for a gown lying on top.
She lifted it out and stood to hold it up for inspection. It was a lovely dark blue gown with a fitted
bodice and pale blue panels in the pleats of the skirt
that would only show when walking.

Heart lifting at her discovery, Evelinde carried the
dress to the bed and laid it out, then returned to the
chest in search of a chemise.

She found one quickly and slipped it over her head while standing beside the chest, wrinkling her nose at the stale smell to the garment as it slid over her face. 'Twas obvious the shift had been packed away for some time. The clothes probably belonged to Cullen's first wife and had simply never been removed after her death.

The thought made her pause as Evelinde fretted that he might resent her donning his dead wife's clothes. She almost took the chemise off, but the prospect of being trapped, naked, in the bedroom was not an attractive one and made anger rise within her. If the man had shown the good sense to ensure she had alternate clothing, she would not have to wear these, Evelinde told herself, shoulders straightening.

Satisfied that she should wear it, Evelinde glanced down at the chemise she wore. It was rather large on her. Cullen's first wife had obviously been much taller, not to mention more buxom, she thought, noting the roomy bodice and gaping neckline. 'Twas obvious she would have to take in the gowns if she planned to wear them, but for now it would have to do. She would start working on the gowns by the fire that night. However, at the moment she wished to see her new home.

Moving to the bed, Evelinde donned the gown, biting her lip when she found the bodice of the dress gaped as much as the chemise. It also pooled around her feet. She tried gathering the material of the gown at her back to see if that improved matters. Finding

it did, Evelinde then glanced around for some way
to pin it there, but she didn't see anything useful.
Finally, she knelt back at the chest and dug through
the contents. When that didn't turn up anything,
she moved on to the two smaller chests. The first
held her husband's clothes; plaids and white shirts.
The last chest, however, held an odd assortment of
items, some that made absolutely no sense.

Evelinde lifted out an arrow with alternating white
and dark feathers in the fletch, grimacing when she
noted that they were tinged with dried blood. Most
of it had flaked off over time and lay in a powdery
residue on the bottom of the chest. Even more of it
fell away as she shifted it aside to peer through the
other items. Evelinde was most relieved when she
found a large broach among the rest of the items. It
was similar to the one her husband used to fasten
his plaid over his shoulder.

She let the chest lid drop closed, set the pin on it,
then quickly regathered the material of the gown
at her back and—with a bit of effort—managed to
fasten the pin through it.

Satisfied, Evelinde glanced around, her thoughts
on a brush to fix her hair, but of course, she didn't
have one of those either. She knelt to Cullen's chest
again and dug through the small knives and other
contents in search of a brush, but could not find one.

Evelinde sat back on her haunches with exasperation, then closed the chest again. Truly, she was glad
to be away from Edda, but—

But nothing, she told herself. Everything would be

fine. She would take in his first wife's gowns, and find a brush, for surely he had one somewhere. The man had long hair and did not run around with it all knotted up, so he must have one. *Everything would turn out*, Evelinde assured herself. These were just little hiccups on the path to happiness, and truly she had little to complain about. These small problems were better than a cruel, coldhearted husband who beat her and was uncaring of her pleasure in their bed.

Buoyed up by these thoughts, Evelinde stood and ran her hands through her hair. Then, hoping it looked passable, she made her way to the door. It was time to explore.

When Evelinde stepped out of the chamber, it was to find herself in a very dim hall. This explained why her husband had had no difficulty making his way to his room in the dark when they arrived the night before. With no windows to allow sunlight in, it was nearly as dark now. He was obviously used to traversing the hall in poor light. Making a mental note to suggest lit torches be placed in the hall during the day, Evelinde made her way carefully to the top of the stairs.

Much to her relief, the light here was better thanks to arrow slits at intervals in the wall rising above the great hall. Evelinde had grabbed up the voluminous skirts of her gown to keep from tripping over them and started down the stairs when the keep doors opened and Fergus entered. The man didn't notice her on the stairs, but strode quickly across

the great hall. His long legs ate up the distance as
he approached the door she had guessed led to the
kitchens when Cullen had carried her through last
night. Once he passed through the door, the great
hall was once again empty.

Evelinde started down the stairs then, finding
it quite odd that the big room was abandoned. At
d'Aumesbery the great hall had always seemed to
have someone in it. When the people and servants
were not crowded around the tables for a meal, there
would be a servant cleaning, a group of knights enjoying an ale before returning to guard the wall,
Edda seated by the fire . . . The list of possibilities
was endless.

Stepping off the stairs, Evelinde hesitated, uncertain what to do. As lady here . . . She bit her lip,
acknowledging she had no idea what her responsi-
bilities would be. She'd known what to do at home
but had no idea how things went at Donnachaidh.

Evelinde glanced toward the door she thought
must lead to the kitchens, took a step toward it,
and paused again. At home, one of her duties had
been to confer with the cook about meals and what
supplies were needed and such, but presumably,
Donnachaidh had run along well enough ere she'd
arrived. She had no idea who did such tasks and did
not wish to step on anyone's toes.

Clucking her tongue impatiently, Evelinde shifted
from one foot to the other, wishing she'd asked
Biddy a thing or two while the woman had been
helping her with her bath. She would next time,

Evelinde promised herself, and she would also ask her husband what he expected of her when she had the chance. For the moment, she would just explore and get a feel for her new home.

Feeling better now that she had a plan, Evelinde caught up her skirt and crossed the great hall to the door Fergus had disappeared through. As expected, she found herself in the kitchens when she stepped inside. What she hadn't expected was to find it completely occupied by females. The kitchen at d'Aumesbery had both male and female workers. Aside from the rotund little male cook who ran the kitchens, there were several younger, strong male servants to do the heavy work, such as preparing boars for the spit and so on. However there wasn't a single male in evidence in Donnachaidh's kitchens. Even Fergus was gone. Obviously, there was another door leading out of the kitchens because he hadn't come back the way he'd entered.

Evelinde's gaze slid around the room, running over the women of varying ages until it landed on Biddy. Much to her surprise it appeared the woman who had acted as her lady's maid was really in charge of the kitchens. At least, she was the one waving a large knife and barking orders at the other women bustling about as she paused in carving up a chicken.

A sudden splash of sunlight drew her attention to the door Fergus must have used to exit, and Evelinde watched curiously as a man, thin and somewhat gnarled by time, entered. He glanced toward Biddy, then almost seemed to tiptoe along that wall of the kitchen until he reached what appeared to be a tray of cooling pastries.

"Get away from those pasties, Scatchy, or ye'll be losing a finger," Biddy snapped without glancing up. "Fergus has already tried that, and I've no patience for ye men this morning."

Old and grizzled, Scatchy stared mournfully at the tray he stood beside and turned a scowl on Biddy. "Yer a cruel woman, me lady, making them and no letting us have any."

Evelinde gave a start at the title. Me lady? Her gaze swung back to Biddy, her eyes widening as she peered at her dress. All she'd noticed in her room was the apron. Evelinde hadn't taken heed of the gown beneath, which was far too rich to be a servant's. Who the devil was she and what was she doing acting as lady's maid and working in the kitchens? Evelinde wondered. Her husband had not mentioned any female family. But then he hadn't mentioned male family either, though she knew he had a cousin named Tavis, at least she thought Tavis was the cousin. One of the few comments Fergus had made to Cullen on the journey to Donnachaidh was that mayhap they shouldn't have left his cousin behind with the others because the man was likely to get waylaid by the first likely female and forget to return. Cullen had grunted and said that the other men would keep Tavis in line.

"Ye can have a pasty at the nooning along with everyone else," Biddy said unsympathetically. "Now be off with ye and go back to yer stables ere I mistake ye for one of me chickens."

She added an exclamation mark to the comment by slamming her knife down and slicing cleanly through a leg on the dead and plucked bird.

Shaking his head, the man made his way to the door, slowing to offer Evelinde a wide, toothless smile as he passed.

"Go on!" Biddy yelled, and glanced up to cast a glare at the man, which was replaced by surprise as she spotted Evelinde by the door.

"Lass!" Setting down her knife, the woman wiped her hands on the apron around her waist as she rushed to her side. "Yer up. Cullen thought ye'd sleep most of the afternoon away when he came back below."

Evelinde tried not to blush. "Nay. I slept through most of the journey here."

"Oh. Well, would ye like something to break yer fast?"

"If 'twould be no trouble," Evelinde said.

"No trouble at all," Biddy assured her. "Just take yerself on out and sit at the table, and I'll send a maid out with some mead and a pasty. Or would ye prefer some cheese and bread?"

"A pasty sounds lovely, but there's no need to send it out. I shall just eat it here. I have some questions to ask if it would not trouble you," she explained.

"Of course ye have questions. Come on over here then." Biddy led her back to where she'd been working when Evelinde had entered, pausing beside a bit of clean counter not far away, then glanced around, her gaze stopping on a young blond maid chopping vegetables. "Mary! Bring that stool over here fer the lass."

The girl stopped her chopping to pick up the stool and hurry over with it as Biddy then shouted for another servant to fetch a pasty and some mead for her.

"There ye are," Biddy said once she had Evelinde seated at the clean bit of counter with both food and drink. "Ye go ahead and ask what yer wanting to ken. I'll just keep working if ye doona mind."

"I do not mind," Evelinde assured her, then hesitated, unsure how to phrase her questions. Finally, she simply blurted, "Who are you?"

Biddy paused and raised surprised eyes to her, and said, "I introduced myself, lass. I'm Elizabeth Duncan, did ye forget? Did ye take a blow to the head in that fall from yer horse?" Frowning with concern, she set her knife down and moved toward Evelinde as if to examine her head.

"Nay, nay, I am fine," Evelinde assured her quickly, holding up her hands to ward her off. "I did not forget your name, 'tis just that Scatchy called you my lady, and I did not realize—I mean, when you helped me with my bath I thought you were a maid, and then I came in here and you are obviously in charge of the kitchens, but Scatchy called you my lady, and yet my husband did not mention having female relatives. Though, he did not mention male relatives either. In truth, he has said little to me at all except to give me orders," she added with irritation.

Then, seeing how Biddy was staring at her, silent
and eyes wide, ended apologetically, "Not that any
of that matters except to explain that I fear I am not
sure who you are."

Much to her amazement, Biddy—or Lady Biddy—
appeared to be struggling not to laugh. For the life of
her, Evelinde couldn't think what was so amusing.
She herself was terribly embarrassed by her lack of
knowledge and more than a little angry at her husband for leaving her in such an ignorant state.

"Eat yer sweet, lass," Biddy said finally, managing to keep a straight face. "I shall explain all while
ye eat."

Heaving out a little sigh, Evelinde reached for her
mead and took a sip as the woman began to speak.

"I am Cullen's aunt," Biddy announced as she returned to pick up her knife once more. "Tavis is my
son, and Darach was my husband."

Evelinde's eyes widened incredulously as she recognized the name of the uncle Cullen was said to
have killed. She bit her lip and watched silently as
the woman set back to work cutting up the chicken
for what appeared to be a stew. "But why are you
working in the kitchens?"

Biddy grinned. "Ye make it sound like some form
of punishment."

"Well . . ." Evelinde glanced around, reluctant to
insult the woman by saying she thought it must be,
but her expression must have spoken for her, because the woman laughed.

"I like to cook," she assured her with amusement.
"I always have. I used to hang about, pestering our

cook at MacFarlane when I was a child. Of course,
my mother deplored the oddity and tried to steer
me away from it, and did manage to until I had a
home of my own, but once here, I returned to pestering the cook here in her kitchens. She taught me
a thing or two just to make me let her be . . . and because she didn't have a choice since I was her lady,"
she added wryly. "And over the years I've done
more and more in the kitchens."

"And your husband did not mind?" Evelinde asked
curiously. Her own father would have been horrified
to find her mother working in the kitchens.

"My husband did not care what I did so long as
I was happy and not nagging after him," she said
wryly.

"Oh," Evelinde murmured.

"And it turns out my pasties and some of my other
dishes are so good, none of the men complain,"
Biddy added with a grin, then said more seriously,
"I am not in the kitchens all the time. I merely help
out on occasion, or take over for Cook when she
needs to be away. Right now she is away for a couple
of days visiting her daughter, so I get to play cook
until her return."

"Oh," Evelinde said again, then cleared her throat,
and said, "Well, thank you very much for helping
me with my bath."

Biddy chuckled. "What else could I do? I'd sent the
servants away. Besides, it gave me a chance to get
to know you a little. I am just sorry I did not realize you had no idea who I was, else I would have
explained. Now"—she waved her knife toward the

pasty she'd had fetched for her, and ordered—"eat. Yer body needs sustenance to heal, and pasties are my specialty."

Evelinde managed a smile and picked up the pasty. She sighed as flavor exploded in her mouth with the first bite, even as the pastry seemed to melt away to nothing on her tongue. "Oh, this is lovely, my lady. So sweet and flaky."

Biddy flushed with pleasure at the compliment. " 'Tis my specialty. Everyone at Donnachaidh loves 'em. Especially Fergus. That man's in here at least ten times a day trying to steal one. They go quick, so I'll be sure to keep a couple extra aside fer ye each time I make them."

"Aye, please do," Evelinde murmured, then took another bite, marveling at how good they were. She'd always thought the cook at d'Aumesbery was good, but he'd never made anything like this. In truth, she didn't think the man was big on sweets, though.

"Would ye like another?" Biddy asked, as Evelinde finished off the first.

"Yes, but I shall get it," Evelinde said quickly. Standing, she moved to where the tray of fresh pasties sat, took one and returned to her stool. Before taking a bite, she asked, "Are you castellan here then, my lady?"

"Biddy," she insisted, blue eyes twinkling. "Or Aunt Biddy if ye like."

"Thank you . . . Aunt Biddy," Evelinde said quietly, touched at such a generous offer of acceptance.

Biddy nodded her satisfaction, and said, "Aye. I was mistress here when my husband was laird, of course. When he died, and Liam—Cullen's father," she paused to explain, before continuing, "Liam's wife had died long ere that, and he had never remarried, so I remained castellan here for him. And then continued to when he died, and Cullen took over. At least, until he married, then little Maggie was mistress here."

"Were you sorry to step down?" Evelinde asked, worried she was about to displace the woman.

Biddy looked surprised by the question, then chuckled, shaking her head. "Truth to tell, I rather enjoyed being free of the burden during those two years. I got to spend more time in the kitchens. Though," she admitted with a grimace, "little Maggie hated when I did that. She thought it was beneath me." Biddy rolled her eyes, and said solemnly, "Trust me, lass, no task is beneath ye if ye enjoy it. There is real pleasure to be found in making a fine meal, especially if ye hunt it up yerself, clean it, and turn it into a tasty feast. 'Tis most satisfying," she assured her. "Much more satisfying than ordering servants about and dealing with tradespeople."

Evelinde nodded solemnly. She looked down at the oversized gown she wore, then back to the woman, as Biddy hacked the second leg off the chicken and threw it in a pot. "Little Maggie?"

Biddy chuckled at the question. "Nay. The woman was huge; tall, round, and buxom. But she was smaller than her mother, big Maggie, by an inch or two so she was 'little Maggie.'"

"Oh." Evelinde tried to imagine a woman bigger

than the one who had owned the dress she wore but found it difficult.

"I'm sure yer mother trained ye well to be castellan, but if ye need any help, lass, or have any questions, ye just have to ask. And I'll even stay out of the kitchens if yer family come to visit and ye'd be too embarrassed to have them know I putter about in here on occasion."

"Thank you," Evelinde murmured, "but that won't be necessary. Both my parents are dead. My mother died some years ago and my father two years past. There are only my brother and stepmother left."

"Oh, I'm sorry, lass," she said sincerely. "There's nothing harder than losing a loved one."

"Aye." Evelinde frowned as she saw the grief flicker briefly over the older woman's face, suspecting she'd made her think of her lost husband. She sought her mind for something to say to cheer them both, raising the pasty to her lips as she did. The sweet melting on her tongue made her add, "Besides, I see nothing wrong with you working in here if you like it. Especially if I get pasties out of it."

Biddy smiled, the grief swept away by pride and pleasure as she assured her, "Ye will, lass."

Evelinde glanced at the women working so industriously as she took another sip of mead, then asked, "Why are there no men in the kitchens? At d'Aumesbery we had men to help with the heavy work."

"Fergus helps out if he's in the kitchens," Biddy said, then added, "And he's often in the kitchens.

The man is thin as a whip, but is always grabbing something to eat."

Evelinde's eyebrows rose slightly at the wry affection on the woman's face.

"It would be a blessing to have a couple of men working in here permanent-like," Biddy continued. "Unfortunately, they are kept busy guarding the walls and training fer battle. It leaves just the women to tend to everything else."

"Are there so few men?" she asked with surprise.

"Nay. Well . . ." Biddy paused, then said, "There are fewer men than women here at Donnachaidh, that's certain. Too many good men have been lost in battles, but it's no as bad as it used to be. Liam worked hard to make alliances after Darach's death, and Cullen himself has continued those efforts. We hardly see battle at all anymore. And then many of the daughters who have married outsiders have brought them home to Donnachaidh with them, which has increased the number of males, too. 'Tis probably close to equal again."

Evelinde nodded slowly before she asked, "If the men are rarely needed for battle anymore, why do some of them not help out in the kitchens now? I realize they still must train, but surely one or two would not be missed, and it would make it easier to have men in here to do the heavy lifting and such."

Biddy paused in her cutting to glance at her with surprise, and finally said, "Well, aye, but . . . 'Tis the way it's always been."

Evelinde let the matter drop but tucked it away

in her mind as something to discuss with Cullen. *'Tis the way it's always been* was not a reason to keep doing something if there was a better way. She saw no reason why a couple of men could not be spared to help out with the heavy work in the kitchens.

"So, the men are all out guarding the wall or practicing in the bailey?" she asked, setting her empty mug on the counter.

Biddy snorted at the suggestion. "Nay. They are all out in the paddock celebrating yer wedding."

Evelinde raised her eyebrows in surprise, and asked, "Celebrating our wedding in the paddock?"

"Aye." Biddy grinned at her bewilderment. "They'll be drinking ale and baiting old Angus. He's a bull," she explained before Evelinde could ask. "A mean old bull with a nasty temper. Anytime there's something to celebrate, the men take a couple of barrels of ale down to the paddock and bait the poor bugger. Then they'll run across the paddock with him chasing them to prove their courage and speed. Some will even wrestle the mean beast."

"This is their idea of celebrating?" she asked with amazement.

Biddy laughed, and said, "They're men," as if that explained it.

Evelinde shook her head, and asked, "And what will the women do to celebrate?"

Biddy paused again, surprise once more on her face. "We've no time fer celebrating, lass. We've too much work to do around here to take the time."

Evelinde frowned. "So the men practice at swords or celebrate while the women do all the work?"

"Aye." Biddy nodded and turned back to hacking at her chicken. " 'Tis the way it's always been."

"I see," Evelinde murmured, "Will my husband be there celebrating as well?"

"No doubt," Biddy said. "He was carrying one of the barrels of ale when he left."

"I think I shall go speak to him, but when I return I shall probably pester you with more questions, if 'tis all right? I was castellan at d'Aumesbery since my mother's death, but every castle is different, and I—"

"Yer stepmother didna take up the role as castellan when she married yer father?" Biddy interrupted with surprise.

Evelinde wrinkled her nose. "Edda preferred to be a lady of leisure."

"Ah." Biddy nodded in understanding. "Well, welcome to Donnachaidh, lass. We have no ladies of leisure here but are glad to have ye. I'd be more than happy to help ye settle in and figure out what is what. Ye come talk to me when ye're ready."

"Thank you." Evelinde squeezed the woman's shoulder in affectionate appreciation as she stood up, then turned to leave the kitchens.

Her gaze swept over the great hall as she crossed it. For a keep kept mostly by women, it was very plain, with little that would not be considered necessities. There were the tables arranged in a squared-off U shape in the center and two chairs by the fire, but both were square and without any sort of cushion. They didn't look particularly inviting. And that was it for the great hall. While there were rushes on the floor, there were no tapestries on the walls, or even any whitewashing, she noted with a frown, and had to wonder if Cullen's first wife had really preferred it this way, or if it had been more inviting while she'd lived but had since been emptied out.

The sight of the barren walls reminded Evelinde of the two tapestries she had left behind. Her father had purchased them for her mother during their marriage. The first depicted Adam and Eve in the garden of Eden, and the second featured a unicorn and a lady. Both had hung in the great hall at d'Aumesbery until Edda's arrival. On learning they had been gifts to his previous wife, the woman insisted they be removed. She'd done away with anything having to do with the first Lady d'Aumesbery.

Evelinde's father hadn't argued. He'd simply ordered the tapestries rolled up and put away, telling Evelinde she could take them with her when she married and moved to her own home.

It was a shame she hadn't been able to bring them, Evelinde thought sadly. They would have looked lovely on the wall here and would have brightened the place. Then there were the cushions she and her mother had sewn of a night. Those would have made the chairs by the fire more inviting. And there were—

Evelinde cut off these thoughts, knowing it was useless to pine for things she could not have.

She could always make more, Evelinde told herself as she pushed through the keep doors and stepped out onto the stairs leading into the bailey. Of course, she couldn't make a tapestry herself. She had neither the skill nor the time for such an effort, let alone a loom on which to perform the task. Tapestry weavers were always male, and it could take two months for two men to weave just a square foot of a tapestry. That was why they were so dear to purchase and why it was such a shame her husband hadn't given her the chance to bring them, or anything else with her.

Scowling, Evelinde caught up the skirts of the voluminous blue gown she wore and started down the stairs, pushing these concerns aside to join the other little irritations she had against her new husband at the moment. They did seem to be building up in her mind. She already had a healthy list of things to hold against the man, and they'd barely been married more than three days.

Evelinde paused to peer around the bailey as she stepped off the stairs. It was nearly as empty as the great hall had been, with just a few women walking this way and that on some endeavor or other. Had she not spoken to Biddy, Evelinde would have wondered about that, but she had and knew exactly where to find the men. The paddock.

She recalled the direction in which Fergus had taken the horses the night before and—supposing the paddock must be near the stables—turned that way, sure she'd find it easily enough. All she need do was look for men and listen for their voices. It was her experience that men got loud and unruly when "celebrating," and she had no doubt she'd hear them long before she reached them.

Evelinde found herself glancing curiously inside

the stables as she walked by. She saw row after row of stalls running its length. From the glimpse she got, it looked as well kept as Mac kept the d'Aumesbery stables.

Lady would have been well cared for here, she thought, then quickly pushed the thought away. She didn't wish to approach her husband angry, for it rarely achieved much except to cause bad feelings. It was always best to approach a matter calmly and while both parties were in a good mood.

To her mind, her husband should be in a good mood right now. She'd certainly felt pretty cheerful after consummating the marriage, at least until all these little problems had cropped up . . . like not having anything of her own here.

Cullen, of course, wouldn't have this issue, and was celebrating, so should still be cheerful, Evelinde decided. It seemed the perfect time to approach him on the subject of what he wished her to do as his wife. At least that was what she told herself. And it wasn't that it was untrue, but, really, the conversation could have waited until that evening after the sup. However, Evelinde found herself eager to see her new husband, and she was sure he would be happy to see her, too. No doubt he would smile, and open his arms, welcoming her to him, then he would kiss her until her toes curled and . . .

Evelinde brought her daydream to a halt as she heard a shout of laughter. As expected, she'd heard the men before spotting them. Stopping to look around, she found she'd reached a series of paddocks that ran up to the outer wall. The first enclosure was empty, and she moved closer to the wooden fence that surrounded it, leaning against a post as she peered across to a small stretch of grassy land where the men were gathered along the rails of the next paddock, watching some activity inside.

Her gaze slid over the mass of bodies, searching for her husband as another roar of laughter went up. Curious, she turned her attention to the paddock itself, eyes widening with horror when she realized the men had either finished with baiting "poor old Angus" or forgone that fun altogether and moved on to riding bareback on a mad horse. Truly, the horse seemed crazed. It was bucking, twisting, and leaping about, doing everything in its power to unseat the man presently clinging to its back.

Evelinde had just decided the man on the beast's back must be as mad as the horse itself when the horse turned, and she realized the madman was her husband.

For one moment, Evelinde simply stood there clutching at the fence post, mouth agape with horror. Visions began dancing in her head of her husband flying off the beast and being trampled to death. The thought of being made a widow so soon after discovering the joys of marriage almost made her swoon. And then her husband *did* go flying through the air, tossed from the beast's back like so much rubbish.

A shriek of horror slipping from her lips, Evelinde immediately began to climb the fence. She was determined to get to her husband as quickly as she could. Her skirt had other ideas, however, and kept catching on the wood. Evelinde just tugged at it impatiently, nearly tumbling on her head as she threw herself into the paddock. She heard a rip, then she was free, tumbling to her belly on the ground.

Grunting at the impact, Evelinde pushed herself to her feet, grabbing at the overlarge skirt and holding it gathered in her hand as she charged across the paddock.

Despite the noise they were making, several of the men apparently heard her shriek her husband's name and turned to watch her rush across the paddock. The horror on their faces made her heart squeeze tight. Evelinde had not seen her husband land, but obviously it had not gone well, she realized, as the men began to shout at her.

Hoping he was not so badly injured he would not mend, Evelinde began trying to recall all Mildrede had taught her about healing as she ran. He probably had a broken bone or two . . . or more. Those would need setting. His head was her foremost concern, however, and she sent up a silent prayer that he'd protected his head as he fell. The man was just healing from his last fall from the horse. What was he thinking, getting on that mad beast? She would ask him that, Evelinde thought, just as soon as she judged him healthy enough she could give him hell without feeling bad about it.

The men's shouts had grown almost frantic, and they were gesturing and waving a bit wildly. Evelinde tried not to let her imagination tell her Cullen was injured beyond repair.

He couldn't be, she told herself. *Surely, God would not be so cruel?*

"Evelinde!"

Startled to recognize Cullen's voice, she pushed her worries away and looked more closely at the crowd on the other side of the fence. Her heart leapt with relief when she spotted Cullen pushing his way through the men who were now pressed up against the fence.

"Dammit woman, *move*!" Cullen roared, beginning to climb the fence to get to her.

Evelinde took in the fury on his face and suddenly wasn't at all certain she wished to see her husband after all. She had no idea what she'd done to cause his fury, but she was definitely sure she didn't want to see him until he'd had a chance to calm down.

It was as she whirled to head back the way she'd come that Evelinde spotted the bull. If her heart had leapt and her blood pounded when she'd seen Cullen thrown from the horse, it was nothing compared to her body's response when she saw mad Angus thundering down the paddock toward her.

Evelinde had never been a particularly physical person. It wasn't expected of a lady. She enjoyed riding and wading in the river, and that was about the extent of her physical activity as a rule, but being chased by a snorting bull was a wondrous motivator. Evelinde caught up her skirts and burst into a run toward her husband. She ran so fast her feet hardly seemed to touch the ground. In fact, she wouldn't have been surprised if someone told her they'd seen an angel swoop down from the skies and carry her those last thirty feet to the fence. Evelinde moved so fast she actually reached the fence before Cullen had finished climbing it.

Her climbing the fence, however, was another matter entirely. She could not climb and hold her skirt up at the same time. Evelinde could hear the pounding hooves behind her and actually feel the hot breath of Angus's angry snorts on her back. She would never climb the fence before he was on her. She was going to be gored, and he would then toss her through the air and stamp all over her where she landed, Evelinde thought dismally even as her hand closed on the rail . . . and then Cullen reached down from the top of the fence, snatched her by the back of the dress, and hauled her out of the paddock.

chapter

Seven

"What the devil were ye doing, ye daft woman!" Cullen roared. It was not the first time he'd shouted the question. In fact, it seemed to be the only thing he could say as he stared down at his trembling wife, not even giving her a chance to answer before bellowing it again.

Cullen couldn't help himself. When he'd spotted his wee wife rushing across Angus's paddock, his heart had lodged firmly in his throat, leaving him gagging on a terror like he'd never before experienced. His terror had only increased when he saw that Angus had spotted the witless woman and was charging down the paddock toward her.

Worse yet, the senseless female had stopped moving when she'd seen him, a relieved look crossing her face. Why the devil she'd looked relieved was beyond him. He'd been too far away to do much but roar at her to move and rush to climb the fence to try to help her. And what had the foolish wench done? She'd done a little turn on the green as if she were at a bloody ball, and *then* sprinted for the fence.

Truth be told, Cullen had been rather impressed by her speed in that final dash, but it didn't lessen his anger. Dear God, he was sure she'd scared ten years off his life with this little adventure . . . and he did not scare easily. In fact, Cullen could honestly say he'd never *ever* experienced that kind of horror and fear before in all the years of his life . . . over anyone . . . and he never wanted to feel it again.

"I—"

"What the devil were ye doing?" Cullen interrupted to ask again. The bull had been a hairbreadth away from goring her when he'd lifted her out of the paddock. And this wasn't the first time she'd put herself in jeopardy with mad behavior either, he recalled. There was that little ride of hers in the meadow with her mare's reins in her teeth, too. The woman seemed prone to dangerous behavior.

"I was coming to speak to you," Evelinde blurted quickly, before he could repeat his words yet again.

"Me?" he asked incredulously.

"Aye. I had reached the first paddock when I saw you get thrown from that mad horse. I feared you had been injured and would need me. Rather than waste time running around the paddock, I climbed the fence to run through. I thought it was empty," she explained in a rush.

"Empty?" Cullen echoed with disbelief. "Are ye blind as well as daft? How could ye no see him?"

Evelinde just stared back at him helplessly, apparently not having an answer for that. It was Fergus who stepped to Cullen's side and placed a calming hand on his arm as he murmured quietly by his ear, "The paddock is L-shaped, me laird. Angus may have been in the inner far corner, where she could not have seen him."

Cullen felt his shoulders sag at that reminder. In truth, a lot of his anger had slipped away at the knowledge that her stupid behavior had been out of concern for him. Fergus's comment simply drained him of the rest. He was terribly happy to know his wife wasn't an idiot. He was even happier to know she had been concerned for him. Though, Cullen couldn't have said why he cared . . . except perhaps because he found he quite liked her, and he had been concerned for her when he'd seen her in the paddock with Angus. In truth, he'd been in a panic when he'd realized the peril she was in.

The sound of throat-clearing made him glance to Fergus to find him first jerking his eyes toward the other men standing around them, gawking at his wife. Cullen glowered at the lot of them and caught Evelinde by the arm to urge her across the grass toward the path.

"I am sorry, husband. I really did not see the bull," Evelinde said quietly, as he marched her up the path toward the castle.

Sighing, Cullen glanced at her as they passed the stables, really seeing her for the first time now his fear and anger had cleared. A frown immediately reclaimed his lips. The woman's hair was a knotted mass on her head, and the gown she wore was so big it was gaping in the front for all and sundry to see what she did and did not have.

"What the devil are you wearing?" he asked with dismay.

"I—" Evelinde glanced down at herself and gasped as she saw the state of her dress. She then reached behind her back, gathering up the excess material into one fist so the front was more fitted and didn't reveal so much.

Cullen scowled as he glanced over the gown. It looked familiar, but wasn't hers he was sure. At least it wasn't one of the ones he'd packed for her.

"Me laird!"

Cullen paused and glanced toward the wall at that shout to see one of the men waving at him. "What?"

"A traveling party is approaching," the man yelled back.

Cullen scowled, then glanced to Evelinde. Not that she noticed. Her attention was on the back of her gown as she twisted about trying to see something, though he wasn't sure what she was looking for, and at the moment, he didn't have time to find out.

"Get to our room and change into something that fits ye," he ordered, giving her a little push toward the keep. "I have to see who this is."

* * *

Evelinde moved toward the keep, but she wasn't moving very quickly. It was difficult to walk quickly with your upper body twisted as far to the side as you could turn it so you could examine the back of your skirt. She was searching for the pin she'd borrowed—without permission—from Cullen's chest. It had obviously come undone, letting loose the material she'd gathered at her back, and she was hoping it was caught in the folds of her gown somewhere. Unfortunately, a thorough search through the fabric proved it wasn't still there.

Pausing, Evelinde bit her lip and glanced back toward the paddock. Most of the men had dispersed; only a few were still making their way from the area. Gnawing at her lip now, Evelinde glanced in the direction she thought her husband had gone and saw him hurrying up a set of stairs carved into the stone wall. No doubt he was heading up to see who was approaching, she thought, and glanced back toward the paddock again.

Evelinde really didn't wish to go anywhere near the bull again, but she also didn't want to have to explain to her husband that she'd lost his pin. What if it held some sentimental value? It could have been his father's, or even his mother's. Even if it wasn't, it had looked valuable. She was sure there were both rubies and emeralds in the broach.

Sighing, Evelinde gave up her position in the middle of the path and headed back to the paddock. She moved slowly, eyes scanning the dirt for the pin as she went, but she didn't see it. By the time she reached the fence, every last man who had been gathered there was gone. It seemed the celebrations were over.

Evelinde paused where she had the first time she'd reached the fence and looked inside the paddock for the bull. Angus was nowhere to be seen, but that was what she'd thought the last time and so looked a little more closely, realizing that it wasn't a rectangle as she'd first assumed, but an L-shape, the back end turning sharply and running along behind the next paddock and out of her line of vision. No doubt that was where the beast had been, back in the area she couldn't see, Evelinde realized, and decided she'd best not try to check the paddock itself now.

Lips pursing, she tightened her fingers on the fence before her with frustration, then suddenly recalled the struggle she'd had with her skirt on climbing the wooden frame. Perhaps the pin had popped open and dropped off there, she thought, and began to search the ground outside the fence, running her slipper back and forth over the grass, hoping to reveal it. When that didn't work, she knelt and began to crawl over the space, running her bare hands over the grass, willing to risk being pierced by the sharp tip to find it. She really didn't want to have to explain she'd lost the pin.

When that turned up nothing, Evelinde sat back on her heels with a sigh and peered into the paddock. The pin might have opened when she climbed the fence, but hung briefly from the material, falling out at some point between this and the other side of the paddock.

Or it may have hung there until she and Cullen

were walking back toward the keep, she thought
with sudden hope. Standing, Evelinde moved back
to the path and followed it past the bull's paddock,
eyes scanning the ground as she went. When she
reached the spot where she thought they'd cut across
the grass between the two paddocks, she got back to
her hands and knees to search the grass along the
path they'd taken.

"Wife!"

Evelinde closed her eyes at that bark, and there
was no other word for it. Cullen sounded angry . . .
again. Not wishing to lose her spot, she turned on
her hands and knees to glance up at him, her eyes
widening as she saw he wasn't alone. There were
two men and a woman with him, she noted with
dismay . . . and every single one of them, Cullen included, were staring at her with a sort of fascinated
horror she didn't understand. Surely it wasn't that
shocking to find her looking for something on the
ground?

"Wife, ye—yer—" Apparently at a loss, Cullen
gestured toward his upper chest, then rushed forward.

Evelinde glanced down at the gesture, a blush of
embarrassment heating her face as she realized her
borrowed gown was gaping wide and—with her on
all fours—she was giving them a lovely view all the
way down to her knees. Gasping, she sat up abruptly
and gasped again as Cullen caught her by the arm
and yanked her to her feet.

Before she could reach back to gather the folds
and make the gown more presentable, Cullen had

already done so. He caught the excess material in a fist and used that hold to turn her toward him as he hissed, "What are ye doing? I told ye to go change."

"Aye, but I lost—" Evelinde paused abruptly when she realized she was about to tell him she'd lost his pin, but he didn't notice, he was already snapping at her again.

"When I tell ye to do something, ye do it, lass." The words were hard and uncompromising.

"I—"

"Obey was one of the vows ye gave," he reminded grimly.

Evelinde blinked at the words, then said sharply, "As I recall I did not vow *anything*, husband. I flopped about like a landed fish."

Cullen growled and opened his mouth, no doubt to give another order, but was interrupted by a woman's voice saying, "Oh my, that sounds an interesting tale, dear. I cannot wait to hear it."

Evelinde turned wide eyes to the woman, noting with distraction that the trio she had first noted with her husband had moved closer.

"You are English," she said with surprise, her gaze moving over the tall, curvy woman with interest.

"Born and raised," the woman agreed with a smile. "And here I feared I'd taken on a Scottish accent after all these years."

"You have a bit of one," Evelinde said. "But not so much I have to struggle to understand you as I do everyone else here."

The woman laughed, but Cullen and the other two men scowled as if she'd insulted them. Obviously, she could not do anything right today, not even speak, she decided unhappily. Her thoughts were distracted when Cullen suddenly urged her forward with the handful of skirt he held, his fist goosing her—unintentionally, she was sure.

"Wife, the Comyns. Comyns, me wife," Cullen announced as he directed them all up the path again. Evelinde rolled her eyes at his idea of an introduction, but then smiled as graciously as she could manage and said, "Welcome."

Lady Comyn—at least Evelinde thought she must be Lady Comyn, though it was hard to say after that introduction, she thought irritably—chuckled and moved to slip her arm through Evelinde's to lead her toward the keep.

"Call me Ellie, dear. My name is Eleanor, but only people I do not like call me that."

"And I am Evelinde," she murmured, glancing impatiently back at her husband, who was still holding the back of her gown and trying to steer her by it. She attempted to brush his hand away and take over holding the gown with her own free hand, but he ignored her efforts and merely scowled. She scowled right back and pinched the back of his hand.

"We heard Cullen had found himself a bride and could not resist coming to meet you," Lady Comyn said, distracting her.

Giving up on her husband for the moment, Evelinde turned back at that announcement and offered a smile. "And I am glad you did."

"So am I," Ellie said with amusement, as Cullen

broke them apart by shifting Evelinde to the right by his hold on her gown.

It was only then Evelinde saw the puddle she'd been about to stomp through. Still, she cast a glare back at her husband and once again tried to free herself from his hold, this time resorting to digging her nails into the skin of his hand rather than pinching him.

A low chuckle then drew her attention to the fact that the Comyn men—one older and probably Ellie's husband, and a younger one of about Cullen's age who she thought might be their son—were grinning at these antics as they followed them up the path.

"Aye, we heard Cullen had found himself a bride, but no one mentioned he'd met his match," the younger Comyn man said, amusement sparkling in his eyes. " 'Twill be interesting to see how the Devil of Donnachaidh deals with a wife who doesna automatically obey as everyone else does."

Cullen released her skirt then in favor of turning a hard glance on the man, but he merely laughed and slapped his shoulder. "Come now, Cullen, cheer up, or I shall tell one and all that you are attached to yer wife by her skirt strings."

Evelinde's eyes widened at the man's baiting, but then glanced to Lady Comyn as she chuckled and caught her arm to urge her forward again. "Do not mind them, my dear. My son, Tralin, and your husband have been friends for ages."

She smiled at the reassurance but cast a glance nervously back to be sure the men hadn't come to blows. However, Cullen was walking between the two Comyn men, listening to something the older man was saying, and didn't look the least annoyed. He also wasn't holding her skirt up anymore, Evelinde realized, and was relieved to take over the task for herself for the rest of the walk.

Her relief only lasted until they reached the keep stairs. Evelinde paused there and caught up her skirt to keep from tripping over it, then gasped as her husband scooped her up into his arms.

"Ye'll trip in that ridiculous gown," he said, carrying her past a now openly laughing Lady Comyn.

Evelinde ground her teeth together and crossed her arms over her chest, wondering where and when it was exactly she'd lost her dignity. She'd think it was somewhere between England and Scotland except for the humiliating events leading up to her wedding. Between tumbling into the river, the debacle when Cullen had fallen from his horse, and being forced to flop her way through her wedding, it did seem she'd had nothing but difficulties from the moment Edda had announced she was to marry the Devil of Donnachaidh. It made her think that must be when luck had turned on her.

And here she'd woken up after consummating the marriage thinking herself lucky to have been wedded to the man. Evelinde snorted at her poor, naive thoughts of earlier as Cullen carried her into the keep. The sound made him glance at her sharply, but she ignored his questioning glance and decided she should have taken heed of her husband's poor luck at the time and reconsidered finding a way to end the betrothal.

And he did have poor luck, Evelinde thought, as he carried her across the hall to the stairs. There was the matter of his dead father, uncle, and wife, and each death blamed on him. That certainly wasn't good luck. It seemed obvious her husband walked under some curse.

Perhaps she should look into good-luck charms to help preserve her through this marriage, Evelinde thought grimly.

"Change." The one-word order was said as Cullen paused at the stairs leading to the keep's second level and set her on her feet.

"Into what, my lord?" Evelinde asked with exasperation. "I have nothing to wear but the gowns in our chamber, and every one of them will be as large as this one."

"What?" he asked, his face gone suddenly blank.

"You heard me," she snapped, some of her temper slipping out despite herself. Her gaze slid to the Comyns then, and Evelinde sighed inwardly as she realized that while they had paused at the tables, they were listening avidly.

"Of course you have something else to wear," Cullen insisted. "Put on one of yer own gowns."

"What gowns of my own?" Evelinde asked, turning sharply back on him as all of her frustrations burst forth. "You carried me away from d'Aumesbery without my maid, my mare, or even a change of clothes, or a brush for my hair. This is the best I can do," she cried.

Cullen grunted with irritation and shook his head. "Of course I brought ye a change of clothes. I packed

them meself while we were supposed to be consummating the marriage."

Evelinde noticed the eyebrow-raising among the
Comyns, but other than shout out to them that the
wedding had been consummated since then, she
didn't know what to do. And really, she was embarrassed enough already.

"And I put a brush in, too," Cullen added, reclaiming her wandering attention.

"In what?" Evelinde asked with bewilderment.
She recalled his moving briefly out of her sight and
hearing rustling that might have been the sound of
packing.

"In a sack. 'Tis in our chamber," he said.

Evelinde stared at her husband, realizing he'd
spoken more words in the last few moments than
he'd yet said since they'd met. While she was relieved
to have this information now, she couldn't help but
be absolutely furious that—had he simply told her
these things at some point during the journey here,
or even before bedding her that day—the whole humiliating afternoon could have been avoided. She
would be wearing one of her own gowns that fit
properly, would have had no need of the pin that was
now lost, would not have unintentionally exposed
herself to their neighbors, and would have greeted
them looking dignified and well put together. This
whole mess was *all his fault*.

Evelinde opened her mouth, several choice words
trembling on the tip of her tongue, but then snapped
it closed again and whirled away. She had already
thoroughly humiliated herself in front of their

neighbors and would not make it any worse. However, she and her husband were going to have a serious discussion later, Evelinde thought, grabbing up
her skirts and stamping up the stairs.

She kept stamping all the way to the room and
into it. Evelinde then stamped around the chamber,
glowering as she searched for the sack he spoke of.
At first, she thought there wasn't one, but then she
recalled the soft whoosh when he'd reached the opposite side of the bed the night they'd arrived and
moved around to the side he'd slept on and glanced
at the floor. Nothing.

She was about to whirl away and stamp back
below to bellow at her husband when she spotted a
corner of cloth sticking out from under the bed.

Moving forward, Evelinde knelt to grab it and
pulled out what turned out to be a sack. The only
thing she could think was he'd accidentally kicked it
under the bed when getting into it last night, or perhaps at some point when he'd come up this morning
to rub the salve into her. Had he mentioned it was
there, she would have thought to look for it.

Closing her eyes, Evelinde held her breath for a
moment, then released it slowly.

"Patience," she murmured, and opened the sack
as she stood up. Setting the bag on the bed, Evelinde
reached in and pulled out the first thing she touched.
It was a dark green gown, one of her favorites. A red
gown followed; another of her favorites. A chemise
came next, then another. Finally, her hand closed
on a handle and she pulled out a brush. Evelinde
then turned the sack over, emptying the remaining

contents onto the bed and sighing as several items tumbled out, including a couple of her best belts, cornets, circlets, gloves, and a smaller sack, which held her mother's jewelry.

Evelinde stared at the items and sank down on the side of the bed as tears filled her eyes. He'd thought of everything. Well, not everything. Her tapestries and so forth were not there, but he'd included everything she would need to dress herself properly at least for a couple of days. It was more than she'd hoped for when he'd said he packed for her. Most men would not have thought to include the gloves or circlets she was sure. But Cullen had, and had done so despite her not being able to remind him of the need at the time. He'd also done so during a more stressful than usual wedding. At least, she thought it had probably been more stressful than the average wedding but couldn't be sure. It was her first.

Feeling a bit mollified, Evelinde forced herself to stand and begin to remove her gown. She would dress and fix her hair as quickly as possible, then return below. They had guests. Her first. She'd made a poor showing at the initial meeting but hoped to repair the impression. If she could.

chapter

Eight

Marriage was horrible.

Evelinde grimaced as the thought ran through her head for about the hundredth time since she'd sat down to mend a small tear in her green gown. It was three days since the Comyns had visited. Evelinde had quite enjoyed seeing them once she was dressed properly. Ellie, Lady Comyn, was a charming, amusing, and elegant woman like her own mother had been. The sort of woman Evelinde had hoped to be, but apparently had failed miserably at becoming.

Sighing, she sewed another stitch, her eyes seeking out her husband where he sat at the table talking to Fergus. Apparently, Cullen *could* speak, Evelinde thought bitterly as she watched his mouth move in what appeared to be a whole sentence rather than one of the grunts he doled out to her.

The man rarely bothered actually to say anything to her. Evelinde tried repeatedly to engage him in conversation with no success. Hoping to encourage him, she'd chattered on about her life growing up, her parents, her brother, her mare, and so on. She'd even managed to slip in a reference to her beloved tapestries and her sorrow that she hadn't been able to bring them. What she'd spoken of most, though, was Mildrede and Mac. She missed them terribly and said so at every opportunity. In turn, Cullen had grunted.

He hadn't even given her an answer when she'd asked what duties he would like her to take on now that she was at Donnachaidh. Met with the usual discouraging silence, she'd let that go to keep her promise to Biddy and asked if he couldn't have some men aid the women with the heavier tasks in the kitchens and elsewhere in the castle. All she'd received for her trouble was a look that suggested the very idea was mad.

If it weren't for the fact that Evelinde had seen his lips move in what appeared to be actual conversations with others, she would have thought the man incapable of forming whole sentences. However, she had, and Evelinde now suspected the truth was that he simply didn't care to trouble himself to speak to her. She was beginning to think he was regretting their marriage. Not that he was mean or cruel, but he also hadn't touched her again since consummating the marriage. It seemed that what she had thought was a beautiful, exciting, and world-shattering event had not even been enjoyable for Cullen. Else why had he not repeated the experience?

That was the question running repeatedly through her mind as she'd lain in the dark next to him at night, listening to him breathe: Why did he not touch her again?

Evelinde was miserable. She missed Mildrede and Mac, felt bereft and lost in her new home, and had not even her husband's kisses and caresses to comfort her. Instead, she moped about during the day and lay awake in bed at night, tears streaming silently from her eyes as she imagined this to be her life from now on: a silent, uncaring husband and not even a friend to speak to.

Well, there was Biddy, Evelinde reminded herself. But Cullen's aunt was forever busy, hustling about the kitchen, directing staff and chopping up chickens or performing other such tasks. Evelinde hated to bother her while she was so busy filling in for Donnachaidh's normal cook, so tried to avoid pestering her too much, which left her lonely, and growing more so all the time, to the point that last night she'd wished briefly that she were back at d'Aumesbery. While Edda could make life unpleasant, at least Evelinde had someone to talk to there, and during those rare moments when she managed to get away from the keep, she'd found peace and a measure of happiness riding Lady or sitting by the clearing. Something she feared she would never find at Donnachaidh.

Aye, it was turning out that marriage was not as wonderful as she'd thought the day after arriving here. Evelinde sighed as she noted that the last few stitches she'd sewn were crooked. Grimacing, she began to tear them out. It seemed she could not do anything right anymore. At least nothing she'd attempted to do here had met with any measure of success. She couldn't get her husband to talk, couldn't sew a straight line, and couldn't even gain a bit of information that would help her sort out why Cullen's uncle, father, and wife might have been murdered.

Evelinde sighed again as she thought on the last subject. When she hadn't been trying to get her husband to talk these last few days, or tending to her duties here as Lady Donnachaidh, she'd spent her time delving into the matter of the three deaths.

All she'd really done was ask questions. Evelinde had started with his aunt, trying to be casual about it, but Biddy had caught on to what she was up to at once and told her to "let it lie. The last thing Cullen needs is another dead wife." Evelinde had reluctantly given up on quizzing the woman and turned to asking her questions of others instead. She'd spoken to several maids, Scatchy—who it turned out was the stable master—Fergus, and a few others, but none of them had been very forthcoming on the subject either. All she'd gained was a stern lecture from Fergus assuring her that her husband had not killed anyone and that she shouldn't believe the rumors and nonsense.

Cullen was a good man, he'd informed her, and she should concentrate on being a good wife to him. Feeling suitably chastened, Evelinde had let the subject drop at once.

So far, she had got nowhere with that effort. It was another failure, in her mind, and it irritated Evelinde because she wasn't even sure why she had troubled herself to ask around about the subject. She'd started out telling herself it was because she wanted to do something nice for her husband in return for his thoughtfulness in packing a bag for her, but suspected the truth was that, like his first wife, little Maggie, she was hoping to win his affection, or at least his attention, by clearing his name.

And was that not a sad state of affairs? Evelinde thought to herself with disgust. She did not even know why she cared. 'Twas a marriage, and marriages rarely included love. They were business associations. Through their marriage, Cullen had gained a healthy dower, and she'd gained a home for the rest of her days. Without it, she would have either been a burden to her brother, living at d'Aumesbery like Edda would, or she would have found herself shipped off to a nunnery. Love wasn't a part of marriage. Her parents hadn't loved each other when they'd first wed, that had come later, and they'd been lucky to find it. Most husbands and wives didn't come to love each other.

"My lady."

"Aye?" Evelinde glanced up to see who addressed her and gasped, "Mildrede!"

The maid laughed gaily as Evelinde tossed her sewing aside and threw herself out of the chair and into the maid's arms.

"Oh, Mildrede, I have missed you so!"

"And I, you," the maid assured her with a laugh as she hugged her back.

"What are you doing here?" Evelinde asked, pulling back just far enough to see her face.

Mildrede's eyebrows rose at the question. "Where else would I be? I am your lady's maid. My place is with you."

"Aye, but—" Evelinde paused, confusion rife within her. She turned to seek out her husband for an explanation, but her gaze caught on the man standing a couple of feet behind the maid, and her eyes widened incredulously. "Mac?"

His dear face split into a wide grin at her disbelief and he nodded. "'Tis I."

Slipping from Mildrede's hold, Evelinde now hurried to the man and gave him a hug as well. "I cannot believe you are here."

"Nor can I," he admitted wryly. "Never thought I'd see me beloved Scotland again, but here I be, and glad of it," he added grimly. "We couldna leave d'Aumesbery quick enough fer me liking. Edda was taking out her temper on all and sundry once ye were no there for her to focus her frustration and anger on."

When Evelinde frowned at this news, he quickly added, "Ne'er fear though. We passed a small traveling party on the way out and stopped to find it was Alexander returning. He'll take Edda in hand."

"My brother is back?" Evelinde asked with a gasp of both happiness and relief. She'd begun to fear he'd been badly injured or killed in Tunis. But he had not, and he was home. It was almost as great a gift as having Mildrede and Mac returned to her, she thought, and turned excitedly to her husband as he took her arm to draw her away from Mac's embrace. "Can we visit him? I have not seen my brother in three years."

"Not right now," Cullen answered. "Later in the year, mayhap. But ye can invite him to visit us do ye wish."

She nodded, excited at the prospect, then gestured to Mildrede and Mac, and asked, "Are they here for good?"

Cullen nodded.

"Mildrede can stay?" she asked, needing clarification.

"She's yer maid," he said simply.

"And Mac?"

"Ye said he was yer friend." Cullen shrugged. "He's a Scot, and Scatchy is getting old, he'll need someone to take his place and direct his daughter in the stables."

Evelinde stilled at these words. She'd known Scatchy worked in the stables, one of the few men who seemed actually to do anything other than practice at sword play, but hadn't realized the man's daughter worked there as well. Not that it mattered much to her at that point. She was more concerned with what her husband had done for her.

"You sent for them because you knew I missed

them?" she asked, tears welling in her eyes as she realized he had actually listened to her after all.

"Nay."

Evelinde glanced around at that word to see a tall, very handsome, fair-haired man moving toward them. She recognized him at once as one of the men who had arrived at d'Aumesbery with her husband, but who had remained behind when they'd left. She had no idea who he was, though.

"Tavis," he introduced himself, apparently reading the confusion on her face. "I'm Cullen's cousin. Yers, too, now that yer wed."

"Oh," Evelinde managed a smile and nodded. "Hello, cousin Tavis."

Tavis's smile widened at her prim greeting, eyes twinkling, then he turned to gesture to the men who had followed and introduced them, "Gillie, Rory, and Jasper."

Evelinde nodded to each of the grinning men in turn, then shifted her attention back to Tavis as he explained, "Cullen ordered your things brought ere leaving d'Aumesbery. While the three of ye left, he ordered us to stay behind long enough for a wagon to be packed with yer belongings and follow."

"Aye, me lady," a short, freckled, strawberry blond Tavis had introduced as Gillie said. "We got here as quick as we could but had to travel more slowly because of the wagon."

Evelinde stared at the men, slowly understanding that this, then, was where they'd disappeared to.

They'd stayed behind to escort the wagon to Donnachaidh; a wagon with her belongings.

"We brought everything of yours," Mildrede said, drawing her attention again. "Edda tried to stop us at first, but Tavis and the men just told her to stay out of the way. We have your tapestries and—"

The maid stopped speaking because Evelinde had whirled away at that point and was rushing for the doors.

"Oh!" Evelinde gasped as she slammed through the door and paused on the top of the keep stairs to stare down at the overloaded wagon waiting in front. She peered at the familiar items on the wagon with wide eyes, then glanced back when the doors opened behind her. A beaming Mildrede and Mac stepped out first, followed by Cullen and the four men who had escorted the wagon.

"You brought my chairs from my room," she said with amazement, turning back and running lightly down the stairs to the wagon.

"Aye. Mildrede wanted to bring yer bed, too, but it wouldna fit," Tavis informed her with amusement, leading the other men down the stairs to follow Mildrede and Mac to the wagon as Evelinde moved around it, touching familiar items as she passed.

It was like having a little bit of home with her. Each item held memories, both good and bad. The good memories were of her parents, the bad were of Edda. Evelinde decided she would only remember the good and forget the bad. She had enough problems at present without troubling about the past. The past

was done. Edda could not hurt or humiliate her anymore, so carrying those memories with her would
only be her hurting herself in Edda's stead.

"My tapestries," she murmured, caressing the end
of one of the rolls, then her gaze moved on. "The
cushions Mother and I embroidered!"

"And all your clothes, and even the embroidered
linens your mother put aside for you," Mildrede said
with a grin, then sobered somewhat as she added,
"And your parents' portraits."

Evelinde felt tears well in her eyes and quickly
dashed them away as she turned to offer her husband a small smile.

"Thank you," she murmured with heartfelt gratitude.

He grunted.

Evelinde frowned, her gaze sweeping back to the
wagon. She shook her head as she recalled how
upset she'd been when she thought she'd never see
these things again. In truth, though, she would have
given them all up to have Mildrede and Mac with
her, but it seemed she'd lost neither her dear maid
and friend nor her things. All her upset and depres-
sion had been for naught.

"Why did you not tell me they were coming?"
Evelinde asked with bewilderment. Had he done so
the last few days would not have been so dark and
gloomy for her. She would have been able to enjoy
the anticipation of their arrival as a much-needed
bright spot in her day.

Cullen shrugged. "Ye assumed I would no see

yer things brought, so I left ye to believe what ye wished."

"What I wished?" Evelinde asked with disbelief, anger stirring in her. "You think I *wished* to don your dead wife's gown and make a complete cake of myself in front of our neighbors because I thought I had naught but the clothes I rode here in? You think I *wished* to weep at night because I thought everyone I loved was lost to me? You think I *wished* I thought I had lost every tie and reminder of my family?"

"Weep?" he asked, zeroing on the word with a frown. "When did you weep?"

"While you slept," Evelinde snapped, feeling embarrassment color her cheeks as she admitted it. She wasn't the only one embarrassed. His men and Mac were all exchanging panicked glances and looking terribly uncomfortable, though Mildrede was looking upset on her behalf rather than embarrassed. Evelinde wasn't surprised when the woman moved to stand behind her in her usual show of support.

"Hmm," Mac muttered suddenly. "Well, guess we should start unloading this wagon." Grabbing Mildrede by the arm, he dragged her to the wagon. Evelinde heard Mildrede hiss at him to let her alone, but he muttered back that she was best not to get between Evelinde and Cullen, then shoved a cushion at her and grabbed a chair himself before directing her toward the stairs. The rest of the men were snatching up items left and right and hurrying after the pair, fleeing the field of battle, Evelinde realized.

"Well, there was no need for crying," Cullen said with a scowl, as the last of the group disappeared into the keep. "If ye had just trusted me to tend to matters as it is my place to do, ye'd have realized I'd see to yer well-being. And," he added with a frown, "ye've no lost all ties to yer family. I am yer family now."

"Family? You?" she asked with amazement. "Nay, my lord. You are a complete stranger to me. And why should I trust a stranger to do what is best for me when my own stepmother— who was not a stranger—would not?"

"I am no a stranger," Cullen said impatiently. "I'm yer husband."

"You may be my husband, my lord, but a couple of head flops in front of a priest does not change the fact that you are a stranger," Evelinde said grimly, then pointed out, "I know nothing about you. While I have told you everything I can think of about myself, you have shared nothing in return. I know Scatchy better than I know you, and all I know about him is that he likes pasties. I have no idea what you like or dislike, except perhaps that you do not like me."

Cullen stilled in surprise, then looked irritated. "What the devil would make ye think I doona like you?"

"Oh, I do not know," she snapped, as a now-empty-handed Mac started back out of the keep followed by the other men. "Perhaps because you have not touched me or more than grunted at me since consummating our marriage."

The men on the stairs stopped abruptly and turned

to head back into the keep without Cullen ever seeing them, Evelinde noted, as her husband's mouth opened and closed twice without issuing a word.

Finally, he glared and snapped, "I was being considerate."

"Considerate?" she asked with disbelief.

"Aye. I didna wish to pain yer bruises. I thought to let them heal more ere bothering you again."

Evelinde was too upset at this point to appreciate the thoughtfulness of the gesture. If it was true, she thought furiously and bit out, "Well, it would have been nice if you had said as much to me, my lord, rather than leave me thinking I was so poor at the duty you wished not to have to attend it again."

Cullen's eyes widened in shock, then he grabbed her by the arm and turned to drag her into the keep.

"Where are you taking me?" she asked with irritation, trying to jerk her arm free as he dragged her across the great hall toward the stairs.

"To show ye I like ye," he snarled.

Evelinde immediately dug in her heels, bringing them to a halt by the trestle tables.

"Have you not listened to a word I have said?" she asked incredulously. "I do not wish to be *shown*, I want to be told, my lord."

Cullen turned back to face her as the men, who had apparently settled themselves at the table to avoid being unwilling witnesses to the fight while it was outside, quickly scrambled to escape the great hall, rushing back out the doors they'd just come in.

"Wife," he said, his expression exasperated. "Ye never judge a man by his words, but by his actions.

A man, *and a woman*"—he added firmly—"can lie to ye with their lips, but their actions will tell the truth."

"That may be true of most people, husband. But I am not most people, I am your wife, and I need both the actions *and* the words," she said firmly.

Cullen stared at her as if she were some exotic creature he'd never seen before, then threw up his hands with exasperation and marched past her and out of the keep.

Evelinde stared at the closed door for several minutes, her mind in an uproar. She wasn't sorry she'd said what she had. For heaven's sake, she hadn't even known Biddy was his aunt until the woman had told her so herself!

Still, she wasn't sure she'd accomplished much either. What Cullen said was partly true. Were she to judge him by his actions, her husband was proving to be a considerate, caring man. He had done everything she would have wished him to do and without her ever having had the opportunity to ask him to do it . . . Everything except ease her mind by telling her what he was doing.

Evelinde supposed that was better than a man who made proclamations of caring, or promised her the world but did not trouble himself to do anything. And it was certainly better than a husband who drank too much and beat her. Releasing a little sigh, she rubbed her forehead where an ache was beginning to grow and acknowledged that things could indeed be worse. She did much prefer a quiet but thoughtful husband to a lying, abusive husband.

Perhaps she would just have to learn to deal with Cullen's telling her nothing, Evelinde thought on a sigh.

At least she had Mac and Mildrede again, she reminded herself, as the door opened, and Mac, the man who had listened to her woes and worries since she was old enough to sit a saddle, entered with a small chest in hand. He was followed by the other men, each of them carrying an item from the wagon.

Mac paused beside her, waited for the others to pass by and start up the stairs, then said, "Lady's been stuck walking behind the wagon for four days and may like a ride. She's no had a proper ride since ye left."

"Lady is here, too?" Evelinde asked, cheering.

"Aye. She was taken to the stables."

Evelinde immediately started past him, pausing to glance back when he spoke her name softly.

"Doona be too hard on the man, lass. Talking is harder for men than 'tis for women."

Evelinde frowned at his words, and pointed out, "You talk to me all the time."

"Aye." He smiled faintly. "But I'm an old man. I've learned the value of talking. Cullen's younger, though, and proud." He shrugged and shook his head. "Empty vessels make the most sound, lass, and he's no empty."

"No, he is not," she agreed quietly.

Apparently satisfied that he'd done what he could, Mac turned away with his burden. "Go on and see yer Lady. She's been pining for ye."

Smiling faintly, Evelinde turned and continued out of the keep. Her smile widened at the prospect of seeing her mare as she crossed the bailey.

She was barely halfway to the stables when she saw Cullen come charging out of the building on his mount. He immediately headed out of the bailey, urging his mount to a run as soon as he'd passed under the gate.

Evelinde wondered briefly where he was going but then pushed the worry away and hurried on to the stables. If Lady did not seem tired, she would take her for a ride. Just a short one since she didn't know the area, but even a short, fast ride would help soothe her.

"My men saw ye from the wall about half an hour ago. So, I saddled up to meet ye," Tralin greeted as he reigned in before Cullen's mount on the edge of the woods surrounding the hill Comyn castle sat on.

Cullen grunted. He would have done the same the other day had Tralin and his parents not already nearly been to the castle by the time his man had alerted him that a party approached. Cullen suspected the men on the wall had been too distracted watching him trying to break the new horse to notice the approaching riders. Or perhaps they'd been watching his wife trying to get herself killed charging across Angus's paddock, he thought with an irritation that soon faded as he recalled she'd been rushing across the paddock because she'd feared he'd done himself an injury tumbling from the horse.

His wife was like to drive him crazy at this rate, Cullen decided with exasperation. One minute he was scared witless, the next furious at her for risking herself so, and the next he was touched that she'd feared for his well-being. Truly, marriage was turning out to be like a ride on a boat in rough weather; up and then down and then up and then down again. Someone should have warned him that marriage could make a man seasick.

"So? To what do I owe this visit? Or need I ask?"

Cullen's eyes narrowed. "What do ye mean by that?"

Tralin shrugged, then arched his eyebrows. "Do I dare ask how married life is treating ye?"

"Nosy beggar," Cullen muttered.

Tralin burst out laughing at the insult, and asked, "Trouble in paradise?"

When Cullen merely sighed unhappily, he reached out to slap him on the back encouragingly and turned his mount back toward Comyn castle. "Come, friend, I suspect ye could use an ale, and I would enjoy one, too."

Cullen hesitated. He shouldn't really be there. It was nearly an hour's ride to Comyn and would be the same back, and he had much to do, but he'd needed to ride off his frustration and confusion and had somehow ended here. Now that he was at Comyn, he might as well have a drink before he returned, Cullen reasoned and urged his mount forward with a nod.

"So," Tralin said, once they were settled at the

trestle table in the Comyn great hall. "How is the fair Evelinde?"

Cullen smiled reluctantly and admitted, "She *is* fair."

"Aye," Tralin agreed, watching his face with interest. "Even in the overlarge gown and with her hair looking as if she'd come straight from her bed, she was fair, but she was fairer still when she came down after changing and fixing her hair."

Cullen nodded, a smile curving his lips as he thought what Tralin said was true, but his wife looked most beautiful when she was naked, her bright blue eyes darkening with the passion he stirred in her.

"She seemed to have a personality to match," Tralin added, when Cullen remained silent. "So I can only assume whatever trouble it is has brought ye here is yer fault."

The image of his naked wife shattering, Cullen straightened abruptly and turned an offended gaze his way. "What?"

"Well . . ." Tralin shrugged. "I doona see her being stubborn and proud. You, on the other hand, are both."

Cullen grimaced at the truth of those words and sighed. "I didna plan to come here, but now that I am . . ." He shrugged, and said, "You are better with women than I. At least they seem to like to talk to ye."

"That's because I actually talk back," Tralin said dryly, then asked, "What happened?"

"I found out she's been crying herself to sleep," Cullen admitted unhappily.

Tralin's eyebrows rose. "Why?"

"She did not realize I had brought her clothes," he admitted. "The woman seemed to think I brought her to Donnachaidh with naught but the gown on her back."

Tralin shrugged. "How could she know otherwise? Did ye tell her ye had?"

"Nay, but she should ha'e kenned that I'd no bring her here without her belongings."

"How could she know that?" he asked with amusement. "She doesna ken ye, Cullen. And ye must admit, you are no the most forthcoming of men."

Cullen frowned at the very suggestion that he might carry some of the blame for her thinking so poorly of him but knew it was true. The man was only echoing her complaint.

"Have the two of ye talked at all since the marriage?"

"She talks," Cullen admitted with a smile tugging at his lips as he thought of the way Evelinde had chattered away to him the last several days. She'd told him tales of her youth, her adventures, her friendship with Mac and affection for Mildrede, as well as revealed the clever ways she'd managed to avoid her stepmother as often as possible.

"*She* talks, huh?" Tralin said, watching his smile. "And what do you do?"

"I listen," Cullen answered, and he did. He'd found himself enthralled, listening to her voice. Evelinde was a fair storyteller, and he'd been able to picture much of what she'd said in his head as she spoke.

"Hmm." Tralin sipped at his ale, and asked, "Do ye like her so far?"

Cullen considered the question and nodded slowly. "Aye. She's clever and sweet and . . . wishes herself back at d'Aumesbery with that perfectly hateful stepmother of hers rather than at Donnachaidh with me," he ended with disgust.

Tralin choked on the ale he'd been in the process of swallowing, and Cullen thumped him a couple of times on the back, understanding the reaction. That admission had horrified him, too. It was hard to accept that she was so unhappy with him that she would rather be back there being insulted and abused by Edda.

"Why?" Tralin got out finally. "From what you said the other day, the woman treated her horribly."

Cullen nodded glumly. He'd told Tralin and his parents about the stepmother while Evelinde was upstairs changing the day they'd visited. He'd described Edda's behavior toward her stepdaughter with a few succinct words that had made it clear she had been badly treated by the woman.

He, on the other hand, never insulted or abused her, Cullen thought. In fact, he'd done everything he could to try to make things easier; leaving right after the wedding to get her away from Edda rather than staying to rest a night after the long trip to d'Aumesbery, choosing and packing gowns and such in that small bag for her when she was unable to do it herself, cutting himself to fake the consummation rather than subject her to the humiliation Edda had insisted on, carrying her before him on his mount the whole way so that her injuries were exacerbated as little as possible . . .

"Are ye rough with her in bed?" Tralin asked suddenly, and when Cullen turned a shocked and furious gaze on him, added quickly, "I am just trying to sort out why she would wish she was back at d'Aumesbery. I ken ye would not insult or abuse her like her stepmother—"

"I called her daft," Cullen admitted, then explained about the bull and her being in the paddock.

"Well, I think that can be forgiven," Tralin said with a frown, then cleared his throat and returned to the bone he'd dug up a moment ago. "I know you would not abuse a woman, but I was just wondering if—I mean, yer no used to dealing with virgins, Cullen, and mayhap you were a little less gentle than you might have been, or she was shocked by what . . . er . . . takes place."

"I have been avoiding bedding her to allow her body to heal," he admitted unhappily.

Tralin's eyebrows shot up. "You mean the wedding has not been consummated?"

"Aye, it has," Cullen assured him and frowned. He'd intended to wait until her body had healed completely and she would not wince in pain when he caressed her. Howbeit, the morning after arriving home, he'd spilled ale on himself and headed up to the room to change his tunic and Biddy had stopped him and asked if he'd take her salve up to Evelinde and tell her she'd be along shortly. He'd agreed, fully intending just to give her the salve, but then he'd walked in and found her laid out naked on the bed on her stomach and all his best intentions had gone out the window.

The next thing he knew his hands were slick with salve, and he was applying it himself, and once he'd touched her, Cullen had been lost. So much so that he couldn't even say if Biddy had ever come up intending to apply the salve. If she had, neither of them had noticed, and she'd slipped away without disturbing them, and he was grateful for it.

Tralin cleared his throat to get his attention, and asked delicately, "And how did it go?"

"It went . . . well," Cullen muttered, knowing he lied through his teeth. It had been incredible. He was no virgin, but bedding his wife had been one of the most exciting experiences of his life. Cullen had never before felt a passion like she'd drawn from him, or the desire to please a woman as much as he'd wanted to please Evelinde. His passion was so all-consuming it had been a struggle to remain gentle and a constant battle to avoid touching any of her sore spots. Reining in the passion she'd stirred so had been a sort of torture . . . a sweet torture. And one he'd wanted to repeat immediately on awaking, too. But, afraid he wouldn't be able to go gently next time, Cullen had forced himself to resist, reminding himself that she needed to heal.

"It went well for *you*," Tralin said. "But what of her? Perhaps—"

"It went well for her, too," Cullen interrupted dryly. "It went *verra* well for both of us. Howbeit, she seems to have mistaken my consideration in not wanting to trouble her again until she is fully healed as an indication that she did not please me."

"Hmm," Tralin murmured.

"And she wants me to explain things to her," Cullen complained. "I told her to watch me actions and no bother so much about the words, but she insists she wants me words *and* actions."

"Demanding wench."

Cullen nodded, only realizing that his friend had been teasing him when Tralin started to laugh.

"Cullen," he said with exasperation. "I ken yer no used to explaining yerself. Yer laird over the people of Donnachaidh and as such need not explain anything to anyone, but she is not just another one of yer people. She's yer wife, and the two of ye are just getting to ken each other. Ye'll need to explain some things at first."

When Cullen just glowered at him, he added, "Look at it from her perspective. Ye showed up, married her, and dragged her off right away, and *she thought* with naught but the gown she wore. Ye then bedded her once, and no doubt left her to her own devices after that, without a word of praise to let her know that ye were pleased with her, or—knowing you—any sort of direction as to her place at Donnachaidh. She is no doubt feeling lost and uncertain in her new home and position."

"But I have done all I possibly can to ease the way for her," Cullen protested.

"Except tell her ye're pleased with her for bride," he pointed out. "And praise is no doubt what she needs after being insulted by her stepmother all these years."

"But—"

"Look at it as just another one of yer duties," Tralin interrupted. "Ye take yer duties seriously, I ken. So, think of this as one. Yer duty is to ensure yer wife kens she is appreciated and necessary at Donnachaidh."

"A duty," he muttered.

"Aye." Tralin nodded. "I promise ye if ye do, she—and hence, ye—will be much happier."

Cullen considered the suggestion seriously, then nodded and stood.

"Where are ye going?" Tralin asked with surprise.

"Home to attend me duties," he muttered, heading for the door.

chapter

Nine

"We are lost and 'tis all your fault."

Lady did not react to either her vexed mistress's comment or her irritated scowl. The horse merely waited patiently for her to decide which way to go. Evelinde made a face at the animal's lack of concern and glanced around the woods.

It really was the mare's fault they were now deep in the woods in the valley at the base of the hill Donnachaidh sat on. Evelinde had never intended to enter the woods, but Lady had had other ideas. She supposed it was her own fault for giving the mare her head. Though, to be fair, doing so had never been a problem at d'Aumesbery. Donnachaidh was

another matter entirely. And not knowing where
she was going had not stopped Lady from charging
down the hill and into the woods.

Evelinde had tried to stop the mare at the bottom
of the hill, but Lady would not be stopped and had
run into the woods like a wild thing. By the time
she'd managed even to slow the beast, they were
well into the forest.

She hadn't thought it a problem at first. Evelinde
had assumed that if she just turned the mare back the
way they'd come, they'd canter happily out of there.
Only they'd been cantering for more than two hours
now without finding their way out of the woods.
Obviously, they'd got turned around somehow and
headed in the wrong direction, but Evelinde didn't
know how that had happened.

Shifting on her mare, she again glanced around
the woods surrounding them. It was a sunny day
outside the forest, but the trees in here grew so close
together, the cover overhead might as well have
been a stone wall. Very little sunlight was getting
through, and it felt like early evening in the heart of
the small forest.

Or perhaps it *was* early evening, Evelinde thought
anxiously, wondering if she'd underestimated the
time that had passed as she'd tried to find her way
back out of the valley. She hoped not, as Evelinde
had no desire to spend the night there.

The crunch of leaves and twigs being trampled
underfoot reached her ears, and she glanced sharply
to the side as Lady shifted nervously, but there was
no one there, and the sound wasn't repeated. Still,

both she and Lady had heard something so Evelinde waited, slowly scanning the woods, the feeling on the back of her neck creeping all the way down her spine.

It was enough to make her decide she didn't wish to sit there any longer trying to think of a way to resolve the problem. It seemed to her that moving— even in the wrong direction—was better than staying in one place.

Turning Lady away from the direction the sound had seemed to come from, Evelinde urged her forward, resisting the urge to look back.

"It was probably just a rabbit or vole," she said, running a soothing hand down the mare's neck. "Certainly not a wolf or anything of that ilk."

Whether Lady was reassured or not Evelinde didn't know, but she wasn't feeling much better herself. Her back was still creeping, and her body had tensed up, waiting for some ferocious animal or other to leap out at them at any moment.

Trying to ignore the anxiety slipping through her, Evelinde slid her gaze over the way ahead, looking both to the left and the right, hoping to spot a break in the trees that would speak to their nearing the edge of the woods. She just hoped it wouldn't be the wrong side.

That thought made Evelinde rein in again. The ride through the valley the night they'd arrived hadn't seemed to take as long as this ride was. Of course, it could just seem like a long time because she was lost, but . . .

It would be very upsetting finally to find her way

out of the woods only to discover she was on the wrong side of the valley and had to travel back through the woods again to get to the castle side.

If only she could see the castle . . .

But, of course, she couldn't, the trees were in the way.

Evelinde glanced upward at the foliage overhead. If she were to climb one of the taller trees until the foliage thinned out, she might be able to see the castle. Then she would know which direction she needed to go to get there.

Once the thought had taken hold, nothing could have stopped Evelinde from making the attempt. Patting Lady's neck soothingly, she slid off her mare and dropped to the ground. She then propped her hands on her hips and peered upward as she turned in a slow circle on the spot, trying to judge which tree was the largest and likely to get her high enough to see the castle, yet had branches low enough that she could reach them to start her climb.

After deciding on a tree, Evelinde moved to stand at its base. She paused there, her gaze sliding between the tree and her skirt, then she bent and reached under the front hem to catch the beck hemline of the skirt and draw it forward between her legs and up as she'd done to wade in the river. Recalling the problems it had caused when the skirt had slipped free of her belt the last time, Evelinde put extra care into making sure it was well affixed, then approached the tree she'd chosen.

She'd thought the branches of this tree were low enough to make it easy, but Evelinde had never climbed a tree before and hadn't a clue how hard it would be. Honestly, she'd seen children at d'Aumesbery shinny up with what appeared to be little effort, but it wasn't as easy as they made it look.

The lowest branch on the tree she'd chosen was low enough that she could hook her arms over it, which she did at once. Evelinde then tried to lift her leg to the branch, but her leg apparently didn't go that high. Grimacing, she moved farther along the branch until she was closer to the tree, then planted one foot on the trunk of the tree and sort of walked up it while hanging from her arms. Evelinde was quite proud of herself when she managed to get her legs hooked around the branch, too, but then hung there, uncertain how to get herself from hanging under it to perched on top.

After she dangled there for several moments, trying to work it out, Evelinde's muscles began to protest, and she let her legs drop and released the tree to stand on the forest floor again. She simply stood there, hands propped on her hips, glaring at the tree until Lady walked up next to her and nudged her in the shoulder. Evelinde immediately turned her scowl to the mare, knowing the creature probably wanted water after her run. She'd always taken Lady to the river by d'Aumesbery after her wild runs there. Unfortunately, while on first arriving at Donnachaidh they had crossed a river on the way through the valley, Evelinde had no idea where it was.

"I would take you for a drink if I could—" she began, then paused as an idea occurred to her. Smiling as the idea blossomed in her mind, Evelinde moved to the mare's side and climbed back into the saddle

"I promise do you help me get up this tree, I shall soon have you drinking water," Evelinde told the mare as she urged her closer to the tree she'd decided to climb, then added, "Hopefully in the stables of Donnachaidh."

Once Evelinde had got the mare as close as she could to the branch, she released her reins and patted her neck soothingly as she whispered, "Pray, do not move."

Straightening in the saddle, Evelinde grabbed the branch next to her and used it to steady herself as she climbed carefully to stand on the mare's back.

Much to her relief, the mare stood perfectly still, and Evelinde was able to get herself to a standing position and simply step onto the branch of the tree. Unfortunately, her slippers were not made for such endeavors and had she not been holding on with both hands to the branch above, she surely would have slipped off.

"Thanks," Evelinde muttered to the mare when she finally felt stable enough to look around and saw that the horse had backed up several steps to get out of the way should she fall. "Nice to know I have your support in this endeavor to rescue us both."

Lady's response was to bend her head to the ground and begin nosing at twigs on the dirt.

Shaking her head, Evelinde leaned against the trunk and held on with one hand while she lifted first one foot, then the other to remove her slippers, dropping each to the ground.

She felt much more confident after that and turned her attention to the serious business of climbing. It was something of a learning experience. Truly, Evelinde had never realized how difficult a task it would be. The branches grew out in all directions, some too close together, some too far apart to make it anything resembling easy. Still, determination pushed her on despite being scratched repeatedly, and scraping an elbow here, and a knee there, along the way.

Evelinde paused when she thought she must be halfway up the tree. She then glanced first up, then down, disappointed to realize that she wasn't anywhere near halfway. It was then she decided that her brilliant idea had not been so brilliant after all.

Sighing, she examined the branches above, trying to decide which would be the best to reach for, and had just settled on one when the snap of a twig made her pause and glance around. Had she been climbing at the time, Evelinde probably would not have heard the small sound. However, she did hear it, and so did Lady she noted, as the mare did the same nervous sideways dance she had earlier and looked in the direction the sound had seemed to come from.

The earlier creeping sensation returning, Evelinde surveyed the trees surrounding them; but no matter how hard she squinted into the dim woods, she couldn't see what had made the sound. After a moment, she reluctantly gave up and glanced back up the tree. If she could just get high enough to see which direction they had to go, they would soon be out of these woods.

Grinding her teeth together with determination, Evelinde started upward again and had climbed up to the next branch when something breezed past her and a soft thunk sounded to her left. Startled, Evelinde removed her left hand from the branch she held and started to turn to see what she'd heard, but the branch she stood on chose that moment to snap under her feet.

Crying out, Evelinde grabbed wildly with her free hand, her fingers catching at a very slim branch and holding on for dear life as she scrabbled to find purchase with her feet. Relief poured through her when she did, and she released a slow breath, and then hugged the tree, her cheek pressed against the rough surface as she waited for her heart to stop its mad thumping. Once it had, Evelinde glanced down toward Lady to see that the mare had moved back several more feet to get out of the way of the branch that had fallen and was now eyeing her with accusation.

"Do not look at me like that, this is all your fault," Evelinde muttered, then sighed and leaned her cheek against the tree again.

She would never enter these woods alone again, Evelinde silently vowed, then raised her head to glance up to the branch she'd grabbed hold of. Her heart, which had just slowed, now seemed to stop altogether as she realized she wasn't holding on to a branch at all, but the shaft of an arrow.

Evelinde was so startled at this realization that she unthinkingly released it at once, leaving her only holding on to the original branch with one hand. Panic reared up in her, and she swiftly grabbed for another branch, relief roaring through her until she heard, "Wife?"

After briefly closing her eyes, Evelinde dropped her head forward to peer down. Sure enough, her husband had found her. The man was even now scrambling off his mount, which he'd stopped beside Lady.

Brilliant, she thought unhappily. Why did he always find her at her worst?

"What are ye doing, ye daft woman?" Cullen roared as he moved to stand beneath her under the tree.

Where have I heard that before? Evelinde wondered, then cleared her throat, and said, "Oh, nothing, my lord. Just enjoying an afternoon out."

"Yer hanging in a tree, wife," he growled. "By yer hands."

"I am letting my legs rest," she responded promptly, then moved her legs about until she brushed against a branch. Setting first one foot on it, then the other, she released a little sigh of relief.

"Get down here!"

He sounded furious, she noted, looking about to see which branch would be safest to step down to next.

"Just let go. I shall catch ye," he ordered.

"Nay. I climbed up and can climb right back down," Evelinde assured him, and proceeded to do just that. Not too quickly, mind. She wasn't eager to face his wrath again and was hoping he would calm down did she give him time.

Evelinde had reached the last branch and dropped to sit on it, intending to push off and drop to the forest floor when she found herself caught in strong hands and eased to the ground instead.

"Thank you," she mumbled, as he set her on her feet.

"Yer welcome," Cullen growled, then snapped, "Now. What the devil did ye think ye were doing?"

Evelinde opened her mouth, closed it, cleared her throat, and said, "Climbing the tree."

"I could see that," he said impatiently. "Why?"

"Because I was lost," she admitted with disgust, and bent to collect her slippers before pushing past him to walk to Lady. "I thought I would climb a tree and see which direction the castle was in rather than wander these woods for the rest of my days like some stupid English ghost trapped in your bloody highlands."

A small silence followed her explanation, then Cullen cleared his throat, and said, "That was clever."

Evelinde stopped next to Lady and turned uncertainly, taking a step backward when she found that he'd followed. Peering up at him suspiciously, she asked, "It was?"

"Aye." Obviously he wasn't going to elaborate on the compliment, but there was nothing in his expression suggesting he was being sarcastic or mocking her.

Biting her lip, she glanced to his mount and back, and asked. "Was it you I heard in the woods then?"

"Probably," he said with a shrug.

Evelinde scowled at the scare he'd given her. "Well, why the devil did you not just call out and let me know 'twas you rather than following and scaring the devil out of me?"

"Following ye?" His eyebrows rose. "I have no been following ye. I just came upon yer mare on me way back to the castle, then spotted ye in the tree as I reined in."

Evelinde frowned and glanced back up to where she thought she'd been perched in the tree. She could not see the arrow from the ground but knew it was there. Her gaze then shifted to his mount to see that there was no bow and arrow on the animal. Cullen also wasn't holding one, she noted. Her husband hadn't loosed the arrow. If it had been loosed at all today, she thought. It was wholly possible that the arrow had sat in the tree for years or longer, and the sound she'd heard had been another branch or even a bird's nest falling from one of the upper branches as her climbing shook the tree.

Unfortunately, Evelinde hadn't got a good look at the arrow and couldn't say if it had looked weathered or not. She'd barely realized what it was before releasing it, then had been preoccupied trying not to fall.

"Why are ye in the woods?" Cullen asked.

"I thought to take Lady for a ride," Evelinde answered absently, her gaze now moving around the woods surrounding them, but there was no one there that she could see. Still, she turned to him, and said, "There was an arrow in the tree."

He shrugged. "There are probably many in these woods, arrows gone astray during a hunt."

"Aye," Evelinde muttered, but then felt it necessary to add. "I did not notice the arrow ere grabbing it while climbing."

Cullen smiled faintly. "I am not surprised. Come."

Evelinde's eyes widened, but she didn't protest when he grabbed Lady's reins in one hand and her arm in the other and urged her over to his mount. He stopped there and released Lady to catch Evelinde by the waist, then paused before applying the pressure necessary to lift her. "How sore are ye still?"

"I am not sore at all. The bruises were mostly healed by the time we reached Donnachaidh. 'Twas mostly my muscles bothering me then, but Biddy's salve and your massage seem to have done the trick," Evelinde admitted, blushing as she recalled what had followed the massage.

Cullen nodded and lifted her onto his mount, then caught Lady's reins again and mounted behind her. Evelinde expected that he'd return them to the castle then, so was somewhat startled when they broke out into a clearing beside a river.

"Ye'll no want to wade here like ye did in England," he announced as he slid off his mount and helped her down. They walked to the riverside and peered at the water.

"Why?" Evelinde asked, her eyes moving over the clear water bubbling past.

"The water runs off the mountains and is cold."

"Oh," she said, but didn't really mind. The clearing was small and the river narrower than the one at d'Aumesbery. There also was no waterfall here, but it was pretty just the same. It would be a nice spot to relax when she needed a moment to herself.

"Yer no to leave the castle alone in future," Cullen announced, turning her by the shoulders and reaching for the laces of her gown.

Evelinde reached for his hands, unsure what he was doing, but then paused and frowned as she realized what he'd said. She wasn't to come here alone? Seeing her vision of peaceful moments alone slipping away, she forgot about what he was doing and lifted a frown to him to ask, "Why?"

"I like ye," Cullen announced, quickly undoing her laces and beginning to ease her gown off her shoulders.

"I cannot come here alone because you like me?" she asked with confusion, wondering a bit distractedly what he was doing and catching her gown to keep it from slipping off her arms.

"Nay, well aye," he corrected himself. "Ye canna come here alone because 'tis no safe . . . and I like ye," he added, giving up on her gown and raising his hands to begin unpinning her hair from the bun she'd place it in on the back of her head that morning.

"Why is it not safe? And what are you doing?" Evelinde asked, trying to swat his hands away from her hair.

"I like ye," he repeated.

Evelinde opened her mouth, then closed it again as his words sank in. He liked her. Her husband liked her. Well, that was just . . . She didn't know how to feel or even what to think. And then his hands returned to trying to remove her gown, and she repeated, "What are you doing?"

"I like ye," was all he said, and it reminded her of his repeating that he was the Duncan the first day they'd met. She hadn't understood what he'd meant then and no better understood him now. Obviously 'I like ye' was some code, but she hadn't a clue for what, then he said, "I've told ye, now I'm going to show ye. Ye said ye wanted both, and so I shall give ye both."

Evelinde blinked as sudden understanding set in. He meant to—

"Here?" she gasped with amazement.

"Aye. Here, in our bed, on the fur before the fire . . . There are a lot of places I've imagined showing ye, and now that yer no sore, I can."

Evelinde's eyes had widened at his words as she realized that while she'd been sitting about fearing he didn't want her at all, he'd been sitting about imagining all these places to—

"You—"

"Wife," Cullen interrupted with a sigh. "Ye may think I speak too little, but ye tend to speak too much. Shut up and let me love ye."

Evelinde stilled at the order, then gasped as he suddenly gave up on her gown and bent to kiss her.

Shut up and let me love ye. The words rang in her

ears, and she sighed as his lips urged hers apart,
wishing that it *was* love. Her husband liked her and
enjoyed bedding her, but she didn't think it was love
. . . not on his part. As for her . . . Well, in truth,
Evelinde was confused about her own feelings. She
found the man exasperating, frustrating, considerate, attractive, sweet . . . and dear God when he
kissed her with the hunger he was showing her now,
he made her very toes curl. How could a man be so
many conflicting things at once, she wondered, then
gave up trying to think and slid her arms around
his neck.

The man really was a very good kisser, Evelinde
acknowledged as excitement began to build in her.
She felt his hands return to her gown, but this time
did not try to hamper his efforts to remove it, even
lowering her arms so he could slide it off. When
it dropped to pool around her feet, leaving her in
nothing but her chemise, she slid her hands up over
his chest, searching blindly for the pin that held his
plaid in place. Evelinde managed to poke herself
once with the tip as she struggled to undo it but finally got it loose. She sighed into his mouth as his
plaid slid away, joining her gown on the ground.

She then broke the kiss long enough to glance
down and drop the pin on the plaid before tugging
his shirt up to remove it as well. Evelinde had barely
removed the garment when Cullen swept her up
into his arms, his mouth claiming hers. With him
kissing her, she couldn't see where he was heading,
but smiled against his mouth when he sat on what

she presumed was a boulder or fallen log, settling her sideways in his lap. It reminded her of their first meeting and her regret at the time that she'd had to end their embrace. This time she need not. They were married.

"Yer smiling," Cullen murmured, his lips moving across her cheek.

"Aye. Because I like you, too," she said simply, and he raised his head to peer at her and kissed her again. He was more demanding this time, one hand tangled in her hair, positioning her head where he wanted it as he plundered her mouth. He kissed her until she moaned and arched, kissing him back with an eagerness and hunger that she would have been embarrassed by had she been able to think at that moment.

His hand slid up over her ribs to one breast, and Evelinde gasped encouragement and pressed into the touch as he kneaded the flesh through her chemise. A disappointed groan slid from her mouth into his when his hand slid away, but then she realized that he was tugging impatiently at the collar of her shift, trying to get it out of the way.

Evelinde immediately moved to help him, shimmying free of the shift until it dropped away to pool around her waist. Cullen's hand immediately covered one breast, squeezing briefly before his fingers concentrated on her nipple, plucking and rolling it between his fingers, drawing a deep moan from Evelinde and making her own kisses a little frantic until he lifted his mouth away and dropped his head to catch her nipple between his lips.

Evelinde slid her fingers through his hair and curled them, catching several strands in hand as he caught the nipple gently between his teeth and rasped his tongue over it. It sent pleasure shooting through her and had her wiggling in his lap, her bottom grinding against the hardness she could feel growing there.

This time, when she felt his hand sliding up her leg, she did not break free and tumble from his lap. Instead, Evelinde opened her legs for him, her breathing becoming fast and shallow and her body stilling in his lap in anticipation. When his fingers reached the top of her thighs and brushed gently over the curls there, she gasped and groaned as he began to caress her. Cullen soon had her almost sobbing with need, her body weeping for him as she writhed in his lap.

Only then did he leave off touching her and lift her from his lap. Evelinde was a little confused as to why he'd stopped when he set her on her feet before him, and shivered when he tugged her chemise over her hips to drop to the ground. He then turned her to face him and caught her by the hip with one hand to draw her closer even as the other urged her legs apart.

Evelinde bit her lip and caught at his head for balance, unsure what he was doing, but then his hand slid between her legs again, and he once more began to caress her.

Gasping, she tangled her fingers in his hair as he began to trail kisses across her hip, then held on to keep from tumbling when he suddenly lifted her right leg to rest her foot on the log he sat on. When he then withdrew his hand to clasp her buttocks and leaned forward to press his mouth to where his hand had been, Evelinde cried out in shock and startled pleasure and found it difficult to stay on her feet. In fact, she wasn't sure she would have been able to had his hands not shifted to her hips to steady her as he ministered to her.

While Evelinde found this most enjoyable, some of her pleasure was tempered by guilt as her mind pointed out that while he was giving her pleasure, she was neither touching nor caressing him but simply clutching at his hair desperately as his mouth moved over her. She tried to move away from her husband then and perhaps take the opportunity to kiss and caress him some, but his hold on her was firm, and he held her in place. Redoubling his efforts, he washed the guilt from her mind with his tongue and drove her up onto the toes of the one foot on the ground.

"Cullen," she pleaded, unconsciously pressing his head closer as her body strained for release. She was vaguely aware when one hand left her hip, but was definitely aware when it joined his tongue. Evelinde cried out at the surge that went through her body as she felt his finger slide inside her even as he continued to suckle at the core of her pleasure, then the passion that had been building inside her exploded and Evelinde threw her head back and screamed as her body convulsed.

Only then did Cullen stop what he was doing and release her hip. When he eased her foot back off the log so that she was standing between his legs, Evelinde sank weakly to her knees before him.

Eyes closed, she hugged his knee as he ran a soothing hand through her hair, waiting for her to catch her breath, then her eyes opened and she found herself staring at his erection waving gently before her with his movements. She eyed it curiously, recalling the pleasure she'd felt when they'd consummated the marriage and he'd plunged it into her, and, without thinking, Evelinde reached out to catch it in hand.

Her eyes shot upward when Cullen groaned at the light touch, and she saw that his eyes had closed, and his expression had tightened. Watching his face, Evelinde drew her hand along its length, a sense of power creeping over her as she felt his fingers tighten in her hair and knew he was experiencing a pleasure similar to that he had given her.

Similar, but not the same, Evelinde thought, and leaned forward to press a kiss to the tip of the shaft, watching him as she did. Cullen's eyes shot open at once, and they were now wide with both surprise and what appeared to be hope. It was the hope that made her kiss him again, but curiosity was what made her slip her tongue out to lick the spot she'd kissed. She wanted to taste him and thought it a strange want, so had rather hoped that did she do it quick enough he might not notice the flick of her tongue. However, Cullen did notice, and his reaction was startling. The man bucked his hips, his hold on her hair becoming almost painful in his excitement.

Evelinde thought she must have discovered something then, and licked him again, the movement slower and covering more area. This time, Cullen cried out, his expression becoming almost pained, she noted, and was inspired to take him into her mouth. The man nearly leapt off the log in response and suddenly dragged her off her knees.

"I did it wrong," Evelinde said with both regret and apology as he drew her onto his lap facing him.

"Nay," he growled, reaching between their bodies to grasp himself with one hand as he urged her body up off his legs so that she stood with her legs on either side of his. "Ye did it right. Too right."

"Then why—?" Evelinde began, but her words ended on a gasp as he urged her back down and slid into her.

"Ye talk too much, wife," Cullen muttered, then his mouth covered hers and he began to urge her to raise and lower herself on him. The moment he had her doing so at a pace he was satisfied with, his hands shifted around to clasp her breasts, squeezing and kneading as he kissed her most thoroughly.

Evelinde was unsure of herself at first, not quite prepared to be in control, but soon found a rhythm and speed she was comfortable with and was just beginning to enjoy it when he suddenly shifted. Pushing himself off the log, Cullen took her with him as he knelt in the grass, then he carried her down to the ground, their bodies still joined at hip and mouth.

When Cullen caught her hands in both of his and

pressed them down into the cool grass on either side of her head, holding her there as he thrust into her, Evelinde groaned and arched into the action, her body moving to meet him as he drove them both toward the explosion of pleasure waiting at the end.

chapter

Ten

ullen pressed a kiss to the top of Evelinde's head, then began to slide out from under her to get out of bed.

"Are you getting up already?"

He heard the disappointment in Evelinde's voice and merely smiled to himself as he found his plaid and laid it out to work folds into the strip of cloth in preparation of donning it. While it was early morning, it was not as early as it had been when he'd woken her with kisses and caresses and made love to her. The memory drew his gaze back to his wife, and he found himself transfixed as she stretched in the bed with a feline grace.

"Are you disappointed?"

Cullen glanced to her face as she drew the linens up, covering herself. "In what?"

"I am not as buxom, or big, or tall as little Maggie," she pointed out quietly.

He almost laughed, but then realized she was serious. Women were a strange breed, Cullen decided. The truth was he liked her body. He'd liked Maggie's, too. They were both beautiful in their own ways. Evelinde's was slim and graceful like a rosebud rising out of the earth. Maggie had been full and ripe like a rose in full bloom. Both were roses and both beautiful.

"Well?" Evelinde asked, the worry in her voice growing more pronounced.

"I'm no disappointed," Cullen answered. When that did not seem to reassure her, he recalled his duty, and frowned. "I like yer body. Yer short, but please me."

"Short?" she squawked, appearing affronted.

"Aye. Yer like to make me a gnarled old man with a twisted back having to stoop to kiss ye all the time, but 'tis worth it," he teased.

Evelinde's expression was priceless. Her mouth opened and closed several times, then she grumbled under her breath, but her cheeks were flushed from her exertions, and her expression was not the troubled and unhappy look he'd become used to. She looked satisfied and at peace.

And all it had taken was giving her a tumble and a compliment or two, Cullen thought with a shake of the head. He'd ridden for three days without sleep to get her away from her stepmother, but she hadn't seemed to appreciate that. Yet he said a couple of words of praise and bedded her—definitely not an effort—and she was happy.

He would never understand women, Cullen thought as he donned his plaid. His gaze slid back to his wife as he drew the end of the plaid over his shoulder to fasten it in front, and he paused when he saw the way she was watching him.

"Stop that, or I shall never get out of this room," he growled, feeling his body respond to the hunger in her eyes. When she just smiled, Cullen shook his head, and forced his attention to finding the broach that he used to fasten his plaid. A frown claimed his lips when he couldn't find it in the rushes by where the plaid had lain.

"What are you looking for?" Evelinde asked curiously.

"Me pin," he muttered, and shrugged impatiently and moved to his chest. He had another there and would find the missing one later. Cullen had knelt and opened the chest when Evelinde suddenly cried, "Here it is!"

Pausing, he glanced toward the bed to see her grab something off the bedside table and scoot off the bed.

Cullen straightened as she rushed over to offer it to him, his eyes moving over her. When Evelinde paused in front of him—instead of taking the pin—he used his free hand to sweep her against his chest and lowered his head to kiss her soundly. He squeezed her behind and urged her closer as he did, but then Evelinde moaned and wiggled against him, and he felt his body responding. Cullen immediately set her away and took the pin from her before temptation could become irresistible.

"Pack a picnic for the nooning," he ordered, temptation nagging at him as he fastened the plaid in place with the pin.

"Why?"

He glanced to the surprised expression on her face, but merely said, "I've a mind to return to the clearing with ye."

Cullen heard her draw in an excited breath as he turned away and smiled to himself as he walked out of the room. He was now very much looking forward to the midday meal.

Evelinde watched her husband go, a slow smile curving her lips and her toes curling into the rushes beneath her as she considered why he might wish to take her back to the clearing. The smile faded, however, as she glanced down at the open chest beside her.

What with one thing and another, Evelinde had quite forgotten all about losing his pin until Cullen had gone in search of it. She was thinking of it now, however, and knew she had to find it, which meant a trip down to the paddocks. Evelinde grimaced at the thought, but it was either that or telling her husband she'd lost it.

Finding it was definitely the preferred option, Evelinde decided, and straightened her shoulders with determination as she moved to the basin on

the table for a quick wash before getting dressed.
She had her chemise on and was just picking up the
gown she'd decided to wear that day when Mildrede
arrived.

The maid helped her, chattering on about her impressions of Donnachaidh as she did. Distracted with
her worry about finding the pin, Evelinde wasn't
really paying much attention until Mildrede said,
"I could hardly believe it when she said the men go
about their swordplay while the women do all the
real work around here."

Evelinde scowled, recalling her intention to talk
to Cullen about the unfair division of labor at Donnachaidh. Perhaps she should do so this evening, or
while they were on their picnic. This evening, she
decided, not wishing to ruin the afternoon's outing
and discourage her husband if he wished to once
again show her that he "liked" her. Evelinde quite
liked being liked. It was turning out to be the best
part of marriage so far.

"Ugh," Mildrede muttered as she followed her out
of the chamber a moment later. "How anyone can
see in this light, I don't know. I am like to do myself
an injury do we not get some light in this hall."

"Aye." Evelinde sighed, taking her arm to lead
her to the stairs. "I shall talk to Cullen about it this
evening."

Mildrede grunted her approval and continued her
earlier chatter as they descended the stairs.

Evelinde tried to leave the keep at once to go start
her search for the lost pin, but Mildrede wouldn't
hear of her leaving without seeing she first broke

her fast. The maid had her sit at the table while she fetched her some mead and one of Biddy's delicious pasties, then sat and told her she thought Biddy was a love while she watched Evelinde eat.

Evelinde listened with amusement and affection, glad to have the woman with her again and grateful to her husband for it. Cullen really was very considerate, she acknowledged. And now that he was speaking to her a little, she was beginning to think everything might be all right after all. Evelinde did not think they would ever have deep and long-winded conversations, but perhaps that wasn't important. She wasn't sure.

Once Evelinde had finished eating, Mildrede rushed off to see to straightening the bedchamber, and Evelinde was finally able to slip out of the keep.

She didn't see her husband as she made her way to the paddock, and was glad for it. Did he ask her where she was headed, Evelinde would not feel she could lie outright and would have had to tell the truth. Something she'd rather not have to do. She would not mind explaining that it had been briefly lost *after* she found it, but would rather Cullen not know until she'd found it again.

Evelinde started her search where she'd left off the day the Comyns had arrived, on the path she thought they'd taken when leaving the area. She followed that path all the way to where Cullen had hauled her out of the paddock but had no success.

Sighing unhappily when she reached the fence without finding it, Evelinde got back to her feet and

peered into the paddock. She didn't see Angus, but
had learned her lesson from her last walk through
the enclosure. Evelinde followed the fence all the
way to the end to check the entire area. The paddock ran alongside the one where Cullen had been
breaking his horse with just a ten-foot span between
the two, then turned and ran along the back of it to
a small barn with doors both in front, opening into
the horses' paddock, and another on the side, opening into Angus's paddock.

The door to Angus's paddock was presently
closed, and there was no sign of the bull. This was
probably the best time to search the paddock for the
pin if she was going to do it, Evelinde realized, and
cast one last glance toward the closed door before
hurrying back along the fence to where Cullen had
pulled her out.

Hitching up her skirt, she quickly climbed the
fence and dropped into the paddock. Evelinde then
paused to glance around one more time to be sure
Angus was still inside the barn before dropping to
her hands and knees to begin searching the grass in
the enclosure. She moved much more quickly here,
just running her hands over the grass in search of
the pin, then moving on to the next spot and doing
it again. She didn't wish to be in the paddock any
longer than necessary. She also wished to avoid
being seen at her search. Evelinde had no doubt that
Cullen would be furious if he caught her in here,
and that was without even knowing that she'd lost
his pin.

She was halfway across the paddock when she spotted the missing broach. Giving a happy cry, Evelinde snatched it up and sat back on her heels to examine it, releasing a small sigh of relief when she saw it was undamaged. She was just getting to her feet thinking she'd been very fortunate to come when the paddock was empty as well as to actually find the pin when the thunder of hooves drew her head around. Her eyes widened at the sight of an angry Angus charging down the paddock toward her.

For one moment, Evelinde was frozen, then she broke into a run, Cullen's pin clutched in her hand like a talisman.

"Ye'll manage?" Cullen asked Mac as he led his mount out of the stables. He'd just finished giving the man a tour of the stables and introduced him as the new stable master to Scatchy and his daughter, Loa.

Scatchy appeared happy enough with the new arrangement. Cullen wasn't surprised. The man had told him more than once that he was getting too old to be sitting up all night with ailing or birthing horses.

Much to Cullen's surprise, however, Loa didn't appear to be taking the new arrangement well at all. She'd been grim and stiff ever since he'd introduced Mac and explained his new position. Cullen would have expected the woman to be relieved to have someone remove the burden from her. Scatchy had been little help the last few years, and the task of managing the stables had fallen on her shoulders.

He glanced to the woman now to find her standing in the shadows of the stable doors, glaring out at them.

"She'll settle," Mac said.

Cullen turned back to see that Mac was watching her, too.

"She just needs a little handling," the stable master added mildly. When Cullen raised his eyebrows, he shrugged. "Women are like horses; keep them fed and watered, rub them down of a night, and whisper a sweet word or two in their ear, and they'll follow ye anywhere."

Cullen released a bark of laughter, but then tried to smother it as Scatchy came out of the stables. The old man walked toward them with a smile that turned into a perplexed expression as he glanced at something to his left.

"Is that not yer lady playing with Angus again, me laird?" the old man asked as he reached them.

Cullen glanced sharply toward the paddocks, his heart lodging itself in his throat when he saw Evelinde in her red gown, running willy-nilly around the field trying to outrun the bull, which was almost on top of her.

Cursing, he leapt onto his mount and spurred him into a dead run. Cullen knew he'd never make it even as he charged toward the enclosure. Evelinde didn't have a chance at outrunning the beast, he thought, but quickly realized he'd underestimated her. While she might not have been faster or stronger than the bull, she was definitely smarter. Just when Cullen thought she would be caught up in the bull's horns and tossed through the air, Evelinde suddenly dove to the side, throwing herself to the ground.

Unprepared for the action, Angus stamped past her a good distance before managing to bring himself to a halt and turn back. By that time, Evelinde had already rolled back to her feet and was again racing toward the nearest fence. Angus was immediately after her again, her red gown drawing him on.

Cullen leaned low over his mount's back and steered him straight at the fence. His horse was leaping the top rail when Evelinde next threw herself to the side to avoid being gored. Angus was more prepared this time, however, and managed to stop and turn much more quickly. But Evelinde had nearly reached the fence when she threw herself to the ground and rather than get up and race the last few steps and try to climb it as he feared—which would have seen her gored ere he could reach her—his clever wife simply rolled several times, rolling herself right under the fence to safety.

Angus came to a halt at once, furiously puffing air from his nostrils as he glared at the woman staring back at him from safety. Cullen's heart was just starting to slow with relief that she was safe when Angus suddenly swiveled his head to glare his way.

Realizing he was now the one in danger, Cullen immediately jerked his mount to the side, heading for the fence and safety as Angus started to charge him. Should the bull take out the horse before they got out of the paddock, Cullen knew they were both in trouble. He dug his heels into the animal's side, demanding more speed, but needn't have bothered.

The horse had no interest in being gored. His mount managed a speed Cullen had never seen from him before, seeming nearly to fly the short distance to the fence.

Even so, Cullen wasn't sure they would make it. The bull's huffing was loud in his ears, and he was sure the beast was about to impale his mount, when the animal suddenly made a leap for the fence. Cullen lowered himself to the beast's neck as they sailed through the air. In his fear, the animal had made the leap early and he suspected they barely cleared the fence, but barely was enough. They came down hard on the other side even as Angus crashed into it from inside with a fearsome force that made the fence shudder visibly. But the fence held, leaving the beast glaring at them and snorting its rage.

Cullen was off his horse and rushing to Evelinde's side almost before his horse stopped.

"Are ye injured?" he asked, anxiously drawing her to her feet.

"Nay. I am fine," Evelinde assured him breathlessly, watching the bull with wide, wary eyes as if she feared he might still get out and come after them.

Cullen closed his eyes briefly with relief and shook his head, thinking that the woman would be the death of him. She was forever getting herself into trouble and scaring the life out of him. One of these times she was going to get herself killed with her foolish stunts, he thought, his relief giving way to anger. The next thing he knew he was bellowing, "What were ye doing, ye daft woman?"

Evelinde turned wide eyes to him, opened her mouth, closed it again, then clucked her tongue irritably and pushed herself away to march toward the path.

Cullen immediately chased after her. He had never been so furious in his life. Half of him wanted to beat her for her stupidity, and the other half wanted to throw her to the ground, pull her skirt up, and love her until she didn't have the strength to try to get herself killed again. He couldn't do either, of course, so he simply caught her by the arm, and swung her around to face him as he repeated, "What were ye doing?"

Evelinde blew her breath upward on a sigh, sending the tendrils of hair that had escaped her bun flying and then muttered, "Where have I heard that question before?"

"Wife," he growled, his temper barely controlled.

"I borrowed your pin the other day to help keep little Maggie's blue gown from gaping."

Cullen frowned at her with confusion, unsure what that had to do with anything until he recalled how she'd been searching the back of her skirt for something when one of the men on the wall had called out to him that a party was approaching. The pin, obviously, he thought.

"But when I climbed the fence it came undone and fell out in the paddock. That is what I was doing when you and the Comyns found me on my hands and knees that day," she explained. "I fear I forgot about it until this morning when you were looking for it. I came down after breaking my fast to find it.

And I did," she added brightly, holding it out in her hand. "I had just found it when I realized Angus was charging on me."

Cullen stared at the pin in the palm of her hand with amazement. "Ye braved the bull for me pin?"

"Aye. Nay," Evelinde corrected, then sighed, and said, "He was not in the paddock."

Cullen realized then that he had never explained to her that the paddock was L-shaped. Fergus had mentioned it the other day to calm him, but the man had spoken so low he doubted she'd heard it. Evelinde must have glanced the length of the stables and not seen the beast before and thought the paddock empty, he realized. This was an instance when his lack of talking was definitely detrimental, he thought grimly, and began to explain what he should have at the time. "The paddock is L-shaped, wife. He was probably—"

"I checked the entire paddock, Cullen." She interrupted. "Angus was not outside, and the door leading from the barn to his paddock was closed when I climbed in."

"She's right, me laird. Angus should have been in his pen."

Cullen glanced around at that announcement to see an older man approaching in a hopping limp. The man was Hamish, who was in charge of these paddocks, and the limp was from an old injury, a gift from Angus some years back.

"I hadn't yet let him out today," the man said once he'd reached them. "Angus went in to eat when the sun was setting last night, and I closed the door and dropped the bar. I have yet to let him out today. He shouldna have been in the paddock."

"Well someone let him out," Cullen said grimly.

The man nodded slowly. "Aye, it would seem so."

Cullen frowned, then both men turned to peer at Evelinde. She stiffened under their gazes and then said impatiently, "Well, I can assure you it was not I."

"Then it was someone else," Cullen growled, anger stirring in him. Whoever it was had nearly got his wife killed. A soft touch on his arm drew his gaze down to see that Evelinde was patting his arm soothingly.

"I am sure whoever let him loose simply did not see me in the paddock," she said, then explained, "I was on my hands and knees searching through the grass for your pin just before I realized he was charging. I am sure it was an accident."

"Aye," he agreed, but was still bothered by the whole incident.

"Well," his wife said with a forced smile, "I shall just go put this back in your chest where I found it."

Evelinde hurried away before he could stop her.

Cullen watched her go, his eyebrows drawn together with worry.

"It was no accident, me laird," Hamish murmured quietly, drawing his gaze away from his wife. "No one ever deals with Angus but me. No one would have a reason to open the door . . . unless they saw yer lady wife in the paddock and wanted to loose him on her."

Cullen stared at the man for one long moment, then asked, "Why would anyone wish to do that?"

Hamish shrugged. "Why would anyone kill your uncle, father, or first lady wife?"

"Those were accidents," Cullen said coldly, though he wasn't at all certain they were. However, he'd never been able to find out for sure one way or the other so had been forced to accept that they were accidents and move on.

"And this would have appeared to be an accident, too," Hamish pointed out.

Cullen stiffened, his head jerking up at the words as if under a blow.

"Just something to think about," Hamish pointed out, and turned to walk along the paddock toward the barn.

Cullen watched him go, his mind crowding with thoughts. His uncle Darach had been the first questionable accident. An arrow to the back had taken him while hunting. No one had ever admitted to loosing the arrow, but it was thought at the time that the individual might not have known he did it. Cullen had been fourteen and on his first hunt when it happened. They'd been hunting wild boar and come upon a family of them. There had been at least twenty men. When the two adult boars had charged, trying to protect the younger ones, every one of those men had scattered, each heading in a different direction to get out of the way. Boars were vicious when provoked.

Arrows had flown from every direction that day as the boars had gone after anything that moved, chasing one way, then another, hardly seeming to notice the arrows that soon stuck out of them until they resembled oversized hedgehogs. It wasn't until both boars were down that anyone realized that Darach, their laird, was not there to help collect their prizes and carry them back to the keep. A search had started, and the laird of Donnachaidh had been found lying in the bushes, an arrow through his back. Darach had still been alive, and told them that he'd fallen from his mount when one of the boars charged him, sending his horse rearing. It was while tumbling into the bushes that he'd felt the arrow pierce him. He'd thought it an accident, that he'd fallen into the path of the already loosed arrow, and everyone had accepted that. When he died three days later with fever from his infected wound, all the keep had thought it a tragic accident.

Cullen's father, Liam, had then become laird and brought peace and prosperity to their people for ten years until the day he'd been found at the base of the cliffs that backed Donnachaidh. The hill that sloped away from the front gates of the outer wall ran along three sides of the castle, but at the very back it dropped away as if God had sliced away the gentle incline, leaving a very steep drop of rocky cliffs. This was where his father had taken the fall that had killed him. Cullen had been at Comyns the day it happened. Tralin and he had grown up friends and often visited each other, and that was where he'd been.

Cullen had returned home from the Comyns' to find his father dead and rumors being whispered that he himself had been seen near the spot where he died . . . and that perhaps it wasn't an accident.

It hadn't been long before people recalled that he'd been on the hunt when his uncle was killed, too. They began to wonder if that had really been an accident at all. It was suggested that Cullen could have loosed the arrow that had killed his uncle. Perhaps he had sought the title of laird even back then, they'd murmured.

Despite the rumors, as Liam Duncan's son, Cullen had been named laird. Weighed down by his grief for a man who had been both a fair leader as well as a good father, and busy with his new position, Cullen had not addressed the rumors. He had tried to sort out whether his father's death really was an accident, but there was no way to know. Liam's horse had wandered back to the stables, a search had been started, and the laird had been found at the foot of the cliffs. There was nothing else to tell what had happened, and while the rumors had said someone had seen Cullen riding away from the spot, he had never been able to find out who the witness was supposed to be. No one seemed to know who it was, just that "it was said" someone saw him.

Knowing he hadn't been there, and how rumors started and grew and twisted as they traveled, Cullen had decided there really was no witness and gave up his search for the truth to concentrate on the task of running Donnachaidh. And then he'd married little Maggie, a betrothal his father had arranged when they were but children. She had been a fine woman, cheerful and kind, and he'd grown an easy affection for her. They would have passed a life of peace and contentment without the highs and lows brought on by his passion for and worry over Evelinde, but two years after fulfilling that contract, she, too, had been found at the foot of the same cliffs.

That had been beyond any possible coincidence for Cullen. Unfortunately, it had been too much for a lot of people at Donnachaidh, too, but while he was looking to them for the culprit, they were all looking to him. No answers were found.

Cullen sighed and ran one hand through his hair in weary frustration. While everything seemed fine on the surface at Donnachaidh, there was actually a division among the people. There were those who believed none of the three deaths was an accident, but that they were murders and that Cullen was responsible for them all. Then there were those who thought the "accidents" might have been murder but were sure he was not the culprit, and, finally, there were those who were not sure either way. It made leading his people a tricky business at times, for while they followed his orders, with some it was slowly and with resentment. Being laird for the two years since Maggie's death had been like being the captain of a ship on the brink of a mutiny.

Unable to prove his innocence, or even protest the unspoken accusations when they were mere rumor and whispers, Cullen had been forced to ignore them and hope they would fade in time. However, every time it appeared to be doing so, something or someone seemed to stir it up again. And then the marriage contract with Evelinde had been offered to him. Cullen needed a wife to bear his bairns, but he'd also hoped her presence would help people

forget the past and let it lie. Instead, Evelinde was
now having accidents, Cullen thought grimly, considering the events since meeting her. Her fall from
the horse on the first meeting had definitely been an
accident, as had her being given the wrong medicinal on their wedding day. He was even sure that her
first adventure in Angus's paddock had been an accident. However, he was almost certain today's was
not. Someone had opened the door and let Angus
out while she was searching the paddock, and he
had nearly lost a second wife.

Cullen frowned and glanced around the bailey,
his gaze sliding over the people milling about. If the
previous deaths and Evelinde's present accidents
had been perpetrated by someone, it would have
to be one of his own people, for a stranger could
not move freely through the gates without his men
stopping them. One of the people he was looking at
right now may have tried to kill his wife, he realized . . . and, perhaps, not for the first time. That
thought came as he recalled the incident when he'd
come upon Evelinde in the woods on the way back
from Comyns.

Cullen was suddenly recalling her mention of an
arrow in the tree she was climbing. He'd assumed
that it was an old arrow, but something about her
troubled look as she'd said she hadn't noted it earlier
was bothering him. And, he recalled, Evelinde had
asked if he was the one who'd been following her
and why hadn't he let his presence be known.

His mouth tightened grimly as the two points combined in his mind with this accident and Hamish's

words regarding it to send fear creeping up his spine. He was beginning to suspect there was more to her comments on the arrow than he'd assumed at the time, and suddenly was very desirous of asking her about the incident.

Climbing back onto his mount's back, Cullen turned him to the path and headed for the keep. He would talk to Evelinde. And hold her. And warn her to stay close to the keep until he was sure all was well. Cullen had been sad when little Maggie had died. He had become used to the woman for wife and gained affection for her over their two-year marriage. But he knew without a doubt that his mild grief at her death would be nothing next to how he would feel should he lose Evelinde. His new lady wife had managed to burrow under his skin with her soft laugh, constant chatter, and welcoming body.

Cullen liked his wife. He might even more than like her, though he wasn't willing to explore that possibility at the moment. He just knew he wanted to keep this wife around.

here you are."

Evelinde let the keep doors close behind her and saw Mildrede seated in one of the chairs by the fire.

"Lady Elizabeth was looking for you a few moments ago," the woman announced, as Evelinde approached.

"Do you know what Aunt Biddy wanted?" she asked, noting that the maid had her green gown on her lap and was apparently mending a small tear in it. It was the dress she'd been wearing the day before. Evelinde must have caught it on a branch during her climb and caused a small tear.

Mildrede shook her head. "She did not say, but I imagine it has to do with meals for the week. Or perhaps she wishes to restock supplies since Cook will soon be back."

Evelinde nodded, then hesitated, briefly torn between seeing what the woman wanted and heading above stairs. In the end, she decided to replace the pin first. The broach had caused her enough difficulties, and with the way her luck was running of late, she feared getting distracted and losing it again.

"If Biddy comes looking again, tell her I have just taken something above stairs and will return directly to speak to her." Evelinde started to turn away then, but paused at a clucking sound from Mildrede.

"You have grass stains on your skirt," she pointed out with irritation. "I swear child, I do not know what has happened. You have ever been careful with your clothes ere this, but seem to be ruining another one each day since the day you married laird Cullen."

Frowning, Evelinde glanced down at her skirt, grimacing when she saw that while she had escaped Angus unscathed, her gown had not. Sighing, she shook her head with irritation, and muttered, "I shall change while I am up there."

"I shall help." Mildrede started to rise, but Evelinde waved her back down.

"I can manage on my own, Mildrede. Carry on with what you are doing."

The maid sank back in her seat with a nod, and Evelinde hurried to the stairs and up. Her first stop on reaching the room was Cullen's chest. She replaced the broach where she'd found it with a little sigh, then closed the chest and stood to cross to her own, removing her gown as she went.

Pausing by her chest, Evelinde took a few moments to examine the gown. It was one of her favorites, and she thought Cullen must like it, too, for of all her gowns, this and her forest green one were the ones he'd chosen to pack when he'd taken her away from d'Aumesbery. Since the man spoke so little, that was the only way she could judge what he liked.

Fortunately, the grass stains were not too bad, and at least there were no rips or tears. A good soaking and a little hard scrubbing should remove the stains she thought with relief and rolled the gown up and set it aside to take below for cleaning. Evelinde then moved to her chest, opened it, and bent to rummage through its contents for another gown to wear.

She never heard the bedchamber door open, and jumped with surprise as arms slid around her from behind.

Evelinde didn't need to look to see who it was. She recognized the hands that suddenly covered her breasts as well as the way Cullen cupped and kneaded them through the cloth of her chemise.

"I came to ask ye something," Cullen rumbled by her ear.

"Oh?" Evelinde sighed, her eyes closing as she leaned back into him. She covered his hands with hers, squeezing encouragingly as he caressed her.

"Aye, but ye've managed to distract me."

She opened her eyes at that, a breathless laugh

slipping through her lips. "I have done nothing."

"Ye were bending over the chest in naught but yer shift," Cullen explained.

"And that distracted you?" Evelinde asked with surprise, tipping her head back to peer at him.

"Oh, aye," Cullen growled, and claimed her lips even as he swept her into his arms and carried her to the bed.

"Wife?"

Evelinde opened her eyes but didn't raise her head from her husband's chest. He had exhausted her with his passion, and she was too spent to bother, so merely tilted her face up to glance at him. "Aye?"

"Tell me about the other day in the woods before I came upon ye."

Evelinde raised an eyebrow at the demand, then shrugged where she lay half on top of him. He was the one who had placed her there, and she had been content to remain. Now that he was talking to her, however, she felt self-conscious about her position and started to shift away to lie beside him, but his hand was suddenly there to stop her. Apparently, he liked her where she was. Relaxing back against him, Evelinde pursed her lips and shrugged.

"What do you wish to know? I got lost, climbed a tree to find the castle, then you came."

"Ye asked if I'd been following ye," he reminded her.

She wrinkled her nose. The events seemed so far away now. They had only been the day before, but so much had happened since then that they seemed a far-off memory, and Evelinde felt foolish about her fear in the woods that day.

"Wife," he growled insistently.

"I thought I heard someone," she admitted slowly. When his eyes sharpened on her, she quickly added, "But 'twas probably just a rabbit or vole."

Cullen was silent, his expression troubled. "And the arrow?"

Her eyebrows rose, but she shrugged. " 'Twas probably there from a long time ago, as you suggested."

"Ye did no seem sure of that at the time," he pointed out.

Evelinde glanced away and shrugged. " 'Tis silly really." She paused and blew out an exasperated breath before explaining. "I was climbing the tree when I thought I heard a whiz thunk, and I—"

"A 'whiz thunk'?"

Evelinde chuckled at his confused expression, but explained. "A whizzing sound as if something had gone past me, then a thunk as if it had hit the tree."

When Cullen's eyebrows drew together on his forehead, she rushed on to say, "It was probably a branch or bird's nest dropping past me and hitting the tree on its way down. I was shaking the branches a good bit with my climbing."

His expression did not clear.

Evelinde continued, "Anyway, I instinctively released one of the branches I held to look around and see what I had heard. The branch I stood on chose that moment to snap, and I grabbed for something to hold on to, and once I regained a safe purchase with my feet and peered at what I had grabbed, I saw that it was an arrow." She shrugged and gave an embarrassed smile. "I know 'tis foolish of me, but at the time I thought perhaps that had been the 'whiz thunk' I'd heard."

Noting how solemn and stern her husband's face had become, Evelinde frowned. The man always looked serious, but this was different and was making her nervous. She decided a change of topic was in order and chose the first one to come to mind.

"Husband, do you not think torches should be set in the upper hall and lit during the day? It has no windows and is very dark."

Cullen shrugged, his voice distracted as he said, ' "Tis the way it has always been. Ye will get used to it."

Evelinde narrowed her eyes with displeasure, but before she could speak he was suddenly shifting her off of him and sliding from the bed.

"Where are you going?" she asked, sitting up to watch as he began to don his clothes.

" 'Tis the middle of the day. I've things to attend."

"But—" She glanced to the window, noting that the sun was hanging directly overhead. It was indeed midday. "What about our picnic in the clearing?"

Cullen hesitated, but then shook his head and continued to dress. " 'Twill have to wait for another day. I have wasted enough time today."

"Wasted?" Evelinde squawked, then scrambled off the bed and hurried after him as he headed for the door. "But I wished to speak with you about some things."

Pausing at the door, Cullen turned back, his gaze
sliding over her, but hardly seeming to see that she
was standing before him completely naked. His
voice was impatient as he asked, "What did ye wish
to speak about?"

Evelinde hesitated, at a loss now that she was on
the spot, but when he shrugged and turned to the
door, she blurted, "About the torches in the hall, and
getting men to help in the castle with the heavier
tasks, and what my duties are?"

"We've discussed the torches, they're no necessary. And why do ye keep insisting ye need men in
the castle?"

Evelinde decided to let the issue of the torches
go for now in favor of pursuing assistance in the
keep, and said, "The women do all the work while
the men play at swords, Cullen. Did they help with
the heavier tasks, the women would not be so bur-
dened."

"The men do not 'play' at swords," he said with af-
front. "They practice to stay in good form to defend
the women and children of Donnachaidh."

"Aye, of course," she said soothingly. "But Donnachaidh has had peace for a long time, and it seems
unfair to make the women work so hard when a
little help from the men would make things so much
easier. Surely you can spare a man or two once in a
while to help them?"

Cullen made a sound of irritation and turned to
open the door. "The women have managed well
enough for decades now. I see no reason to change
things. 'Tis how it has always been."

"But—"

"And yer duty as wife is to obey me," he added. Pausing again, now that he had the door open, Cullen turned back to say, "Stay in the castle from now on."

He departed then, pulling the door closed behind him and leaving a stunned Evelinde staring at the wooden panel with disbelief. She wasn't at all pleased with how their "talk" had gone, but that last order had her absolutely flummoxed.

Turning away from the door, Evelinde wandered back to the bed and sat down, her shoulders slumped with dejection. It was amazing how quickly her marriage went from wonderful to horrible to wonderful and back again. What had happened? Moments ago she'd been lying on her husband's chest feeling satisfied and even blissful, and now she wanted to wring his bloody neck.

" 'Tis how it has always been," she muttered aloud with disgust. What kind of argument was that? And her duty was to obey? Ha! What exactly were his duties then? She seemed to recall words like "comfort" and "honor" and "cherish" being a part of their wedding vows. Evelinde didn't feel particularly comforted or honored, but especially she wasn't feeling cherished.

Sighing, she dropped back on the bed and stared at the cloth draped overhead. Truly, marriage was turning out to be a most frustrating business. At least it was with *her* husband. He seemed to see her as helpless and useless and—

That was it! Evelinde sat up abruptly. No doubt

Cullen did see women that way. He'd been raised to think of them as the weaker sex needing defending. That being the case, it would be hard for him to see her as strong in her own right. She needed to show him that she was strong and capable and intelligent. Perhaps then he'd be more willing to listen to her ideas and thoughts.

The problem was how to do that, Evelinde thought, standing and moving to wash at the basin. She simply wasn't as physically strong as a man.

But she also had never been short of intelligence, Evelinde reminded herself encouragingly. With a little thought, surely she would come up with something.

In the meantime, she decided, if Cullen would not tell her what he wished her to do, she would decide for herself what her duties were . . . and the first task she set herself was to address the issue of getting men into the kitchens. Her husband might not be willing to set a couple men permanently to the task, but there were other ways to get them there, she thought.

Evelinde had noticed that the men tended to find excuses to go to the kitchens on the days that Biddy baked her pasties. Perhaps they could make them more often as a lure to get the men into the kitchens, and in exchange for a pasty, she and Biddy might get them to do a bit of the heavy lifting or some such thing. It could not hurt to try. As for the torches in the hall, if he would not order some set there, then she would bloody well do it herself. He might fuss about it at first, but would surely see the benefit when he could see his way clearly to their door without risking a stumble or fall. At least she hoped he would, Evelinde thought as she finished washing and quickly dressed.

While she was seeing to these things, she would consider how best to show him she was intelligent. Perhaps by solving the mystery of the accidents/ murders of his family members, Evelinde thought grimly, aware that she might be discovering the source of her own latest "accidents" that way. This last "accident" in the paddock and Cullen's questions regarding the arrow in the woods made her think someone might be trying to make her husband a widower again, and she wasn't ready to rest in peace.

Aye, Evelinde thought as she headed for the door, solving the matter would surely prove to her husband that she wasn't the weak, defenseless creature he thought her.

Her determination to light up the hall gained some strength as Evelinde stepped out of their room, pulled the door shut, and found herself enclosed in darkness.

"'Tis not strong or brave to walk around in darkness," she muttered irritably as she stepped carefully away from the door. "'Tis just stupid."

Shaking her head, Evelinde moved toward the stairs but then paused as a rustling from somewhere behind made her glance around. Her first thought was that it was one of the maids coming from a task in one of the rooms, but the moment she stopped the sound did, too.

"Who's there?" she said, staring into the darkness.

Silence was her answer.

Evelinde peered into the gloom, straining to see. It was possible it was just a mouse who'd taken up residence in the hall or one of the empty rooms. There were five of them on this level. She'd toured them all during the miserable days before Mildrede and Mac had arrived. The three rooms along the hall opposite their bedchamber were smaller bedchambers, one of which was Biddy's. The room next to their own, however, was a large solar. It was empty at the moment, but Evelinde hoped to change that at some point in the future. It was one of the other things she'd thought to speak to her husband about. Now she decided she'd simply take care of the matter herself. It would be one of the duties she set herself.

No further sound had reached her ears. It seemed it really had been a mouse or something, still her "accidents" had made her wary, and Evelinde was on the alert and moved much more slowly than usual as she approached the stairs. In the end, that probably saved her life when she stumbled over something on the floor. She was only a step from the stairs and had she been moving at her usual bustle, probably would have pitched headfirst down the steps. Although she still fell forward toward the stairs, her slower speed allowed her to cry out and reach for the railing as she did so.

A concerned shout from the great hall below answered her call, but Evelinde hardly noticed, she was grabbing wildly for the railing. Her hand slapped down on the wooden rail, and she clutched desperately at it. While it didn't completely stop her fall, it slowed her further. Evelinde's upper body swung toward the railing, her shoulder slamming into the sturdy wood as the rest of her body kept going. Her legs slid past her to the side, their weight dragging her down several steps so that a squeal sounded as her palm slid along the wood before she was able to tighten her hold again and bring herself to a complete halt.

"Wife!"

Cullen was there almost the moment Evelinde came to a halt, and she suspected that his was the concerned shout she'd heard, but she was stunned and breathless from the scare and merely peered at him with wide eyes.

"Are ye hurt?" Cullen asked the question as he scooped her up in his arms and hurried down the stairs to the trestle table. The way she was jostled around in his arms as he went kept her from answering, however, and Evelinde merely held on and waited. Unfortunately, he took her silence as a yes. So did Mildrede, who rushed over as he set Evelinde on the table, the maid's face a picture of combined worry and fury.

"I'm fine," Evelinde gasped a little breathlessly, as Cullen straightened from setting her down, but no one heard her over Mildrede's furious voice.

" 'Tis that damned dark hall. 'Tis a menace! Why are there no torches up there?" Mildrede snapped as she hovered beside him.

Evelinde waited for the hated line, "Because 'tis how it's always been," to sound, but Cullen didn't speak to the question. He was busily running his hands over her body on top of her gown.

"I am fine," Evelinde repeated, trying to sit up, only to find herself pushed flat again.

"Stay put till we're sure nothing's broken," Mildrede insisted, holding her shoulder down flat on the table. She then glanced to Cullen, and asked worriedly. "Is anything broken?"

"I doona think so," Cullen muttered as he finished his examination and straightened, his eyes searching out her face. "Are ye all right?"

"Aye—" she began, but Mildrede cut her off.

"Of course she is not all right!" the maid snapped. "She just took a tumble down those accursed stairs."

The maid urged Cullen out of the way to examine Evelinde for herself. While he'd concentrated on her limbs, looking for breaks, Mildrede moved her hands over her stomach and urged her to sit up so she could run them over her back as well.

"I am fine, Mildrede," she muttered, trying to wave her away.

The maid merely tightened her lips, and said, "You are not fine. You will be black-and-blue . . . again," Mildrede added heavily, glowering at Cullen, obviously blaming him for this latest accident.

"What's happened now?"

Evelinde glanced around at that exasperated question to see Fergus approaching the table. Tavis was not far behind.

"She fell down the stairs," Cullen answered in a growl that drew Evelinde's eyes to his face. He was scowling at her as if this were all her fault, she noted with irritation.

"Has she always been this clumsy?"

Evelinde's head shot back around at that question from Tavis, and she glared at the man despite the teasing voice he'd used. He merely grinned back, eyes sparkling with amusement.

"Nay!" Mildrede snapped, apparently no more amused than Evelinde was, "In fact, she rarely had accidents at all ere the day *your* lord arrived at d'Aumesbery. But, then, 'tis not the first accident that has happened around him."

Evelinde's eyes widened, but then she realized Biddy must have told Mildrede the tale of how Cullen's father, uncle, and first wife had died. Ere coming to the castle, all either of them had known was that he was supposed to have killed them, not that their deaths were the results of suspicious accidents. Her gaze slid to Cullen to see how he was taking the words, only to find his face expressionless as usual.

"Are ye suggesting our laird had something to do with this?" Fergus demanded, elbowing Tavis out of the way so that he could glare at the maid.

"Mildrede," Evelinde said in a warning tone as the woman opened her mouth to answer.

The servant hesitated, but held her tongue. Evelinde was just relaxing when Cullen suddenly scooped her off the table and moved toward the stairs.

"What are you doing?" she asked with a frown.

"I am taking you to our room to rest."

"I do not need to rest, Cullen. I am fine really. I do not think I even got hurt this time, I was able to save myself," she assured him quickly, ignoring the slight ache of her arm from that saving. It was little enough compared to what she could have suffered.

"I shall fetch some mead and mix a tonic," Mildrede announced, hurrying for the kitchen.

"Husband," Evelinde said impatiently. "I am fine. Really."

"You are not fine. You nearly broke your neck and will rest to allow your body to recover."

Evelinde opened her mouth to respond, but they'd reached the top of the stairs and instead she cautioned, "Be careful. I tripped over something on the floor just before I reached the stairs."

When Cullen paused to glance at her, she nodded. " 'Tis what made me fall."

He met her gaze silently and for a moment Evelinde thought he didn't believe her, but then he turned to shout over his shoulder. "Bring me a torch."

Tavis appeared behind them shortly after that carrying a lit torch in hand. At a gesture from Cullen, he moved around them and stepped onto the landing.

"Wait," Cullen said, when Tavis started to lead the way to the bedchamber. "Move the torch over the landing before the stairs."

Evelinde saw an eyebrow rise on the man's forehead, but he lowered the torch, lighting up the floor before them. Evelinde frowned on seeing that there was nothing there to see. The way was clear.

"But I tripped over something," she muttered, and

twisted in Cullen's arms, trying to look at the top few stairs. It was possible she'd sent whatever she'd tripped on skittering down the stairs ahead of her as she stumbled over it.

"Settle yerself," Cullen ordered, and nodded to Tavis to continue forward.

"But I really did trip over something," she insisted.

"Probably yer own feet," Tavis teased as he led the way up the hall.

Evelinde's alarmed gaze slid between the fair-haired man and her husband. Cullen's face was its usual unreadable self, even his eyes were giving nothing away, and she feared he agreed with Tavis's teasing and thought she'd just tripped over her own feet. But she really had tripped over something and couldn't for the life of her sort out where that something had disappeared to.

It must have rolled down the steps, Evelinde thought with frustration.

"Thank ye," Cullen rumbled, and Evelinde glanced around to find that they'd reached their bedchamber. Tavis had opened the door and now stood aside for Cullen to enter.

Her husband's cousin began to close the door behind them once they'd passed him, but before he could, Cullen ordered, "I want torches in the hall from now on."

Tavis paused, eyebrows rising slightly. "We've never had torches in the hall here before."

"We will now," Cullen said firmly. "And I want them lit each morning and kept lit until we are abed. Tell Fergus, and make sure he arranges it."

The man's eyes slid to Evelinde, a curious expression on his face, but he nodded, then pulled the door closed.

"Thank you," Evelinde said quietly as he set her on the bed. It seemed her near fall had done what her own requests had not. There would be light in the hall.

Cullen's answer was a grunt as he turned away and headed for the door.

Evelinde heaved a sigh as the door closed behind him, sure he didn't believe she'd tripped over anything but her own feet. She supposed she couldn't blame him. There had been nothing that he could see for her to trip over. Making a face, Evelinde slid her feet off the bed. She was perfectly fine. Her arm muscles were a little tender, but that would pass quickly, and she had no intention of "resting." She had a plan of action she wished to set in motion and now, more than ever, was determined to follow it.

chapter

Twelve

"Yer plan is working like a charm."

Evelinde smiled at that gleeful greeting from Biddy as she entered the kitchen and paused to peer toward where Fergus and another man were carrying in large cloth bags of vegetables that were to be prepared for the evening meal.

"Good," she said with a pleased sigh. It was her first success at Donnachaidh, but Evelinde sincerely hoped not her last.

"In fact, I've more help than I can use at times," Biddy added wryly, her lips curving into a smile when Fergus grinned around the pasty in his mouth as he passed.

Evelinde peered after the man curiously. It wasn't the first time she'd seen him smile, but she'd come to realize he only seemed to do it around Biddy. The rest of the time he was as grim-faced as Cullen normally was.

Dragging her attention back to what Biddy had said, Evelinde suggested, "If you've more help than you need, then only make the pasties every other day. Or perhaps only when you think you'll need the help."

"Aye. I'll do that," Biddy decided, and shook her head. "I should have thought to use bribery years ago. 'Twould have eased our burden mightily these years." She peered at Evelinde solemnly. "Yer a clever lass."

Evelinde flushed at the compliment. " 'Tisn't bribery. 'Tis a bit of sweet to tempt them is all."

Biddy chuckled at her discomfort, and said, " 'Tis bribery, and it works, and no one is hurt by it, so . . ." She shrugged, then asked, "Were ye lookin' to break yer fast? I've made a fresh batch of pasties."

"Aye, but I'll settle for an apple if we have any," Evelinde said, not wishing to take any of the valuable bargaining chits thus forcing the woman to make more.

"Ye'll take a pasty and enjoy it," Biddy responded at once, shuffling off to get her one. She collected a mug of mead and the originally requested apple for her, too, and returned. "Now take them out and settle yerself at the table while ye eat. Ye've been busy all week and need to look after yerself."

Evelinde murmured her thanks and left the kitchen

with her treasure, feeling a little guilty anyway. She hadn't truly been busy this last week since her near fall down the stairs. She had simply taken on her duties as castellan.

Her gaze slid over the great hall as she crossed to the table, and a sense of pride slid through Evelinde as she took in the changes wrought. The barren walls had been freshly whitewashed and now sported her beloved tapestries, the chairs by the fire bore the cushions she and her mother had embroidered, and the floor was covered with fresh rushes. It looked much brighter and welcoming, she thought, and only wished her husband had troubled himself to notice, but he had been terribly distracted of late.

Evelinde snorted at her own thoughts. Her husband had been much more than distracted lately, he had—

"Is that one of Biddy's pasties?"

Distracted from her depressing thoughts, Evelinde glanced at Gillie with surprise as she found him suddenly at her side, escorting her to the table. He and Rory seemed always to be underfoot over the past week, she'd noticed, and was beginning to find it a bit wearying.

"Aye," Evelinde said as she settled at the table, then suggested, "Why do you not go see if Biddy needs anything done? She may give you a pasty if you assist her."

The man glanced longingly toward the kitchen, then shook his head and settled on the bench beside her. "Nay. I am not hungry. I shall just sit and keep you company."

Evelinde managed not to grimace as she concentrated on tearing her pasty in half. Where before it had been hard to find a man anywhere near the keep during the day while the women worked, now there seemed always to be at least two there. Fergus was forever finding some excuse or other to visit the kitchens, though Evelinde was used to that. He had done that from the start, and she suspected the man had feelings for Biddy. However, Cullen had also taken to popping into the keep several times a day, which would have been nice had he been there to see her, but he never said a word to her. And then there were Rory and Gillie. Now that they'd returned from escorting the wagon, the two men appeared always to be in the great hall, and they were not just passing through, but always underfoot. Evelinde wouldn't have minded so much except that they seemed always to be nearby, staring at her. She had no idea why they did but wished they wouldn't; it was making her daft.

Deciding she might as well take advantage of his presence, she asked, "Gillie, were you here when Darach died?"

"Aye, but I was only four. I doona even remember the man," he said, his eyes longing as he watched her take a bite of pasty.

Evelinde swallowed the food in her mouth along with a lump of disappointment, but asked, "Then you would have been fourteen when Liam died?"

"Aye. But I was visiting me mother's family at the time," he said distractedly, then licked his lips as he watched her take another bite. "I'm bound that's a tasty bit."

She ignored the question, and asked impatiently, "Well, surely you were here when Maggie died?"

Gillie started to nod, then shook his head. "Nay. I was out hunting with Rory."

Evelinde clucked with exasperation that, yet again, she would not find any answers. Everyone she had asked thus far had either been elsewhere at the time or evaded her questions. Shaking her head, Evelinde decided she might as well continue with her duties as castellan and stood as she popped the last of the pasty into her mouth.

"Where are you going?" Gillie asked, immediately on his feet.

She raised her eyebrows at the question but swallowed the last of the sweet, and admitted, "I thought to go take a look at the solar and see how much work it needs doing to make it habitable again."

"Oh." Gillie hesitated, his gaze sliding from her to the door to the kitchens. "Well perhaps I will nip into the kitchen then and just see if I cannot beg a pasty from Biddy."

Evelinde raised her eyebrows but merely headed for the stairs. She glanced back twice as she mounted the steps to the second floor, both times finding Gillie still standing by the table watching. She was actually to the door of the solar before she heard the squeak of the kitchen door opening and paused. Evelinde waited a heartbeat, then retraced her steps, a relieved sigh slipping from her lips when she saw that the great hall was empty. Gillie had obviously gone into the kitchens.

She immediately picked up her skirts and rushed back downstairs. If she was quick, she might slip out before he returned, Evelinde thought hopefully, casting anxious glances toward the kitchen door as she rushed across the great hall. She wouldn't have dared try to leave while Gillie or anyone else was around, for fear they'd report her to Cullen. He'd surely be upset to know she was leaving the keep. It was against his express orders. Her husband had made it plain she was to stay within. Evelinde had no idea why he insisted on it, perhaps he feared her visiting the paddock again, but she was growing heartily sick of being inside all the time. Surely a quick nip down to the stables to visit Lady wouldn't hurt. At least, it wouldn't if she wasn't caught, Evelinde thought wryly as she slipped through the double doors and out onto the steps.

The bailey was nearly empty at that hour, the men all busy with her husband practicing at battle. Evelinde managed to make it all the way to the stables without running across anyone she feared might carry tales to Cullen of her being out and about.

Slipping into the cool, dim stables, she peered about, relieved to find it empty as well. Relaxing a little then, Evelinde retrieved the apple from her pocket and made her way to her mare's stall.

Lady was happy to see her. It just made Evelinde feel guilty for the time that had lapsed since their last ride. No doubt the mare was as bored as she was, she thought unhappily, and considered taking her out for a quick ride.

"Does yer husband ken ye be out here?"

Evelinde jumped guiltily and turned to face Mac as he moved up the aisle toward her, leading a dappled mount.

"I just wished to look in on Lady," Evelinde said, watching him lead the horse into a nearby stall and set about unsaddling him.

"Last I heard ye werena to leave the keep."

Evelinde made a face as she moved out of Lady's stall and walked over to lean against the door of the one he worked in. "Who told you that?"

"Yer husband," he said dryly.

"Oh," she muttered with a little sigh. "Well, I am tired of sitting in the keep. I have been stuck inside for more than a week."

Evelinde didn't need the look Mac turned her way to know how petulant she sounded at that moment. But all he said as he set the saddle aside was, "I'm sure ye can find enough that needs doing inside to fill your time."

"Aye," Evelinde admitted. "But 'tis nice to get out, too."

"How did ye slip yer guards?" Mac asked, taking a brush to the horse. Spotting her confusion, he said, "Gillie and Rory. Cullen set the two lads to watch ye."

"What?" she asked indignantly. "I do not need watching."

"Oh, aye. Ye'd never get yerself into trouble." Mac snorted, then asked meaningfully, "How are yer bruises from yer last accident, yer fall down the stairs?"

"I didn't fall down the stairs," Evelinde said with an impatient cluck, then added, "At least not far. I caught the railing and saved myself. My arm was sore for a few days, but that is all. Besides, that was not my fault. I tripped over something . . . Not that anyone believes me. Everyone appears to think I am just clumsy," she added bitterly.

"Yer husband believes ye," Mac announced.

"He does?" Evelinde asked eagerly.

"Aye. 'Tis why he has guards on ye. Because he thinks someone put something there for ye to trip on, then took it away while everyone was fussing over ye."

Evelinde's eyes widened at the suggestion, and despite having wondered about that herself this last week, asked, "Why would anyone do something like that?"

Mac shrugged, not even looking away from the horse he was tending. "Why would anyone kill his first wife? Or his father? Or his uncle? Cullen's trying to find out."

Evelinde peered at the old man more closely. "He has been talking to you."

"Aye."

A growl of exasperation slipped from her lips. "I wish he would talk more to me. I am his wife."

"Truth to tell, I doona think he talks much to anyone," Mac commented. "He gives his men orders and such, but—" He shrugged.

Evelinde peered at the man. She already knew from Biddy that he was right, but was more interested in the stable master's willingness to talk to Cullen. Mac understood people as well as he did horses. He said 'twas why he preferred the animals; he didn't think much of people in general. She and Mildrede were the only people he'd bothered with at d'Aumesbery, but now it seemed he'd included Cullen in that small circle.

Evelinde found it reassuring to know he thought Cullen deserving of his time, it said he thought well of her husband. But she was also jealous that her husband would talk to Mac and yet did not speak to her.

"He doesna ken who to trust here," Mac volunteered. "I am an outsider and have not been involved in the matters presently plaguing him. He values yer opinion in trusting me and so came to me to talk after yer fall down the stairs."

Evelinde's eyebrows rose. Cullen valued her opinion in trusting Mac? That was encouraging. At least she thought it might be. "Why does he trust no one here? Is it because of the deaths and rumors?"

"Aye. He doesna ken what is what. He thought the deaths of his father and uncle were accidents, but when little Maggie died in the same spot as his father, he suspected foul play. He isna sure if all three were murder, or just hers. And then there are the rumors. He had too many say to his face that they knew he had nothing to do with the deaths, only later to overhear them tell another that *'Aye, he was behind it for certain.'"* Mac shrugged. "He has not known who to trust and has been forced to keep his own counsel."

Evelinde bit her lip at this news. It seemed a horrible way to live, surrounded by people who thought you a killer but said one thing to your face while saying another behind your back. And they were *his own* people. Even worse, as laird, he was the one responsible for their well-being and safety. It said much for him that he did not shirk that duty or use his position to avenge himself for their shabby treatment.

"I still do not understand why he will talk to you and yet does not see fit to talk to me," she said now, pushing those thoughts away. "I was not here then either."

"Some men do not speak much," he said, turning back to his horse. "Yer husband has been forced to be one of those men since the trouble here. But he does talk, and if he isna talking to ye, then 'tis probably because he fears revealing something he is not ready fer ye to ken."

Evelinde was puzzling over what that could be when he added, "But he follows ye everywhere with his eyes, and constantly finds excuses to go into the keep during the day to be near ye, and his worry over ye and anger about these accidents is excessive, at least the anger is. It suggests deep feelings."

She was silent for a moment. The week since her near fall down the stairs had been rather trying for Evelinde. She'd found herself with a husband who had suddenly turned cold and angry. He had not

touched her since the incident and had been short
and easily provoked. Between that and the fact that
he never spoke a word to her, she'd thought he was
angry with her for what she feared he saw as her
clumsiness. Learning that he was not angry at her
but angry about the possibility that she'd been attacked was rather reassuring, Evelinde thought,
then realized what Mac had said.

"He thinks that other incidents besides the one
on the stairs may have been attacks?" She had come
to that conclusion herself, but was almost afraid to
hope her husband might agree. It meant he might
not see her as a completely clumsy fool.

"Aye. He suspects the bull being loosed in the
paddock was deliberate, too," Mac said. "Hamish
has managed that barn for many years. Not once
in that time has anyone but he let Angus out . . .
until the day ye were in the paddock. And then
there is the arrow while ye were in the tree in the
woods. The laird suspects someone was following
ye through the woods, and the arrow was shot at ye
while ye were climbing."

Evelinde sagged against the stall door. "Why has
he said none of this to me?"

"More importantly, why would anyone want ye
dead," Mac said dryly. "Cullen and I have tried to
sort that out. But 'tis most difficult. The problem
is that if someone is trying to kill ye, 'tis probably
tangled up in the other deaths, but 'tis hard to sort
out who would have committed all three murders
because we cannot find a common motive. If the
uncle's death was murder, the most likely culprit

would have been Cullen's father, Liam. He was the only one to gain from it. He became laird," Mac pointed out.

Evelinde's eyes widened at the suggestion.

"But, then, if Liam's death was murder, and 'twas the same murderer, then Cullen is the most likely suspect since the death of both men saw him become laird."

She stiffened then, but Mac was already continuing, "But it isna him."

The conviction in his voice made Evelinde curious. "How can you be sure?"

"Cullen's spoken of his father to me, and I can hear the affection and respect in his voice. He'd no have killed his father to gain a title. But, even if he hadn't felt so about Liam, he wouldna," Mac said solemnly, then admitted, "I listened to his men speak on the way here, and have watched him since arriving and—" Mac turned to her, letting her see his very serious and certain expression as he said, "The boy is one of the most honorable men I've ever met."

Evelinde nodded slowly; she had already begun to see that herself and to appreciate his thoughtful and kind ways . . . despite his frustrating silences.

Mac turned back to the horse, before adding, "It takes a strong man no to take advantage of his position to punish those who have wronged him, but Cullen has done nothing to gain retribution for the rumors and whispers. And then there is how he has treated you."

He paused again to glance at her. "Cullen recognized what Edda was right away, ye ken. Despite having traveled and camped out for five days to reach d'Aumesbery—he didna take the opportunity to rest there a day or two ere returning. He headed straight out with ye, riding night and day so ye'd no have to endure her abuse a minute more than ye had to."

Evelinde's eyes widened incredulously. "That is why we left right after the wedding?"

"Aye."

"I wish he had told me so," she said with frustration. Truly, it was such a sweet and thoughtful thing to do. The man had ridden himself to near exhaustion just to prevent her having to bear any more insults from her stepmother, and she hadn't even known.

"He isna the sort to flaunt his good actions," Mac said with a shrug. "The point is, I am sure Cullen isna the one behind his father's death. So, while he is the only one we can tell gained anything from it, someone else must have gained something, too." He was silent for a moment, then added, "Without Maggie's death, I would consider Tavis a likely suspect. He may have hoped to gain the title of laird for which he had been passed over."

"But he was just a boy when Darach died," Evelinde protested.

"Aye, but that one may truly have been an accident," he pointed out. "If it was, Tavis may harbor a secret bitterness that he did not become the laird on Darach's death, the title going to Liam, then on to Cullen when Liam died."

Evelinde's eyebrows rose slightly. She hadn't considered this.

"However," Mac went on. "Did Tavis want the title, it should have been Cullen killed, not little Maggie, and as far as we can tell, no one at all gained from her death." He shook his head. "Hers is the one that really suggests the other two werena accidents e'en though hers is inexplicable. And then there are these attacks on you. No one would gain from yer death either."

Evelinde bit her lip and then admitted, "Biddy thinks little Maggie was killed because she was asking questions about the other deaths. She thought little Maggie was trying to gain Cullen's love by clearing his name."

Mac stopped working and turned to glance at her in surprise. "Was she now?"

"Aye," she said, then shifted uncomfortably under the sudden narrowing of his eyes.

"Ye wouldna be doing the same, would ye, lass?"

Evelinde avoided his gaze. "Doing the same what?"

"Ye've been asking about the deaths," he accused with certainty in his voice.

"I have," she admitted reluctantly. "Not that I've learned anything."

She could see the conflict on his face as he stared at her and knew he was torn between giving her hell and asking her something. In the end, he asked, "Who did ye ask questions of? Was Tavis one of them?"

"Nay. He was not here at the time. I asked Biddy,

and several of the other maids in the keep. I talked to Scatchy, too, and Fergus and Gillie."

Mac frowned. "And yet none of the accidents occurred until after Tavis returned from escorting yer wagon, Mildrede, and me here."

"Nay," she agreed.

"One of them could have mentioned it to Tavis," Mac said with a frown.

"You think 'tis Tavis, then?" Evelinde asked with interest.

Mac's expression was conflicted, then he admitted, "Me instincts tell me no. He seems a lighthearted sort, more interested in women than the responsibility of laird, but . . ." He shook his head. "If the motive is to gain the title of laird, then he is the most likely suspect besides Cullen."

"Should he not then be trying to kill Cullen?" Evelinde asked slowly.

"Aye, and mayhap he will, 'tis hard to say when we are unsure of the reason for any of the murders," Mac said slowly as he shook his head. "If all three were murdered, this killer is not just clever enough to escape discovery but almost frighteningly patient. There were ten years between the uncle and Cullen's father, then four between that and little Maggie's death."

"And now two between her death and these accidents," Evelinde muttered, then fretted. "Cullen was nearly injured when he tried to save me from the bull. He could easily have died that day. If Angus was deliberately loosed, whoever did it may have realized Cullen was nearby and would try to save me."

"That is a lot of hope on the killer's part," Mac pointed out. "Besides, he was not the target when you fell on the stairs."

"Mayhap," Evelinde said quietly, then pointed out, "but he left the room just ere me to go below that day. He may have been the target then and, with his long strides, simply missed whatever it was I later tripped over."

Mac frowned, and asked, "He wasna there when the arrow was loosed though, was he?"

"Nay, but as Cullen said that day, the arrow may have been in that tree for years. It may simply have been something else I heard," she pointed out.

"That is the trouble here," Mac said with disgust. "We are not sure what are accidents and what are not. Everything is so uncertain. We may be imagining murderers where there are none. 'Tis no wonder it has remained a mystery all this time."

"Aye." Evelinde sighed. She didn't know what to think about anything now.

"Ye never did say how ye managed to slip free of Gillie and Rory," Mac prompted, changing the subject. She suspected he was trying to prevent her worrying about things, but it wasn't going to work. She would let him change the subject, but worry about Cullen had now firmly buried itself in her thoughts.

"I said I was going to the solar, and—"

"I knew I'd find ye here."

Evelinde closed her mouth and turned guiltily to

peer up the aisle as that impatient comment interrupted her. Cullen stood, glaring at her from the stable doors, exasperation on his face. When she merely peered back at him, he moved forward so that he could loom over her and glower up close.

Evelinde glowered right back. Truly, the man was a trial to her. If he spoke at all, it was only to order her about or snap and snarl like a rabid dog. How a man could behave with such consideration and thoughtfulness on the one hand but not manage to speak other than to growl was beyond her.

"I was most displeased when Gillie came to find me to say ye'd slipped his guard. I ordered ye to stay in the castle."

"Aye, and mayhap if you had told me *why* you wished it, I would have," she told him. "Though, it seems to me I'm hardly safer there since one of the accidents you worry over took place in the keep itself."

Cullen frowned. "That's why the men are watching ye. To keep ye safe."

"And what if one of them is the culprit?"

"Gillie and Rory were barely more than bairns when my uncle was killed," he pointed out with a dismissive wave.

"And if his death really was an accident? They were older when your father and Maggie died."

"That's why there are two watching ye. If one is the culprit, the other surely isn't, and ye be safe. Now get ye back in the keep where yer supposed to be," Cullen growled, moving past her to enter his horse's stall and begin saddling him.

Evelinde ignored the order and followed him instead. "Where are you going?"

"I am riding out to Comyn."

"By yourself?" When he merely turned and peered at her as if that was a stupid question, Evelinde asked, "Can I come?"

"Nay."

"Why? Surely I am safe with you?" And you are safer not alone, too, she thought, worried that he might be a target as well.

"Wife—" Cullen paused, and shook his head, apparently at a loss.

Mac had been watching their exchange with amusement, but now said, "Ye may as well give in, lad. She's persistent is that one. Besides, 'twill do the girl some good to get out for some fresh air. She has been trapped inside for near a week now."

Cullen hesitated, then gave in with a sigh.

"All right," he said, turning back to finish saddling his mount. "But ye'll ride with me."

Evelinde didn't protest. She would have preferred riding her own mount, but wasn't risking putting up a fuss and possibly making him change his mind about allowing her to accompany him.

"Cullen and Tralin used to get up to such mischief! His mother and I would spend half our time fretting and the other half laughing at their frolics."

Evelinde returned Lady Comyn's smile, and asked curiously, "Did Tavis never play with them?"

Lady Comyn hesitated, her gaze thoughtful as she peered down at her mead. "Tavis was four years younger, and the two of them were forever leaving him behind. He tended to stay close to his mother."

"And you and Biddy didn't keep up your friendship after Cullen's mother died?"

Lady Comyn smiled sadly, then admitted, "We did at first, but . . ." She sighed. "It was very hard. Being together afterward was rather sad. It made us remember what we had lost. We still visited each other, but not as often. After Darach died, Biddy seemed to retreat somewhat. She spent more and more time in the kitchens." Ellie Comyn shrugged. "We drifted apart."

Evelinde was about to ask another question when the doors to the great hall opened to allow Cullen and Tralin to enter.

" 'Tis time to leave," Cullen announced as he reached them.

Evelinde nodded and thanked Lady Comyn for a lovely time. She then allowed her husband to escort her out of the keep to where his horse was already awaiting them. Within moments they were passing out of the bailey and heading back to Donnachaidh.

They had ridden for quite a while when Cullen suddenly asked, "Did ye enjoy yerself?"

Evelinde twisted her head around to glance at her husband. He so rarely spoke, his asking the question was a pleasant surprise.

"Aye. Lady Comyn is lovely. We had a nice talk," she answered, and it was true. While Cullen and his friend Tralin had disappeared down to the stables to look at a new horse, Lady Comyn had shown

Evelinde her gardens. They had enjoyed a pleasant walk before stopping to rest and chat over a refreshing mead. She really had enjoyed herself. Evelinde had learned some things she hadn't known ere this. It seemed that Tralin and Cullen had been friends for some time. Lady Comyn had been friends with Cullen's mother while she still lived, and the two women had visited back and forth quite frequently while the boys were young.

"Did you?" she asked in the hopes of keeping her husband talking.

"Aye. Tralin is a good friend."

Evelinde grinned and admitted, "She told me of some of your exploits when you and Tralin were children. It sounds as if the two of you got into a good deal of mischief."

A small smile tugged at Cullen's lips, but all he did was grunt.

Evelinde hesitated, then asked, "Husband, would you show me where your father went off the cliffs?"

The request seemed to startle him, and he glanced down at her sharply. "Why?"

Evelinde hesitated, then admitted, "I just thought perhaps if I saw the spot, I would get a better idea of what might have happened. No one seems to be sure if 'twas an accident, or nay, and that just adds to the confusion."

Cullen was silent for so long, it seemed obvious he was going to ignore the request. Evelinde sighed to herself and settled back against him, resigned to not having her request fulfilled. It was another twenty minutes before she realized that rather than approach the front of the castle, they were riding toward the back of it and the cliffs there.

Sitting up before him, she peered curiously around as he drew his mount to a halt on a windswept cliff behind the curtain wall at the back of the castle.

It was a narrow spot, Evelinde noted, as Cullen dismounted and lifted her down. The area that ran along between the high stone wall and the edge was only about ten feet wide, but ran on for quite some way.

Cullen caught her arm as she moved to peer over the edge, holding her back as if he feared she might tumble to her death. Evelinde was glad he did when she looked over and saw how steep it was and how far it was to the ground below. It was dizzying. The fact that a strong wind was swirling around her, rushing up the cliff wall to catch at her skirts, tugging at her gown as if to pull her over the edge did not make her feel any better.

"He had his horse with him?" Evelinde asked, easing back from the edge and trying to eradicate the image that had entered her mind of an older version of Cullen lying broken and battered on the stones below.

"Aye."

"Do they think he dismounted and somehow fell over the edge? Or that his horse was spooked and he was thrown from the saddle?" she asked with a frown.

Cullen shook his head. "No one kens, or at least no one I have been able to find yet. If there truly was a witness, he may be able to tell us."

"And if 'twas murder, his murderer could tell us," Evelinde said quietly.

Cullen nodded.

Sighing, Evelinde turned away. Coming here had not really helped her envision how the "accident" might have happened. There was nothing here but some sparse grass and a pile of stones; nowhere for an animal—or a man—to have leapt out from to startle Liam's mount and send him rearing. More to the point, she could see no reason for the laird to have been here in the first place.

Her curious gaze slid to the pile of stones. She'd thought it just a rocky outcropping, but suddenly noted 'twas not a natural formation. Evelinde moved toward it. "What is—?"

The question died on her lips as she suddenly thought that it might be a cairn for his father. Or his first wife.

" 'Tis Jenny. Biddy's sister," he explained.

Evelinde hesitated, then asked, "You mean she is actually buried under those stones?"

Cullen nodded.

"Why?" Evelinde stared at him with dismay.

" 'Tis where Biddy wished it," he answered simply, and when she turned a confused face his way, explained, "She killed herself and could not be buried in hallowed ground. But she liked this spot and spent a good deal of time here, so Biddy decided this should be her final resting place."

"She killed herself?" Evelinde turned her gaze back to the stone grave. "Why?"

Culled frowned. "I was only fourteen at the time, but I've since learned she was supposed to marry the Campbell."

"The Campbell?"

"Aye. He's been dead these last five years, but he was an evil bastard, cruel and heartless. They said she killed herself rather than marry him."

Evelinde nodded, but her mind was not really on the Campbell. "You were fourteen when she died? That was the year your uncle died, too, was it not?"

"Aye. She died just two weeks ere the hunting accident."

Evelinde turned to peer at the spot where the cliff fell away. It was a barren spot, lonely and cold. "Did she really like this spot?"

"Aye. She used to come here often the first time she visited."

"The time she killed herself was not the first time she was here?"

"Nay. She had been here once before that, about two months earlier," Cullen said. "She was much younger than Biddy, and that was the first time she came. She was supposed to stay for a month, but only remained three weeks. Tralin was most disappointed. He thought her the prettiest lass he'd ever seen," he confided.

Evelinde smiled at the confidence, pleased that he was actually talking to her. Eager to keep him talking, she asked, "And did you?"

"She was pretty enough," Cullen allowed with a shrug, "but I was not as enamored as he."

Evelinde was secretly pleased at these words, but simply said, "So she returned two weeks before your uncle died?"

"Aye. She arrived unexpectedly and asked to speak to Uncle Darach."

"Why your uncle?" Evelinde asked with surprise. "Why not Biddy?"

"Darach was laird," Cullen said with a shrug. "If anyone were to offer her sanctuary, he would have to be the one. He took her for a ride on his horse so she could have her say, but must have refused her sanctuary, because she was sobbing when she returned and ran up to her room and would not come out. Biddy found her the next morning. She'd hanged herself in the solar."

Evelinde's eyebrows rose. That explained why the solar was empty. She supposed Biddy had emptied the room and never set foot in it again. Every time she entered, she would have been reminded of her last sight of her younger sister.

"Come." Cullen caught her arm and urged her back to his mount.

As pleased as she was that he was finally speaking to her, Evelinde remained silent as he set her on the saddle and joined her. Her mind was taken up with thoughts of what she'd learned. Biddy's sister had died two weeks before Cullen's uncle, and had been buried in the very spot where Cullen's father and first wife had later died. It was a strange coincidence . . . if it was a coincidence at all.

Thirteen

T hank you," Evelinde murmured, as Mildrede refilled her cup of honey mead. Her gaze then slid around the great hall. Cullen had left her sleeping that morning, and everyone had broken their fast ere she'd come below. Now there was just herself, Rory, and Gillie, though the two men were seated farther along the table, quietly talking to each other. They were guarding her as usual.

"You seem very distracted this morning," Mildrede commented as she settled herself at the table beside Evelinde. "In fact, you have been rather quiet since returning from Comyn's yesterday. Did something happen while you were there? Did it not go well?"

"Nay. I had a lovely time," Evelinde assured her, and it was true. However, she *had* been distracted since returning to Donnachaidh. Her mind had been worrying over the problem of how to approach Biddy on the subject of her sister, Jenny. Evelinde was sure it couldn't be coincidence that Jenny had died two weeks ere Darach and that Cullen's father and first wife had later died at the spot where the young woman had been laid to rest.

There must be some connection. She simply wasn't sure what it could be and wished to cause Biddy as little upset as possible while trying to find out.

"Well," Mildrede said, when Evelinde fell silent. "Unless you have ruined another gown you have not told me about, I have finished the mending. Would you like me to start on the solar today? You mentioned that you would like to clean it out and perhaps start using it again," Mildrede reminded her.

Evelinde nodded with a frown. She had considered doing that, but that was before she'd learned about Jenny killing herself in the room. The fact didn't bother her, but she didn't wish to upset Biddy.

"It could be a lovely room, a nice spot for you and Cullen to get away from the crowded great hall of a night. Perhaps enjoy a quiet meal together without having to retire to your room."

"Aye," Evelinde murmured, then sighed, and said, "However, I am not sure Biddy would be pleased; tis sure to bring back bad memories for her."

"Bad memories?"

Evelinde remained silent as her mind turned the situation over. An idea had occurred to her. Mildrede and Biddy had spent a lot of time talking of late. The two women often sat together by the fire after the sup, chatting about this and that while mending, or embroidering, or some other task. It wasn't unusual for a lady and her maid to be friends, though it was somewhat unusual for them to be friends with another's maid. On the other hand, the two women were around the same age, and Evelinde had thought nothing of it, but now asked, "Mildrede, has Biddy ever mentioned her sister to you?"

The maid peered at her blankly. "Her sister?"

"Jenny," Evelinde explained.

"Nay. I had no idea she had a sister."

Evelinde noted the hurt on the maid's face, and said quietly, "Jenny killed herself some years ago, Mildrede. No doubt 'tis painful for Biddy to discuss."

"Oh," Mildrede said, some of the hurt slipping away to be replaced with sympathy, and she asked, "Why would cleaning up and arranging the solar bring back bad memories?"

"Jenny hanged herself in the solar a couple of weeks before Biddy's husband, Darach, died," Evelinde murmured.

Mildrede's eyes widened incredulously, then a soft breath slid from her lips before she breathed, "Poor Lady Elizabeth. She has had grievous times."

"Aye," Evelinde agreed, and popped into her mouth the last bit of bread and cheese she'd chosen to break her fast. After chewing and swallowing, she murmured, "I suppose we could ask her if 'twould be all right. She may not wish to use the solar herself but might not mind our using it."

Mildrede hesitated briefly, but then nodded. "I am sure she would not mind."

Evelinde drank the last of her mead, nodded, and stood. The moment she did, Gillie and Rory got to their feet as well. Irritation flickered through her when they did, but she forced a smile and waved them back to their seats. "There is no need to trouble yourself, gentlemen. I am merely going above stairs to take a look at the solar to see what needs doing. You can see the landing and the solar door from here."

The two men hesitated, exchanged glances, then settled back into their seats, and Evelinde immediately turned and headed for the stairs, aware that Mildrede was on her heels.

The stairs and upper hall were much more pleasant to manage since the torches had been added. The hall was just a hall, long and empty, with doors coming off it, but at least they could see where they were going and not fear tripping over something they could not see.

Evelinde grimaced at the very idea. She'd had quite enough spills and falls of late and would happily avoid another for a while. If she could manage it, she thought, as she led the way to the closed door of the solar.

Despite having looked into the room before, Evelinde still found herself a little surprised at the wave of stink that met them when she opened the

door. A musty, moldy smell rolled out, making both
women wrinkle their noses with disgust. She supposed that was why she'd done little more than stick
her torch in to see the general size and shape of the
room at the time before beating a hasty retreat. Now,
she didn't have that luxury. If they were to use the
room, they would have to clean and air it.

"Bring one of the torches from the hall, please, Mildrede," Evelinde ordered, and moved a few cautious
steps into the room, waving one hand before her as
she went in an effort to brush away the cobwebs in
her path. She recalled from her first look into the
room that there were shutters on the windows. The
sooner she had them open, the sooner she would not
only be able to see what she was doing, but the fresh
air should help dissipate some of the odor.

"Here we are."

Evelinde turned to her maid with relief as she re-
appeared in the doorway, torch in hand, sending
shadows dancing across the room. Taking the torch
from her, Evelinde held it out before her, waving it
back and forth to sweep more cobwebs as she made
her way to the nearest set of shutters. They were a
bit shaky after seventeen years, but opening them
sent light splashing into the room. However, it also
allowed a breeze in to stir the dust and cobwebs,
causing a cloud of the fine powders to rise and swirl
in the room.

Mildrede was standing at a second set of shutters,
opening those. Evelinde would have warned her not
to, for it would only cause more of a stir, but before

she could, the dust in the air got into her nose and mouth, and she found herself sneezing, then bending over under a coughing fit.

Evelinde turned to the window she'd opened and inhaled the fresh air until the need to cough had passed. She straightened and turned cautiously to face the room, her gaze sliding over the interior.

Truly, she almost wished she'd not opened the shutters. The room hadn't looked nearly as bad by torchlight as it did under the harsh glare of the sunlight pouring through the open shutters.

It was obvious the chamber had not been used during the seventeen years since Jenny had died. Every minute of that time showed in the room, in the dust layering every surface, the gossamer cobwebs billowing in the breeze, and the rushes that were half-rotted away and half-petrified with the passage of time. The room also had an unpleasant, musty odor that hit you like a wave on entering.

"There is a lot of work to be done," Mildrede murmured.

Something about the tone of her voice made Evelinde glance at the maid, and her eyebrows rose as she saw that her gaze was lifted toward the high ceiling, no doubt searching for where Jenny might have hanged herself. Evelinde had wondered that herself, but this was the first time she'd entered the room since learning of the young woman's death. Her own gaze slid over the room now with new eyes, but then, deciding she really didn't want to know and have that image in her mind, she turned her attention away from the ceiling and toward the rushes. They would have to go. Removing them would improve the smell in the room greatly. However, it would mean walking through countless cobwebs to do so did they not remove those first.

"I shall go fetch a besom and such," Mildrede decided.

Evelinde watched her go and turned her gaze over the room again. It was definitely going to be an effort to clean up, but worth it . . . she hoped.

Wrinkling her nose at the negative direction to her thoughts, Evelinde turned and peered out into the bailey below, enjoying the fresh air leaning out the window allowed her. Truly the smell in here was most unpleasant, and Evelinde suspected she would find that even more mice than was usual had taken up residence in the empty room. There would doubtless be a nest or two, and likely even corpses of the little rodents in among the rushes.

Evelinde was trying not to consider that unpleasant possibility when a small cough made her straighten and glance around.

"Aunt Biddy," Evelinde said, guilt pouring over her in a wave as she spotted the woman in the doorway.

"Yer going to use the solar," Cullen's aunt said quietly, her gaze seeming to fix on Evelinde to avoid looking at the room itself.

"I was going to talk to you first, but, aye," she admitted uncomfortably. "If 'twould not be of distress to you, I thought it might be pleasant."

"Of course ye should," Biddy muttered, her gaze dropping to the rushes, then down to her own skirt. " 'Tis a waste not to use it."

Evelinde hesitated, then admitted, "On the way back from Comyn yestereve, Cullen took me to the cliff where Lord Liam and little Maggie died."

Biddy's face froze briefly, but then she managed a neutral expression. "Oh?"

"Aye," Evelinde hesitated, then pushed ahead. "Cullen told me about Jenny. I am sorry, Aunt Biddy."

Biddy nodded but remained silent.

Evelinde blew out a short breath, and continued on determinedly, "He said she killed herself rather than marry the Campbell?"

Biddy remained silent, her fingers beginning to clench and unclench on the cloth of her skirt.

"I am sorry, I know this must distress you," Evelinde said quietly, finding the conversation rather difficult herself. She liked Biddy and didn't wish to pain her, but . . . "You do not think your sister's death had anything to do with your husband's death. Do you?"

Biddy suddenly slammed one hand into the doorframe beside her with enough violence to make Evelinde jump a little nervously and watch her wide-eyed.

"Spider," Biddy muttered for explanation, brushing off her hand.

Evelinde nodded and almost gave up questioning her, but then blurted, "I was just wondering if there might be a connection."

That caused the woman to raise her head. Eyes sharp and expression tight, she stared at her.

Evelinde bit her lip under that hard stare, and said apologetically, "It just seems odd that she is somehow connected to each death. She died here two weeks before your husband's death, then Cullen's father and first wife both died on the cliffs where she was laid to rest. Is it possible someone blamed Darach for her death because he would not offer her sanctuary from marrying the Campbell?"

"Sanctuary?" Biddy asked with surprise.

Evelinde frowned. "Aye. Is that not why she wished to speak with Darach when she returned?"

"Lass," Biddy began grimly, then paused abruptly, her head jerking around toward the door as Tavis suddenly appeared behind her. The two peered at each other for a moment. Evelinde couldn't see Biddy's face, but Tavis's expression was neutral, and Biddy turned back. "Yer more than welcome to open up this room. 'Tis well past time 'twas done, but I'll no likely be using it much meself."

Biddy's gaze shifted to the corner where a wooden chandelier hung by a chain from the ceiling. It was very simple, two pieces of wood crossing each other with prickets at each end of each piece of wood so that four candles could be fixed on them. Evelinde peered at the chandelier, wondering if it was what Jenny had hanged herself from, then decided it most likely was. She could see no other choices within the room.

Her gaze dropped back to Biddy, only to find that the woman had slipped away while Evelinde was examining the chandelier, and Tavis had stepped back into the hall and was staring after her. A troubled expression on his face, he glanced back to Evelinde.

"Doona mind her," Tavis said as he stepped back into the doorway. "She was very fond of Jenny."

Evelinde nodded solemnly, finding herself torn between guilt at obviously upsetting the woman, and frustration that she hadn't learned anything from it.

"We came to tell ye that Cullen called Rory and Gillie away and set us to watch ye," he announced, when she remained silent, caught up in her thoughts.

"We?" Evelinde asked, glancing up curiously.

"Fergus and I," Tavis explained. "He came above stairs with me to find you, but I think he's hied himself off to the kitchens to find something to eat."

Evelinde smiled faintly, and said with amusement, " 'Tis not food that draws him to the kitchens all the time."

"Nay. But food is all he will get," Tavis said.

Evelinde tilted her head, eyeing him curiously. It seemed obvious he, too, suspected Fergus had feelings for Biddy.

"Are his feelings so hopeless then?" she asked curiously.

Tavis shrugged and moved forward, his gaze shifting curiously around the filthy room. "Me mother loved me father dearly. Forgave him all his sins, and has shown no interest in any other man since his death. In truth, she has shown little interest in anything but cooking. His death changed her."

"His death or her sister's?" Evelinde asked.

"His," he assured her solemnly. "Oh, she was broken-hearted when Jenny died. Wept and wept she did. My father spent a deal of the two weeks before his death just holding and comforting her. But after he died." Tavis shook his head. "She retreated into herself, started disappearing all the time, either to the cliffs to sit by Jenny's grave or into the kitchens and away from the rest of us. I think her heart was broken, and she just couldna bear to love anymore. Not even me," he added with a wry little smile that was both sad and charming.

Evelinde frowned, her heart twisting for the young boy Tavis would have been at the time. At the tender age of ten years old, he'd found himself orphaned by one parent and abandoned by the other. "Who looked after you?"

Tavis shrugged. "Uncle Liam did what he could for me. And the rest of the ladies around here offered comfort as they could."

The wicked grin on his face suggested that comfort wasn't always just hugs, and Evelinde frowned, wondering just how old the boy had been when he'd been initiated into manhood.

"Do you remember Jenny?" she asked abruptly, wishing to change the topic.

"Aye." Tavis smiled faintly. "She was great fun the first time she was here. Happy and gay, always laughing. Cullen and Tralin used to run off all the time. They thought they were too old to play with me, but not Jenny. She let me trail her about all the time." He frowned suddenly, then admitted, "Well, at first she did, then she took to sitting out on the cliff, looking out over yon valley below, and she started sending me away more often than not. I could follow her anywhere but the cliff."

"Why?" Evelinde asked curiously.

Tavis grimaced. "She said 'twas because it was dangerous and that she wished to be alone to think."

"But you didn't believe her?"

Tavis shook his head. "I followed one day. There is a door in the outer wall at the back of the castle. There is a trick to opening it, and I didna ken the way back then, but I could climb the tree and did . . ." A wicked smile came to his lips again. "She wasna alone, and they werena thinking."

Evelinde's eyebrows rose. "Who was she with?"

"I doona ken," he admitted. "I couldna see very well. All I saw were a man's legs entwined with her on the ground. The branches of the tree I was in were in the way. I barely caught a glimpse before I leaned out too far and fell out of the tree." He smiled wryly, and admitted, "I didna want her to ken I'd been spying on her and be angry, so I took myself off back to the castle for my mother to tend me scrapes and bruises."

They were both silent for a moment, then Tavis said, "It wasna long after that she left. A couple of days, mayhap. Mother was out hunting rabbit to make some of her stew to give Cook some ease, and

Aunt Jenny disappeared to the cliff, only to come running back sobbing fit to die. I thought she'd hurt herself, but she didna appear to have an injury. When I tried to ask her if she was all right, she yelled at me to leave her alone and pushed me out of her room. She came out a few minutes later with just a small sack with a few gowns in it and hurried down to the stables." He shrugged. "She rode off, just like that, without even a word to me mother, or anyone."

"By herself?" Evelinde asked with amazement.

"Nay, three men escorted her."

"Who?" she asked at once, thinking that Jenny's lover may have been among the trio.

Tavis considered the question, but then shook his head. "I am no sure. I was standing on the keep stairs. 'Twas too far away to see more than that there were four in all riding out of the stables."

"Well someone must have arranged for her escort," Evelinde pointed out. "Your father, perhaps?"

Tavis considered the question, then shook his head. "I doona remember seeing him about. He had ridden out on his horse before Jenny went for her daily walk to the cliff."

Evelinde was frowning over this when Mildrede entered. The maid was lugging several items with her; a besom, a pail of water, rags, and other cleaning items, and Evelinde rushed forward to take the besom and a bundle of rags as Tavis took the pail from her to prevent everything from tumbling from her hold.

Tavis set the pail aside, then straightened and

moved toward the door. "Well, I'd best go below and get out of yer way. We'll be in the great hall if ye need us."

He then slipped from the room before she could ask any more of him. She supposed he was afraid he'd be asked to help clean, something the men were more likely to do now, but only in exchange for pasties and she had none with her. She could have sent for some of the women to help, but the room was small enough the two of them could manage. Evelinde turned her attention to beating away the cobwebs overhead while Mildrede began sweeping the rushes toward the door.

As she'd feared some wee beasts had taken up residence. Both she and Mildrede were sent squealing a couple of times when the mice were disturbed and sent running. That brought Tavis and Fergus running each time, until Evelinde got the pair to help remove the rushes she had drawn together in one huge pile by the door. Both balked at the very suggestion, but after some promising to ask Biddy to bake a whole batch of pasties just for them, it was decided that one could help while the other continued to act as guard. It fell to Tavis to help Mildrede cart the rushes away while Fergus remained in the great hall and watched the solar door as they'd been doing. Evelinde, they insisted, was to continue about her work in the solar. Neither man thought it would be good to annoy Cullen by letting her leave the castle.

Supposing that was better than nothing, Evelinde watched Mildrede and Tavis gather as much of the old rushes as possible. As they left the room, she considered the dent they'd put in the pile and guessed it would take the pair at least two more trips back and forth to get it all out.

Turning back to the chandelier she'd lowered to clean, Evelinde continued digging away the candle wax that had accumulated over the years, her mind going over what she'd learned from Tavis.

She wasna alone, and they werena thinking.

It sounded like young Jenny had a lover. A foolish mistake when she'd known she was going to marry the Campbell, a man known for cruelty. The only thing Evelinde could think was that the girl had hoped her lover, whoever he was, would marry her and save her from the Campbell. It would have taken a powerful lord to be able to do that and withstand the retribution that would have followed from the Campbells. But the only powerful lord at Donnachaidh was Darach, and he was already married, in no position to marry and save her. As far as Evelinde knew there hadn't been any other powerful lord visiting at the time . . . Though, she thought suddenly, there had been the son of a powerful lord who had come to the keep back then and still did. Tralin.

Evelinde slowed in her work on the chandelier as she considered that. Cullen had said Tralin had thought Jenny the prettiest lass he'd ever seen. What if she had liked him in return? Jenny had obviously been meeting her lover at the cliff for privacy. Could it have been Tralin? Could she have hoped he would marry and save her from the Campbell?

Evelinde blinked and straightened as she realized

there *had* been another powerful man . . . Cullen's father, Liam.

Nay, she realized in the next moment and bent back to her work right away. Liam had not been powerful in his own right until after his brother's death, when he'd taken on the title and position of laird . . . and that left her considering Tralin again.

Jenny's leaving in tears could only mean that whoever her lover was, they'd had argued. Evelinde wondered briefly who he might have been, but there was something else troubling her. Tavis said Jenny had left without a word to her sister. If so, then who had arranged the three-man escort for her? Darach?

Evelinde chipped away another large piece of wax, wrinkling her nose as the acrid scent of smoke wafted to her. It was as if the scent was embedded in the wood itself, she thought with disgust, then frowned as she realized that the smell was not of burning tallow, but—

She glanced around sharply, eyes widening in dismay as she saw that the torch Mildrede had set in the holder by the door had somehow fallen on the rushes piled in front of the door, and they were aflame.

Evelinde snatched up one of the damp rags she'd been using to scrub off the window ledges and moved toward the fire with some vague intention of beating it out, but dry and ancient as the rushes were, it was spreading quickly, the flames shooting up and out with a hunger that was alarming. She would not be able to beat them down, and she could not go for help, the fire blocked the door. Evelinde was trapped.

Cullen's expression was grim as he rode into the bailey. The incident with the arrow in the tree had bothered him since he'd begun to suspect some of his wife's accidents might not have been accidents at all. Finally, today he'd ridden out to the woods to find the tree his wife had been climbing and climb it himself to get a look at the arrow. One look had been enough to tell him that the arrow had not been long in the tree. It hadn't rained since the incident, and the fletching was pristine. Also, the wound in the bark around the arrow was new, not old and healed. Someone *was* trying to kill his wife.

Cullen had tried to pull the arrow from the tree, but it had sunk in deep enough he'd had to give up. He'd then examined the shaft and fletching to see if there was anything unusual about it that might lead him to the person who had loosed it, but the fletching was of common goose feathers. Most used goose, and some, very rarely, used swan feathers when making arrows. Some used a combination to make them more distinctive, but this was very common fletching and could have belonged to any number of Donnachaidh people.

Disappointed that the arrow wouldn't tell him anything about the person who had shot it, Cullen had climbed back down the tree and headed straight back to the castle. He'd suspected someone was trying to kill his wife since Hamish had spoken up at the bull's paddock, but having it confirmed like this made him anxious for Evelinde. Seeing her and assuring himself that she was well was the only thing he could think of to help put him at ease.

Cullen was debating whether he shouldn't put four men on her rather than just the two as he slipped from his horse and entered the keep, but all his thoughts scattered when he spotted Fergus seated at the great hall trestle tables alone.

"Where is Tavis?" he asked, his gaze sliding toward the chairs by the fire in search of his wife. When he didn't see her there, he frowned, and added, "Where is me wife?"

"Tavis is helping Mildrede cart dirty rushes out to be disposed of," Fergus answered slowly. "And yer wife is in the solar."

"By herself? Yer supposed to be guarding her," Cullen snapped.

"Aye, but she said she did not want us standing about getting in her way, and we can see the solar door from here," Fergus pointed out. "No one could get past us down here to trouble her."

Cullen scowled at the words, his head swiveling toward the bit of landing visible from here and the only door one could see from below. The solar door. His heart leapt into his throat when he saw that it was ablaze.

"Evelinde!" The name tore from his throat in a roar of agony as he bounded up the steps two at a time. Cullen recognized the fear and pain in his own voice but hardly heeded it. His ears, his mind, his whole body was straining for some answering call from his wife to tell him she yet lived. However, it brought him little relief when he heard her answering call as he reached the landing. Her voice had come from the solar, and now he knew for certain that he had something to fear.

Cullen charged to the door, then came to an abrupt halt as he found himself confronted with a wall of flame. It was as if someone had built a giant bonfire right in the doorway. The flames were nearly as tall as he, and what he could see of the room was full of smoke.

"Water!" he roared, turning on Fergus as the man reached his side.

The soldier turned away at once to charge back down the stairs. Cullen glanced back to the room, his heart twisting as he saw a dark shape he thought was his wife, bent over and coughing by the window. She could die in there from the smoke ere Fergus managed to return with water.

Cullen ground his teeth together and backed away from the door a few steps.

"I'm coming, wife. Get out of the way," he roared.

Cullen heard her shout something in response, but was already running forward, charging the flames. He would not lose Evelinde. He could not lose her. He loved the silly, talkative, sweet woman.

chapter

Fourteen

"Nay, husband, I have water!" Evelinde shouted between coughs, then gave up her protest to leap to the side as she saw Cullen rushing the flames from the hall.

The stupid man is going to get himself killed when if he'd just waited a moment, I could have put out the fire, she thought impatiently.

It had taken Evelinde a moment to recall the pail of dirty water in the room, a precious moment during which the fire had grown wildly, and she'd heard her husband shout for her. She cursed that moment of stupidity as she watched Cullen try to leap the flames. He might have managed to do so were it not for the doorframe. There simply wasn't enough room for his tall body between the top of the flames and the upper ledge of the door.

Much to her relief, Cullen had the sense to tuck his head down as he jumped, but his shoulders still hit the doorframe, and he crashed back down short of safety.

Evelinde screamed in alarm, her heart lodging itself in her throat as he came down at the edge of the burning rushes, but in the next moment, he'd thrown himself forward and rolled away from the fire.

"Are you all right?" she gasped, hurrying to his side as he regained his feet.

"Aye," Cullen growled, grabbing her by the arm and urging her to the window as she began to cough again. Once she'd drawn in a couple of fresh breaths and stopped coughing, he asked, "What happened?"

Ignoring the question, Evelinde peered over him a bit frantically for any sign of burns or injury, repeating, "Are you all right?"

He had given her such a fright! The likes of which she hadn't experienced since the day her father had died. She'd had that same sickening lurch in her stomach when he'd clutched his arm, turned grey, and tumbled from his seat, but it was a sensation she'd never experienced before or since then . . . until now, with this man. It told Evelinde that her feelings for her husband were much stronger than she'd imagined. Somehow, despite his frustrating silence, the man had found his way into her heart.

"I'm fine," Cullen assured her, catching at her fluttering hands. "We have to get out of here."

Evelinde's eyes widened with alarm, and she scrambled away from him and across the room when he reached for her. She had no doubt he intended to scoop her up in his arms and carry her out of the room, but there was no need.

"Wife!" he snapped, following, but paused when she picked up the pail of water in the corner. However, when she headed toward the flames to throw the water on them, he was suddenly at her side.

"Give me that," Cullen snapped, taking the heavy pail. When she released it easily and bent to cough as the smoke irritated her throat and lungs again, he ordered, "Wait by the window. The air is better."

Evelinde grimaced at his sharp tone, but when she opened her mouth to protest and ended coughing again, she gave way and did as instructed. She watched worriedly from the window as Cullen braved the heat of the flames quickly and efficiently to douse the fire. The water didn't put it out entirely, but it was enough that he was able then to beat out the rest of the flames with the damp rags she fetched for him.

"What happened?" Cullen asked as he beat out the last of the flames.

"I am not sure," Evelinde admitted, using another damp rag to try to wave the slowly dissipating smoke out through the window. "I think the torch fell out of its holder and onto the rushes."

His expression told her he doubted it had done so on its own, but she continued, "I had just remembered the pail of water when I heard you shout. I tried to yell at you not to risk yourself until I had doused the flames, but . . ." She shrugged, not bothering to point out that he hadn't listened.

Cullen merely grunted, and bent to peer at something in the embers. Giving up on the smoke, Evelinde moved up behind him to see what it was, her eyes moving over the torch lying in the center of the pile. When his gaze then lifted to the holder beside the door, she followed his glance, noting that the holder was tipped to the side as if to suggest the brace had slid, and the torch had fallen out. The problem was that even she could see that had the torch fallen out, it would have fallen closer to its holder, not the good foot and a half it had somehow traveled to land in the center of the rushes.

"It was not an accident," Cullen growled, straightening.

"Nay," Evelinde agreed quietly, but wasn't surprised. She hadn't heard it fall. Surely had it tumbled from its holder in some natural fashion, she would have heard it hit the floor? There should have been a thump, or at least a rustle of the rushes. However, there had been no sound to warn her. The smoke had been her first and only warning.

"But it would have looked like one had the fire done its work and destroyed the torch ere we got it put out," he continued grimly. "The tilted holder would have suggested it had fallen out on its own."

"Aye." Evelinde sighed, then watched silently as he straightened and moved around the embers to the iron holder fixed into the stone wall by one large bolt. There had been two when Mildrede had put the torch in earlier. Evelinde swept the floor with her eyes but didn't see the second bolt anywhere. She then glanced back to Cullen as he turned the holder upright and saw his mouth tighten when it moved silently. When he then gave the bolt still in the wall a tug, it came out easily and equally silently, which explained why she hadn't heard a thing.

Tossing the torch holder aside with disgust, Cullen turned back to sweep her into his arms and step over the still-smoking embers. They met Fergus as Cullen carried her into the hall. The older man was out of breath, a pail of water in each hand and several women behind him with more.

"The fire is out, but the embers are still hot. Douse them well," Cullen growled, then carried Evelinde to their room.

She could have walked, but already knew from past experience that there was no sense arguing with Cullen. The man would carry her when he wished, and, apparently, he wished to now. Evelinde remained still in his arms as he strode to the door of their chamber, reached out to open it when he growled the order to do so, then waited patiently as he carried her inside, kicking the door closed behind them. However, the moment he stopped beside the bed, she kicked her legs and asked him to set her down.

Cullen hesitated long enough that she thought he would refuse, but then he reluctantly set her on her feet. The moment he did, Evelinde dropped to her knees before him and began examining his legs for burns.

"What are ye doing?" Cullen asked, trying to step away.

Evelinde hooked one arm around his leg to hold him in place and continued her inspection, even going so far as to lift his plaid to check his upper legs and thighs.

"Wife!" He tried to brush her hands away, and she glanced up, surprised to see that the man was actually blushing at her efforts.

"I wish to be sure you suffered no burns when you landed in the flames," she explained, and pushed his plaid up again, surprised to find a growing erection staring back at her. While her interest was purely out of concern for his well-being, it appeared Cullen was finding it all rather . . . interesting.

Shaking her head, Evelinde continued to peer over his skin, crawling around him to check the back as well. She had just lifted the back of the plaid and noted that he really had a very nice bottom when Cullen appeared to reach his limit. Turning swiftly, he caught her under the arm and dragged her back to her feet, his expression exasperated.

"I am no burned," he growled. "And I am more concerned with you at the moment. Ye breathed in a lot of smoke. Does yer chest hurt?"

"Nay," she assured him solemnly, then couldn't resist grinning and adding, "Would you care to check me for burns?"

Cullen's mouth dropped open at the bold invitation, then he shook his head on a reluctant laugh as he pulled her into his arms for a hug. The chuckle ended on a sigh as he rested his chin on her head, and said, "Yer going to be the death of me, wife."

Evelinde's own smile faded at the soft words as fear claimed her that she might indeed be the death of him did such "accidents" continue. While the fire suggested she was the target, Cullen could have been killed today trying to save her from it. Had she not had the bucket of water inside the room, they would both have been trapped in the smoke-filled chamber. Evelinde was sure he couldn't have leapt back through the burning rushes carrying her, and was equally sure he would have tried rather than leave her there to stay and smother to death in the thickening smoke. She had no doubt Cullen would have saved her, but he could very well have burned himself badly doing so, and burns often ended in infection and death.

"Have I told ye yet today how much ye please me fer a wife?"

Evelinde stilled at those soft words and leaned back to peer at him. Something about the softness in his eyes made the breath catch in her throat. She thought it might be more than the simple caring of a husband for his wife.

"What the devil happened here?"

"Where is my lady?"

Evelinde and Cullen both glanced toward the closed bedchamber door at the startled cries from the hall. It seemed Mildrede and Tavis had returned from their first trip to remove rushes. Not that they would have to make many more trips, she supposed wryly. The rushes were now a pile of charred and soggy ashes on the solar floor. A frown claimed her lips as she wondered if the floor would now need repairing.

A sigh from Cullen drew her attention back to him as he eased her away and turned toward the door.

Evelinde started to follow, but he paused at the door and glanced back to order, "Stay put. I shall send a bath up to ye."

Evelinde scowled at the door when he pulled it closed. She was reaching to open it when she heard Cullen begin shouting in the hall. He was giving Fergus and Tavis the sharp side of his tongue for not staying with her but leaving her to work in the solar alone. She considered going out to explain that she'd told them there was no need, but then thought better of it. Cullen wouldn't see that as a good excuse for their not following his orders. He blamed the men, and nothing she said was going to change that. In fact, Evelinde suspected her intervention would just annoy him further and make it worse for the men.

Sighing, she turned away from the door and moved back to the chair to await her bath.

"No one went above stairs," Fergus repeated for the fourth time. "The torch must have fallen out by itself."

"It didna fall out by itself," Cullen growled with frustration.

"But no one went above stairs," the older man insisted. "I was watching the whole time."

"Ye didna look away even fer a minute?" Cullen asked grimly.

"Nay," Fergus assured him.

"Well . . ." Both men paused and glanced to Tavis as he spoke the word. The man cast an apologetic glance to Fergus, then pointed out, "Ye did come help with the door."

Fergus's shoulders sagged, and he ran one hand wearily through his hair. "They both had their hands full with the rushes, so I hurried over to the door to open it for them," he admitted on a sigh, then rallied and added, "but that only took a moment, surely not enough time for someone to get upstairs without me noticing."

"Apparently it was," Cullen growled, furious that the man had failed him like this. Fergus was usually the most dependable of men. It was why he had been first for so long, first to Cullen's father, then for himself.

"Well, they could not have got up *and* down in that time," Fergus pointed out, sounding frustrated. "It had to have been an accident."

"They could have waited up here and slipped away while I was in the room, and you were below fetching water," Cullen pointed out.

The point did not please the man. He shook his head stubbornly, and insisted, "It had to have been an accident. I cannot believe anyone would—"

"It wasna an accident," Cullen interrupted furiously, then added, "In future, whoever is guarding my wife is to remain in the room with her, or follow wherever she goes. Understood?"

"Aye," Fergus and Tavis said as one.

Cullen let his breath out on a pent-up sigh. He wasn't satisfied. Evelinde had nearly died, and it was leaving him with an urge either to make love to her and hold her close for a good several hours or, alternately, to smash something. Unfortunately, Mildrede had rushed off to the chamber to see that her mistress was all right as soon as he'd begun yelling at the men, and the servants even now were trudging up the stairs with the tub and water he'd ordered before laying into Tavis and Fergus for allowing this to happen. Making love to his wife was out, and as much as he'd like to, striking one or both of the men before him was not an acceptable choice at the moment either. Angry as he was, he might very well kill one or both of them.

He needed an outlet, however, and turned abruptly away from the men to head for the stairs. A rant with Mac, then a hard ride on his mount should help him use up some of the heated blood pouring through his veins, Cullen thought, but paused and scowled with frustration as he realized he couldn't get down the stairs until the women got up them with the tub.

His angry glare was on the women as he waited impatiently, but then it turned to a concerned frown as he noted the struggle the women were having with the tub. It was taking four of them to cart the item, which made negotiating the stairs with it a tricky business, and Cullen suddenly recalled his wife's claiming that a couple of men to work in the keep would ease the burden somewhat. It would only have taken two men to handle the tub, which would have speeded up the process and made it less difficult.

As he was thinking about the matter of men in the castle, Cullen was recalling the last time they'd had boar for sup. The beast had been spice and cooked on the spit, then stuffed and presented on one large platter. It had taken six women to bring the beast out, and the animal had landed in the rushes when one of the women stumbled and the tray tipped and the carcass slid off. They'd quickly stopped and replaced the beast on the tray and continued forward, and the meal had still been good, but they'd had to pick off the pieces of rushes and other unsavory bits that had stuck to the animal after the fall.

Men to help with the heavier kitchen tasks might have saved such an accident. It also would have freed the women to serve the other dishes more quickly. And really, having three or four men in the castle to help with such tasks would hardly leave him lacking men to train, and the men could take turns at it; a day in the castle, three or four at practice perhaps. His wife's suggestion really was a good one he admitted reluctantly. He would have to arrange it.

"I wish to take a bath and cannot do so with the two of you standing there watching," Evelinde repeated with exasperation, finding it impossible to believe her husband had really ordered the men to stay in the same room with her. What had he been thinking? Obviously, he hadn't been thinking at all when

he'd given that order. At least he hadn't been thinking about the fact that he'd ordered a bath for her as
well. Good Lord! Were the two men going to crowd
into the privy with her when she needed to use it?

Evelinde tried to push that thought out of her
mind the moment it entered. Just thinking about it
was likely to make her need to relieve herself, then
she'd be in a real pickle.

"The laird ordered that we are to stay in the same
room with ye," Fergus repeated stubbornly. He was
looking a bit angry and annoyed at the whole business. Obviously, he was displeased with getting into
trouble and unwilling to risk disobeying Cullen's
order. Tavis, on the other hand, was grinning like
an idiot at the idea of her having to bathe in front
of them.

"Now, this is just folly," Mildrede said with exasperation, weighing into the fray. "You cannot stand
there while she bathes."

"And we cannot leave," Fergus said firmly. "She
will just have to wait until Cullen returns to bathe."

"Oh, that would be a waste," Tavis protested. "The
water will get cold, and after the ladies worked so
hard at heating and bringing it up here."

Evelinde scowled at her husband's cousin, knowing he didn't care a fig for all the work the women
had put into preparing the bath. Otherwise, he
would have helped carry up the bloody tub. Shifting impatiently, she headed for the door, asking,
"Where is my husband?"

When she got no answer, Evelinde glanced back
to see that while they were following her, their ex-

pressions suggested they had no idea where the man had gone. Shaking her head with exasperation, she pulled the door open and sailed out of the room, aware that the men were still following. Evelinde paused at the top of the stairs, her gaze sliding over the great hall below with irritation. She'd hoped to find him below dealing with some business or other, but he was absent from the nearly empty room and could be anywhere. He might have been in the bailey, the stables, working in the practice field or he may even have left the castle. How annoying!

Evelinde stood at the top of the stairs, undecided as to what to do. Then she nodded firmly to herself and swung back around. Fergus and Tavis broke apart to make way for her and followed as she moved quickly back along the hall, but when she reached her room, Evelinde opened the door just enough to slip inside, then slammed it quickly closed as the men realized what she was doing and rushed forward. She barely managed to slam the bar into place before they thumped against the other side of the wooden panel.

"Me lady!" Fergus snapped from the hall. "Open this door! We are not to let you out of our sight."

"I shall open the door as soon as I have finished my bath," Evelinde announced serenely as she started across the room toward the tub, where Mildrede was chuckling softly as she checked the temperature of the bathwater.

"Oh, now, Evie," Tavis wheedled, making Evelinde's eyebrows rise at the use of the nickname only Mac had ever used. "Ye'll be getting us in trouble. Open the door, lass, and let us in. We promise not to look."

Evelinde snorted at the claim as she quickly began to strip off her gown. She would have believed that Fergus might not look, but Tavis? Not likely. The man was as ruttish as a bull and with every single female around as far as she could tell. There didn't appear to be a woman the man didn't like. She'd seen him with the young, the not so young, blondes, redheads, brunettes, and women with ebony hair. She had seen him with thin women, large women, and every size in between. She suspected he was trying to fill the void left by his mother's apparent withdrawal when he was young, but couldn't be sure. And it mattered little anyway. He would never be able to fill that void by hopping from woman to woman.

"In you get, love," Mildrede murmured as she finished helping Evelinde to remove her gown and chemise.

Thanking Mildrede for her help, Evelinde stepped into the tub, releasing a little sigh as the warm water closed around her soot-stained skin. The temperature was perfect, and it would have been a lovely bath were it not for the continued bellowing and shouts from the men in the hall.

Really, their increasing volume and panic over her refusal to let them in rather ruined the whole experience for her. Grimacing, Evelinde moved quickly through her bath, washing away the soot covering her as swiftly as she could. Apparently she wasn't the only one to find their bleating annoying. She had never known Mildrede to wash her hair so quickly, and it seemed like just moments before Evelinde was hurrying out of the tub, running a dry linen over herself, then donning clean clothes.

" 'Tis well past time we sort out all these accidents and who is causing them," Mildrede said grimly as she helped Evelinde with her laces. "I think I shall ask some questions myself. Perhaps I can learn something of use from the other maids here."

"Nay," Evelinde said sharply. "I shall not have you endangering yourself that way."

"But—"

"Nay," Evelinde repeated firmly. "Leave it to me. I shall figure it out and sort the matter myself."

Mildrede's mouth tightened, but she didn't argue further, and Evelinde moved toward the door. Her hair was still damp and needed brushing, but she was bathed and dressed, and that would have to do. She could not stand the noise Fergus and Tavis were making for another moment. If they were so determined not to let her out of their sight, they could stand about and watch the less-than-titillating show of her brushing her hair by the fire to dry it. No doubt it would be like watching wheat grow for them, Evelinde thought, and hoped it bored them to tears.

It was midday when Evelinde finished drying her hair and led the way below to the great hall. Mildrede had a small smile of amusement on her face as she descended the stairs next to her, but she was the only one of their group enjoying herself. Fergus and Tavis had paced about her room, sighing repeatedly and loudly as they'd waited for her to finish with her hair. Evelinde herself was finding their presence less than enjoyable. If her husband had been below when she stepped off the last step, she would have had a word or two for the man.

However, he was nowhere in sight. Evelinde released a heavy sigh and started toward the head of the high table for the nooning meal. She had crossed perhaps half the distance when the great hall doors opened, drawing her gaze. Evelinde stopped abruptly on seeing Tralin Comyn entering, and nearly tumbled forward to the rushes when one of the men didn't stop quickly enough and crashed into her back.

"For heaven's sake," she said with exasperation when someone quickly caught her to keep her on her feet, and she turned to see that Tavis was the culprit. "There is no need to walk on my heels. I am not going to run off anywhere."

"Sorry," Tavis muttered, appearing amused despite the word.

Clucking under her tongue with irritation, Evelinde turned away and crossed toward Tralin rather than her seat.

"Good day, my lord," she greeted. "My husband is not here at the moment, but I am sure he shall return soon."

"Aye." Tralin smiled. "Mac said Cullen had gone out for a ride when he took my mount. He thought he should return soon, too."

Evelinde felt her mouth tighten with irritation. It did appear everyone else seemed to know things she didn't, and truly it was annoying. Would it really have been such an effort for Cullen to have sent someone to tell her he was going for a ride?

Shaking the thought away, she said, "Well, you are welcome to join us for the nooning meal while you wait."

"I did not realize it was so late in the day when I left," Tralin said apologetically. "But, aye, if 'twould be no trouble, I would be pleased to join ye in a meal."

"'Tis no trouble at all," Evelinde assured him, slipping her arm through his to guide him to the head table. In truth, she was glad to have the opportunity to speak to the man.

"Mac also told me there was some trouble this morning," Tralin said quietly, as they settled at the table. His gaze slid over her. "Ye appear to have come through well enough."

"Oh, aye, I am fine," she assured him, pausing to scowl at Tavis as he settled himself so close next to her that he sat on the skirt of her gown. Tavis merely grinned and shifted a little to tug the skirt out from under him as Fergus took a seat on his other side.

"'Tis not the first bit of trouble ye've had since arriving," Tralin murmured, reclaiming her attention. "Cullen told me about the paddock, the arrow in the tree, and your fall down the stairs when the two of ye last visited at Comyn."

Evelinde hesitated, then said carefully, "I appear to be troubled with accidents of late."

"Cullen didn't appear to believe they were accidents," Tralin said solemnly. "'Tis why I rode over today. I thought to come to the two of ye and be sure all is well."

Evelinde's mouth tightened. He'd come to see if all was well, only to discover there had been another accident. "We are fine," she finally said. "Fortunately, whoever is causing these accidents appears to be rather ham-handed since none of the attempts has succeeded."

It had been an offhand comment, one to ease her own discomfort, but the effect it had on the men on either side of her was interesting. Tralin looked startled and concerned, while Tavis gave a burst of laughter that drew several eyes their way. Fergus, on the other hand, was scowling.

" 'Tis that attitude that will get ye killed, me lady," Fergus growled with irritation. "Ye've been lucky so far, but do ye no let us guard ye as we've been ordered to do, ye may find yerself no so lucky with the next attempt."

Evelinde rolled her eyes at the reprimand, then, catching the curious arching of an eyebrow Tralin was giving her, she explained, "Fergus is just upset because I wouldn't let him and Tavis watch me bathe."

Tralin's jaw dropped at her words, then he grinned at the older soldier. "Why, Fergus, ye ruttish devil. I'd expect that of Tavis, but no of you."

"Cullen ordered us to stay with her at all times," the man snapped, his face reddening. "But she tricked us into leaving the chamber and locked us out."

"I am sure my husband did not mean for you to oversee my bath," Evelinde said calmly.

"He—" Fergus began, but fell silent as several women rushed from the kitchens and paused before them with platters of food.

"Thank you," Evelinde murmured as she peered over the selection and chose some meat and cheese. They all fell silent as they began to eat, but when Evelinde felt Tralin's shoulder shaking as it brushed against her own, she glanced over to see him silently laughing, his face wreathed in amusement as he glanced at a still-disgruntled Fergus.

Tavis, she saw, was also looking rather amused. Evelinde smiled faintly herself, then her gaze slid down to one of the lower tables, where Mildrede had seated herself, and her smile faded away to concern as she noted the concentration on her maid's face as Mildrede nodded and listened to the old woman seated beside her. Evelinde was suddenly quite sure that—despite her ordering her not to—the maid was trying to find out what she could in an effort to put an end to these accidents. Evelinde understood her desire to do so, but really had no wish for the woman to endanger herself by drawing the attention of the culprit behind them. However, she knew the only way to stop her was to resolve the matter herself.

Biting her lip, she glanced to Tralin again, noting absently that he was really quite handsome. His easy smile and sparkling eyes were most attractive. However, while her own husband rarely smiled, his features were more noble and . . . well, she found Cullen more attractive for some reason. Perhaps because she had come to care for him, Evelinde acknowledged.

Despite her frustration over the lack of communication between them, his actions really did seem to speak louder than words at times. Ordering the men to stick with her every minute—while annoying—was also really quite sweet and showed a caring and concern she thought she'd seen on his face when he'd told her that she pleased him as wife. His expression had seemed to be . . . well, loving. It gave her heart hope, for Evelinde feared she might very well be falling in love with her husband. Although, if she were to be perfectly honest with herself, she suspected she was not falling so much as already there. And really, she had no idea how that had happened. While she enjoyed his kisses and caresses, found an excitement beyond anything she'd heretofore experienced when he bedded her, and was often and repeatedly touched by his consideration and kind acts . . . Evelinde also found Cullen somewhat frustrating because she often learned about these kindnesses through someone else or after the fact when it was rather too late to appreciate them.

"That was a heavy sigh."

Evelinde glanced to Tralin with a start, then forced a smile. "I was just thinking."

"They must be heavy thoughts to have produced such a sigh," he murmured.

She considered him briefly, then glanced around the room, becoming aware that most people had finished eating and were leaving the great hall. There were few still seated. Mildrede had left the table and was now mounting the stairs to the second level, no doubt to see how much damage the fire had done in the solar, she supposed. Tavis had left his seat and was presently flirting with one of the maids clearing away the lower tables. Even Fergus had left the table and now stood talking to Gillie by the keep doors, no doubt giving him instructions about something. Despite the fact that he was talking to Gillie, the man's eyes were on her, she noted, and her mouth flattened with displeasure. She suspected she would have eyes on her every moment of the day until she resolved the matter of who was behind these accidents and the deaths in the past.

Turning back to Tralin, she announced, "Cullen and I stopped at the cliff where Jenny is buried on our return from Comyn the other day."

Tralin raised an eyebrow, curiosity clear on his face. "Oh?"

"Aye. He said you fancied Biddy's sister, Jenny, when she visited here."

A slow grin broke out on his face. "And ye wish to ken if he fancied her, too."

"Nay," Evelinde assured him quickly. "I just wondered if 'twere true."

He considered her with raised eyebrows for a moment and nodded. "Aye, I fancied her."

Evelinde was trying to figure out how to ask if he'd been her lover when he added, "No that it did me any good. She had eyes for another."

"Another?" she asked with interest.

"Darach."

Evelinde stiffened, her eyebrows rising. "Biddy's husband?"

"Aye." Tralin laughed at her expression, then explained, "Darach was—Actually, he was much like Tavis is now," he said with a shrug, his gaze sliding to the man.

Evelinde followed his gaze to see that Tavis was whispering something in the maid's ear that had her blushing and giggling.

"He was very similar in looks, too," Tralin continued. "Darach was fair-haired and handsome as Tavis is, and even more charming if you can imagine it."

Evelinde narrowed her gaze on Tavis as he slid an arm around the maid and drew her against him as he continued at her ear, though it was hard to tell if he were speaking or nuzzling the lass. The maid was looking a bit dazed, and Evelinde actually felt sorry for the girl, sure she was finding his attentions somewhat overwhelming. The man was definitely comely, and more than charming when he tried. She'd seen him working that charm on a few occasions since the men had arrived with the wagon. Just the night before, Evelinde had watched him tease, and flatter, and whisper to one of the maids she'd thought was more sensible until the girl allowed him to lead her to a quiet corner for more than talk. It looked to her as if this maid would hold up no better against his charms.

"Tavis causes quite a stir among the women, but Darach—" Tralin shook his head "He had every single female who came into his presence aflutter;

from the very youngest to the oldest. How could a youth like I compete with that?"

Evelinde turned her gaze back to Tralin to see the wry expression on his face as he shook his head, and continued, "I was just a callow youth to Jenny compared to Darach's attentions. He teased and flattered her, and she soaked up every word like a flower desperate for attention."

"And Biddy did not mind?" Evelinde asked slowly, wondering for the first time if Darach *were* the lover. If he were, he had been a despicable cur, taking advantage of a young noblewoman like that. Not to mention his own sister-in-law.

"Nay." Tralin waved the thought away. "She knew it was all teasing. We all did. Although, I think Jenny might have been naive enough to believe every word he said. As much as she thought herself so much older and more sophisticated than Cullen and I—we were a whole year younger than she," he added, rolling his eyes. "In truth, she was terribly naive."

"She was only fifteen then?" Evelinde asked with a frown.

"Aye," Tralin said, and shook his head sadly. "And a young fifteen. She never would have survived marriage to the Campbell."

Evelinde nodded, and murmured, "Cullen mentioned that she was betrothed to marry him."

"Aye. I doona ken what her father was thinking agreeing to the match." He shook his head, but then added cynically, "Or, actually, perhaps I do. The man was imagining all that Campbell wealth and the powerful connections that the marriage would bring him. 'Tis no wonder the lass killed herself."

Evelinde considered that, her gaze sliding to Tavis, who was seated on the bench where the maid had been working. She was no longer working, however, but was seated in his lap, her arms around his neck, the rag she'd been cleaning the table with trailing down his back as he kissed her most thoroughly and eased one hand up her skirt.

Evelinde turned her glance quickly away, shaking her head at the man's idea of guarding her. Fergus was still watching her closely, of course, but . . . Her gaze slid back to Tavis, and she frowned. She had no difficulty believing Tavis might think nothing of charming his way under an unmarried noblewoman's skirts . . . if he thought at all before doing such things. Evelinde suspected the man didn't think at all, at least not with his head. And if Darach was as Tralin described . . .

Turning back to Tralin, she asked, "You are sure Tavis's father would have left Jenny alone?"

Tralin frowned at the question, and for one moment she saw uncertainty flicker on his face, but then he shook his head. "Nay. Darach was a bit of a rogue and liked to lift the skirts of the willing servant or wench, but he would never have dallied with a young noblewoman. And he would hardly ruin his own wife's sister. Biddy would have killed him did he try."

chapter

Fifteen

*B*iddy would have killed him did he try.

Evelinde stared at the crack of light coming through the window a couple of feet from the bed and yawned wearily. She hadn't slept well last night. Her mind had been taken up with what she'd learned from Tralin. Cullen had returned to the keep after Tralin had spoken those words, preventing her asking further questions, but it hadn't stopped Evelinde from thinking over everything she'd learned.

While Tralin had said he was sure Darach wouldn't have ruined Jenny by taking her as a lover, he hadn't appeared certain. The only thing that might suggest

Darach hadn't been Jenny's lover was that Tavis had told her that his father had ridden out of the bailey just before Jenny had gone for her walk the day she'd come back weeping and fled. However, it was possible Darach had ridden out and around the curtain wall to the cliffs. He could have been the girl's lover.

It didn't speak well of either Biddy's sister or husband if they were lovers, but if Darach was as bad as Tavis, Evelinde didn't think his conscience would trouble him much. She certainly didn't see much in the way of conscience in Tavis when it came to the way he dallied with the women here. He got what he could from each woman and went merrily on his way to the next like a bee flitting from flower to flower, uncaring of the havoc he left behind.

As for Biddy's sister, Jenny had been betrothed to a horrid man known for his cruelty and abuses. She may have been desperate enough to get involved with her sister's husband in a bid to save herself, or simply for a last grab at happiness before being forced into the marriage.

Evelinde could almost understand that herself. Her own behavior the day she'd learned she was to marry the Devil of Donnachaidh had been less than exemplary. She had let Cullen kiss and touch her in ways she still found difficult to believe. And she had justified it by using the horrid marriage she'd thought was in her future. Telling herself it was the only pleasure she might experience in her life. She couldn't even honestly say she would have pushed him away sooner had she known he was married, though she'd like to think she would have had she had a sister and he been her brother-in-law. And she wasn't even as young as Jenny had been.

Evelinde yawned again and sighed as she thought that a child like Jenny might be able to justify taking her sister's husband as a lover that way. She might even have hoped the man might somehow find a way to save her from the marriage.

She frowned at the possibilities floating around in her mind. Had Biddy found out her sister and husband were lovers? Was this one indiscretion she hadn't been willing to forgive Darach? And why had Jenny returned after leaving so abruptly? Had she even really killed herself. It was possible she'd felt bad about dallying with her sister's husband and killed herself, but it was also possible her death was just another murder covered up.

Biddy could have murdered Jenny and her husband after finding out about them, she supposed, but if so, why kill Cullen's father all those years later, she wondered. Had Cullen's father, Liam, somehow figured out what had happened all those years earlier, confronted her, and brought about his own death? Or perhaps that had simply been an effort to correct the injustice Biddy might have felt she'd caused by killing Darach while her son was too young to take over the position of laird. Her own son had been passed over due to Darach's premature death. She may have hoped the title would be passed on to her son rather than Cullen if she killed Liam.

As for Maggie, either the questions she'd asked

had made Biddy nervous enough to make her kill her, or Maggie had actually somehow stumbled onto the truth, bringing about her own death.

Evelinde scowled at her own thoughts. While it all made a sort of sense, she found it hard to see Biddy as a ravening murderer, running about killing off all those people; her own sister, her husband, her brother-in-law, and her nephew's wife. Besides, Evelinde liked Biddy and didn't want to believe the woman was trying to kill her.

She really had to sort the matter out and quickly, Evelinde decided, but just wasn't quite sure how. Talking to Biddy wasn't likely to get her any answers. The woman would either be insulted if she was innocent or just lie and deny everything if she was guilty.

Evelinde supposed she could try sneaking into Biddy's room when she wasn't around and seeing if there was something that would help her find out what had happened. Letters from Biddy to her sister and back, a diary . . . or maybe a written confession lying around, she thought dryly, and shifted impatiently in the bed. Still, it was worth doing.

"What has ye all upset?" The sleepy question sounded by her ear as Cullen cuddled up behind her, one arm slipping around her body.

"What makes you think I am upset?" Evelinde asked rather than answer, her hand covering his where it rested beneath her breast on top of the linens and furs.

"Because ye were sighing and huffing loud enough to wake me," he answered, and began to nuzzle her ear.

"I was not," Evelinde said a bit breathlessly, her eyes drooping closed as his lips moved over her neck.

"Aye, ye were," Cullen assured her, tugging down the linens and furs that covered her to expose her naked breasts to his seeking hand.

"Oh," Evelinde breathed, as his hand closed over one breast and he began to fondle her, his hips pressing more firmly forward so that she could feel the hardness growing between them.

"What were ye thinking about?" he asked, nibbling at her shoulder now.

Evelinde swallowed, finding it difficult to think while he was touching her so.

"Tell me," he insisted on a whisper, his hand leaving her breast briefly to slip between them to rearrange himself so that his hardness pressed between her legs and against her wet core.

Evelinde groaned as he then shifted his hips, rubbing himself across the bud of her excitement as his hand moved back to her breast.

"Tell me," Cullen repeated, plucking at her nipple as he continued to move his hips.

"About Jenny and Darach and whether they were lovers and Biddy didn't find out and kill them and—" Her words died abruptly as he suddenly stilled.

"Jenny and Darach?" he said blankly, and Evelinde twisted slightly so that she could see his face. He was looking stunned by the very suggestion.

"I know it seems unlikely," Evelinde said apologetically, "but Tavis said that Jenny was meeting a lover out on the cliffs, and Tralin suggested that Darach paid the girl a lot of attention and she seemed to have feelings for him. If Darach was like Tavis is with women, and if Jenny was really as naive as everyone thought . . ."

She didn't finish the words but let him come to his own conclusion, then added, "It may be a coincidence that Jenny died two weeks before the accident that killed Darach, but I find it hard to believe that she is not somehow involved. Both your father and little Maggie died in falls from the same cliff where she killed herself and was laid to rest."

Cullen was completely still and silent, but she could see the thoughts racing through his eyes, then suddenly he was rolling away from her and getting out of bed.

"Husband?" Evelinde frowned and tossed the linens aside to follow. She frowned again when she saw he was dressing, his expression grim. Biting her lip, she asked worriedly, "What are you going to do?"

"Leave it to me. I shall tend to it," Cullen said firmly as he fastened his plaid.

Evelinde worried her lip as she watched him don his sword and sgian dubh, then said, "Pray, husband, do not take this to Biddy. I may be completely wrong about all this and would not see her hurt until we are sure one way or the other."

"Leave it to me," Cullen repeated. When he saw the worry on her face, he frowned and moved before her to take her by the arms. "I'll not have ye fretting over this. Ye've suffered enough under all these attempts on yer life. I want ye happy and content wife. I love ye."

Evelinde's eyes widened, and her mouth dropped open at the blunt announcement, which was rather fortuitous because it meant Cullen didn't have to urge her mouth open when he bent to kiss her. It was a very quick but thorough kiss, then Cullen set her away and headed for the door. "Get dressed. I'll be sending the men up to watch ye the minute I get below."

Evelinde was still blinking over his words when the door closed behind him. He loved her. He'd said he loved her. Dear God, her husband loved her. She moved to the bed and dropped to sit on it, then in the next moment was popping back up and rushing to dress. Cullen was going to send up whoever was guarding her today the minute he got below, and once her guards were on her, there was no possibility she could search Biddy's room. Not that Evelinde thought she was likely to find anything of use in the woman's room. Still, it was worth trying.

She had her clothes on in a trice, and didn't bother with her hair except to pull it back. Hurrying to the door then, Evelinde eased it open and peered out into the hall, relieved to find it still empty. The men had not yet made their way above stairs. She was about to slip out of the room when the door to Biddy's room suddenly opened and she saw the little woman bustle out and head for the stairs. Fortunately, Biddy never even glanced in her direction.

Thanking her lucky stars that she hadn't already

been trying to creep into the woman's room when Biddy had come out, Evelinde waited until Biddy was out of view on the stairs, then slid from her own room, eased the door closed, and crept silently up the hall.

Cullen was in the solar, examining the floor. He'd been headed for the stairs when it occurred to him that Evelinde and Mildrede would probably wish to continue with their project to clean out the room. Suddenly worried the floor might not be stable after the fire, he'd changed direction and come to the solar instead, which was why he was on his haunches when he heard the door and saw Biddy bustle past. He didn't say anything to draw attention to his presence in the shadows of the room, but simply listened to her rapid tread as she hurried to the stairs and down.

He then lowered his gaze to the floor once more, but his mind was on what his wife had said in their room. Tavis thought Jenny had a lover? And Tralin thought the girl had had feelings for Darach?

It appeared he'd been a very unobservant lad, because Cullen hadn't seen any of this at the time. Though, now that his wife had said the words, he did recall that Jenny used to light up like a torch put to flame every time his uncle entered the same room. And he could recall his and Tralin coming upon her once when her cheeks had been flushed, her lips swollen, and her gown wrinkled, the lacings not properly done up. They'd even teased her about it at the time, suggesting she must have been kissing one of the squires though they hadn't really believed it. As pretty as she'd been, Jenny always seemed so prim and snobby that Cullen found it difficult to imagine anyone wanting to kiss her. She really appeared to be a proper little thing. He was sure she never would have been caught riding around in nothing but a wet chemise, her horse's reins in her mouth and her wet gown held overhead to dry.

The memory of his first sight of his wife made Cullen smile. Evelinde, he was sure, was special, unlike any other woman in the world. She chattered away like a child one moment and snapped at him like a harpy the next, but when he kissed her, she melted like butter on a warm bit of bread. She was everything he could have wished for in a wife if he'd taken the time to worry about such things before marrying her. His only hope at the time he'd agreed to the wedding was a woman he could bear to live with, but Evelinde was much more than that, she was a woman he could, and did, love.

Cullen just wished he hadn't blurted the words out to her this morning as he had. He hadn't meant to. That had just happened. Unfortunately, Evelinde's response had been less than flattering. Her eyes had gone wide and her mouth had dropped and she'd stood there staring at him as if he'd suddenly sprouted horns. Cullen had then kissed her just to keep her from saying something he might not want to hear, but knew he'd have to hear her response eventually. He wasn't foolish enough to hope the woman loved him in return. As she had pointed out more than once, she hardly knew him thanks to his

tendency not to speak. That was something he supposed he should do something about.

First, however, he had to unravel the matter of who
was trying to kill her, Cullen thought, and what she'd
said that morning had turned his suspicions firmly
in Biddy's direction. He stood slowly, considering
the matter. Asking his aunt questions wasn't likely
to get him anywhere, but a talk with Lady Comyn
might shed some light on things. She hadn't visited
as often then as she had when his mother was alive,
but she had visited a couple of times while Jenny
was at Donnachaidh and might have picked up on
a thing or two.

He could also search Biddy's room, Cullen supposed, and see if there was anything in there that
might help him solve this matter. Although he
couldn't imagine what that might be. Still, he knew
Biddy wasn't in there at the moment, and it wouldn't
hurt to look around . . . but first he had to wring his
lovely wife's neck, Cullen thought, as Evelinde suddenly crept past the open door of the solar.

Evelinde was concentrating so hard on her feet
to keep from making a sound that she—like Biddy
before her—didn't even cast a glance into the solar
where he stood. If she had looked his way, what
she would have seen was one very angry husband.
Cullen had made it very clear that she was not to
go anywhere without her guards, yet here she was,
creeping about.

Cullen moved silently forward to follow his wife's
progress. His eyebrows rose when she paused at
Biddy's door and slid silently inside. It seemed he

wasn't the only one who'd thought to examine his aunt's room. It was no wonder he liked his wife, Cullen decided. It seemed obvious they thought much alike.

Shaking his head, he stepped out of the solar, intending to follow Evelinde and probably scare the goodness out of her by entering while she was inside. He'd feel bad about that prospect, except that it was little more than she deserved for putting herself at risk by creeping around on her own when she knew someone was trying to kill her. If she didn't care for her own well-being, she could at least consider his feelings in the matter. He loved the woman and had no desire to experience life without her. That was odd, he supposed. Until a very short time ago, he couldn't have imagined life with a woman like her, and before meeting her, his life had seemed just fine, not horrible or lonely, but . . . fine. Now, however, he knew that life would be a much gloomier, unhappy existence without her there.

Cullen had just stepped out of the solar when a sound by the stairs made him pause and swing back. His eyebrows rose with alarm when he saw Biddy stepping onto the landing and bustling toward him, obviously headed for her room.

Once safely inside Biddy's room, Evelinde leaned against the wall with a little sigh. This sneaking about business was all rather worrying.

Grimacing, she peered around the room, only to glance nervously toward the door as she thought she heard the murmur of voices from the hall. No doubt it was Gillie and Rory, or Tavis and Fergus, or perhaps some other combination of the men, sent up to guard her, Evelinde thought, then frowned as she realized that she had trapped herself nicely. With the men in the hall it would be impossible to leave unnoticed. That gave her pause. Why hadn't she considered that when she'd had this brilliant idea?

Sighing, Evelinde glanced back to the room. There was little she could do about the men now. She was here and might as well look around. If, by some chance, she did find something in the room to help sort out the past and what was happening now, Evelinde wouldn't care if the men saw her leaving the room and knew she'd been searching it.

That was her greatest hope at the moment. She was determined to resolve this matter. So far she'd gotten lucky and survived these attempts on her life relatively unscathed, but Cullen could have been seriously injured or even killed trying to save her from the fire, and she would not see the man in such a situation again. She loved him. And he loved her.

A small smile curved her lips. "I love ye," he'd said like he was saying he liked her hair. Leave it to her husband to announce it like he was telling her the time of day. The man was definitely not a romantic, but she could live with that. She could even live with his distressing refusal to speak much. However, she didn't think she could live without him in her life. Evelinde found she'd begun to depend on his silent strength and consideration.

She also had no desire to die before enjoying their love for a while . . . and perhaps having a babe or two. A little Cullen would please her. She would enjoy watching him grow into as fine a man as his father. Hopefully, her influence would make him a little more talkative, she thought with amusement, then turned her attention to the room.

What had Maggie discovered? Evelinde wondered as she peered around the chamber. It was a much smaller room than the one she shared with Cullen. There also wasn't much in it. A bed was pressed up against the far wall. There was a small table next to it with a half-used candle in an iron holder on it, and there was a bow and a quiver of arrows leaning up against one of three large chests against the wall at the foot of the bed.

Evelinde moved farther into the room, intending to start with the chests, but then paused and moved to the bed, some instinct making her kneel to peer under it. Despite having thought to look there, she was surprised to see something in the shadows underneath. Reaching in, she grabbed what felt like a leather bag and tugged it partially out, frowning when she saw that it was merely another quiver of arrows. Evelinde was about to push it back under the bed when she noticed the fletching on the arrows. Pausing, she drew it back out and examined them more closely. Each one was a combination of white and darker feathers in an alternating pattern. Just like the arrow in the chest in the chamber Evelinde shared with her husband. The one covered with dried blood, she recalled, and wondered what that might mean. It seemed obvious the arrow in the chest in their room was probably from this quiver.

But why was it in the chest, and whose blood was on it?

Shrugging the problem away for now, she slid the arrow back into the quiver and returned it under the bed, then stood and moved over to the second quiver leaning against one of the chests. A quick glance proved that the fletching in those arrows was all made up of darker feathers, probably goose, she thought. That was what was most commonly used.

Evelinde wasn't sure what the white feathers came from. Her guess would be that they were swan feathers, but those were rare to be found in an arrow. Not unheard of, but rare. At least they were in England. She wasn't surprised that Cullen's aunt had a bow and arrows. Biddy had mentioned that she liked to hunt for animals for her pot on occasion. It did surprise her that she had two different sets of arrows, however.

Shrugging that aside, Evelinde turned her attention to the chests. She knelt before the first one and opened it to find that it looked to be full of gowns. She quickly rifled through the clothing inside, doing her best not to disarrange the gowns too much and give away that they'd been searched. It slowed her down a little, but Evelinde wasn't yet sure that Biddy was guilty of anything and didn't wish to upset her unnecessarily . . . at least, not until she was sure.

When clothes were all she found in the first trunk, Evelinde eased the chest closed again and stood to move in front of the next of the three. The first held linens and pillows and other such items, but nothing more than that. Disappointed, she closed it and turned to the last chest. The moment she opened it, Evelinde let her breath out on a little sigh. This one immediately showed more promise. It held items obviously belonging to a male, Darach's things, she supposed, but more importantly, there was a stack of letters at the bottom of the chest.

Evelinde lifted them out and began to open them, feeling guilty for invading Biddy's privacy as she did but determined to learn what she could. There were many letters. Evelinde went through them quickly, but had nearly reached the bottom of the pile before she came across letters between Jenny and Biddy. She slowed then and actually began to read them.

The first letter was simply about Jenny's planned visit to Donnachaidh. Jenny had been excited at the prospect of seeing her older sister. It seemed Jenny had never been to Donnachaidh and Biddy's own visits back to her childhood home of MacFarlane, had been few and far between. Both seemed happy at the prospect of seeing each other.

The second letter was more of the same, but had been written much closer to the actual trip and the young woman's excitement and anticipation nearly leapt off the page.

It was the last note, however, that made Evelinde sit back on her heels to read more carefully rather than merely skim it. It was the last letter Jenny had ever written and the tone was much much different from the others. That Jenny had been weary and unhappy and the note was to tell Biddy that she was about to kill herself and why.

Evelinde let her breath out slowly as she closed the

letter. It was poignant and sad and so full of betrayal and hopelessness that tears had welled in her eyes as she'd read it. Closing the chest, she got wearily to her feet and tucked the letter into her pocket. She had to talk to Biddy, and this time she wouldn't let the older woman avoid answering her questions.

chapter

Sixteen

ullen stared at Biddy, watching her lips move as she spoke, but not really hearing her. He was too busy trying to figure out how to keep her from continuing on to her room. He'd managed to forestall her by asking if she had any suggestions on how he could remove the burn marks on the solar floor. Biddy had followed him back into the solar and been talking ever since. But he knew she would stop giving her various suggestions soon, and he would have to find another way to keep her from going into her room.

"That should work," Biddy finished finally, then glanced briefly toward the corner of the room where the wooden chandelier used to hang before forcing her gaze away and turning to the door. "I should return to the kitchens. I was just going to my room for a clean apron. Cook says we are out of pasties, and I thought I'd bake up a fresh batch."

"Nay," Cullen said firmly, stepping in front of her when she went to walk around him.

Biddy paused, eyebrows rising. "Nay?"

"Nay," he repeated, searched his mind frantically, then blurted, "I'm wanting ye to come to Comyns with me today."

"Comyns?" she asked with surprise.

"Aye. Someone's trying to kill me wife, and I'm wanting to get to the bottom of it. I need some questions answered about Jenny and Darach, and I hope that between you and Ellie Comyn, I can get those answers."

Biddy's head went back as if he'd slapped her. She also paled sickly. She didn't say a word, however, but hurried around him and out into the hall. Eyes wide with alarm, Cullen followed, but the woman moved surprisingly quickly for her age. She'd crossed the few steps to the door of her room and opened it before he could grab her back.

Cullen froze as the door slid open, waiting for Biddy to begin yelling, but all she said was, "I'll get me wrap for the trip."

The door closed behind her with a thud, and Cullen hesitated, uncertain whether to open it and go in, but there was no sound from inside to indicate that Evelinde had been discovered. There wasn't even a whisper. Frowning, he stepped closer to the door, listening intently, and that was how Biddy found him when she opened the door.

Straightening guiltily, he backed away.

"Afraid I was going to try to flee?" Biddy asked dryly as she stepped out of the room, then she shook her head as she donned her wrap and started up the hall toward the stairs. "I'm getting too old to bother with such nonsense, nephew. 'Tis time it all came out."

Cullen stared after her wide-eyed, those words sending a chill down his back. He had always liked his aunt Biddy. The woman made the best damned pasties in Scotland and used to sneak them to him and Tralin when they were younger. But her words just now weren't encouraging. He very much feared there really was something to Evelinde's theory.

Reminded of his wife, Cullen turned back to Biddy's door. Obviously, she'd hidden when she'd heard the door open. Thank God she'd had the sense to do that. He'd get Evelinde out of Biddy's chamber and back to their room before he gave her hell rather than risk his aunt returning and finding them in there. Afterward he would take her below and hand her over to Gillie and Rory to watch with the express order that they were not to let her out of their sight under threat of death . . . or at least some sort of horrible punishment. He would decide what when he was actually speaking to them, Cullen thought as he reached for the lever on the door.

"Are ye coming or not?"

Cullen let his hand drop and turned to see that his aunt hadn't continued downstairs as expected but had paused at the top and was now waiting impatiently for him to follow. He hesitated briefly, but then decided Evelinde would be safe enough making her way back to their room on her own, especially if his aunt was the culprit, as she seemed to be suggesting.

Turning away from the door, he followed Biddy below. Leaving her to walk to the stables without him, he paused just long enough to tell Gillie and Rory to guard his wife when she came below. And then, before he followed Biddy out to the stables, he explained quickly to Fergus that he was heading to Comyns and that Fergus would be in charge until he got back.

"What is this?"

Evelinde stopped brushing her hair and turned. Her eyes widened with alarm when she saw the paper her maid was taking out of the hanging pocket that was inside her skirt.

"Nothing," she said quickly, setting down her brush and crossing the room to retrieve the letter. Evelinde had returned to the chamber after leaving Biddy's room, grateful to find the hall empty of her usual guard. She'd heard voices from the solar as she'd passed and seen her husband in there talking to Biddy. Wishing to speak with her alone when she confronted her, Evelinde had decided to wash and change before seeking out her explanations, hoping that by then Cullen would have finished the discussion he was having with his aunt and left for his daily duties.

She'd made it safely back to the chamber and been undoing the laces of her gown when Mildrede had entered to help her dress and fix her hair. The maid had frowned at the gown Evelinde was wearing, thinking she was dressing rather than undressing. The woman had immediately begun to help Evelinde undress, chattering the whole while about her thinking to wear the gown from the day before and hadn't she folded and set the gown aside when she'd helped her disrobe last night? The nattering had only gotten worse when Evelinde had confessed that she hadn't even washed yet. Mildrede had then subjected her to a lecture about taking on the heathen ways of these Scots as she quickly got her out of her chemise and over to the basin of water to wash herself.

Evelinde had briefly debated explaining what she had been up to and why she was wearing her gown from the day before, but she really found herself reluctant to reveal what she'd found in her search of Biddy's room, at least until she'd spoken to the woman. She felt she owed her that much at least.

"Shall I put up your hair for you?" Mildrede asked.

Evelinde opened her mouth to say yes, then shook her head instead. She had washed and dressed while Mildrede had tended her clothes but felt her hair was fine down. She couldn't be bothered to take the time to fuss with it. Evelinde was eager to get the talk with Biddy over with.

"Nay, I shall wear it down today, I think."

Mildrede nodded, and said, "Come along then. You need to break your fast."

The letter gripped in her hand, Evelinde allowed her maid to usher her out of the room.

"You are late enough everyone has eaten and gone," Mildrede commented, as they descended the stairs. "Do you wish to eat at the table, or by the fire, where I can keep you company while I embroider?"

Evelinde's gaze slid to the tables where Gillie and Rory sat watching her descend the stairs, then to the two chairs that sat by the cold hearth and didn't even have to think about her answer.

"By the fire with you, but I shall fetch it, Mildrede," she added. "I should like a word with Aunt Biddy anyway."

Mildrede nodded silently and headed for the chairs by the fireplace as Evelinde headed for the door to the kitchens. She pushed into the steamy room, fully expecting to find Biddy there as usual, but the woman was absent.

"Oh, me lady! Ye'll be wanting to break yer fast."

Evelinde glanced toward the cook and offered a smile. The woman was red-faced and sweating and looking harassed, but then she had looked like this every time Evelinde had seen the woman since her return from her visit. Truly, Biddy appeared to run the kitchens much better than Cook, who seemed forever to be struggling under the burden.

"Go sit yerself down, and I'll send one of the lasses out with something," Cook said, waving her out of the kitchen.

"Thank you," Evelinde murmured, but didn't leave right away, instead pausing to ask, "Where is Biddy?"

Cook frowned and shrugged. "She was talking about making some of her fine pasties when she broke her fast, but hasna been here since. She'll be along betimes, I'm sure."

Nodding, Evelinde backed out of the kitchen and turned away, her gaze sliding to the men at the table. If they had been seated at the table since Cullen had gone below, no doubt they knew where Biddy had gone. At that, she was rather surprised that they had waited below at the tables rather than making their way above stairs to oversee her activity. It made her wonder if her husband had actually listened to her last night when she'd berated him about ordering the men to stay in the same room with her when she had personal things to do such as bathe, use the privy, and such. Cullen hadn't appeared to be listening at the time. He'd merely kissed her until she forgot what she was angry about and distracted her with other lovely diversions.

And then this morning he'd told her he loved her, she recalled, a smile tugging at her lips.

A burst of laughter drew her gaze to the men at the table, and she recalled the task she'd set herself. She needed to find and speak to Biddy, and the sooner the better. Shoulders straightening, she crossed to the tables. It was no longer just Rory and Gillie. While she'd been in the kitchen, Fergus had joined the two men, and they were all laughing softly at something as she approached.

"Have you seen Biddy?" Evelinde asked once she'd reached them.

The three men turned to peer at her.

"She left the keep just before the laird," Gillie informed her helpfully.

Evelinde was frowning over that when Fergus said quietly, " 'Tis Jenny's day."

She raised her eyebrows, shifting guiltily as she noted his curious gaze on the letter in her hand, then asked uncertainly, "Jenny's day?"

"The anniversary of her sister's death," he explained, his gaze shifting from the letter to her face. "Biddy always goes to take flowers to her grave on this day."

"Oh. Thank you," Evelinde murmured, and turned away, moving toward the chairs by the fire where she'd last seen Mildrede. The woman wasn't there anymore, but she'd left her embroidery behind, so should return soon Evelinde supposed a bit absently, her thoughts on Biddy. Evelinde was eager to talk to the woman, but not so eager she was willing to hunt her down at the cliffs. That was the last place she wanted to meet Cullen's aunt. His father and first wife had already died there, and Evelinde had no desire to chance making her own the third death on the spot.

She would just have to wait for Biddy to return, Evelinde supposed. Were she foolish enough to go out there and get herself killed, no doubt the blame for her own death would somehow land at Cullen's feet as well, Evelinde thought on a sigh. She paused as she suddenly realized that perhaps she *could* go looking for Biddy at the cliffs. After all, unlike Cullen's father and first wife, she would have Rory and Gillie to escort her. They should be able to keep her safe.

Pleased that she would not have to wait to confront the woman after all, Evelinde turned back to the tables, but her smile faltered when she saw that Fergus was alone at the table now. Her gaze slid to the doors of the great hall in time to see Rory and Gillie slip outside and the doors swing closed.

"Where are Gillie and Rory going?" she asked, moving back to the table.

"I'm no sure," Fergus admitted. "They just asked me if I'd keep an eye on ye for a few minutes. Why? Is there something ye need?"

Evelinde hesitated, unsure she should risk going out to the cliff with only one man, but then she felt rather silly. Biddy was an old woman. She might have taken Cullen's father by surprise, and might have won out against Maggie by herself, but surely both she and Fergus would be able to manage her?

"I killed Darach."

Cullen reined in sharply and glanced at his aunt at those softly spoken words. They hadn't been riding long and had done so in silence until she'd spoken that confession. The words had come out of the blue and hit him like a stone to the head. He stared at her with incomprehension for a moment, then asked, "Why? Ye loved the man. I ken ye did. Everyone knew it. Ye forgave him every slip with other women, every—"

"Aye well, he finally did something even I could not forgive," she said bitterly.

"Jenny?" Cullen asked, recalling Evelinde's suggestion that morning.

Biddy nodded, sorrow mingling with anger on her face before she turned away to peer over the hills ahead of them. "I didna have any idea at the time. Oh, I knew he flattered and teased her like the others, and perhaps I should have seen, but I never imagined . . . *My own little sister.*" She said the words with bewildered disgust.

"How did ye find out?" Cullen asked quietly.

"I didna until it was too late," she admitted. "I truly thought she'd killed herself rather than marry the Campbell, as everyone else thought. For two weeks I mourned. And all that time, Darach—" She shook her head. "He was so sweet. Always there to comfort me, always murmuring reassuring words that the lass was beyond Campbell's reach now and she was safe at least from that. I truly thought that was the proof of how wonderful he really was despite his wandering ways.

Biddy let her breath out on a little sigh, and added, "And then I found Jenny's letter. It must have been in the solar all that time, but I did not find it until I finally ventured back into the room to find the embroidery I'd been working on before she died. I read what Darach had done . . . to my own sister! 'Twas bad enough watching him sniffing after every other female around, but my sister?"

She ground her teeth and shook her head. "He

ruined her. Jenny was a child, and he treated her like a common whore. In her naivety she thought it was love, until the last time they were together he said some very cruel things, and she fled Donnachaidh." Biddy turned furious eyes to Cullen, and said, "The night she left, Darach actually had the spine to tell me that she'd taken all his teasing and flirting seriously and that he'd had to set her straight and explain to her that he loved me," she added bitterly. "He forgot to mention that he deflowered her first and bedded her several times more."

Cullen let his breath out on an unhappy sigh at her acid words.

"Jenny was so ashamed of what she'd done, she planned to keep the whole matter to herself," Biddy said sadly. "But when she realized she was with child—Darach's child—she knew there was no way to hide it from the Campbell. She fled here scared witless and desperate for Darach's help." Her mouth tightened, and she said, "Do ye ken what that heartless bastard did?"

Cullen shook his head.

"He said 'twas not his problem and that he would deny it was his if she tried to drag him into her shame. *Her shame*," she said furiously. "He said if she tried to come tell me the truth, he'd get three or four of his men to claim they were her lovers, and she was nothing more than a common whore."

Biddy took several deep breaths, obviously trying to calm herself, then continued sadly, "Jenny did not know what to do. She knew the church said taking her own life would see her in hell, but felt sure she was headed there anyway for betraying me, and so she killed herself."

"I'm sorry, Biddy," Cullen said quietly, and the face she turned to him was stark.

"I forgave him for so much, Cullen, for so many women . . . But I could not forgive him Jenny. I would not, not after I read that letter."

Biddy fell silent for a minute as she apparently reflected on the devastation Darach had wrought, then she sighed.

"I stormed below stairs, determined to confront the bastard, but you had all gone out to hunt boar." She ground her teeth. "I grabbed me bow and quiver, and rode out. I had no difficulty finding ye all. I trailed the hunting party, and when ye rode up on the boars and chaos broke out, I took me opportunity. I shot Darach as he fell, got him with the first try, and felt such peace when 'twas done."

Her expression was almost rebellious as she admitted that, but then Biddy sighed again, and continued, "It did not last long. By the time I got back to the keep the guilt had set in. It was almost a relief when ye men arrived back, and I learned he was no dead. I vowed I'd mend him, and at first he seemed to be improving, but . . ." She shook her head unhappily, and added, "In the end, I wasna able to save him."

Cullen stared at his aunt as the silence fell around them again. His feelings were a mixture of many emotions: pity for Jenny, grief at her abuse and wasted life, rage at his uncle for acting in such a callous and heinous way with his own wife's sister, and even pity for Biddy. Had he been the one to find that letter and read it, Cullen could not be at all sure that he himself might not have shot the bastard with an arrow. Surely, Darach had deserved to die for ruining Jenny and probably many other young noblewomen and others over the years. If her being so young and his sister-in-law—his responsibility while visiting— had not stopped him, then no woman had been safe from his unspeakable ways.

In that moment, Cullen might have assured his aunt she had done right and that they need never speak of the matter again . . . Except that Darach wasn't the only one dead. There were his father and little Maggie to consider, as well as the attempts on Evelinde's life.

Clearing his throat, he sat up a little straighter in the saddle, and asked, "And me father?"

"Liam?" Biddy glanced at him with confusion, then understanding crossed her face, and she shook her head. "I had nothing to do with that. I killed Darach, but I never would have harmed a hair on yer father's head. Liam was a good man. An honorable man. He loved yer mother. He never behaved as Darach did. Nay," she repeated firmly. "I did not kill him. I truly thought his death was an accident."

"Ye thought?" Cullen prompted.

"It was Maggie's death that made me wonder. She started asking questions about the deaths of yer father and Darach, and when she was found at the bottom of the cliffs, I wondered if Liam's death had been an accident after all," she admitted. "I won-dered if perhaps it had been murder, and her questions made someone nervous. It seemed too much of a coincidence that they both died from plunging off the cliff where Jenny was laid to rest."

Cullen nodded silently. That was exactly what Evelinde had said that morning.

"And then," Biddy continued, "when the accidents began happening to Evelinde, I could not but worry. I have been trying to think who could have killed Liam and little Maggie."

"Did you come up with anyone?" Cullen asked, but she shook her head.

"Nay. I simply do no understand why anyone would have killed Liam. Ye're the only one who benefited from his death."

He was just stiffening at those words when she hurried to add, "But I ken ye loved yer father, Cullen. Ye would ne'er have killed him. Ye were fond of little Maggie, too, and wouldna have harmed her either. But even if I had doubted that, I ken beyond a shadow of a doubt that ye love yer Evelinde and most surely would not be trying to kill her."

Cullen relaxed, but asked, "How did ye ken I love Evelinde?"

Biddy smiled faintly. It was a small smile, but the first she'd worn since he'd encountered her in the hall. "Lad, yer love is plain to see in yer eyes every time ye look at the lass."

He smiled faintly now himself and nodded, his mind turning to the question of who could be behind his father's and Maggie's deaths as well as the attacks on Evelinde.

"Do ye believe me?"

Cullen glanced to his aunt in question.

"That I didna kill Liam or Maggie and am not responsible for Evelinde's accidents," she explained. "I know ye thought I was when ye brought me out here, but do ye believe me now that I—"

"I believe ye," he interrupted, and it was true. Cullen did believe her. Biddy was not the sort of woman who could kill in the normal course of events. He suspected that had she had a chance to think after reading her sister's letter, she would not have killed Darach then. But she had done so in a fit of passion. There wouldn't have been that same rage and passion with his father, and certainly not with little Maggie. Nay, she hadn't killed Liam or Maggie . . . which meant there was still a killer at Donnachaidh trying to make him a widower.

"Come," Cullen said, and turned his horse back the way they'd come. He suddenly wanted to get back and make sure Evelinde was safe. While he had solved a part of the puzzle that was the past and found one killer, there was another more dangerous one yet about.

"Nephew."

The firm tone of her voice made him rein in and glance back. Biddy was eyeing him solemnly, and asked, "What will ye do with me now?"

Cullen hesitated, a frown claiming his lips. He wanted to tell her that he would do nothing, that Darach had reaped what he'd sown, but he had a responsibility as laird to uphold justice and wasn't sure he could do that.

"I am no sure," he admitted finally. "I need to think on it."

Biddy peered at him silently for a moment, then nodded and urged her horse forward.

"Yer a good laird," Biddy told him quietly as she rode past him back toward the keep. "Ye'll sort it out, and I shall accept yer decision. In truth, 'twill be a relief finally to be punished fer what I did."

Cullen didn't say anything as they rode back, but it occurred to him that Biddy had been punishing herself for the past seventeen years for killing her husband. She'd withdrawn from those she loved, banished herself to the kitchens, and refused any and all of the little luxuries that had been her right all those years. It hadn't gone without his notice that her bedroom was small and cramped and that she'd put away all her fine linens and pillows long ago, sleeping in a small, hard bed in a room as austere as a monk's cell. She also rarely purchased cloth to make new gowns, and when she did, what she chose was never the more luxurious weaves or fiber, but cloth as coarse and cheap as a lady could dare wear without shaming her family.

Aye, Cullen thought, Biddy probably would be relieved to be punished. Then she could stop doing it herself. He just wished he was not the one who had to decide what that punishment should be. It was times like these he wished his father were still alive to take on the burden of laird.

They rode back to the keep much more quickly than they'd ridden out. Cullen had set a slow and steady pace on the way out, thinking that they would have the long ride to Comyn and back to contend with and not wishing to tax his aunt by racing there and back. But now that the long ride was unnecessary, he urged his mount to travel at speed, checking every once in a while to be sure that Biddy was having no difficulty keeping up.

Once in the bailey, he steered his mount to the stables, and Biddy followed. However, in his eagerness to reach the keep and check on Evelinde, Cullen left his mount for Scatchy's daughter to tend while Biddy stayed behind to see to her own horse.

He crossed the bailey quickly, but Cullen's thoughts were distracted enough that he had nearly reached the keep before he noted Gillie and Rory talking to Mac at the foot of the steps. He gave a nod of greeting to the old man as he came to a halt, then turned a scowl on the two younger ones. "What are ye two doing here? Yer supposed to be watching me wife."

"Rory and I were beginning to fall asleep in the great hall so Fergus said we could take a turn out here. He said he'd watch her if we wished to stretch our legs for a few minutes. It gets fair boring sitting in there all the time, so we took the opportunity," Gillie explained apologetically.

Cullen scowled at this news but could hardly fault them. Fergus was his first, and he'd left him in charge while he was gone. Part of the man's job was giving the men rest if they appeared to be lagging. A man would hardly be alert when he was falling asleep, and 'twas better an alert man on guard than a weary one, slow to notice trouble and equally slow to react.

Nodding, he turned to continue on to the keep.

"Me laird?"

Cullen paused and glanced back. "Aye?"

The men exchanged a glance, then Rory asked, "Did Biddy's sister no die in autumn?"

"Biddy's sister?" he asked, startled to hear them mention the woman he'd just spent so much time talking about. Gillie and Rory were ten years younger than he. He was surprised they even recalled the woman.

"Aye," Rory said. "I helped Biddy take some flowers out to the cliff last autumn because she said it was the anniversary of her Jenny's death. But Fergus told Evelinde that Biddy was at the cliffs and that today was the anniversary of her death."

"He's mistaken. Yer right, Jenny died in the fall, no summer," Cullen said, and shook his head with exasperation. He was sure he'd mentioned to Fergus that he was taking Biddy with him to Comyns. Apparently, the man had forgotten that.

"I thought so," Rory said with satisfaction, and elbowed Gillie. "I told ye the old man was losing his wits to age."

Cullen grimaced, worried that he'd soon have to find himself a new first if the man's memory was slipping away. Did he not have enough problems at the moment? he thought with irritation, then shrugged the worry away and—eager to see his wife—continued on his way up the stairs.

Mildrede was coming out of the kitchen as Cullen

entered the keep, but other than that, the great hall was empty. Frowning, he glanced at the maid. "Where is me wife?"

Mildrede's eyebrows rose—probably at his sharp tone of voice rather than the question itself—and she gestured back the way she'd come. "She left through the kitchen door some moments ago. She is not alone," the woman added quickly. "Fergus is escorting her."

Cullen frowned. "Escorting her where?"

"I am not sure," she admitted uncertainly. "I did not get the chance to speak to her. Fergus was ushering her out the door and into the back courtyard as I entered the kitchen."

When Cullen continued to frown, she added, "I know she was looking for Lady Elizabeth earlier. Perhaps they have gone in search of her."

"Who's looking for me?"

Cullen turned to the doors behind him as Biddy let it swing closed and started across the great hall toward them.

"Evelinde," Mildrede answered.

"Well, here I am. What's she wanting?" Biddy asked, as the keep doors opened again, and Gillie, Rory, and Mac trailed Tavis inside.

Mildrede shook her head with bewilderment. "I do not know."

"Fergus told her ye were at the cliff," Cullen muttered. "But I told him ye were coming with me to Comyns."

Cursing, he headed for the door to the kitchens.

"What is wrong?" Mildrede asked, following on

his heels, worry evident in her voice as she added, "Is not the cliff where your father and first wife died?"

"Aye," he bit out, fear racing through him now.

"Surely it canna be Fergus behind the accidents and deaths?" Biddy asked, but her tone told him she very much feared it might be.

"Fergus?" Tavis echoed the name with surprise as he and the other men began to follow as well. "It canna be Fergus, Cullen. There's no profit for him in these deaths. What would he have to gain from killing me da? Or yours? Or even Maggie?"

"Some of the deaths might have been accidents," Gillie pointed out.

"Aye," Rory agreed. "But 'tis curious he's taking the lass to the cliffs if he kens Biddy isna there."

That comment caused a silence to fall over the group as they hurried out of the kitchens and along the path to the back of the curtain wall. Cullen almost wished they'd continue their blathering. At least it kept him from thinking about what might be happening to his wife right that moment. If Fergus hurt her, he would kill the man with his bare hands. He was not going to lose Evelinde.

Seventeen

Evelinde stepped through the door in the castle's curtain wall when Fergus held it open for her and moved out onto the small bit of land between the stone wall and the edge of the cliff. Her gaze slid over the lonely, desolate spot, but there was no sign of Biddy. Her attention then moved to the pile of stones that was Jenny's resting place, but there were no flowers there to speak of Biddy's recent visit.

Frowning, she turned back to see Fergus pushing the stone door closed behind them. "She is not here."

The soldier peered over the area and shrugged. "Mayhap she's already going back."

"We would have passed her," Evelinde pointed out.

"Nay, there is more than one path. I just picked the quickest one. Biddy may have gone another way." He shrugged again, then raised an eyebrow. "What diya want with Biddy?"

Evelinde managed a crooked smile. She'd been trying to think how to tell him what she'd learned and what she suspected all the way out here and simply been unable to decide how to start her explanations. Evelinde supposed it was actually a good thing that Biddy wasn't here else she'd have led the man blindly into a situation that might have been dangerous.

"Lass?" Fergus prompted. "What are ye needing with Biddy? Mayhap I can help."

Evelinde smiled wryly, knowing he couldn't answer the questions she had for Biddy, but after a moment, she asked, "Fergus, what do you recall of her sister's death?"

"Jenny." He said the name sadly. "Losing her upset Biddy something terrible. She was very fond of her sister."

"Fond enough to kill the man who was responsible for making her kill herself?"

Fergus was silent so long she didn't think he'd answer, but finally he moved over to the grave of stones and peered over them. "Ye found the letter."

Mouth suddenly dry, she asked, "The letter?"

"Aye. Maggie found it some years ago. I should have destroyed it then, but they were Jenny's dying words, and I didn't have the heart to take it from Biddy." He turned a sad face to her and shook his head. "So I tucked it back in her chest so she never even knew it was gone."

"Maggie found the letter?" Evelinde asked faintly, realizing she'd made a big error in judgment. A foolish one when she really thought about it. She'd known in her heart of hearts that Biddy wasn't a killer. She'd also known that Fergus held feelings for her and that he *was* capable of killing. As a soldier, that was all he trained for—defending his home and people by killing others. She never should have come out here with him.

"I doona ken why ye had to stick yer nose in, lass."

Evelinde took a wary step back as he started forward.

"If ye'd just let the past lie . . . Now I'll have to kill you, too, to protect Biddy."

"To protect Biddy from what?" she asked grimly, continuing to back away as he approached.

"To protect her from anyone finding out she shot the arrow into Darach."

Aware that she was drawing close to the cliff's edge, Evelinde began to move sideways rather than back as she asked, "You have known all this time that she killed him and have been protecting her?"

"Nay, she didna kill him," he countered firmly. "I did."

"But you just said she shot the arrow into Darach," she pointed out with confusion.

"Aye, she did," he acknowledged. "But that isna what killed him. He was mending, so I smothered him in his sleep on the third day after he was shot."

Evelinde stopped moving. Relief had washed through her as she learned that Biddy wasn't a murderer after all, alas that news didn't help her now. Hoping to keep him talking while she figured out a way to escape him, Evelinde asked, "It was not the infection that killed him?"

Fergus shook his head. "It was his own stupid inability no to follow his cock that killed him."

Her eyes widened in shock, but he didn't apologize for cursing in front of her. She doubted he even noticed he had. The man was suddenly furious.

"He had a good woman to wife, did Darach!" Fergus said, suddenly shouting. "Biddy *loved* him. The woman thought the moon and stars rose in his eyes and forgave him every transgression," he said almost plaintively. "Dear God, any man would kill to be loved like that."

Evelinde nodded her understanding, "Or kill others to gain it."

Fergus scowled, but said, "Aye. He didna deserve her. It was bad enough that he was crawling under the skirts of every servant and wench he came across while she wept her eyes red, but then to go after her sister?" He spat on the ground. "Biddy forgave him those other women, but I knew she wouldna forgive that. She loved Jenny something fierce."

"You told her?" Evelinde asked uncertainly. She was more than a little confused by the suggestion that he had. The letter she'd read had seemed to imply that Jenny was telling Biddy something she didn't know when she revealed the affair and subsequent events.

"Nay. I wanted to, but couldna hurt her like that . . . but I knew. I came across the pair of them, Darach and Jenny, here in the third week of the first visit. He was charming his way under her skirt like he did every other female. 'Twas like a sickness with him. The man just couldna resist. And Jenny, she was so taken with him, crying out how she loved him, and was so grateful to be loved by one such as the laird." Fergus shook his head with disgust. "Darach didna love her. The man never loved anyone in this world but himself."

"He didna even have enough kindness to lie to the lass. He grunted away on top of her until he spilled his seed, and when she again begged him to tell her he loved her, Darach just laughed, and said, 'Of course I love ye, I love all women, they are flowers to be plucked.' And then he chucked her under the chin like a child who'd just performed a fine trick, and said, 'That was fun. Mayhap I'll give ye another tumble later in the day,' and walked off, leaving her here, crushed."

Evelinde bit her lip. She couldn't imagine the humiliation Jenny must have suffered in that moment.

"Aye," Fergus said, reading her expression. "He was nothing but a rutting animal. And he left her here in a terrible state. The stupid chit tried to throw herself off the cliff that day, and maybe I should have let her, but instead I stopped her and calmed her down. In the end, she decided she wasna ready to die. She begged me not to tell Biddy and to help her leave early, and I did. I got the lass out of here before Biddy could realize something was wrong with the girl and force it out of her. I wouldna see Biddy hurt by it all."

"But Jenny came back," Evelinde pointed out.

"Aye," Fergus said heavily. "I wasna here when she arrived two months later or what followed might no have happened." He sighed and shook his head. "She was with Darach's child." Fergus paused and eyed her briefly, then said, "If ye've read the letter, ye ken what happened next."

Evelinde nodded solemnly. "Aye. Darach rejected her, and she killed herself."

Fergus frowned. "We tried to stop her. She had slipped the letter under Darach and Biddy's chamber door before she hanged herself. I was coming above to light the torches—we kept them lit then— and I saw their bedchamber door open. Darach started to step out, then paused and bent to pick up the letter from the floor. He opened it, read it, cursed, and went to Jenny's room, but she wasna there, so he hurried past me and rushed below.

"I followed. He was heading for the curtain wall. He must have thought she'd planned to throw herself off. Halfway there, Darach crumpled up the letter and shoved it in his sporran, but it wasna all the way in and fell out without his noticing after just a couple of steps.

"I picked it up and read it, then tucked it in me own sporran and turned back to the keep. I, too, thought the girl had probably thrown herself off the cliff. I had no desire to see her broken body, so headed back to await the news in the great hall. But when

I walked back into the keep, Biddy was screaming. She'd found her sister hanging in the solar."

"If you had the letter, how did Biddy get it?" Evelinde asked.

"Two weeks after Jenny died, I put it in the solar where she'd find it. I hoped she would think the lass had left it."

"Why?" she asked with dismay. The man had just spent several minutes telling her he couldn't do this and couldn't do that because it might hurt Biddy. But in the end he had done the one thing most likely to crush the woman.

"I was sick of watching that bastard Darach act like the loving, caring husband. He'd caused the death, he'd caused the sorrow, and Biddy was grateful for the arm he gave her to cry on about it!"

Fergus closed his eyes briefly and shook his head. "I didna think it through. I wanted her to see him for what he was, but didna consider how she would react. I left the letter and went out on the hunt with the others, happily anticipating her confronting him when we returned and revealing him to all and sundry. Instead, she shot the bastard."

"Are you sure she did?" Evelinde asked hopefully. "Mayhap it truly was an accident."

"Nay. It was Biddy's arrow. The fletching gave it away," he explained. "She'd had a pet swan when she first married Darach. It had died some years earlier, but she'd kept the feathers and always did her own fletching, alternating white swan feathers with those of a goose or whatever was available. I recognized it at once and knew Liam would, too. There wasn't time to remove and replace it with another, so I covered the fletching with blood and dirt, hoping it wouldna be noticed. And it wasna at the time."

"But her arrow didn't kill him," Evelinde pointed out. "You said you did."

"Aye. I smothered him in his sleep, but all just thought it a result of the wound," he explained, then added with regret, "Biddy was devastated . . . But I knew it was just guilt, and she'd mend in time."

Fergus fell silent, his gaze on the stones covering Jenny, but she suspected that wasn't what he was seeing. Evelinde was sure his thoughts were in the past and took the opportunity to glance around, her eyes seeking a path of escape or at least a weapon she might use to save herself. She never really completely took her attention off Fergus, however, and when he apparently finished his ruminations, raised his head, and took a step toward her, she quickly asked, "Why kill Cullen's father, Liam?"

"Liam." He uttered the name almost like a prayer.

"Ten years had passed," she pointed out. "Why kill him so long after the first death? Surely you had got away with Darach's murder by then?"

"Aye, I thought so. Those years passed peacefully, and I had almost forgotten all about Darach . . . until the arrow came back to haunt me." He clucked unhappily. "I didna ken it at the time, but Liam had apparently taken Biddy's arrow to his room the day it was removed from Darach. I thought it had just been thrown away else I would have stolen into his room and taken it at the time, but I had no idea and thought all was well."

"That mistake forced me to killed Liam," Fergus said with what she thought might be true regret. "I didna like to do it. Cullen's father was a fine man, much finer than his brother ever was, and his death was truly unfortunate."

"And still you killed him," Evelinde said quietly, her gaze sliding quickly around the area again. There were several rocks she might be able to put to good use but little other than that.

"It was for Biddy," Fergus explained, reclaiming her attention. "It was all my fault, and I couldna let Biddy pay for it."

When she just stared at him silently, he explained, "Liam apparently kept the arrow because something about it bothered him. The blood obscured the coloring, so it must have been the length that did it. Biddy was as short as the boys', and so were her arms and arrows," he pointed out, then shrugged. "It may have been that, but whatever it was, it was enough to make Liam keep the arrow in that chest in his room, bloodied and all."

Evelinde's eyes widened as she realized the arrow she'd seen in the chest in their room was the one that Darach had been shot with.

"But the blood dried up and over the years got brushed off every time he took something out of, or put something into, the chest. By the time he noted that there were white feathers among the darker ones, he thought little of it . . . until the day he came down to the cliff and found me cleaning rabbits."

"Rabbits?" Evelinde asked with bewilderment, not sure what one thing had to do with the other.

Fergus nodded. "Biddy hadna been hunting since Darach's death. She used to like it before that, but after shooting her husband, she never picked up her bow again until I convinced her to join me hunting almost ten years to the day after Darach died. She'd been sick for a couple of weeks and stuck indoors else I doona think I'd have convinced her to accompany me, but in the end she decided she would and would catch some fresh rabbits to make a nice stew for supper.

"I soon regretted pushing her into it," Fergus said on a sigh. "When we returned, I sent her in to start chopping her vegetables while I brought the rabbits here to clean and skin them." His gaze slid to the pile of stones. "As much as Biddy liked to come here to visit her sister, I did, too. I often visited Jenny and talked to her while doing some task or other. The first time it was just to assure her that Darach was rotting in hell for what he'd done to her. But 'tis a peaceful spot, and I kept returning."

He shrugged unhappily, and said, "That day, I brought the rabbits here to tend them, and Liam came looking for me. When he praised me on the number of rabbits, I wryly admitted they were all Biddy's catch. It was only then I noted the recognition in his eyes. Had I realized he'd know the arrow's fletching I would have claimed they were my own and let him execute me for killing Darach, but 'twas too late. I could not convince him then that it had been me who had killed Darach. He would not listen, and I had to kill him.

"Liam never saw it coming," Fergus assured her

as if that might make a difference. "He had dismounted and was standing with his back to the cliff.
I launched myself at him and pushed him over the
edge without a fight."

"And little Maggie?" Evelinde asked, her gaze now
slipping to the door in the curtain wall. She knew
that once he finished explaining everything, he
would turn his attention to killing her. She needed
to figure out a plan to save herself, and Evelinde
was thinking that she might hit him with a rock and
make a run for the door in the curtain wall.

"I was sorry to have to kill little Maggie."

Evelinde's mouth compressed at the words. It
seemed to her that Fergus had been awfully sorry
over each of the murders, but it hadn't stopped him
committing them, or following them with others.
He'd no doubt be sorry to have to kill her, too, she
thought with disgust, then stiffened as she noted
that the door in the curtain wall was open a little.
For a moment, she thought Fergus had simply not
closed it properly, but then she noted that several
faces were crowded in the narrow opening. She recognized Cullen at once, as well as Mildrede, Tavis
and—Her heart squeezed as she spotted Biddy and
noted the expression on her face. Evelinde had no
idea how long they'd all been there listening to Fergus's confessions, but it was long enough to leave
Biddy shaken and pale.

"Little Maggie was a sweet lass."

Evelinde forced herself to turn her gaze back to
the man lest her distraction warn him they were no
longer alone.

"But she had to poke her nose into this business. Like you," he added grimly. "The only difference was she came to me first with her plans to resolve the matter. She fancied Cullen would be so pleased to have his name cleared, he'd vow his undying love for her . . . the little fool.

"I tried to sway her from looking into it, but she, too, thought Jenny's death might be involved, and turned her suspicions on Biddy. The moment she did that I knew I'd have to kill her. But I liked the lass, and hesitated until the day came when she searched Biddy's room as you obviously did this morn."

Evelinde's gaze skittered in apology to the door, but Biddy's attention was focused solely on Fergus as he spoke.

"When she found the letter, Maggie came running straight to me. I hurried her out here to the cliff. She was so excited telling me of her find, she hardly noticed where I was steering her. If thinking Biddy had killed Darach wasna bad enough, the lass also concluded that Biddy must have killed Liam because he somehow sorted it out.

"And then we stepped through the door and out here onto the cliff, and the wind near to stole the breath from both of us. She turned to me with confusion, asking why we were here and I struck her, knocking her out at once. I then set her on Jenny's grave and tried to sort out what to do. Maggie had to die to protect Biddy, but how? And then I decided just to throw her off the cliff while she was still unconscious. She would just never wake and never suffer."

"And my accidents?" she prompted when he fell silent. "That was you as well."

"Aye. I've been trying to make it look like an accident so no one could turn on Cullen, but ye keep escaping with yer life." He grimaced, then admitted, "And I am sorry about having to kill you, too, as it seems obvious the lad loves ye, but he'll get over ye in time."

Evelinde's mouth tightened at the words. The man had no idea what love was if he thought it was so easily forgotten. However, he was moving forward again, and she searched her mind for another question to keep him talking.

"What of the rumors?" she asked, grabbing at the question, as Cullen began to slide through the partially open door behind the man. "Did you start those, too?"

Fergus paused again. "Not a purpose. It was after Liam's death they started in whispering about murder and wondering about Darach as well. I worried they'd look to Biddy. So, to turn the gossip away from her, I mentioned to someone that I'd heard someone else had seen a dark man fleeing the area about the time that Liam would have died. The next thing I knew the rumor returned to me with Cullen's name inserted in place of 'a dark man.' I have ever been sorry for the trouble that's caused ye, Cullen."

Evelinde had been watching her husband creep slowly and silently up behind Fergus as she listened to the man speak, but his last words made her stiffen as she realized some sound or perhaps her watching had given away Cullen's presence. She glanced sharply to the soldier and was somewhat surprised to find that while she'd been watching her husband, Fergus had been sidling closer to her. Now he was little more than an arm's length away. Before she could rectify the matter and move out of reach, he lunged forward, catching her upper arm and hauling her back up against his chest as he turned to face Cullen, and added, "But ye've handled it well, lad. Yer father would have been proud."

Cullen had stilled, his jaw clenching with frustration as she was caught, but that was the only reflection of his feelings as he glared at Fergus, and said, "He might be were he still alive."

"Fergus," Biddy said quietly, slipping through the door in the curtain wall and moving up beside Cullen. "Let Evelinde go."

The sharp prick of a knife against her neck told Evelinde he wasn't ready to do that. She stood completely still, holding her breath lest she accidentally slit her own throat as she waited for an opportunity to free herself or otherwise bring an end to the situation.

"I did it all for you, Biddy," Fergus said solemnly.

"But I didna want it done," Biddy said sadly.

"Ye shot him," he pointed out with exasperation.

"Aye, but—That was in a moment of rage over what he'd done to Jenny," she said, trying to explain her feelings. "Murder is wrong. I should have—"

"It isna murder when 'tis someone like him. Darach deserved to die," Fergus insisted. "He was a cold, heartless bastard. Had he lived, he'd have just broken yer heart over and over again, made ye more miserable and ruined countless other young lasses."

"Aye, but at least I'd have not suffered the guilt I've suffered all these years thinking I'd committed a mortal sin and murdered my own husband," Biddy countered, sounding angry for the first time. "And Liam and little Maggie didna deserve to die. They were both good people, both friends and loved ones whose passing I've mourned."

Her gaze flickered to Evelinde's face, and her lips tightened before she added, "And then there is Evelinde. Ye planned to kill her, too, did ye not? Who would have been next? Cullen, when he tried to find out who killed his wife and sought vengeance? Would ye kill everyone I love in your supposed effort to 'protect' me? I'd rather ye'd killed me that night than any of the others, including Darach. Ye've done nothing but cause me more pain, Fergus. Do ye no see that?"

Evelinde swallowed and shifted her eyes to the side, trying to see Fergus. He was still as stone behind her, but his breathing was rapid, and she wasn't sure how he was responding to Biddy's words.

"Let Evelinde go," Cullen said grimly, drawing her gaze back to his stony face. "Her death will win ye nothing now. 'Tis over."

"Aye, 'tis." Fergus sighed by her ear, then began to back up. "I'm sorry, Biddy. All I ever wanted was to make ye happy and protect ye. Ye deserved better than the cards ye were dealt. But I've managed to muck everything up."

"Fergus, let Evelinde go, and fight me," Cullen

growled, moving forward as Fergus continued to drag her back toward the cliff.

"I've no desire to fight ye, lad. I feel bad enough fer killing yer father. I'll no add yer death to the list of me sins."

"Well then, doona add Evelinde either," he said desperately.

"Please, let her go, Fergus," Biddy said quietly. "Cullen and Evelinde love each other. They deserve the happiness neither of us found."

"Aye, mayhap they do," Fergus agreed, but backed up several more steps before pausing to say by Evelinde's ear. "I'm going to let ye go, lass, and when I do, yer to walk straight away from me to yer husband."

"What are you going to do?" she asked with concern.

"Never ye worry about that," he said. "Ye just go to yer husband and love him. Biddy's right, ye deserve each other."

Evelinde opened her mouth again to ask what he was going to do, but Fergus suddenly pushed her forward. Unprepared for it, she stumbled, but Cullen was there to catch her, steadying her with one hand even as he lunged past her to catch at Fergus. Evelinde whirled as his hand left her, eyes widening in horror as she saw Fergus pitching off the cliff and Cullen throwing himself forward to catch him.

Evelinde wasn't the only one to scream out, but she was the only one close enough to make a grab for Cullen as he caught at Fergus and was pulled off-balance. She caught him by the back of the plaid and followed him to the ground as he fell. Cullen landed with his legs on the cliff but his chest hanging over the edge. Fergus, however, was hanging in midair, kept from plunging to the bottom of the rocky incline only by Cullen's hold on his tunic. When his weight began to drag Cullen forward, Evelinde scrambled onto his legs, adding her weight to his own to anchor them.

"Let me go, lad," she heard Fergus say almost kindly.

"Nay," Cullen growled. "Take me hand, yer plaid may rip."

"Take his hand, Fergus," Tavis coaxed, as the men rushed forward to try to help.

Evelinde relaxed a little as Gillie and Rory knelt on either side of her and caught at Cullen to help keep him from going over the cliff with the man he held.

"Take me hand, ye stubborn bastard," Cullen snapped, as Evelinde heard the faintest tearing sound. "I'm trying to save yer life here."

"Why? So ye can later hang me fer murder?" Fergus asked dryly, then repeated, "Let me go. I'm ready."

Cullen was stiff and silent, and Evelinde knew he was hesitating, unwilling to let go the man who had been a first to him for years and probably had trained him in his youth, but also aware that did he save him now, he would then have to punish him for three murders. It *would* mean hanging him.

Evelinde's heart went out to her husband, knowing how agonizing a decision this must be for him, but then the choice was taken out of his hands. The hard wind that had been pounding at them suddenly died an abrupt death, a brief hiccup just long enough for her to hear the sound of Fergus's tunic tearing away; and then the wind roared back, slapping at them as Fergus plunged downward. He never screamed, the only sound was the shriek of the wind around them.

Eighteen

There is no need to carry me, husband. I am not hurt. I can walk," Evelinde repeated for about the tenth time since Cullen had been pulled back up on the cliff, swept her up in his arms, and headed for the keep. And for the tenth time he ignored her and continued silently on his way.

Giving up on the possibility of walking, Evelinde peered over his shoulder to the small group following. Biddy, Tavis, and Mildrede were in front with Mac, Rory, and Gillie following. Her gaze settled on Biddy, taking in her lost expression. The older woman's face was pale, and her trembling was visible across the ten-foot span between them. Mildrede had her arm around Biddy's waist and was helping to support her as she walked, while Tavis had his mother's arm clasped in his hand in the first show of familial support she'd seen between the two since arriving at Donnachaidh. Cullen's cousin also looked shaken by the revelations this day, and Evelinde wondered if learning what he had about his father might not steer him toward changing some of his ways. She hoped so, but would just have to wait and see what happened.

She was not willing to wait and see when it came to Biddy, however.

"Husband?"

He didn't speak, but his eyes did flicker toward her briefly before returning to the path ahead. Knowing that was the equivalent of a "Yes, wife?" from him, she said, "What will you do about Biddy?"

One corner of his mouth twitched toward a frown before settling back into its usual expressionless pose, but she could see the fretting in his eyes and knew he wasn't sure what to do about his aunt and what she'd done.

"She did not kill him," Evelinde said softly. "She shot him with an arrow, 'tis true, but that is not what killed him. Darach deserved that and more for what he did to Jenny. Can you not just forget what she did and let it go?"

"Aye." Cullen sighed. "In truth, she has been punishing herself for years for what she thought she'd done. I do not feel any great need to punish her further."

Evelinde tightened her arms around his shoulders

in a brief hug, then relaxed in his hold and smiled.

"Ye shouldna be smiling. Ye should be furious with me," Cullen growled, as they reached the door leading into the kitchens at the back of the castle, and he kicked it open with one booted foot.

Evelinde's eyes widened in surprise, but she waited until they had passed out of the kitchens and were crossing the empty great hall before asking, "Why?"

"Because once again me refusal to speak has caused ye grief, and this time it nearly got ye killed."

"It did?" she asked, perplexed.

"Aye," he said as he started up the stairs with her. "He wouldna have been able to lure ye anywhere had I but spoken of my uncertainties where he was concerned."

Evelinde glanced at him sharply as they reached the landing. "You suspected Fergus?"

"Nay," he admitted, pausing to allow her to open the door to their chamber. He then stepped inside, kicked the door closed, carried her to the bed, then simply stood there holding her, as he said, "But the business with the fire in the solar troubled me. He claimed to be in the great hall and should have seen anyone ascending the stairs, yet said he hadn't and was very insistent it had to have been an accident. Even when I pointed out that the torch had fallen too far from the cresset to be accidental, he insisted it had to be." Cullen grimaced. "They claimed he'd looked away briefly to open the door for Tavis and Mildrede, but I ken Fergus. He takes his duties seriously and woudna have looked away from the solar even as he crossed the hall and opened the doors for them, so it troubled me. Mayhap if I had mentioned that to ye, ye would have thought twice about going anywhere with him alone."

"Aye, I would have," she agreed calmly, but there was no anger in her words. She simply wasn't experiencing any.

"I'm sorry," he said solemnly, then vowed, "I shall change. I will tell ye everything in future. I will—" Cullen paused, his eyes widening with surprise when she covered his mouth with her hand, forcing him to silence.

"You need not change, my lord husband. You—"

"Aye, I do," he insisted earnestly, twisting his face away to dislodge her hand. "I love ye, Evelinde. I do. And I ken ye doona love me back. How could ye when ye hardly know me? 'Tis all me own fault. As ye pointed out, ye've told me everything about yerself. I know about yer childhood, yer family, yer beliefs . . . everything. But ye ken nothing about me. I would change that. I would have ye love me, too."

"I do love you," Evelinde said quickly.

Cullen blinked. "Ye do?"

She chuckled softly at his startled expression, then hugged him tightly. "Aye, husband. I do."

How can ye love me when ye hardly know me?" he asked with confusion.

"But I do know you," Evelinde assured him solemnly. "I know that you are strong and honorable. I know that you have and will always do your best to see to my well-being and happiness. I know that you are fair and compassionate in your dealings with your people . . ." She shook her head. "Cullen, what you said earlier in our relationship was true. Your actions do speak louder than words."

When he didn't look convinced, she pointed out, "Look at Fergus. He kept saying that he loved Biddy. That he could not hurt her this way or that, and yet all he *did* was hurt her."

Evelinde paused a moment, then asked, "What would you have done in Fergus's place had you come upon Jenny and Darach and known what he was doing?"

Cullen's mouth thinned out. "I'd have challenged him to a battle and killed the bastard."

"Aye." She nodded. "And what would you have done after Jenny killed herself and Darach played the sympathetic husband?"

"I'd have called him out in front of everyone and let them know what I knew. And then I'd have challenged him and killed the bastard."

Evelinde bit her lip to keep from smiling. There was a definite pattern here. It seemed Cullen found his uncle's behavior despicable and would have "killed the bastard." She wasn't surprised, but merely pointed out, "Instead, Fergus arranged for Biddy to find out and waited for *her* to confront the man. And when she shot Darach, but it didn't kill him, Fergus finished the job, but not for Biddy as he claimed. She was trying desperately to save him. He did it for himself, in the hopes that he would then have a chance with her. He merely justified it by claiming it was for love of her . . . and he did so with little concern for the guilt she would suffer."

"He also did not kill your father or little Maggie for Biddy. Would your father not have listened if Fergus had admitted that he'd killed Darach when he was mending? You do not doubt it, do you?" Evelinde waited until he shook his head. And then she shrugged, and said, "And neither would your father. But Fergus did not, because it would have meant putting himself at risk, and so he justified killing them by saying 'twas for Biddy . . . leaving her to suffer that guilt now as well," she added dryly, and shook her head. "That is not love, Cullen. Fergus *spoke* of love, but his actions didn't support his words."

"You, on the other hand," Evelinde said quietly, raising a hand to press it to his cheek. "While you rarely give me words, your actions have ever spoken loudly of who you are and what you believe in. Your honor shines through, and I love you for it." She smiled wryly, and added, "Well, once I found out about the actions I did."

Cullen hugged her closely, then bent to kiss her. It started out a sweet kiss, loving and gentle, but soon began to change, passion slipping in and taking over. They were both breathless when he broke the kiss.

"I love ye, Evelinde," he repeated solemnly, his fingers moving to begin undoing her lacings. "When I rode out to d'Aumesbery to collect and marry ye, my best hope was that ye'd be someone I could deal with at least middling well, but I found better than that. I liked ye on our first meeting. That liking just increased with every moment we spent together, Ye were like no woman I had ever before met."

"I liked you, too," Evelinde murmured, as he paused to push her gown off her shoulders. "Though I have been fortunate enough to know men as fine as you ere this."

When he stiffened, she grinned, and added, "You are very like my father was, and I hope my brother still is. I have been fortunate in having good men in my life and am proud to be your wife."

Cullen relaxed, but then something flickered in his eyes, and Evelinde tilted her head curiously.

"What is it?"

"I just recalled something I fergot to tell ye," he admitted.

She raised her eyebrows curiously.

"We've had a letter from yer brother," he announced. "Alexander's coming to visit."

Evelinde smiled widely at this news, her heart lifting with joy. Noting that Cullen was appearing less than happy though, she asked, "Do you not wish him to do so? You did say I could invite him," she reminded worriedly.

"Aye, and I am not displeased that he's coming, I just should have told ye days ago when I received the news," he said, then promised, "I shall not forget things like that in future. I'll tell ye, and I'll tell ye anything ye wish to ken about meself. I'll tell ye about me childhood, and me father, and me mother, and anything else ye want to hear about."

He let her chemise slither to the floor. "I'll tell ye about me first hunt, me first wife, me—"

"Husband," Evelinde interrupted, as his hands slid over her body.

"Aye?" Cullen asked, his hands pausing briefly.

"Tell me later," she whispered, then leaned against his chest and slid her hand around his neck to urge him down to kiss her.

"Aye, wife," he breathed before his mouth covered hers.

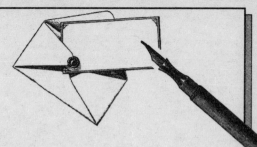

Dearest Reader,

You are in for a treat!

In the coming months we'll read about two sexy devils, one wicked Scotsman, and a little black gown in these four irresistible Avon Romances—all sweeping, sensuous historical romances by four bestselling authors at the top of their game.

Turn the pages
for a sneak peek and be the first
to fall in love with
Avon Books's latest and greatest!

Coming January 2009

Tempt the Devil

Anna Campbell

Olivia Raines has ruled London's demimonde with an iron will and a fiery spirit. Sought after by London's most eligible men, she has never had cause to question her power until she meets the notorious Julian Southwood, Earl of Erith. From the moment he first saw her, Julian knew he must possess her. So when he discovers a secret that could destroy her livelihood, Olivia has no choice than to bargain with the devil.

London
April 1826

Across the packed, noisy salon, Julian Southwood, Earl of Erith, studied the notorious strumpet who would become his next mistress.

He was in the middle of Mayfair on a fine spring afternoon. Yet the reek of sex for sale was as pungent as in the slave markets of Marrakesh or Constantinople.

The crowd was mostly male, although a few provocatively dressed women mingled in the throng. Nobody paid them the slightest attention. Just as nobody but Erith seemed to notice the startling and realistically detailed frescoes of rampant Zeus seizing swooning Ganymede.

From a corner dais a pianist and violinist doggedly plowed through a Mozart sonata. The music came from a different world, a cleaner, purer world untainted by animal carnality.

A world the Earl of Erith would never again inhabit.

Erith shook off the bleak self-reflection and turned to the man beside him. "Introduce me, Carrington."

"Shall do, old chap."

Carrington didn't ask the object of Erith's interest. Why would he? Every man here, including his companion, focused on the slender woman reclining with studied nonchalance upon the chaise longue.

Without being told, Erith knew she'd deliberately chosen her setting in front of the tall west-facing windows. Late afternoon sun flooded her in soft gold and played across her loosely bound tumble of tawny hair. In the clear light, her vivid red dress was like a sudden flame. The effect was worthy of the Theatre Royal.

Even he, familiar to ennui with courtesans' tricks, had felt the breath catch in his throat at first sight of her. One glance and the blood in his veins hummed a deep, dark song of desire, and his skin prickled with the compulsion to make her his.

And she achieved this remarkable effect from half a room away.

Of course, this was no ordinary courtesan.

If she were, he wouldn't be here. The Earl of Erith only bought the best. The best tailoring. The best horses. The best women.

Even by his exacting standards, this particular cyprian was a prime article.

Two extraordinary women had set London on its

ear in the last ten years. One, Soraya, cool, dark, mysterious as moonlight, had recently married the Duke of Kylemore, igniting the scandal of the decade. The other, radiant sun to Soraya's moon, arrayed herself now before Erith like a spectacular jewel.

He assessed her as closely as he'd contemplate an addition to his stables.

Lord, but she was a long Meg. A sheath of crimson velvet displayed her lean body to dramatic advantage. She'd fit his tall frame to perfection, even if his taste usually ran to plumper, more voluptuous bedmates. His memory filled pleasantly with the fleshy blond charms of Gretchen, the mistress he'd left in Vienna a month ago.

Gretchen couldn't contrast more strongly with the jade before him. Where the Tyrolean beauty offered soft, yielding curves, this woman was all spare elegance. The bosom under her gown's low neckline wasn't generous, and her waist was long and supple. He guessed the narrow skirt hid legs as graceful and elongated as a thoroughbred's.

Gretchen had been dewy with youth. This woman must verge on thirty. By that age, most bits of muslin frayed at the edges. But this bird of paradise continued her unchallenged reign over the male half of the ton. Her longevity as the most sought-after courtesan in London made her yet more intriguing.

His gaze slid up to her face. Like her body, it was unexpected. After the rhapsodies he'd heard in the clubs, he'd imagined less subtle attractions. The unmistakable greed he'd heard in her admirers' voices had led him to imagine a brassier, more overtly available bawd.

Her jaw was square, almost masculine. Her nose was a trifle too long, her cheekbones too high. From where he stood in the gilt-framed doorway, it was impossible to tell the color of her eyes, but they were large and brilliant and set at a slant.

Cat's eyes. Tiger's eyes.

Her mouth . . .

Her mouth perhaps explained what he'd heard about her preternatural allure. It might be too large. But who would complain? No man could look at those succulent lips without wanting them on his body. Erith's groin tightened at the decadent pictures rocketing through his mind.

Undoubtedly, she had . . . *something*.

She wasn't a great beauty. She was well past first youth. Nor did she flaunt her charms like tawdry trinkets on a fairground stall. If he'd encountered her at a respectable gathering rather than this louche brouhaha, he'd almost believe she belonged to his own class.

Almost.

After the hubbub, all this was surprising. Disappointing.

But even as he dismissed the wench's heralded charms, his eyes gravitated back to that spare, strangely aristocratic face. To that sin of a mouth. To that luxuriant hair. To that long, graceful body curved in complete relaxation upon her couch while men eddied around her in an endless whirlpool of fascination.

She was the most powerful figure in the room. Even at the distance, he felt the sexual energy sizzling around her.

She swept the room with a contemptuous glance. The raised angle of her chin and the irony that teased the corners of her mouth indicated defiance, courage, challenge.

He tried to deny the sensual pull she exerted. While

his reckless heart kicked into the emphatic rhythm of a drum beating an army into battle.

No, she wasn't what he'd expected, but he didn't fool himself into believing she was anything less than quality.

She lifted her head and smiled at something the effete fellow standing at her elbow said. The lazy curve of those lush red lips shot another jolt of lava-hot arousal through Erith. That smile spoke of knowledge and sharp intelligence, and a sexual confidence he'd never encountered in a woman. Never, even though he'd dealt with the fallen sisterhood for the last sixteen years. Every drop of moisture dried from his mouth, and his interest, wearied through playing this game too long, engaged with an intensity that astonished him. The covetous buzz in his blood notched up a degree.

Oh, yes, she was going to be his.

Not just because she was the elite of London's courtesans and his prestige would accept nothing less as his *chère amie*. But because he wanted her.

More than he'd wanted anything in a long, long time.

Coming February 2009

Devil of the Highlands

Lynsay Sands

*They call him the Devil, the most notorious laird in all of
Scotland. But Cullen, the new Laird of Donnachaidh, pays
them no heed. He cares only about the survival of his clan,
and for that, he needs a wife. He wants someone stout to bear
him sons. He wants a pliable woman who wouldn't question
his dictates. He wants a passionate woman to warm his bed.
Then he meets Evelinde . . . one out of three isna bad.*

Cullen was the first to see her. The sight made him rein
in so sharply, his horse reared in response. He tightened his thighs around his mount to help keep his seat,
moving automatically to calm the animal, but he didn't
take his eyes off the woman in the glen.

"God's teeth. What is she doing?" Fergus asked as
he halted beside him.

Cullen didn't even glance to the tall, burly redhead
who was his first. He merely shook his head silently,
transfixed by the sight. The woman was riding back
and forth across the clearing, sending her horse charging first one way, then the other and back. That in itself
was odd, but what had put the hush in Fergus's voice
and completely captured Cullen's tongue was the fact

she was doing so in nothing but a transparent chemise while holding the reins of her mount in her teeth. Her hands were otherwise occupied. They were upraised and holding what appeared to be a cape in the air so it billowed out behind her above her streams of golden hair as she rode back and forth . . . back and forth . . . back and forth.

"Who do you think she is?" Rory's question was the only way Cullen knew the other men had caught up as well.

"I doona ken, but I could watch the lass all day," Tavis said, his voice sounding hungry. "Though there are other things I'd rather be doing to her all day."

Cullen found himself irritated by that remark. Tavis was his cousin and the charmer among his men; fair-haired, handsome, and with a winning smile, it took little effort for him to woo women to his bed of a night. And the man took full advantage of the ability, charming his way under women's skirts at every opportunity. Were titles awarded by such an ability, Tavis would have been the king of Scotland.

"I'd first be wanting to ken why she's doing what she is," Fergus said slowly. "I've no desire to bed a wench who isna right in the head."

"It isna her head I'd be taking to me bed." Tavis laughed.

"Aye," Gillie said, his voice sounding almost dreamy.

Cullen turned a hard glare on his men. "Ride on. I'll catch up to ye."

There was a moment of silence as eyebrows rose and glances were exchanged, then all five men took up their reins.

"Ride around the meadow," Cullen instructed, when they started to move forward.

There was another exchange of glances, but the men followed the tree line around the meadow.

Cullen waited until they had disappeared from sight, then turned back to the woman. His eyes followed her back and forth several times before he urged his mount forward.

It hadn't appeared so from the edge of the meadow, but the woman was actually moving at high speed on her beast, slowing only to make the turn before spurring her horse into a dead run toward the other side. The mare didn't seem to mind. If anything, the animal seemed to think it was some sort of game and threw herself into each run with an impressive burst of speed.

Cullen rode up beside the mare, but the woman didn't immediately notice him. Her attention was shifting between the path ahead and the cloth in her upraised hands. When she finally did glimpse him out of the corner of her eye, he wasn't at all prepared for her reaction.

The lass's eyes widened, and her head jerked back with a start, unintentionally yanking on the reins she clenched in her teeth. The mare suddenly jerked to a halt and reared. The lass immediately dropped her hands to grab for the reins and the cloth she'd been holding swung around and slapped—heavy and wet—across Cullen's face. It both stung and briefly blinded him, making him jerk on his own reins in surprise, and suddenly his own mount was turning away and rearing as well.

Cullen found himself tumbling to the ground, tangled in a length of wet cloth that did nothing to cushion his landing. Pain slammed through his back, knocking the wind out of him, but it positively exploded through his head, a jagged blade of agony that actually made him briefly lose consciousness.

A tugging sensation woke him. Blinking his eyes open, he thought for one moment the blow to his head had blinded him, but then felt another tug and realized there was something over his face. The damp cloth, he recalled with relief. He wasn't blind. At least, he didn't think he was. He wouldn't know for sure until he got the cloth off.

Another tug came, but this was accompanied by a grunt and a good deal more strength. Enough that his head was actually jerked off the ground, bending his neck at an uncomfortable angle. Afraid that, at this rate, he'd end up with a broken neck *after* the fall, Cullen decided he'd best help with the effort to untangle himself from the cloth and lifted his hands toward his head, intending to grab for the clinging material. However, it seemed his tormentor was leaning over him, because he found himself grabbing at something else entirely. Two somethings . . . that were covered with a soft, damp cloth, were roundish in shape, soft yet firm at the same time, and had little pebble-like bumps in the center, he discovered, his fingers shifting about blindly. Absorbed as he was in sorting out all these details, he didn't at first hear the horrified gasps that were coming from beyond the cloth over his head.

"Sorry," Cullen muttered as he realized he was groping a woman's breasts. Forcing his hands away, he shifted them to the cloth on his head and immediately began tugging recklessly at the stuff, eager to get it off.

"Hold! Wait, sir, you will rip—" The warning ended on a groan as a rending sound cut through the air.

Cullen paused briefly, but then continued to tug at the material, this time without apologizing. He'd never been one to enjoy enclosed spaces and felt like he would surely smother to death if he did not get it off at once.

"Let me—I can—If you would just—"

The words barely registered with Cullen. They sounded like nothing more than witless chirping. He ignored them and continued battling the cloth, until—with another tearing sound—it fell away, and he could breathe again. Cullen closed his eyes and sucked in a deep breath with relief.

"Oh dear."

That soft, barely breathed moan made his eyes open and slip to the woman kneeling beside him. She was shifting the cloth through her hands, examining the damaged material with wide, dismayed eyes.

Cullen debated offering yet another apology, but he'd already given one, and it was more than he normally offered in a year. Before he'd made up his mind, the blonde from the horse stopped examining the cloth and turned alarmed eyes his way.

"You are bleeding!"

"What?" he asked with surprise.

"There is blood on my gown. You must have cut your head when you fell," she explained, leaning over him to examine his scalp. The position put her upper body inches above his face, and Cullen started getting that closed-in feeling again until he was distracted by the breasts jiggling before his eyes.

The chemise she wore was very thin and presently wet, he noted, which was no doubt what made it transparent. Cullen found himself staring at the beautiful, round orbs with fascination, shifting his eyes left and right and continuing to do so when she turned his head from side to side to search out the source of the blood.

Apparently finding no injury that could have bloodied her gown, she muttered, "It must be the back of your head," and suddenly lifted his head, pulling it up off the ground, presumably so she could examine the back of his skull. At least that was what he thought she must be doing when he found his face buried in those breasts he'd been watching with such interest.

"Aye, 'tis here. You must have hit your head on a rock or something when you fell," she announced with a combination of success and worry.

Cullen merely sighed and nuzzled into the breasts presently cuddling him. Really, damp though they were, they were quite lovely, and if a man had to be smothered to death, this was not a bad way to go. He felt something hard nudging his right cheek beside his mouth and realized her nipples had grown hard. She also suddenly stilled like prey sensing danger. Not wishing to send her running with fear, he opened his mouth and tried to turn his head to speak a word or two of reassurance to calm her.

"Calm yerself," was what he said. Cullen didn't believe in wasting words. However, it was doubtful if she understood what he said since his words came out muffled by the nipple suddenly filling his open mouth. Despite his intentions not to scare her, when he realized it was a nipple in his mouth, he couldn't resist closing his lips around it and flicking his tongue over the linen-covered bud.

In the next moment, he found pain shooting through his head once more as he was dropped back to the ground.

Coming March 2009

Bride of a Wicked Scotsman

Samantha James

The Earl of McDonough is determined to reclaim, at any cost, the Circle of Light, which the Druids many centuries ago declared would keep the Clan McDonough prosperous, so long as they were the guardians of the mystical silver bands. But the Circle was stolen, and the Clan began to wither, and no one knew the identity of the thief or his descendants until now. For in Lady Maura O'Donnell lies the key to the clan's salvation . . . and to McDonough's heart.

Alec watched as she downed the remainder of her wine. "Why have I not seen you before today? Are you a guest of the baron's?" Lord above, he'd have remembered those emerald eyes. He'd never seen such brilliant green . . . as green as the landscape of this rocky isle.

"Only for tonight."

"Then perhaps introductions are in order." He wanted to know who she was, by God. "I am—"

"Wait!" She held up a hand. "No, no! Do not say. This is a masquerade, is it not? A night to disguise our true selves. What say we dispense with names?" That tiny smile evolved into seduction itself.

Alec laughed. She was sheer delight. And an accomplished flirt. "As you wish, Irish."

"That *is* my wish, Scotsman."

Alec settled down to enjoy the thrust-and-parry. "May I get you something? A plate perhaps? The desserts are quite exquisite." God help him, the dessert he had in mind was *her*.

"I am quite satisfied just as I am."

He was not, thought Alec with unabashed lust. "Well, then, Irish, perhaps you would care to dance?"

Alec didn't. But manners dictate he ask. Beneath her eye mask, her cheekbones were high, the line of her jaw daintily carved. He longed to tear it away, to see the whole of her face, to appreciate every last feature.

Their eyes met. Alec moved so that their sleeves touched. Her smell drifted to his nostrils. Warm, sweet flesh and the merest hint of perfume.

He wanted her. He was not a rogue. Not a man for whom lust struck quickly and blindly. He was not a man to trespass where he should not. He was discreet in his relationships. He was not a man to take a tumble simply for the sake of slaking passion.

Never had he experienced a wash of such passion so quickly. He'd wanted women before, but not like this. Never like this. Never had Alec desired a woman the way he desired this one. What he felt was immediate. Intoxicating. A little overwhelming, even. Not that he shouldn't desire her. She was, after all, a woman who would turn any man's eye. It was simply that the strength of his desire caught him by surprise.

Perhaps it was this masquerade. Her suggestion that they remain anonymous.

He cupped his palm beneath her elbow. "There are too many people. The air grows stale. Shall we walk?"

Laughing green eyes turned up to his. "I thought you would never ask."

A stone terrace ran the length of the house. They passed a few other couples, strolling arm in arm. All at once, she stumbled. Quite deliberately, Alec knew. Not that he was disinclined to play the rescuer.

He caught her by the waist and brought her around to face him. "Careful, Irish."

"Thank you, Scotsman." She gazed up at him, her fingertips poised on his chest, moist lips raised to his.

Alec's gut tightened. She was so tempting. Too tempting to resist. Too tempting to even *try*.

A smile played about his lips. Behind her mask, invitation glimmered in her eyes. "Is it a kiss you're wanting, Irish?" He knew very well that she did.

"Are you asking permission, Scotsman?"

The smoldering inside him deepened. "No, but I have a confession to make." He lowered his head so that their lips almost touched. "I've never kissed an Irish lass before."

"And I've never kissed a Scotsman before."

"So once again it seems we are evenly matched, are we not?"

"Mmmm . . ."

Alec could stand no more. That was as far as she got. His mouth trapped hers. He felt a jolt go through her the instant their lips touched. It was the same for him, and he knew then just how much she returned his passion. His mouth opened over hers. He'd wanted women before. But not like he wanted this one. It was as if she'd cast a spell over him.

And he kissed her the way he'd desired all evening,

with a heady thoroughness, delving into the far corners of her mouth with the heat of his tongue. Tasting the promise inside her. Harder, until he was almost mindless with need.

She tore her mouth away. She was panting softly. "Scotsman!" she whispered.

Alec's eyes opened. His breathing was labored. It took a moment for him to focus, for her words to penetrate his consciousness.

"I . . . what if we should be seen?"

So his Irish lady-pirate was willing—and he was quite wanting. Oh yes, definitely wanting.

"I agree, Irish. I quite agree." He tugged at her hand and started to lead her toward the next set of double doors.

"Where are you taking me?"

He stopped short. "What! I thought you knew, Irish."

"Tell me."

He slid his hand beneath her hair and turned her face up to his. "Why, I'm about to kidnap you, Irish." He smiled against her lips. "I fear it is the pirate in me."

Coming April 2009

Confessions of a Little Black Gown

Elizabeth Boyle

When Thalia Langley spies a handsome stranger in the shadows of her brother-in-law's study, she knows in an instant she's found the dangerous, rakish sort of man she's always dreamt of. But Tally suspects there is more to Lord Larken than meets the eye, and she has the perfect weapon to help tempt the truth from him: a little black gown she's found mysteriously in a trunk.

"Oh, Thatcher, there you are," Tally said, coming to a stop in the middle of her brother-in-law's study, having not even bothered to knock. She supposed if he were any other duke, not the man who'd once been their footman, she'd have to view him as the toplofty and unapproachable Duke of Hollindrake as everyone else did.

Thankfully, Thatcher never expected *her* to stand on formality.

"One of the maids said she saw a carriage arrive, some wretchedly poor contraption that couldn't be one of Felicity's guests and I thought it might be my missing . . . "

Her voice trailed off as Brutus came trotting up behind her, having stopped on the way down the stairs to give a footman's boot a bit of a chew. Her ever-present companion had paused for only a second before he let out a little growl, then launched himself toward a spot in a shadowed corner, as if he'd spied a rat.

No, make that a very ill-looking pair of boots.

Oh, dear! She didn't know Thatcher had company. She tamped down the blush that started to rise on her cheeks, remembering that she'd just insulted this unknown visitor's carriage.

Oh, dash it all! What had she called it?

Some wretchedly poor contraption . . .

Tally shot a glance at Thatcher, who nodded toward the shadows, even as a man rose up from the chair, coming to life like one of the Greek sculptures Lord Hamilton had been forever collecting in Naples.

Yet this one lived and breathed.

Thatcher's study was a dark room, sitting on the northeast side of the house, and with the sun now on the far side, the room was all but dark, except for the slanting bit of light coming in from the narrow casement. But darkness aside, Tally didn't really need to see the man, whose boot Brutus had attached himself to, to *know* him.

A shiver ran down her spine, like a forebear of something momentous. She couldn't breath, she couldn't move, and she knew, just knew, her entire life was about to change.

It made no sense, but then again, Tally had never put much stock in sense, common or otherwise.

Perhaps it was because her heart thudded to a halt just by the way he stood, so tall and erect, even with a devilish little affenpinscher affixed to his boot.

Heavens! With Brutus thus, how could this man ever move forward?

"Oh, dear! Brutus, you rag-mannered mutt, come away from there," she said, pasting her best smile on her face and wishing that she wasn't wearing one of Felicity's old hand-me-down gowns. And blast Felicity's tiresome meddling, for if she'd just left well enough alone and not insisted the trunks be changed around, her own trunk wouldn't have become lost.

"You wretched little dog, are you listening to me? Come here!" She snapped her fingers, and after one last, great growling chew, Brutus let go of his prize and returned to his usual place, at the hem of her gown, his black eyes fixed on the man, or rather his boots, as if waiting for any sign that he could return for another good bite.

"I am so sorry, sir," Tally began. "I fear his manners are terrible, but I assure you his pedigree is impeccable. His grandsire belonged to Marie Antoinette." She snapped her lips shut even as she realized she was rambling like a fool. Going on about Brutus's royal connections like the worst sort of pandering mushroom.

"No offense taken, miss," he said.

Oh, yes. His simple apology swept over her in rich, masculine tones.

Then to her delight, he came closer, moving toward Thatcher's desk with a cat-like grace, making her think of the men she'd imagined in her plays: prowling pirates and secretive spies. It was almost as if he was used to moving through shadows, aloof and confident in his own power.

Tally tamped down another shiver and leaned over to pick up Brutus, holding him tightly as if he could be the anchor she suddenly felt she needed.

Whatever was it about this man that had her feeling as if she were about to be swept away? That he was capable of catching her up in his arms and stealing her away to some secluded room where he'd lock them both away? Then he'd toss her atop the bed and he'd strip away his jacket, his shirt, his . . .

Tally gulped back her shock.

What the devil is wrong with me? She hadn't even seen the man yet, and here she was imagining him nearly in his altogether.

Oh, dear heavens, she prayed silently, *please say he is here for the house party. Please . . .*

"I daresay we have met," she continued on, trying to lure him forward, force him to speak again, "but you'll have to excuse me, I'm a terrible widgeon when it comes to remembering names."

The man stepped closer, but stopped his progress when the door opened and Staines arrived, a brace of candles in hand, and making a *tsk, tsk* sound over the lack of light in the room. The butler shot the duke a withering glance that seemed to say, *You are supposed to ring for more light.*

Poor Thatcher, Tally thought. He still had yet to find his footing as the Duke of Hollindrake and all that it entailed.

"Have we met?" she asked, and to further her cause, she shifted Brutus to one hip and stuck out her hand, which must compel the man, if he was a gentleman, to take it.

"No, I don't believe we have ever met, Miss—"

Oh, heavens, his voice was as smooth as the French brandy she and Felicity used to steal from their teacher's wine cabinet. And it would be even better if he were whispering into her ear.

Tally, my love, what is it you desire most . . . ?

Oh, now you are being a complete widgeon, she chided herself, closing her eyes, for she couldn't believe she was having such thoughts over a perfect stranger. A man she'd never seen. She only hoped this ridiculous tumult he was causing on her insides wasn't showing on her face.

Taking a deep breath, she unshuttered her lashes and, much to her horror, found herself staring at a complete stranger.

Certainly not the man she'd imagined.

Whoever was this ordinary, rather dowdy-looking fellow blinking owlishly at her from behind a pair of dirty spectacles, his shoulders stooped over as if he'd carried the burden of the world upon them?

Where had he come from? She leaned over to peer past him, searching for any sign of the man she'd expected, but there was no one there.

Tally swayed a bit. Heavens, she was seeing things. If she didn't know better, she'd say she was as jug-bitten as their London housekeeper, Mrs. Hutchinson.

But no, all the evidence was before her, for instead of some rakish character in a Weston jacket and perfectly polished boots, stood a gentleman (well, she hoped he was at least a gentleman) in a coat that could best be described as lumpy, cut of some poorly dyed wool, with sleeves too short for his arms. Far too short, for his cuffs stuck out a good six inches. Then to her horror, she glanced at his cravat, or rather where his cravat should be.

For in its place sat a vicar's collar.

A vicar?

At Avon Books, we know your passion for romance—once you finish one of our novels, you find yourself wanting more.

May we tempt you with . . .

- **Excerpts** from our upcoming releases.

- Entertaining **extras**, including authors' personal photo albums and book lists.

- Behind-the-scenes **scoop** on your favorite characters and series.

- **Sweepstakes** for the chance to win free books, romantic getaways, and other fun prizes.

- Writing **tips** from our authors and editors.

- **Blog** with our authors and find out why they love to write romance.

- **Exclusive content** that's not contained within the pages of our novels.

Join us at
www.avonbooks.com